The Apocalypse Survivors
The Undead World Novel 2
By Peter Meredith

Peter Meredith

Fictional works by Peter Meredith:

A Perfect America

The Sacrificial Daughter

The Horror of the Shade Trilogy of the Void 1

An Illusion of Hell Trilogy of the Void 2

Hell Blade Trilogy of the Void 3

The Punished

Sprite

The Feylands: A Hidden Lands Novel

The Sun King: A Hidden Lands Novel

The Sun Queen: A Hidden Lands Novel

The Apocalypse: The Undead World Novel 1

The Apocalypse Survivors: The Undead World Novel 2

The Apocalypse Outcasts: The Undead World Novel 3

The Apocalypse Fugitives: The Undead World Novel 4

Pen(Novella)

A Sliver of Perfection (Novella)

The Haunting At Red Feathers(Short Story)

The Haunting On Colonel's Row(Short Story)

The Drawer(Short Story)

The Eyes in the Storm(Short Story)

Cast of Characters:

Yuri Petrovich: One time Chief Biologist of the Stepnagorsk Scientific and Technical Institute for Microbiology—a secret biological weapons manufacturing facility. Afraid that he would soon be out of a job due to budget cuts, Yuri sells the Soviet concocted *Super Soldier* virus to North Korean operatives who in turn sell it to an extreme Al-Qaeda linked faction, who ultimately release it. The virus destroys the cognition centers (i.e. the thinking portion) of the brain while simultaneously arousing the aggression centers of the brain and greatly increasing the production of adrenaline. The end result is the creation of real life zombies.

Victor Ramirez: Once a DEA agent, Ram is smart, skilled and highly trained. He's a formidable person, yet still only a man and thus subject to all the fears and stresses that affect the rest of us. Haunted by the murder of the woman he loved, Ram is on a quest for vengeance and little will stand in his way.

Jillian Shaw—AKA: Jillybean. Six year old Jillybean has been on her own for the last four months with only a stuffed animal for companionship. She relies on the subconscious manifestation of her father in the form of "Ipes" the zebra, as well as nature's wisdom to survive—imitating rabbit, squirrel, or fox as the need arises.

Neil Martin: Once a soft Wall Street raider with the heart of a mouse, Neil has grown during the Apocalypse—not in size. He is as small and thin as always. Instead he has grown as a man, finding courage in the face of death.

Sadie Walcott—Seventeen-year-old Sadie has flowered during the Apocalypse, becoming, for the first time in her life a member of a real family—a family she would kill for.

Sarah Rivers—With the disappearance of her daughter in the hell of New York City, Sarah saw herself as failure of a mother, however now she is a mother again twice over:

Eve age seven months and Sadie age seventeen. Still Sarah dreams of Brit and retains a mother's fierce love for her first born.

Cassandra Mason—Cassie sees the world through the prism of racial hatred, causing her to imagine enemies where none exist. Her hatred breeds evil all around her, turning man against man. She is the murderer of Julia, Ram's love.

Prologue

Since the Apocalypse, the world had become quiet in a manner most of the few remaining humans could not quite wrap their minds around. No longer did jets ply the air at unheard of speeds, nor did boats in the tens of thousands split the waves of the oceans, and no longer were the highways abuzz with what everyone had always assumed would be infinite and insufferable traffic.

Man, in his conceit, had figured that he would always be. The universe had other plans.

Now, the Earth demonstrates its own power through the use of eternal silence. The quiet isn't just oppressive; frequently it verges on the maddening. Untold numbers of survivors draw death to them in their need to hear and be heard. Those unfortunate enough to find themselves alone for too long will invariably pick up the habit of singing or humming to keep the quiet at bay. Eventually, these loners will begin to talk to themselves.

And the zombies will hear and come for the feast.

Yuri Petrovich was not like these weak individuals. He liked to be alone, but he rarely was; in fact no one aboard the *Nordic Star*, a 50's era cruise ship, could say they were ever really alone. Built to house just above four-hundred passengers and crew, the *Nordic Star* was now crammed with three times that many people. And were it not for the fact that the boat was also loaded top to bottom with fuel and food it could have held more.

Every square inch of the boat was being utilized. The Sky Bar, which had once had been aglow with gleaming brass and polished wood and women in fancy dresses, now only held hundreds of barrels of diesel oil, while the ship's main restaurant was a maze of boxes from ceiling to floor that only the ship's logistics officer could truly fathom. Even the six life boats, hanging from their stanchions, practically over-flowed with canned goods.

It wasn't likely the lifeboats would be needed. There

wasn't much chance that the *Nordic Star* would sink, not snugged just up the East River as it was. It had been moored in the shallow tidal strait that separated Manhattan from the Bronx since January for two reasons: first, to hide from the remains of the US Navy which had turned into little more than a grasping gaggle of pirates, bent on plundering what was left of the world, and second, to preserve fuel.

The *Nordic Star* went through diesel oil at a prodigious rate—an alarming rate even. Just holding her bow into the Atlantic wind had sucked down hundreds of liters a day. Now they used only enough to power the generators, and even that was being rationed since the weather had turned fair.

There was one area on the ship that demanded and received as much power as it needed: Yuri's lab.

Everyone aboard knew how important that laboratory was to their survival. It was where a cure was being fabricated from glass tubes and stainless steel machinery. At least that was what they had been led to believe. That Yuri was a scientific genius had been well established as fact through the careful use of propaganda.

All the old hands—those who had been hired on to crew the vessel before the zombie virus had even been known in America—were the chief propagandists and they spread their tales with the ardor of zealots for that was exactly what they were.

They looked upon Yuri as their savior—part seer, part savant. Only he had foreseen the coming apocalypse and only he had prepared in a meaningful way. The truth of course was that after selling the virus to the North Koreans he had kept a close eye out for oddities that would point to a looming catastrophe. They were not long in coming, and as most of the world's scientists marveled at the new breed of hardy and vicious rats springing up around the Mediterranean, Yuri had flown into action.

He chartered the largest boat he could afford and then,

like some modern day Noah, had begun to fill it with people, each carefully chosen for their special abilities or training. Electricians, mechanics, metal workers, engineers, surgeons, architects, nurses…the list went on-and-on.

Each person he accepted was given a stipend to simply be "ready" when the time came.

Most had taken the money, never expecting to see the mad Russian again, however when the Apocalypse hit and the quarantine zones began to expand and multiply, Yuri's boat had filled rapidly.

It wasn't long before the "mad" Russian was being spoken of in tones that bordered on religious awe. This was wholly unexpected, yet Yuri took full advantage of it, using it to dominate the stronger personalities around him and thus securing his hold as leader.

When the religious awe began to slip, Yuri turned to what Russian leaders had historically relied upon: violence.

On the one hand, any who even rolled their eyes at an order were severely dealt with—bones were broken, skulls split, and fingers went missing—in other words, routine stuff for what he was fast becoming: a mob boss. On the other hand, Yuri made promises of a new start with a cure to the zombie plague as the means to a glorious future.

At the time, Yuri wasn't in the least worried that he would be able to follow through since he had the antigen already. All that was required was to mass produce it by entering a small portion of it into a cell culture where it would multiply. Now, he wasn't sure at all.

The virus had "jumped" as the Americans put it. It had mutated, rendering the antigen, and thus the vaccine partially useless. "At least it was the good part of useless," he reminded himself.

The vaccine was just effective enough to keep the fever at bay, meaning a person could be bitten or scratched and still live. However not only would the person be a carrier of the disease for the rest of his lives, and thus a danger to everyone around him, he would also turn into a zombie if he was ever killed in a normal manner.

This just wasn't good enough, not for someone who had allowed claims of divine providence to swirl around him without saying a word to stop it. If this little fact got out not only would his position as *Boss* be in jeopardy, his life would be as well.

"Maybe we should switch adjuvants," Dr. Wellsmith suggested. "Like I've said before, we should at least try using the paraffin. Studies show its effectiveness in the rat population."

Yuri said nothing. He only watched as a newly-killed rat began to twitch. It had been bled just to the point of death and now it was coming alive again as the virus gained control. The virus was indeed a wonder. Somehow it took over the rat's brain, forcing the dead body to release epinephrine, which in turn constricted vessels to get the maximum out of its remaining blood.

In a minute it was on its feet and hissing at the glass, eager to get at Yuri, eager to kill.

When Yuri didn't answer him, Wellsmith cleared his throat loudly and tried again, "I don't see why we don't at least give the paraffin a try," Wellsmith said, obstinately. "Nothing else is working."

Wellsmith had been Yuri's biggest mistake. Holding a doctorate in microbiology meant Wellsmith was the only person on board the *Nordic Star* who could undermine Yuri's authority and he was the one person that an opposition group could coalesce around. Yuri couldn't have that.

"No paraffin," Yuri said in his accented English. Adjuvants such as paraffin and aluminum hydroxide were additives designed to maximize the immune response of the vaccine, which in the case of a jumped antigen was useless. "Do they teach you nothing? It is waste and we have only little. The samples hold enough of antigens to keep rat healthy."

"Then it's the antigens that are the problem," Wellsmith said.

An angry sound escaped the Russian. Promises of a golden future weren't something one just took back. "Antigen is good enough. Maybe we do not speak of side effect is all," he ventured aloud, speaking more to himself than to Wellsmith.

"You mean the side effect of not really being vaccinated?" the American scientist shot back. "I can't believe you'd lie to everyone just so you can claim some glory. They'll find out eventually and when they do there'll be hell to pay, and it'll be your head on the line, not mine."

"You make big issue out of little thing," Yuri growled. "The antigen is good, just not perfect."

"Science is about truth," Wellsmith replied haughtily. "There is no room for falsehood in science."

Yuri didn't care for the tone of the man's voice or the suspicious look in his eyes. He had known for quite some time that Wellsmith would be trouble, the sort of trouble that would end badly. The Russian had seen plenty of this type of trouble back in the days when he wouldn't even dare to claim being a Russian, back when he had been a proud and very fearful Soviet citizen. The thought gave him an idea.

He could fix the little problem of the ineffective vaccine and his issue with Wellsmith, by using the tried and true Soviet method of overcoming internal department issues. He would denounce Wellsmith as a saboteur and have him killed. Simple.

Yuri was just imagining the show trial and how it would unfold—a headache for sure since the man was an American and would demand rights that were clearly now nonexistent—when he had a better idea. Yuri could "catch" Wellsmith in the act of sabotage. There would be a struggle, a fight to the death, and then the sad news that the cure was delayed. Though to be sure it couldn't be too long of a delay, since he had already begun to advertise. All he needed was a few more weeks to isolate the issue and fix his antigen.

"I suppose you are correct," Yuri said with a sudden easy grin. "We try it your way first, before we give up. Could you hand me paraffin in bottle?"

"Sure. It could work. You never know," Wellsmith said, turning.

Yuri knew it wouldn't work. The rats were already getting triple the dose needed to fight the virus; the paraffin would only amount to overkill. With that thought in mind, Yuri took a fire extinguisher from the wall and used it to cave in Wellsmith's skull.

Chapter 1

Jillybean

Philadelphia, Pennsylvania

Jillybean now lived in a chalk world where everything was black and white and gritty, and where nothing lasted; nothing good at least.

The first grade had been good, though for her it had been only six weeks long before the monsters had come and ruined it. Despite that, she smiled when she thought of those six weeks—they had been a golden time of sleepovers and soccer and chase on the playground at recess. And friends. She had so many best friends: Janice and Becca and Paula and even Billy from across the street, though he wasn't a best friend, just an old friend, since she knew him for like, forever.

And it was a time of parents. The right kind of parents. The kind where the mommy made breakfast in the morning and daddy went to the work every day except for leaf-raking day and football day, and every night there was a bedtime story, and cuddling, and usually tickling, and always a kiss good night.

But then the monsters came and made it all wrong.

Jillybean's daddy was a fighter...or maybe he was a warrior. She thought the words were similar yet could never make the connection between the two beyond the fact that he was very brave. He dared the streets to get them food, only always he was gone longer and longer and always he came back with less food than before. Once daddy came back all scratched up and bitten, and his eyes were no longer daddy's. They were eyes that were ascared.

"I was bitten, Jillybean." Her name was Jillian, but he

and Ipes called her Jillybean and she liked it better. Though just then, with him shaking and crying, she ignored her special name and tried to hug him because that's what he always liked if he got hurt somehow. Only this time he pulled away. "No, don't touch me. I can't risk getting you infected, too."

"What are we going to do?" her mommy asked. She looked almost as pale as he did. "You know I can't do this alone."

He slumped at this, resting his cheek on the cool wood of their kitchen table, and said, "You have to try."

But she didn't. Daddy left, crying and groaning in pain and mommy went to bed and never left it. Even when the snow came and Jillybean could see her breath right there in the house, mommy just laid in bed, staring at the ceiling, and didn't even eat.

At first, Jillybean scooped water out of the toilet tank and dribbled it into her mommy's mouth but that ran out quickly. Then she used snow that she let melt. It didn't seem to help. Her mommy died in her bed. She was alive one second, her skin like white paint over the bones of her face and her eyes wet blue gems that sat deep in her head, and then, she was dead.

Jillybean didn't go into that room anymore. She spent her nights in the attic, within the walls of a pillow fort she had constructed, curled up in a nest of blankets. In the days of winter she nibbled her way through the last of the food and, fortunately for her, the early winter turned into an early spring so that when necessity forced her out of her home to scavenge for food, she didn't have to add the element of freezing to death to the rest of her fears.

That first time, when she stepped foot across the threshold of her front door had been an absolute horror. Her gnawing hunger had overridden her native wisdom and she had gone too fast, drawing a monster to her when she was barely forty feet from her front door. She had hidden under a car and when it came shuffling by, moaning like a dead wind, she had peed herself.

Now, four months later, she had a way of doing things that Ipes called the "Rabbit system".

That morning she began it as usual, with *Jillyrabbit* slinking up to the edge of each of the windows in her home and slowly, ever so slowly, peering out to check to see if the streets were clear. The monsters didn't like the sun so much. They hid from it—all except Mrs. Bennet. No, she came out in the daytime and stood in the street or poked about in the remains of her flower garden as though she was looking for something lost.

"I didn't like her none before," Jillybean said to Ipes, giving him a quick glance as she did. The zebra caught the look and smartly kept his lips shut tight; he was in *time out* and as everyone knew, you didn't get to talk in time out.

He had been too...what was the word? "Eager," she answered herself. "That's it. We can't be too eager even if we are hungry." And Jillybean was *very* hungry. "I hope the soup is going to be done soon."

"Ahem," the zebra murmured.

"What? You aren't apose to even make noise when you're in..." She stopped suddenly and blinked, remembering that she had forgotten to move the soup. In the afternoon it sat in the dining room where the sun could get at it and in the morning it was supposed to be in the kitchen catching the early rays. "Oh poop! You should have said something."

I'm not supposed to talk in time out, remember? Ipes said, with pure innocence in his voice.

"If you're going to be like that, maybe you won't get any soup today," she said, with the raised eyebrows and imperious tone of a mother reining like a queen in her own kitchen. The little zebra dropped its beady black eyes down and she nodded, satisfied.

She then hurried for the soup. It sat in a glass pitcher

that mommy had used to make sun tea in. Now it held Pine Needle Soup. The recipe being nothing more than water and chopped up pine needles. She had discovered it by accident, playing tea with Ipes, Todd-the turtle, and Teddy-the-bear. Though they had all been there, Ipes took credit for the discovery, which was just the usual for him.

Next to the pitcher was the big spaghetti pot where fifty acorns floated in water that was a thin yellow. The water would have to be changed soon, but first things first: she grabbed two of the bitter nuts and popped them in her mouth, one going into the pocket of each cheek—like a squirrel.

That's how she survived. Like an animal. Ipes taught her everything he knew, and for a stuffed zebra wearing a little blue t-shirt that read: *Too Cute*, he was very wise. She ate like a squirrel and, when she went outside, she moved like a bunny, freezing in place at the first sign of danger, scampering under bushes or beneath cars where the monsters couldn't get her. When she had to run, she was fast as a cat. Unstinting speed was the remedy when stealth and luck failed her.

What helped her the most was she was smart like a zebra. Ipes was always going on about the inherent and unrecognized genius of the zebra, which was funny since he was always getting in trouble. Yet he did teach her things. Once when Mrs. Bennet had treed her like a dog, Ipes had suggested throwing acorns at her for fun. It was hilarious watching them *thunk* off her noggin or drop into her open mouth. When Jillybean missed once and the acorn bounced off the Henderson's car to go bopping down the street, Ipes was quick to point out how Mrs. Bennet had gone after the sound.

Now, Jillybean kept marbles in her pocket just in case she needed to distract one of the monsters.

That particular spring morning, which was the finest she could remember, Jillybean plunked the soup down on the windowsill and stared out at the world with a hunger that Pine Needle Soup wasn't going to satisfy. "Do you know where my backpack is?" she asked Ipes, forgetting that he wasn't supposed to talk in timeout.

I could help you find it if I wasn't in the corner, he said.

Jillybean made a noise in her throat. Ipes was the best finder. It couldn't be denied. He knew everything just like daddy. Back before, daddy had known everything, while mommy had known how everything was supposed to be. They had been a great combination.

"Ok, fine," Jillybean said. "You can come out of timeout. But only if you stop teasing Todd about being slow, and if you help me find my backpack."

Ipes walked...waddled really, out of the corner, saying, *Todd's a turtle and everyone knows he is the slowest thing on four feet.*

"Yeah well, you meant he was slow in the head, and that's just mean."

If the dunce-cap fits... Ipes started to say but Jillybean's blue eyes went to angry squints and he quickly changed the subject. *Your backpack's on the porch where you left it. Are we going scouting some more? I hope we find some cookies. I'm dying for cookies.*

The little girl carried her zebra to the porch and after a cautious minute of gazing all about she bent to get her school bag. It had once been a fancy, brilliant pink that had been the envy of the first grade since it was a *Power-Puff* backpack, but now it was scuffed and growing tattered. Ipes went in one of the mesh pockets on the side, where he had a good view and could act as look-out.

Jillybean needed all the help she could get. The world was dangerous for an almost fifty pound girl who didn't know the first thing about weapons or monster fighting. She slipped down the porch stairs of the porch and crept through the tall grass to the back fence where there were two broken slats. She squeezed through, confident that no monster could ever follow her.

A kid monster could, Ipes mentioned.

This stopped her just as she was about to begin the dangerous part of her trek. "Do they have kid monsters?" she asked.

They have daddy and mommy monsters, so...

The thought made her stomach go wacky and her downy brows came down in consternation. "I guess there could be kid monsters. I don't ever want to see one, that's for sure." Shaking off the idea she made her way, sly as a fox, through the Gunderson's backyard. She didn't bother with the shabby two-story home; it had been picked over long before. Instead she went along the overgrown bushes that ran nearly to the edge of Highview Drive.

She'd been in every house on Highview Drive, even the ones across the street. Her destination that morning was the next street over, Springfield Road—a very daring undertaking for such a tiny girl. Springfield was a major road. It was four lanes wide and always had gobs of monsters.

Like the tiniest commando, Jillybean slunk from bush to tree and then to a parked car and then...

Monster on your left, hissed Ipes.

She slunk back behind the car and put both of her hands up, palms facing out, looking for the "L" that would tell her which way left was. Only when she had her sense of direction did she nudge herself high enough to see the monster over the hood of the car; it had once been a policeman, though now its blue uniform was just rags across its grey body.

"Should I chance it?" she asked Ipes. The zombie was turned partially away and it would be fifty-fifty whether she would be seen.

It's always the ones you don't see that are the most trouble, Ipes told her. *Use a magic marble.*

Though she had only a few left, it was a good plan with

so many lanes to cross. She took out one of the marbles, kissed it to activate the magic and chucked it as far as she could, hoping that it would land beyond the monster—it didn't.

Still it was close. The marble struck once behind the monster with a loud glass "clack" sound and then, before the monster could turn, the marble was past it and bouncing a second time and a third. The sound of the marble on the street was loud in the dead air and, out from the shadows, a few more monsters went after the little glass sphere like dogs chasing a ball.

Now for the hard part, Jillybean thought. With her heart whomping in her thin chest, Jillybean darted across the road at full speed, racing for a parked jeep.

That was close, Ipes said when they were safely across the street and sitting just in front of a fine old two-story home. After only a second she started forward again, but he tapped her on the back. *What are you doing?* he demanded. *Don't go for the front door where everyone can see you.*

He was right of course. If she went that way she would be seen up and down the block. Jillybean changed course at once and went around the side to the backdoor.

Listen first, he warned as she opened the door inch-by-inch.

Monsters rarely stayed quiet for very long and in a house it was easy to hear them move or moan, but she knew this already and didn't need to be told for the hundredth time. "You're the one being loud this time," she said, placing her balled fists on her nonexistent hips. "And beside I already...knew...that...what is that smell?" she asked.

It's food! Ipes cried happily as he wiggled in excitement.

Someone was cooking meat and the aroma, stretching along the air, was like a magnet. She left the house, following the tantalizing smell through its backyard to a chain-link fence and saw another suburban street. Across that was a cookie-cutter home that resembled its neighbors so much that it was like an ant among ants. Two things set this particular house apart: there was a black Humvee sitting in its driveway, and a thin trail of smoke that turned in the air above the chimney.

There were three monsters on this street and because of the smell they were moving about restlessly, looking here and there for the source. Jillybean started forward.

Don't do it, Ipes warned.

But it was too late. The monsters had their back to the girl and she took off in a sprint across the street, giving in to the desperate need, not only for food but for the company of people, too. She wasn't like Ipes who could sit with Teddy and Todd for hours and be happy. A part of her needed actual human interaction.

This drove her in a sprint—with her backpack bouncing and her legs flying—all the way to the Humvee, where she flattened against its side and then stared, with her eyes bugged, back to see if the monsters had seen her. They hadn't, however they had heard her slapping sneakers and now they turned her way. In a restoration of some sense, she slunk low and used the black vehicle to screen her as she scurried along the side of the house.

Movement in the house stopped her cold at a window. Going up on her tippy-toes, she peered in and nearly choked on her acorns. There was a man in the house! She had expected exactly that, and still the shock of seeing another human had her in a strange, but happy panic. It made her chest all aflutter.

As she watched he ran a hand through his black hair and put on a thick leather coat.

"He's leaving, Ipes. What should I do?" Ipes did not answer. "Ipes!" she demanded testily. Turning, she made to cast a fierce glance at him for being jealous, because that was the way he was with anything new, however the zebra wasn't in the side pocket where he had been only moments before.

"Ipes!" she hissed, staring all around at the ground. She then pulled off the pack and dug through it to see if he had climbed into the main pouch. He wasn't there either. Just then she heard the throaty roar of a big engine. She rushed to the corner not knowing what to do without Ipes there to help her—he always helped with the big decisions.

Should she flag the man down? Should she continue to hide all by herself? Should she...the questions in her mind stopped cold as she finally saw her friend. The little zebra was sitting in the middle of the street and the Humvee was heading right for him.

"Ipes!" she cried. Paralyzed with fear for him, she could only stand there with her mouth open as the fat, black tires grazed his big zebra nose before turning to speed away.

Without thinking—her main problem when Ipes wasn't around to help—she dashed into the middle of the street. Thankfully every zombie in the area had oriented on the Humvee and completely missed the little girl scampering low.

That wasn't too smart, Ipes scolded when she made it back to the safety of the house. *First you drop me and forget all about me. Then you risk everything to come get me. You never do that! The monsters won't hurt me, remember?*

"Oh hush," Jillybean said. She didn't like to be told she was wrong, and certainly not by some silly stuffed animal. "Maybe they would've smelled me on you and eaten you thinking you are tasty, which I'm sure you're not...speaking of smell, what is that?"

It was food.

The man had cooked something and the smell sent her stomach rumbling like a motor. She hurried to the back door of the place and was happy to find it unlocked. "Oh, my gosh!" she said, rushing in, overcome by the odor of cooked food. There, next to the fireplace, was a frying pan; within it were the remains of the man's breakfast. It had been meat of some sort, fried in oil with a touch of teriyaki sauce.

The little girl spat out the bitter acorns that she had been storing in her cheeks and ate the scraps greedily. The meat was strangely tangy, yet to her starved taste buds it was heaven. The scraps filled Jillybean's tummy nicely, and though it was still only mid-morning, she pulled a large comfortable chair close to the glowing embers in the fireplace and took a nap, curled up like cat.

Chapter 2

Ram

Philadelphia, Pennsylvania

Victor Ramirez stopped the Humvee in the middle of the street and clicked off the engine. The silence of the new world clung to him, wrapping itself around the lone man. He wasn't completely alone, though: a corpse, wearing the black rags that had at one time denoted it as a master chef, turned slowly on its spindly grey legs and gazed at the Humvee from sixty yards away, its dull mind trying to remember if the vehicle had been there minutes before.

Sitting completely still, holding a long handled axe, Ram stared back, his deep brown eyes focused on the zombie until it turned its head. Zombies were easily confused and the fading echo of the Humvee's engine had the thing looking about uncertainly.

When it began to shuffle on, Ram scarcely gave it another thought. Instead he flicked his eyes at the shadows beneath the eaves of the colonial houses. He stared hard into the gloom below the tall trees and glanced into the open doors around him; it was in these dark places that the real threat lurked. The zombies you didn't see were the most dangerous. They hung back, skulking like spiders, waiting for the unwary to become their next meal.

Nothing stirred; especially not the body lying on the street. It was this that had made him stop.

Stepping out of the Humvee, Ram glanced down at it with his hackles up, nervous at first. However when he saw that it was dead beyond any chance of reviving, he relaxed. There was a bullet hole, neat as you please, right in the center of its head.

Another body, face down on the lawn of a brick home drew his attention. With the axe in his right hand and his

Beretta in his left he eased toward the house. Using his boot he kicked the body over; again dead and again a perfect shot between the eyes.

"Hmmm," he said. On a whim, Ram entered the house and ghosted around the lower floor, seeing nothing of note but a ball of snot hawked up on a wall. The snot was old, maybe a day, maybe two; it was hard to tell in this new world of theirs.

Other than the relics of cities and towns and the empty rivers of concrete that had once been highways, the earth was quickly reverting to its pre-human form so that any recent human activity seemed to stand out and linger against the backdrop of nature. Cooking meat could be smelled for miles; cars or gunshots would waft along the air further than any thought possible, at least until it was experienced; and the sight of a person—a real, live person was like a lighthouse beacon on a black night.

Coming north from the CDC, Ram had seen only thirteen people, none of whom had heard the first thing about the killer he hunted. These thirteen had varied in terms of friendliness. Some had come forward, grinning and eager to shake his hand, while others kept their weapons at the ready. All had the same questions: Where was the government? Where were people? Where was food? Where was it safe?

He pointed them south to Atlanta, while they warned him about going further north. They wasted their breath. *She* had gone north—Cassie, the murderer—so he had to, also.

Outside the little town of Braselton, Georgia, north of the CDC, he had found the Suburban she had stolen after killing Julia. It had been weathered by the winter, yet he had recognized it immediately by all the bullet holes. Three days later, just across the border into South Carolina he discovered where Cassie had squirreled herself away for at least part of the winter: a well-constructed barn close to a medium-sized farming community.

It hadn't taken any of his skills in law enforcement to

figure out it had been Cassie staying there. In her boredom she had scrawled messages of hate on almost every surface, with his name being one of the most pronounced.

Now, ten days later in the suburbs of Philadelphia, he stood eyeing the snot. It was the third hint of humanity that he had come across in the last five days. Had Cassie actually been in this house? Was that her shoeprint in dried mud by the front door? Were these her sooty fingerprints on the mantle? The snot on the wall had his gut telling him this was Cassie's handiwork; she had always been casually vulgar, and he could imagine her spitting in contempt as she left the house. Of course he had no way of really knowing if she'd been here.

Still it was these faint rumors of her passing that kept him going north, though he had nearly abandoned the search after Washington DC. That city had been a running hell, one that even a demon such as Cassie would not have stomached. If there were humans left in that sad city, they were deep in its brick bowels and perhaps forever lost to the world.

Philadelphia was different. The zombies weren't nearly as numerous. Ram laid aside his axe and holstered his weapon before pulling out his battered Rand McNally. After marking his present location in red ink, he studied the map and its three red Xs, looking for a pattern. Each represented some sort of human activity, and if they all had been made by the same person then that person was clearly searching for something and not trying to bypass the city...but what were they searching for?

Food? Weapons? A last vestige of humanity? These were what everyone was searching for, which didn't help him at all.

"If I were Cassie, where would I go?" Ram said and then sighed, turning the map. The flat cartoonish nature of it: streets in white, water in blue *other than city* in green, wasn't much help. He decided to get a better view from above and tromped up to the second floor where he spied a pull down ladder to an attic. Without thinking anything of it, he gave the hanging rope a sturdy yank.

The stairs opened like a black mouth and out of it tumbled a pile of human corpses. They had been gnawed down to the bone, with little left but shreds of skin and tissue clinging to the remains. They rained down on him and the smell had him going dizzy.

"Oh...oh, that's horrible," he moaned. Gagging, he almost hurled up his breakfast, however, at that moment when the zombie which had done all the gnawing fell down the attic ladder, practically on top of him.

It had once been the owner of the home; a man with a family, a large mortgage and a ballooning gut, but now it was a sly zombie with only nine worn-down teeth left in its dank mouth. Its skin was grey and aged: puckered, wrinkled, and fissured. Its claws, on the other hand, were long and sharp.

As it fell, it flung out a hand and raked Ram, catching his shirt and shredding it at the neck. "Jesus!" he cried, in alarm. He put a hand to his neck, felt the skin was intact and breathed a sigh of relief. He then, casually, pulled the Beretta from its place in his hip-holster.

He was too casual by half, while the zombie was far quicker than he expected. To Ram, it looked to have come down in a jumbled heap, but it had actually landed in a crouch. Now it sprung at Ram, who flung himself backwards firing the pistol, running a nasty groove diagonally through the thing's face from left to right. The burning hunk of lead made a horrible gaping hole, but that didn't stop the zombie from attacking Ram with everything in its vicious arsenal.

Claws slashed at him and its jaws snapped crazily. Before Ram knew what was going on, the zombie had bowled into him, knocking him off his feet. Only years of training saved him. He pivoted as he fell—letting the left side of his body drop back while powering with his right, effectively turning the tables and landing atop the zombie.

This made only the barest of improvements.

Any time a man was within arm's reach of a zombie, it meant he was within arm's reach of death. Ram pulled back, gathering his feet beneath him and standing in a single quick move. As he did the zombie's claws made a scritching sound as they tore down his jacketed arm; the sound drew Ram's attention away from what really mattered. The zombie's other hand reached out and just managed to graze the bare skin of Ram's throat.

The sudden burning sensation focused him quickly. "Oh, no," he whispered, touching himself gingerly and feeling suddenly vulnerable and soft, and jittery. His hands began to shake.

In front of him, the zombie clambered to its feet and despite still toting a loaded pistol, Ram panicked. He took one step back, and then another as the zombie lunged again, looking suddenly much larger and fiercer than it had only seconds before.

Unbelievably, Ram found himself fleeing away from it. He raced down the stairs, his eyes blinking largely as if his ability to perceive reality had come unglued, while his mind could not get past the concept that he had been scratched. He was bleeding! It was just a trickle but, because of the virility of the zombie disease, it meant so much more.

It meant he was a dead man.

"This isn't happening," he moaned as he ran, heading out the door and into the yard with the zombie right behind. It stretched out a long arm and grabbed Ram, who could hear its eagerness, its insatiable hatred and hunger. The sound made him jerk and dodge away. Only then did he raise the pistol once more; though he was still sufficiently freaked out that his shot went awry.

The bullet missed low, striking the creature below the left eye; there was no exit wound. Staggered, the zombie took a step back giving Ram time to take better aim. This time he used two hands to steady the gun and it spat out the blazing lead, forming a neat hole in the zombie's forehead.

Ram didn't see the thing fall over. Nor did he notice that all up and down the street a horde had begun to swell, attracted to the sound of the shooting. The beasts came charging at the lone human who all but ignored them. Instead, Ram jumped up on the hood of the Humvee and began to dig in one of the pieces of luggage that he had tied to the roof rack. In it was a med box and in that box was a bottle of rubbing alcohol.

He had no idea if what he was planning would do a damned bit of good, but he felt that he had no choice. Ram poured the alcohol on his neck, and despite the swift sharp pain he worked the clear liquid into the wound and prayed silently as he did.

Other men had turned with lesser wounds. There had been a man in Glendale who'd had his hand nicked with the tiniest nick. It had been so small that a rumor had sprung up among the men that he had contracted the virus through the air. People had shunned him, even more than they normally would have—no one wanted to be close to an infected man, ever—but this had been far worse.

"I was scratched," the man had moaned. He had stood apart, trembling with the chills of his fever and with his overwhelming fear. *"Look."* He held out his hand, showing a wound that looked smaller than a cat's scratch.

No one had much sympathy. The fact was that in many people's minds, a person ceased to exist once the fever kicked in. The man was urged to kill himself and be done.

Ram would cease to exist as well. It was this realization that had him staring with unseeing eyes as the zombies began to close in. He only had hours left as a person. The idea of becoming one of these horrible creatures that he hated with such an intense loathing was a strange feeling indeed.

One of them grabbed his ankle and pulled. Ram shot it in the top of the head and again the unknowable variances in bullet trajectories caused the spinning lead to blast out the front of its face, sending grey teeth and brain splattering onto Ram's shoe. Sickened by the sight, he groaned, sounding like the monster he would eventually turn into.

When he heard himself, he cried, "No, this can't be happening."

Yet it was. Another beast, a tall, skinny zombie with long arms, got hold of his belt at the hip and pulled hard. Ram slid down from the Humvee, practically into the bosom of the monster. He shot it as it craned its open mouth toward him. Flinching from the rain of blood, Ram staggered away.

He became like a pin ball—bouncing from zombie to zombie, killing each but never with any purpose or plan of escape. He shot until the barrel of his pistol was scalding and the clip empty. With the same uncaring attitude he loaded the first of his three spares and began again the same slow killing. One after another they fell at his feet and he wondered why he bothered.

What was the use? He had maybe ten hours left…and that last hour didn't even count. The last hour would be spent in delirium and the one before that would zip by as he cried, clutching his pistol and hoping to find the courage to use it on himself. The hour before that one would be spent alternating between pleading to God for mercy and cursing his name as the heat of his fever began to bake his brain.

So how many hours did that *really* leave him? Six? Seven?

The bolt of the Beretta clunked back and Ram blinked stupidly while his index finger pulled uselessly on the trigger. Slowly he came to realize he had shot himself dry. Automatically he grabbed the second clip from his belt as he stared at the zombie horde which had him surrounded. It was small as far as hordes went, maybe a hundred tops, still it was enough. In his fugue state he had managed to trap himself.

The front yard of the house was bordered by an

impressive run of shrubbery standing at about six feet. There was no getting over it, or through it. Worse, some two dozen zombies had managed to get between him and the house, while the driveway, the only opening in the hedge, was practically clogged with the beasts. Cursing at his stupidity, Ram slowly fired each bullet with deadly accuracy as he backed to the green wall behind him.

And still they came on-and-on.

"I guess I won't have to worry about a fever," he whispered. With the heat of the battle, he felt, at least for the moment, somewhat like his old confident self again and he dropped the zombies one after another. This confidence lasted only the span of time it took him to go through the remaining bullets in the clip. When it was empty, his first thought was that he was going to have keep track of how many times he pulled the trigger.

It was his last clip and it was very important that the fifteenth bullet be saved for himself. The fever scared him to no end, however the very notion of being eaten alive made his skin crawl.

The only problem was that his last clip wasn't where it was supposed to be! He yanked aside his coat and stared down at where the third magazine should've been sitting in its stiff leather holder. "It was there. I put it right there as always," he said in a pleading voice, as his bulging eyes searched the grass beneath the feet of the surging zombies.

It wasn't in sight, but so desperate was the man to find the lost magazine that he let the undead close the distance quickly as he wagged his head from side to side staring intently down. A grey hand took a hold of his jacket while another just missed his face with its sharp talons. They were all around him pressing in close, their long arms reaching and their open mouths grinning in anticipation of their next meal. Despite his training and his deep experience Ram was on the verge of real panic; the kind that went hand-in-hand with madness.

On the edge of insanity, he stepped back uncertainly, and it seemed to him that the air around him grew hot and nasty so that he couldn't pull in a real breath. The beasts pressed close and there was nowhere left to run. Ram could feel himself suffocating as his panic grew. This was because he possessed the certain knowledge that they would drown him in their disease before the eating would commence, and in the end he would be just as they were.

And that, more than anything else, was what released his mind from its delicate hold on reality.

Chapter 3

Jillybean

Philadelphia, Pennsylvania

In a house on Juniper Lane that smelled of fried meat and hot ash, a little girl lay curled up in an arm chair drooling onto the sleeve of her tattered winter coat. In sleep her worries vanished and her face was angelic, seeming to have been created out of the whitest, smoothest porcelain.

When a tiny sound came to her consciousness, her blue eyes opened yet, beyond that slight flicker, she remained so motionless that she might have been porcelain indeed.

She knew that movement drew the monsters' attention. Once, she had sat, scarcely breathing and huddled like a rock, not three feet from one of *them,* and had not been seen. It had taken all her will not to go running off with a panicked scream in her throat. That would have meant sure death.

This was how she survived—with a mental toughness light years beyond her physical maturity.

Now, she froze on the chair in the pleasant home. Without moving her head, she ran her eyes all around while listening intently; the monsters wheezed or moaned when they breathed. She neither heard nor saw anything and so she slowly sat up. It was then she realized that Ipes was missing again.

"Ipes?" she whispered.

Down here. You dropped me, he scolded from the floor. *I nearly fell into the fire and what would you have done then?*

Jillybean fished the zebra from the floor and poked his big nose. "I would have all the cookies to myself for once. What do you think woke me?"

The wind I would say, Ipes ventured. He pointed with his flappy hoof at the window, beyond which trees could be seen swaying.

The little girl yawned and stretched, asking, "How long did I sleep?" She was a child of the digital age and thus was baffled completely by clocks with pointing hands although there were very few of them still moving anymore. She hadn't known the true time since her father had died.

Only a few minutes, Ipes replied. *And it's just as well. What would have happened if you had slept the day away? We have exploring to do and you know you can't travel at night.*

She knew all too well. Getting up she traipsed along to the kitchen, knowing instinctively in what direction it was. "You think that man left us anything?"

If you mean food, probably not.

Ipes was correct. The drawers had all been yanked and the cupboards were laid open and bare...all save a little white tin. "What's that say?" She held it up to Ipes who squinted his two black beads at it.

Or...orag...orange-ano, he said at last. *It's a spice.*

Opening the top of the tin she gave it a look. "Orange-ano? Why would they call it that if it's green?" After giving it a sniff her eyes went wide in recognition. "Momma used to put this in *bascetti*. We should keep it, right?"

Ipes agreed they should and she stored it away in her pink backpack. The pair then went through the rest of the house quickly, finding only one thing worth reclaiming: a four pack of D-batteries that Jillybean didn't want to take because they were heavy.

They're for flashlights, don't you know, Ipes told her. *And you can't see in the dark.*

"Neither can you," Jilly shot back.

Yeah, but I'm not afraid of the dark, like some people I know, Ipes said pointedly, to which the girl only replied: "Humph." Nonetheless she took the batteries. After that she decided to go home. Slipping out the back door she made her way around the side of the house just as she had come, only now there was a strong wind to contend with. It masked the fact that a monster had wandered close.

She neither saw the rotten-skinned thing nor heard it until it was practically on top of her. Only her natural instinct for survival kept her whole. The little girl went from a tentative, mousy walk to a flying, gazelle sprint in a fraction of a second. She eluded the zombie only to nearly run into the arms of another that had been sleeping on its feet in the shade of an elm across the street.

Stifling a useless shriek, she darted around a minivan parked in the street and then slithered under it crawling like a gecko with Ipes still in the crook of her arm. This sometimes worked with the brainless monsters who were easily confused when their prey suddenly disappeared. This time it didn't. One of the monsters, a thing that seemed to have spider-like long arms came down to street level and was just thin enough to wriggle under the minivan, while the larger of the two went down on hands and knees to stare at Jillybean, hungrily.

"What do I do?" she asked Ipes. "Do I try a magic marble?"

After turning his fuzzy head back and forth at the two monsters, Ipes said, *Not yet. Get a marble ready just in case and squinch to the front.*

She was only too glad to obey. It meant getting further from both the monsters. When she crawled away, the one on all fours got up and she could see its feet as it came around to cut off any escape attempt. *Now!* Ipes hissed in her ear. *Throw the marble behind it.*

With a backhand motion she whisked the marble out into the street. Immediately the bigger monster turned and stared at the marble as it skittered away. Unfortunately the one already under the van, the one with long squiggly arms, kept coming after her.

Over there. Ipes pointed. *Don't worry, you'll fit.*

What he had pointed at stopped Jillybean cold. It was a

storm drain, a black hole in the earth that led down into the worst nightmares of her imagination. In her little kid mind, she envisioned grotesque horrors living there—after all, if monsters walked the earth in broad daylight, what sorts of insidious things lurked in the dark and wet where light would not venture.

"Ipes, no," she said in an uncharacteristically whiney voice.

Now! he thundered in a manner that was very much like her father's.

Only this could have got the scared little girl moving. She crabbed her way as fast as she could to the gutter and slid into the storm drain with no room to spare. Her hands caught something on the wall that felt like a metal bar and held on as she pulled her legs in as well. This left her dangling above what looked like a drop into an endless abyss.

Let go! yelled Ipes. This time however the power in his fatherly voice wasn't enough and the girl refused to release her grip. Then a clawed hand, grey and scabby reached down from above and began fishing about, searching for her. Only then did she drop—twelve feet straight down—and had there not been an autumn's worth of moldering leaves at the bottom of the shaft, she would've been injured.

She sat in a thick gloom, looking up at the groping hand, wishing that it would go away. It didn't. Instead the monster's arm could be seen and then its shoulder, and finally it scraped its nasty head through the narrow opening and stared down at the girl.

Now Jillybean traded her fear of the dark for the more urgent fear of being stuck in a constricting tube with a monster. Before it could come further in, she was up and feeling about the walls of the catch basin. In seconds she found a gently sloping secondary tube. It was a feeder line. She went down it on her hands and knees, crawling along as fast as she could. She hurried because the pipeline wasn't small enough for her needs; the monster was a skinny one and she knew it would be able to fit as well.

The tube only went so far and then it branched into a much larger one. It was what was called a trunk line and was so absolutely black that Jillybean hesitated. It was the dark of hell and the sight of it going on for infinity turned her soul cold.

In the gloom behind her came an odd tha-dunk sound and then the rustle of leaves. *It's coming*, Ipes warned.

This was all the incentive she needed to get moving again. Stepping into the trunk line—it was large enough for her to stand stooped over—she turned to her left, feeling the curved walls of the drain and regaining a bit of her composure, which was considerable for a six-year-old. Still her hands shook and her lower lip jabbered up and down as she walked along.

Behind her were odd, slapping sounds like the pattering of webbed feet. They echoed, loudly at first but eventually grew faint.

"I think he went the other way," she whispered.

The zebra shrugged, a move lost by the dark. *Or he's squatting back there waiting for you to come back. Either way we have to go on, and whatever you do, don't drop me.*

Jillybean understood. There was an awful rotting smell wafting through the darkness. "Is this sewer for poop?"

I don't think so, Ipes replied. *It smells more like a dead animal, or one of the monsters, so we should be very quiet.*

That made sense, so Jillybean went into mouse-mode, giving up speed in the name of silence. Time beneath the earth had little meaning and she could only mark progress by the number of large side openings she passed. Each yawning, black opening gave her a queer turn and she was afraid to venture down any, thinking that they would only mean getting lost for good.

Of the smaller feeder tubes that went upwards there were surprisingly few. Nonetheless she explored each, finding three blocked with gratings, while one had a zombie practically standing in the gutter next to it.

Each time, Jillybean slunk back to the trunk line and the wretched dark, carrying on in the direction she had been. Doggedly she walked like a hunchback for what felt like hours, growing ever more tired, while simultaneously, her fear ebbed away.

"If we keep going, how am I going to make it back home again?" she asked her friend. This particular anxiety grew with each step.

Maybe we shouldn't try, Ipes suggested. *We didn't leave anything behind except for some pine needle soup.*

Jillybean pictured the house: her own bedroom with the flowered wallpaper and the carefully arranged Barbie dolls; her parent's room with the mummified body of her mother hidden under layers of blankets; the attic where she had made her nest and where the rest of the stuffed animals sat patiently waiting.

They aren't real, Ipes said, reading her mind as he could whenever the whim struck him. *They're not like me as you know.*

She walked on for a bit, her tiny feet making less sound than her fingers did as they caressed the walls. "What about daddy? What if he gets better and comes home?" Ipes sat tucked in her embrace and said nothing. He waited instead for Jillybean to answer her own question. "He's not coming back is he?"

No, he's not.

Jilly walked on, not saying anything, thinking of her dad and, to a lesser extent, her mom. She had always loved her mom, but it was her father to whom she had been especially close. Ever since his disappearance she had clung to the hope that he would return one day like he used to: with presents in hand and a huge, bearlike hug for her.

From her lips a sigh ran out into the dark only to be answered by a low moan.

All thoughts of her father disappeared.

Don't say a word, Ipes said in such a low voice that she had to wonder if he even spoke the words aloud or if they had originated somewhere in her mind. Either way it was wasted advice since even her breath had become stuck in her throat as surely if she had swallowed her acorns.

Gently now, he said. *Turn around but don't let...*

Too late. As she had turned, her *Power-Puff* backpack scraped against the invisible wall making a noise that could only be defined as human-made. Almost immediately there came a quick thumping and slapping from down the trunk line. It was a quirky noise and the girl could imagine the monster crawling like a giant mechanical insect right at her.

Jillybean fled, running with one hand above, to keep her head from whacking on the low ceiling, and one hand on the wall. *There'll be an intersecting tunnel soon. Hurry!* Ipes cried.

She couldn't hurry any faster. Even before the zombie, she had been tired and now only a minute into her race she felt the air in her lungs burn and soon a stitch stabbed into her side and yet the monster came on without pause. It drew steadily nearer until Jillybean began to make a fear-filled noise in her throat as terror built—she wouldn't make the other tunnel, it was too far.

With the monster huffing just feet behind her, Ipes cried, *Drop the backpack, but don't drop me!* She let it fall and within two strides there came an odd sound behind her as the monster found the backpack. In the dark, it attacked the pack without a second thought, thinking there was still a little girl attached to it.

Now stay quiet, Ipes warned. She was tired and it hurt to breathe, while her back was on fire from running hunched over as she had been, yet not for a second did she consider voicing a complaint. Complaints were for the weak and the decadent, for the people of before, the people who could afford to complain. Jillybean couldn't. Not anymore. She inhabited the world of black and white, life and death. Whining wasn't a part of that world.

She blew air in and out of her puffed cheeks as she hurried on, walking, not running, hoping to come to a side tunnel before the monster quit with the backpack. The hope was in vain. Very quickly, or so it seemed to her, the monster tossed aside the pack and again there came the nasty wet slapping of flat palms on cement and the thumping of knees.

You're almost there, Ipes said as she began again to run. Even quicker than before her breath grew labored and loud. *Just breathe nice and easy. We're going to make it. Ok? Can you get a marble out as you run?*

With her high-water pants being so tight, it was a struggle. After a few seconds she got one out, but she had no idea what good it would do her, not with the monster so close behind her. Then her hand left the wall suddenly and struck the nothingness of a side tunnel. She ducked into it and, just like that, she knew what to do with the marble. With an easy motion she threw it down the old tunnel giving the monster something to chase.

It went after it like a rabid dog and not twenty feet away there was a scrabbling of claws on cement and a ferocious growling. Jilly began to back away down this new tunnel, slowly, running air in and out of her lungs as though she wasn't dying to suck it in as quickly as possible, feeling light-headed in her need for oxygen.

Nice and easy, Ipes said in her mind. *It'll be alright. Just keep going nice and easy.*

She breathed as gently as possible, taking step after step away from the monster who was still in the other tunnel scrambling after the marble like a playful kitten—a giant fanged kitten with dead eyes and a hungry mouth.

Suddenly, it went quiet, and she knew the monster was listening for her. Now she became perfectly still, not even shaking in her fright.

Don't freeze up, Ipes said and again it felt like an echo in her mind rather than real, spoken words. *Keep backing up. Remember, it can't hear you. You're like a tiny mouse that walks unheard.*

Step-by-step she backed away, putting more than the length of a football field between her and the zombie. Just when she felt she was far enough away to breathe easier a new danger came to her in the form of gunfire. The sound of the gunshots, which were slow and steady and loud, like a blacksmith's hammer, came vibrating down the tunnel to stir the black air.

Her first impulse was to slink down and go "bunny", holding completely still until the possibility of danger passed, however Ipes knew better.

Run, he urged.

"Which way?" she asked. Running forward to where someone was shooting seemed as bad an idea to her as running back to the monster. Certainly the person was either shooting at other people or shooting at a *lot* of monsters, and neither option was a good one in her mind.

Straight ahead! Ipes insisted. *The monster can hear the gun too. He's coming.*

Sure enough, the sound of the monster's slapping palms came to her as though from far away. Because of the perfect dark the sound seemed to be coming from below her as if the tunnel had somehow turned on its side and had become a deep hole in the ground that went straight down.

The monster in the dark was an immediate fear and so she fled from it, heading toward the steady gunfire. Having heard plenty of gun play in the last year, this steady bam...bam...bam...like a deadly metronome was strange to her. Why would anyone shoot with such bland repetition? Normally, back when there were more people and more gunfights...that sort of normal, the shooting would erupt suddenly and build to a crescendo before petering away to nothing.

This sounded more like someone shooting without a real purpose. It lacked a sense of urgency and that made it easier for Jillybean to run along toward it. After only half-a-minute she found one of the smaller feeder tunnels which seemed to pulsate along with the gun. It ran at a diagonal upwards while a feeble light washed downward making her blink. The light had all the color and strength of old dishwater, yet it dazzled her wide eyes and sent a surge of hope through her chest.

She crawled up until it leveled off for a span of three feet, ending at a solid wall from which rusting iron rungs sprouted. It was a tall climb, especially for such a young person, however she didn't even pause. She could hear behind her that the monster had found the feeder tunnel as well and the nasty slapping turned into a grunting as the thing slithered on.

Up-and-up she climbed, with Ipes continually warning her not to look down, until the real light of day struck her full in the face and had her eyes watering. She was just about to squeeze herself out of the sewer when Ipes warned: *Don't move! There's a monster right there.*

A lady zombie stumped awkwardly past. It was barefoot save for the fact it had the remains of a high-heeled shoe dangling from an ankle. Though this made for an uncertain stride, it kept on going as fast as it could toward the shooting, ignoring completely the little bundle of rags that Jillybean appeared to be, huddled in the gutter.

When the thing passed her by, the girl scampered up and hid behind the split trunk of a crab-apple tree. Peering between the "Y" formed by the boughs, she watched as the sewer monster emerged into the light of the morning.

It was nasty even compared to its brothers. Crawling around in the unyielding concrete tunnels had worn away the skin and tissue of its hands and knees so that only shreds covered the exposed bones. The top of its head was similarly eroded except here the bone had been cracked and looked like a dented egg shell. None of this seemed to affect it in the least. Like an unoiled and rusted robot, it lurched into a standing position and immediately followed after the growing crowd which was in the process of converging on a single man just down the street from Jillybean.

She recognized him and his Humvee. It was the same person she had seen earlier.

"What do we do?" she asked Ipes in a whisper. The man was completely surrounded and despite the pistol hammering away she didn't think much of his chances. Neither did Ipes.

What can we do besides get out of here?

"I can't just leave him," she shot back. "Oh, why doesn't he run?"

Ipes sighed so that his little shoulders drooped theatrically. *I think it's too late for him to run. We should go. You don't want to see him...uh-oh.*

Uh-oh, indeed, thought Jillybean. It was clear even to the six-year old that the human had run out of bullets. Frantically he began searching his clothes and, seeming to imitate him, Jillybean dug about in the pockets of her high-water jeans as well—he searched for ammunition, while she was after the last magic marble.

But it's your last! Ipes cried.

"We can get more," she said, finding the marble at last in the depth of her pocket. She dug it out, kissed it, and without another word let it fly. Her practice at beaning the old monster Mrs. Bennet paid off and the marble flew straight down the street unleashing its magic with every loud *clack, clack, clack* it made as it struck the pavement.

The grey skinned beasts turned to stare at it as it bounced around and Jillybean knew the man would be ok. He would get away. He'd run for his big SUV and get away. But what of her? She knew the answer to that as well; it would be the same as always: she'd be alone in a world of monsters.

Chapter 4

Ram,

Philadelphia, Pennsylvania

After so much firing, the gun in Ram's right hand felt as though he had just plucked it from a furnace, though to be certain he hardly noticed. What concerned him completely was that it was empty. So were his pockets. His last clip had straight-up disappeared and with it his chance at the only good death left in this new world.

Trapped and alone, the horrifying idea of being eaten alive sent terror, like a bolt of lightning, racing through every fiber of his being. This overdose of adrenaline resulted in a berserker's charge that bowled over the zombies in front of him. With the virus already in him, he no longer feared the touch of the beasts and so he attacked, kicking with his powerful legs at those in front and then as one came at him from the side, he grabbed it and heaved it into a throng of its horrible mates.

Another, a slight zombie: what once had been a fifteen year-old sophomore with a baby face, Ram used as a battering ram to try to smash his way out of the yard, but it was too light and it didn't work. Out of ideas, he then ran through the enclosed yard, dodging this way and that, hoping to get to the house or maybe the street where his Humvee sat alone and untended, only he couldn't, the zombies formed a wall three deep that he dared not try to bust through.

This game of Red-Rover could only end with him becoming a feast. With no other choice, he spun and saw the slimmest of chances that he could add a few more minutes to his life. Two of the zombies that had succumbed to his head shots had dropped one atop the other just feet from the hedge that ran along the adjoining property. Without hesitation he took off at a sprint heading right for them.

Only someone inebriated to a point well past stupidity or someone in the most desperate of straits would have thought his idea a good one. His plan was to use the dead as a springboard to try to clear the hedge.

Ram had an image in his head of him clearing the shrubbery with enough room to land cleanly, enabling him to hop up and make a decent run for safety. Things didn't turn out quite the way he had envisioned it. What happened instead was that he only partially cleared the hurdle and became stranded with one leg up in the air and his face in a moldy pile of leaves on the other side of the hedge. Now there came a pause, a moment of confusion and he dared not move.

The zombies still in the yard were confounded by his leap and wandered back and forth trying to find a way through the hedge, while the ones in the street hesitated for only a moment before they collectively began to head Ram's way.

He could see their legs through the lower part of the hedge and the sight, ensnared as he was in the shrubbery, hanging upside down, made his panic double. He could feel it like a bomb in his chest set to explode and that was when he heard a sound like slapping glass on pavement. Quickly, his mind assessed the noise: unbelievably it was the sound a large marble would make if it had been tossed in the air to land on cement.

It didn't make sense to Ram or to the zombies. The undead on the front side of the hedge turned and began to gape as the marble bounced crazily along knocking into cars and dancing to an unknown and unheard tune. What was left of the minds of the undead was such that their incomprehension rendered them almost paralyzed as they tried to process this new thing—the human had suddenly disappeared and now there was this...this thing bopping about. They stared, their heads bobbing in time with the marble's progress, trying to render the marble into meaning.

To Ram the erratic *clack, clack, clack* was a thin slice of miracle. Every zombie head had turned to watch the passage of the ball of glass and as they did he lifted his hooked shoelace off a branch and, righting himself, then ran, low and hunched, along the hedge until he made the street where running in such a manner was no longer prudent. He sprinted past a group of gawking zombies and made it to the safety of his Humvee before any of the beasts could even comprehend what had just happened.

They were quick to catch on however that their meal was escaping and in a second the zombies were pounding on the side window and clawing at the door. Feeling a need to cackle madly at his luck, Ram started the engine and tore out of there, but not before glancing in the rearview mirror.

There, a good thirty yards or so behind the zombies was a little girl with fly-away brown hair and huge blue eyes in a pale face. Her skin was of such alabaster that the word vampire ghosted through Ram's mind.

The world had so turned on its head that for a split second he actually entertained the idea that she was a vampire. After all, she couldn't be human. She was standing alone and apparently fearless within a few feet of a host of undead. It just couldn't be. A little girl on her own would have died long ago. She would've been caught and killed and then turned...now he understood, she was one of them.

"Just a white zombie," he rationalized. He glanced once to the road and when he looked back she had disappeared behind the horde that followed after the retreating vehicle.

"It's just as well," he said before turning the mirror to look at a more pressing matter for him than funny looking zombies: the three scratches that ran from the hollow of his throat to the top of his chest. They were raised and angrily red.

The sight killed the relief he'd been feeling over his close call. He hadn't saved himself, after all; he'd just put off his death for a while longer.

With a growing depression settling in, he drove and barely saw the road; his haunted eyes wouldn't leave the mirror showing him the marks that were a badge of his imminent death. Eventually, when he found an open stretch of road that was clear of stiffs, he pulled over and went about reloading his Beretta with a new clip.

And then he wasted one of his precious remaining hours simply sitting there with the gun in his large brown hands. At first his mind was blank; it dwelt on nothing at all. He stared at the gun and for a while that was enough. But then he turned it around so that the round bore pointed at his left eye. It seemed inviting.

"Why wait to die?" he asked in a whisper. There was no good answer to that, except to acknowledge that waiting wouldn't help him in the least. In fact it would hurt very much.

Very, very much.

"I should just..."

Impulsively, he stuck the gun to his temple. "I should just..." A second time he couldn't finish the sentence.

How many soldiers had he seen in exactly this same position? A hundred at least, and he had always urged them to just do it. Pull the trigger. Get it over with, but none ever had, not so early. Most of them waited until the pain and the fever kicked in, while a few never did pull the trigger.

Now Ram knew why.

What if the virus doesn't work this time? What if I'm immune? What if some scientist pulls up in the next ten minutes with a cure? These questions ran through his head, just as, he was sure, they had gone through those other men's heads.

When they couldn't pull the trigger Ram had secretly called them fools.

"Am I the fool now?"

The gun had slipped from his temple. He brought it up again and was prepared to pull the trigger right then, however he paused and for some reason glanced into the rearview mirror. Instead of seeing the reality of himself with a gun to his head, he saw the memory of another person with a gun to her head: Julia.

There she was in the reflecting glass, twisting the gun into her red hair, grinding the sight of the barrel into her skin. He had begged her not to kill herself. In retrospect, Ram thought that had been a mistake. She had died anyway. And for what? Nothing.

Ram's right hand bunched, drawing the trigger ever closer to the point where the inner springs of the gun would take over and complete the process of sending a bullet into his brain, but then the woman in the mirror seemed to speak to him:

I didn't just die, she reminded him. *I was murdered. And I didn't die for nothing; I died to save my baby. Don't you remember? Don't you know why you're here?*

He knew. He was here for revenge. Before that morning, the demand for revenge had been a fire in his gut. Now, it suddenly seemed like an empty concept. It seemed like a mirage. Then again life was now little more than illusion to him. It consisted of bits of time broken into tiny pieces of which he had very few left.

Ram blinked away the memory and took to staring into his own eyes in the mirror, seeing the truth of his predicament: he was afraid to both pull the trigger and afraid not to. It was an impossible decision.

Something drew his eye. Far away, above Philadelphia there was a distant smudge in the air. Smoke on the horizon. It meant humans. Maybe, it meant Cassie.

The gun dropped onto the seat next to him. The decision whether or not to pull the trigger was too much for him, so he decided not to decide. Not just yet. In order to delay it he turned the Humvee back east, toward the smoke, hoping to find...something, but what, he had no idea.

Chapter 5

Jillybean

Philadelphia, Pennsylvania

When the hummer surged away from the little girl, knocking over the monsters in the street and running them down, she felt her insides drop. She only stood, listlessly, staring after it. A few minutes later the monsters gave up their chase and began to mill about.

I'm proud of you for saving that man, Ipes told her. *But you really need to get inside before they figure out you're not one of them.*

Wordlessly, she obeyed. For her, one house was as good as another and so she went up the walk of the closest and entered it as if she had always lived there. It was a quaint little place: knick-knacks on the shelves and pictures of a happy little family of four, hanging on the walls. There was even a set of hooks by the door with a leash dangling from one. It had such a homey feel that Jillybean had the temptation to yell out: *Mommy, I'm home*! She squelched the desire and strangely, found it hard to do so.

She missed her mommy and she missed coming home from school to a big smile and a plate of Oreos next to a glass of cold milk. She missed her old life.

As always the girl headed right for the kitchen—it was painfully empty, barren in a way that bespoke of a meticulous search. Someone had even gone through the junk drawer and had taken the small packets of ketchup and *Kikkoman's* soy sauce that Jillybean was sure had been there at one time, nestled beneath the take-out chopsticks, the thumbtacks, and the pens that had long before run out of ink and that for some reason no one had thrown away.

"Darn," she said and then, with a heavy sigh, went upstairs, dragging her feet. The place was more than a little depressing. It was a family home, however the fact that the family had long ago been turned into monsters seemed to have altered something about the house in a subtle way—it was as if the house was waiting to die as well.

What once had been lively and fun was now drab with dust and settled in a gloom. Everything sat in its proper spot...waiting. The TV in its alcove waited to be turned on; the book on the bedside table waited to be opened, the skates by the front door waited with their laces out and inviting.

However Jilly felt that the period of *expectant* waiting had long past. The home waited, but it waited without hope. Now it waited for the earth to reclaim it and the little girl could feel its sadness with each breath.

The master bedroom with its dark furniture held little interest for her. There was a boy's room, filled with boy stuff: army men fighting a mock-battle on a cluttered desk, a long skateboard sitting dangerously just inside the door, a bunk bed with an *Eagles* bedspread on the lower bunk and a dead turtle in a dry tank. She barely gave this last item a look—the details of death repulsed her.

What really got her attention was Carrie's room. She knew it belonged to a girl named Carrie because of the sign on the door that read: *Carrie's Room—Trespassers Beware*! The sign went ignored as far as the threat was concerned and Jillybean went into the room with a flutter in her chest.

It was everything she had hoped for. It was girlie-girl wall-to-wall with pink everywhere, but one thing stood out from it all.

"Oh my God! Ipes, look at this dollhouse," she gushed, hurrying to the gabled miniature mansion that was as tall as she was. Gently she pried back the front half of it so that she could stare in awe at the intricate beveled woodwork, the attention to detail, the perfection.

"There's little people!" she cried, going down to her knees on the beige carpet and gently touching the little family of figurines that lived in the house.

We don't have time for this, Jillybean, Ipes said. *I'm sorry, but there are a whole mess of monsters out there. We have to get what we can and go.*

"But, I don't want to," she said in a soft petulant voice. "I want to stay." Of course she knew he was correct, but the dollhouse was everything she could have wished for. There was a mom and a dad, and two girls and a boy. A dog sat just by the front door and there was even a leash just like downstairs in the real house. Every room was furnished just as it should be, right down to tiny forks and spoons that sat at each of the place settings on the dining room table.

There were eight settings. "I think they're going to have people over," she whispered. "Maybe a dinner party for the grode-ups. I bet the kids will have to stay in the kitchen and eat there."

Ipes swiveled his ears at her, nervously. *Jillybean, please. We can't stay.*

"But I want to!" she cried, slamming her little fist into the plush carpet; suddenly there were real tears hanging on her cheeks and eyelashes. "I don't want to leave. I don't want to do this anymore."

Do what, honey? Ipes said in a voice that sounded like her father's.

"Run away and be hungry and not have anyone," she explained in a voice that cracked with emotion. The tears were hot on her face and they blurred her vision so that the perfect little house wobbled and doubled in her eyes. "I want to play. And I want something to eat. And I don't want to leave. Ever!"

The stuffed zebra in the light blue t-shirt considered this while little Jillybean cried with her lips bent down and her chin shaking and her heart all a mess.

Ipes reached out his soft cotton hoof and gave her hand a pat. *How bout we do this: we write down where this house is and then when we find some people, someone to take care of you, we can come back and get this pretty dollhouse. And maybe even some of those stuffed animals on the bed. What do you think?*

She thought his suggestion was all poopy. Since her father had died she hadn't seen anyone but the man with the Humvee and he didn't seem all that smart. For one he had almost run over Ipes and for two he had needed a six-year-old's help to escape the monsters.

The trouble was that she didn't have a better idea. Staying here would mean starving and despite her meal that morning her tummy was already getting an angry rumble going.

"Ok, I guess," she said, calming by degrees. She wiped her nose across the sleeve of her jacket and added, "But you'll have to do the writing." She was the first to acknowledge that her penmanship had degraded since she had missed so much school. Now her blocky letters would sometimes come out backwards and she wouldn't notice until she tried to read her own writing.

By the front door they found a stack of mail and Ipes, who could barely hold a pen, thought it smarter to just rip off the address from one of the envelopes.

"So where are we going?" Jillybean asked as she peeked out of the window. In the street a number of the monsters still milled about, but it was the ones that were hidden from sight that made her stomach go queasy. "And how will we get there? You don't think we're going down that road, do you?"

Ipes gave the street a glance and made a face. *No, not the road. We should go back to the sewers.*

Jillybean's mouth came open at this. "No way. It's too dark. And there could be more of the monsters down there. You know we barely got away last time."

I don't see any other way, Ipes replied. *This neighborhood is infested with monsters and all that shooting probably brought more from miles around. I bet there are a dozen on every street and down every alley.*

"But it's so dark down there. I don't like the dark. Could we bring a flashlight? I saw one in the boy's room."

Before Ipes could answer she was running up the stairs and with a grin held up the Maglight. It was a heavy thing in her little hands, and it didn't work.

"Shoot!" she exclaimed and tossed it on the bed.

Ipes made a noise of irritation. *Not so fast. I bet it's only got dead batteries and we know where we can get more, right? Your backpack; I know exactly where you dropped it. And look*, Ipes pointed at the long skateboard. *Transportation. You can either lie or sit on that and paddle with your hands. We can go along nice and quiet. What do you think?*

"I guess," she said without much enthusiasm. But then she brightened. "Do you think it'll be alright if I try on some of Carrie's clothes?" Jillybean's ankles showed beneath the cuff of her jeans and her shirt sleeves stopped well up her wrist.

Ipes allowed that it would be more than alright. Unfortunately, Carrie had been ten when she died and her clothes were all much too large. Jilly was forced to make-do with Carrie's brother's clothes instead. She wore a look of disgust when she slipped on a t-shirt with a picture of some once-famous wrestler on the front; over that she pulled on a *Philadelphia Eagles* sweatshirt, while for pants she found a pair of jeans that draped just over her toes.

"I look like a boy," she griped, rolling up the bottoms of each leg.

You kinda smell like one as well, Ipes added. To this she made a little angry noise in her throat. Boys had always been the enemy and to look and smell like one put her in a bad mood. Still, she was warm and less constricted. What's more, just as she turned to leave the room her eyes fell on a jelly jar that overflowed with marbles. The glass beads held every color she could name and many more that she couldn't. Some were striped and others pure, but the ones she liked the most reminded her of cloudy planets. She took the very largest of these and stuffed her pockets with them.

When she was all ready to go, she took the skateboard in one hand, the flashlight in the other and stuck Ipes under her arm; she then slunk out the front door, moving so slowly that she appeared to be a manikin with wide and staring blue eyes. The monsters were all far too close to satisfy so she went into a squat and hunched her way down to the street using a row of shrubs as cover. She went undetected.

Then she was down into the storm sewers, and once again blind. Strangely, the intense dark did not bother her as much as she had feared it would. It was comforting, really, because she knew she was invisible.

By feel she edged to the trunk line and then followed Ipes' whispered instructions, retracing her steps until she ran into her backpack. Though she had expected it with each step, hitting it with her foot caused her to jump, and she knocked her head.

"It's not funny," she said when the zebra began to snort laughter.

It is a little, Ipes replied. *Be careful when you try the flashlight. Shine it into the backpack. Just in case.* He meant just in case a monster was nearby.

With a fresh set of batteries the flashlight worked...too well. Even though she turned the light on and then off again quick, Jillybean's eyes still danced with wild floating spots—purple blobs against a black background. She blinked them away as she listened for any monster-related noises. There were none, so she stowed the flashlight away, put Ipes in his cargo pocket on the backpack and then settled down on the skateboard.

Neither the stuffed animal nor the little girl gave any thought to their destination. In one direction, the way they had been going before running into the monster, there was a slight downward angle to the tunnel and this was the deciding factor. It was simply easier to go that way and that was good enough for them.

Jilly lay, belly-down on the board and alternated paddling with either arm. Sometimes she'd hit a lip of cement or dried leaves that would crackle alarmingly, however mainly it was a smooth, near silent ride. When she grew tired she rested and when her tummy began to hurt from lying on it too long, she changed to a sitting position and still she swept along.

She kept up a steady speed that wasn't very taxing and which allowed her keen ears to focus on any sound emanating from the dark. Twice she heard the telltale moans of the grey-skinned monsters, but luckily both came from one of the many branching tunnels that intersected the main trunk line. When she passed these she held her breath, while her tummy went squirrely with fear. To make sure that she didn't make even an accidental sound, she rode lying on the board, so that she could feel ahead of her with a free hand.

Nothing came of these incidents and so the day wore away and yet Jillybean wasn't quite sure of its passing. Time was wiggy in so much dark. She knew she was growing ever more hungry and thirsty, and yet these states had become such a constant part of her life that hours couldn't be measured by missed meals anymore.

On and on she paddled the board as though she was drifting down a sluggish river and in fact she was heading toward one: the Schuylkill River, one of the two rivers that cut Philadelphia into thirds.

The first indication that her tunnel was ending was the smell; it wasn't pleasant.

"Do you think it's a monster?" Jillybean asked Ipes between sniffs.

I don't think so, he replied, his voice unnaturally high. *It's too strong to be just one.*

She was slow to get moving after that, but eventually she eased the board forward until she saw a meager light ahead. As she got closer, it grew to dazzle her, while at the same time the smell got stronger until she was sure she was going to throw up.

The tunnel ended abruptly at a hinged gate. With meek little steps Jillybean went to it, and, looking out at the Schuylkill she discovered the source of the smell. Rotting bodies by the hundreds in various degrees of decomposition lined the shores or gently drifted along in the murky, river water.

Jillybean's beans face contorted at the sight. "Are those monsters, or…"

They're people, Ipes said sadly. *Or they were people. Here, don't look at them. Instead look across the water. There's smoke behind those buildings.* Sure enough across the river, just behind an industrial complex, a thin ribbon of smoke stretched into the blue afternoon sky. And smoke usually meant people—living people.

"Do we chance it?" she asked, lifting her chin to her left.

There was a bridge not more than a hundred yards away and though it was cluttered with cars, there wasn't a single monster anywhere on it. Nodding, Ipes pointed at it and then he swung his hoof to aim at the far bank directly across from them.

I think we should. See that over there? It's another storm tunnel. We can go up that for a mile or so and come out and look around. If it doesn't curve at all we should be right near that smoke.

She didn't ask about the possibility of monsters in the tunnel—there was always that possibility. They were everywhere, or so it seemed to her. With skateboard in hand, the little girl slipped easily between the bars and then ghosted through the tall river grass, barely parting it with the slimness of her form, until she came to the bridge where cover was sparse.

With what felt like the world staring down at her, Jillybean followed her instincts and slowly drifted from car to car, pausing at each to spy all about her. Had anyone seen the little thing moving with careful steps they might have thought, by her demeanor, to be a timid, frightened wisp of a girl, however a closer inspection would've revealed that her face was hard and her eyes sharp, and that there wasn't a flicker of fear anywhere about her.

Skill, luck, and the western sun behind her allowed her to cross the Schuylkill unnoticed by anything larger than the hungry, squawking seagulls. Once on the far bank she dashed to the tunnel, waited with a cocked ear for all of a minute, and then when no sound came to her she pushed between the bars.

Again the dark was on her like wet on a fish. It seemed to invade her lungs so that she struggled for breath. *Take it easy*, Ipes said coolly. *Just start walking and you'll get used to it again. There you go. Do you want to use the board? It'll be easier than…*

A rumbling from above them stopped the flow of his words. At first Jillybean stepped back in fright, ready to run, but then she understood what she was hearing: a car was passing overhead.

"There's people for sure, Ipes! Come on." She began to rush forward but the zebra stopped her.

Now is not the time for the hare, he intoned. *Now is the time for the tortoise. Slow and steady wins the race.*

Chapter 6

Ram

Philadelphia, Pennsylvania

On his way to discover the source of the smoke, Ram spent a few of his remaining hours wasting gas and wearing out his patience trying to drive the eight or so miles into the city. Someone had systematically blocked all the roads into Philadelphia.

When he came upon the obstruction at the intersection of MacDade Boulevard and Ridgeway Avenue, a seven car pileup that not even his hummer could get around, he thought it was just happenstance. He turned back and skirted north, but found the very same thing at Baltimore Avenue and then again on the West Chester Pike.

With gun in hand, he had inspected the vehicles closer and saw that the windows of each had been smashed, and not by vandals. Glass in the driver's side seats but not the in the passenger seat was the telltale evidence left by a front-end loader equipped with pallet forks. Someone had purposely blocked the roads.

"What a friggin' headache," Ram griped, pushing at the starred window of a Lincoln Continental. The safety glass made it a mesh that resisted his hand, bending without breaking. For some reason it had a calming effect on the man.

"So what's in there that you don't want me to find?" he asked, staring eastward toward the city and the little smudge of smoke that rose above it. The barricade of cars was obviously meant to dissuade humans, not zombies. Either could climb over the cars without too much difficulty and go on to the city by foot, though it was only a zombie that would do so. Any human making the attempt would last only as long as his ammunition did.

This was why Ram kept skirting north, poking east at every street that went in that direction. Eventually he found a way around one of the barricades, or rather, through it. On a street called Ridgewood, the jumble of cars went across the road and right up to the houses on either side. Ram was just in the midst of a curse laden K-turn when he had an idea. His turn had been sloppy; he nicked part of a white picket front yard fence and for just a moment he had reverted to his pre-apocalypse programming and felt an immediate contrition.

Then he laughed at himself since the owners were all long dead—and then he laughed at himself some more. He was in a badass Hummer H2 with a heavy grill in front. What was to stop him from just plowing through this fence and through the one in the backyard? That one was six foot privacy fence that wouldn't last a second in a tussle with his hummer.

A minute later, the fence came down with a very satisfying crash.

Now there was only one more barrier to the city: the Schuylkill River, and again, just like the streets, the bridges were blocked, only this time brute force wasn't going to be much help. One after another he found his way across the water stymied by piled cars, so that he was forced ever northward. After another wasted hour and with aggravation setting in, he passed through the tony area of Wynnfield Heights, where the smallest homes were mansions and the largest were veritable palaces.

Here, he came across a new sign of humanity: a long wall of rusty steel that would stop even the most aggressive zombie. Someone, likely the very same someone who had blocked up the city, had hauled cargo containers up from the port and had set them end-to-end so that they encircled, strangely enough, a golf course of all things.

"Now that is an exclusive course," he said with a smirk.

An entire country club with many posh homes and buildings were within the walled-off area. Because the land was so flat, Ram couldn't see much beyond a few ill-tended fairways. Intrigued, he drove his Humvee closer and parked it just up the street from a tall tree that sat near one of the cargo containers. The tree, with its many branches, looked like a snap to climb and so, forgetting his illness and the fact that climbing trees was the sport of kids, he decided to hoist himself aloft to see what there was to see.

In spite of dark clouds that had begun to mass in the west, it was still a fine afternoon and although the nearest zombie was a tiny figure far down the road, Ram slung his M16 on his shoulder and proceeded on foot toward the tree. It wasn't more than a forty yard tramp through the new grass, but it proved nearly too far.

He was halfway to the tree, humming a bit of nonsense, when a strange noise made him turn. There in his tracks raced a pack of zombie dogs, charging at him with fearfully large teeth bared in either anger or hunger. In a split second Ram judged the distance between them, calculating how many he could bring down with his rifle before the rest were on him and tore him into shreds. It was far too few.

Because it would only slow him down, he let the M16 fall with a clatter—he still had his Beretta at his side with more than enough ammunition to take care of the dogs—and raced for the tree. Though he had a good head start and wasn't exactly slow, the dogs gained on him so quickly that there wasn't time to climb; instead, as he neared the tree he leapt for one of the lower branches and not three feet behind him, the lead dog leapt along with him as well. It was a strange and unnerving sensation to feel the razor sharp teeth of a German Shepherd close on his ankle just enough for him to feel a hard pinch and then let go.

Gasping, Ram clawed the bark, struggling higher into the tree, while below the dogs snapped and snarled, yet none barked. Instead they made an odd hu-reh, hu-reh noise deep in their throats. When he finally got a good perch beneath him, he pulled his pistol thinking he would kill these devil dogs and get back to his search for Julia's murderer, only now that he wasn't running and climbing for his life he saw that these were not zombiefied dogs after all. They were real.

"Wow," he whispered, eyeing the motley pack. Besides the Shepherd and an array of mutts, there was a Pug, three Dobermans, and a Labrador. These were the first live dogs he had seen since, well, he couldn't remember when. "And they're certainly not wild," he added, realizing what their strange, quiet barking meant: their vocal cords had been surgically severed.

Ram holstered his gun. He wasn't about to kill a real dog. Instead, he eased lower and began to croon a long stream of happy sounding nonsense hoping that it would calm the beasts down. It did, to a degree, just not one that allowed him to feel safe enough to climb down.

"Well this sucks," Ram said, giving up after a while. "Look fellas, I can't stay up here all day. I've got to get going…"

Just then a pair of pick-up trucks came racing down the road toward him; the beds of both were crammed with men, each armed to the teeth. When they got close, the trucks slowed and the men came piling out, calling the dogs to them.

Ram eyed the men closely and noted, with disappointment, that they were all white, which meant it wasn't likely that Cassie was within the bounds of the walled golf course. Still, they might have heard something of her passing.

With a little wave of friendly gratitude, Ram climbed down and came forward to greet them. "Thanks. It's not every day a guy gets treed like a…"

"Shut the fuck up and get those hands in the air!" one of the men ordered, adding, much to Ram's astonishment, "Spic."

"Spic?" Ram repeated, half in shock, half in anger. He was about to throw down a challenge, however the man's clear hatred wasn't singular; all the men glared at him and it was only then he noticed that their guns were still trained straight on his chest. "What's going on here?" he asked, raising his hands to shoulder height.

"Get those hands higher," an older man with a patchy grey beard growled. "And turn around nice and easy."

Ram shrugged and did as he was told. He wasn't exactly scared of being shot since his life's meter was running down anyway, as evidenced by the fact that he was already starting to feel a little queer inside. His main worry was that out of spite they would allow him to turn; a fate worse than death in his mind.

When he spun in place to face the rows of cargo containers, rough hands yanked out his Beretta and then he was pushed to his knees where he was thoroughly and properly frisked. "I also dropped a M16 over there in the grass," he said helpfully. When they had gone through his pockets he began to get up.

"Stay down, Spic," one of them demanded, threatening him with a rifle.

With a roll of his eyes, Ram got up anyway. "Are you that afraid of me? There are ten of you and you're all armed for goodness sakes. Now really, what's going on? What's with the rough treatment?"

One of the men came forward and his blue eyes were like hard diamonds. He pressed a long barreled shotgun into Ram's chest and said in a soft voice, "I should plug you right now."

The older man, the one with the grizzled beard put a hand out and said, "Let's find out what he knows first, Scott. There'll be time for revenge later."

The word revenge got Ram's attention more than the shotgun did. "Revenge? What happened?" he asked quickly. "Was there a girl? A black girl? I'm looking for a girl named Cassie. She's a murderer. She killed my…someone close to me."

"Doesn't surprise me," the younger man drawled with a stony sneer. "We learned the hard way you can't trust the blacks…or the spics." Ram began to splutter in anger over this, but the man nodded to his friends who grabbed Ram and wrestled him down to the ground. And then, when he was trapped beneath them, Scott pushed the shotgun down onto Ram's left palm, pinning his hand to the dirt. "You're going to tell me what you're doing here or I'm going to take off this hand in a manner you won't much like."

It was clear he wasn't playing games, yet Ram was so bewildered that the threat of the gun still wasn't striking home. "I already told you," he said. "I'm after a girl…a young woman of about nineteen, named Cassie. She's around five and half feet, 135 pounds, African-American with a dark complexion. She's a murderer. She killed a woman named Julia with an axe. That's why I'm here."

The older man stood above Ram and stared down; he wore an old *Phillies* baseball cap with a sweat stained bill. He took it off and scratched his bald pate. "And you think she's with us? Is that what the *Blacks* told you?"

"The *Blacks*? If you're talking about black people, then no. You guys are the first people I've seen since I got here," Ram said. "I just came up from the CDC in Atlanta."

A man lying across Ram's chest pulled back slightly and said with some excitement, "The CDC? Is there any news of a cure, or a vaccine? A free one, I mean?"

Scott stepped on the man's shoulder, forcing him back down onto Ram. "Don't be an idiot, Herm. This guy's not from the CDC, he's from North Philly. You can make book on that."

"You'd lose that bet," Ram said in a muffled voice. Herm had been heavy to begin with, but now that Scott was resting his foot on his back the weight across Ram felt doubled. "I'm from Los Angeles. Whoever took my wallet can check."

"He is," someone said in a quiet, guilty voice. "And he

was a DEA agent."

There was a murmuring and the men began to get off Ram one after another and now it was Scott who looked puzzled and uncertain. "What are you guys doing?" he asked. "We aren't going to let him go. He's one of them, damn it!"

"One of who?" Ram asked, though he had a gut feeling he knew already.

Some of the men toed the dirt, while others gave a glance to a flock of birds that were mere dashes in the blue sky they were so high up. The older man introduced himself as "John," stroked his beard and told a story that had Ram shaking his head.

"Philly is not a good place these days," he said quietly. "When the zombies came, those that survived sort of clumped together, you know? There were a lot of white people out here in the suburbs and most of us came here when we heard that the walls were holding. In South Philly there was a big trucking company that ran out of this warehouse. It had been almost a fortress to begin with and supposedly it was chock full of food and fuel. That's where the blacks went.

"No one knows where the Latinos first congregated, but it was in North Philly someplace, but it turned out to be too close to the blacks. They quarreled over territory and before we knew it there was a full-fledged war going on. That was about two months ago."

"A race war? Really?" Ram asked with disgust in his voice. "This is the thing about humans I just don't get. We have plenty of enemies all around us, yet we insist on fighting ourselves. So how did you guys get involved?"

"We're not really sure. Maybe because we were trading with both sides," John said. Ram gave him a sharp look and he grew defensive. "We have fourteen hundred people to look after and trading is the best way to get what we need in bulk. It benefits both sides, you know."

Ram gave him a little shrug, "I suppose…sorry."

"It's ok. In retrospect I wish we hadn't traded with either of them. Both the Latinos and the Blacks demanded that we stop trading with their enemy and, when we didn't, bad blood turned into spilt blood. Ever since, it's been constant strife. We keep to our side of the river, but that doesn't seem good enough and there isn't a one of us who hasn't lost someone close."

All the men, including Scott, nodded along at this. Now that they were no longer pointing their weapons at him they seemed to be just a normal group of guys.

"Maybe I can help you," Ram offered. "I have to go into Philly. If I live long enough maybe I can give the *Blacks* the message that you want a cease fire. That's if you plan on letting me go."

John scratched beneath his cap again and asked in a surprised voice, "Why on earth would you want to go in the city after what I just told you?"

Ram flicked his eyes to Scott and said, "Revenge. Retribution."

"If you're going into the city, you won't live long enough for either," Scott said. "They don't take prisoners. If they get you alive, they feed you to the zombies. And then, just as you turn, they'll set you free among your own people. I don't know if you know what that's like, seeing a friend in that state. It's horrible what they do."

The idea made that queer feeling inside Ram ramp up in tempo. It was like the distant clouds—a storm was coming and there was nothing he could do about it. "I've seen my share of friends who have turned, and had I known all this crap was happening I don't know if I would've come. You can only take revenge so far, however…" Here he paused and opened his shirt to show the angry scratches that were at his throat. "I got careless this morning and now I don't have much to lose."

The men backed away.

"There's one thing you have to lose," Scott replied. "A good death. A proper death. It's something you can't take lightly these days."

Ram knew that was true, but he didn't know how true until an hour later when he sat trussed to a tetherball pole in an elementary school playground as three angry men took turns punching him in the face.

Chapter 7

Ram

Philadelphia, Pennsylvania

"Don't do it, man," Scott said. "Don't go. It'll only end badly for you." He made to put out a hand to Ram, however the presence of the virus in Ram was like a force-field that kept the man at bay. He pulled his hand back, curling his fingers in as an extra precaution.

"Listen to him," John advised. He squinted at Ram. "How long do you have left? Two hours? Three?"

Ram touched his face with gentle fingers as if to assure himself that he hadn't changed already. "Four hours I think...I hope. Do I look that bad?" His insides had really begun to bother him and now he could feel a fine sweat at his brow.

"You don't look good," Scott said. He then glanced down to the ground where the grass was still bent from the scuffle and added, "I'm, uh...I'm sorry for how we treated you. My brother disappeared a few days ago and I'm not dealing with it well."

"It's alright," Ram said, still with his fingers on his face. He had a deep sense of expectancy about him as if his doom was in the air he breathed. "It's understandable, I guess. But I have to go. I can't just sit around waiting to die." He had seen too many of his fellow soldiers wallowing in their own sweat, pissing themselves in the extremes of the fever. That couldn't be him, and yet the Beretta at his hip never seemed further away.

"It's too bad this had to happen to you right now," one of the others mentioned. "That's some real bad timing."

This brought a rueful chuckle out of Ram. "When's it ever good timing to get scratched by one of them?"

"You don't know?" the old man asked uneasily. "You

haven't heard?"

"Heard what?" Ram asked with a sinking feeling.

John glanced at the others as if asking for help, but they seemed more interested in the everyday minutia than in catching his eye. "There's a vaccine," John said, finally. "Some guy in New York City figured out how to make one and he's selling them for a thousand a vial."

Stunned at his ill-luck, Ram sagged at the news and could only ask, "A thousand? A thousand dollars? That's weird, you can get money anywhere."

"No. A thousand rounds of ammo or a hundred gallons of gas, or their equivalent. There was some kid who came through the other day with this big ass missile launcher. He's gonna try to get ten vials"

"And the vaccine works," Ram said, heavily. It wasn't really a question, it was more of a statement concerning the present state of his luck which wasn't good.

"That's what they say," Scott put in. "There's some who are skeptical so they're doing a demonstration. It's supposed to be in a few days. John and I, and a few others are hoping to go as representatives, but we'll have to see."

The subject seemed to cast a pall over the group of men and Ram took a guess at what the issue was from the tenor of the man's words. "You don't have enough ammo or gas?"

Scott gave a half-shrug, lifting only his right shoulder as if a full shrug was simply too much work. "We do, but we really can't spare that much, not when we're at war."

"You can have mine," Ram offered. "And the gas in the hummer. I just need my Beretta and enough fuel to make it into the city." He certainly wasn't going to need much else. If he came across a horde of zombies he'd shoot fourteen of them and use the last on himself. And if the *Blacks* were in the mood to fight...he didn't think he would. Not so close to death. Not with heaven or hell on the line. However, he would kill Cassie if he got the chance, and do so with a clear conscience.

His offer pleased the men, who went right to work draining the Humvee of its excess gas and stripping it of anything that Ram wasn't going to need: extra food and water, clothing, and medical supplies.

While they did this, John offered him a beer. "It's warm, but they say warm beer is better than no beer." The old man drank his with relish, and among the many things he talked about as they sat in the darkening afternoon was of a way into the city. The *Whites*, as they called themselves, had turned a midnight blue Volvo upside down on one of the bridges and by using the bumper of his hummer he could spin it like a revolving door. "Just make sure you spin it back," John reminded him.

Ram decreed that he would and then pretended to give his warm beer another swig. The little of it he had drunk made him so nauseous that he was forced into hurrying his goodbyes. As soon as he was out of sight of the tall tree and the little group of men, he pulled over and stood, bent at the waist until he vomited.

Over and over he hurled until at last, dizzy and weak he went to his knees and knelt over the hot mess until he was sure he was done.

"Damn," he whispered to the pale man in the hummer's mirror. With the heavy clouds glooming the sky, his skin was already a shade of grey that portended things to come. Groaning, he felt his neck, however the adenoids hadn't swollen yet, and neither had his fever progressed beyond *mild*. Mostly the virus was in his guts, turning them to knots, and in his muscles, making him feel kitten-weak.

"A little further," he added and then turned his attention to driving, making sure to keep his pace slow enough that his precious-little fuel would last him to his destination. The bridge with the overturned Volvo was five miles to the south and when he saw it he gave a sad little laugh; he'd seen the blue Volvo earlier that day and had not suspected a thing.

Now he came up to its edge with the hummer and

gently turned it sideways. It scraped back, grinding loudly on pebbles and loose grit. When he had gone through the new lane he kept his word and backed the hummer around to use its power to swing the car back into place.

Then it was just him, a few hundred thousand zombies and the city, hiding its remaining human population. Like all major cities, Philadelphia was thought to be a veritable nests of zombies. John had filled him with tales of uncountable numbers of stiffs streaming down the streets like dead grey waves, killing and eating everything in their path.

Yet, as Ram drove around the many obstructions in the streets, he hardly saw upwards of a hundred and these were like their suburban neighbors and seemed content to mosey about as if in a fog. Though to be on the safe side he either steered well clear of them or crushed them beneath the wheels of his beastly SUV.

Although he was thankful for the lack of zombies the constricted streets had his head beginning to pound, which in turn made his stomach feel all the worse. Frequently he had to stop the truck as a shiver of steel seemed to lance through his innards, and once he had to race into a nearby bank to squat in a pitch black bathroom stall in order to relieve himself of a mass of watery stool.

He came out sweating and moaning. "Just a little longer," he pleaded with the universe as he started the hummer up again. His pleadings went unanswered and he grew ever sicker as he wound slowly along not bothering to pay much attention to where he was going. It didn't matter whether he paid any attention or not: his route had been chosen for him. The streets were clogged in such a way that he had only two options: forward or back.

Fifteen minutes from the bank a disabled pick-up truck resting on deflated tires forced him off the street and into an alley where the next obstruction was a dumpster. Thankfully this was the sort of dumpster that had wheels. Ram hopped down from the hummer to push aside the obstruction and that was when a man emerged from the shadows, pointing a gun square into his face.

"That was easy enough," the man said with a grin.

Ram had to agree. He'd been caught so effortlessly that he had to wonder if the virus had already begun to destroy his brain. He was about to make a pleasant greeting when a second man came up from behind him and smashed him in the side of the head with something heavy.

The once DEA agent dropped like a rock and found himself staring up as though from the center of the world or from the bottom of a vortex. The dark clouds above turned wide circles, while nearer at hand the buildings leaned in and raced around Ram, faster and faster. The two black men were joined by a third and it felt as though Ram was on a merry-go-round.

Moaning he put a hand out to one of the men who slapped it away.

"Shit, Trey! Now we're gonna have to carry his sorry ass," the man said.

"Just…just a minute," Ram said, blearily as he tried to sit up, but failed. "I'll be…ok." Somewhere in his rattled mind he thought he had done something wrong.

The man who had hit him, the one called Trey, dropped a brick onto the floor of the alley and then smiled benignly, saying, "See that? He'll be ok in a minute. In the meantime, I don't think you'll be needing that gun anymore." Trey frisked him and when he didn't find anything beyond the gun his smile disappeared.

"Ain't nuffin' in the hummer, neither," said the third man. "Not even no gas."

"Shit," Trey said.

"Shit," the third agreed. "No guns, no gas, no food? What the fuck?" It was a moment before Ram understood that *what the fuck* was a question rather than an exclamation and that it was directed at him.

"Oh, I'm supposed to be finding someone…I think," he

said. Just then his mind was so rattled that he couldn't remember who it was he was supposed to find. "Julia?" he asked, but then remembered she was dead. She had been killed by Cassie. Cassie...now it all came rushing back.

"Don't know no fuckin, Julia," Trey said. "But if I did I'd fuck the shit out of her and turn her into grey-meat before giving her back to you."

Ram took all this in with slow blinking eyes. "Right," he said at last, as the world stopped its mad turning. "I'm not actually here for her. I'm supposed to be brokering a cease fire between you and the *Whites*."

One of the men snorted. "Damn Trey, you scrambled this mother-fucker's eggs. He don't even know what color he be and shit."

Trey laughed as well. He squatted down in front of Ram and asked, "Has you looked in a mirror lately. Sorry to break it to you, spic-n-span, but you ain't white."

"I know," Ram said. "I'm not from Philadelphia, so I'm not a part of all this. I was just trying to do the right thing. I'm supposed to see your leader and set up a meeting." John had suggested a month long cease-fire followed by a meeting on the Passyunk Bridge to try to hammer out a real truce.

At this, the first man who had stopped Ram said nothing but only sneered at him with deep hatred brewing behind his eyes. Trey made a noise of disgust. "Shit, that ain't happening. She gots a hard-on for killing Whitey."

Ram's face went hard. "She? Your leader's a woman? Is her name..."

Without warning, the tall, quiet one stepped forward and kicked Ram in the chest; his steel-toed work boots sent Ram to the paved floor of the alley and left a wide boot print square in the middle of his shirt.

Trey nodded along gently as Ram struggled for breath. "Let me interpret the meaning of Jermy's foot for you Mister Spic-n-span. I think he was trying to let on that it's us who'll be asking the questions, and it's you who will be doing the answering. That right Jermy?"

"Dat right," Jermy intoned. "Let's get him moved."

Before Ram was even half-recovered the three men hoisted him and carried him across the alley to a playground behind the local elementary school. It had been a somewhat rundown schoolyard even before the apocalypse, but now it looked as though a tornado had struck. There seemed to be more of the school littering the playground than was left inside. Desks, chalkboards, chairs, and kindergartener's cubbies were flung about or stacked in piles as tall as a man.

Ram was brought through all this and then stood up against a tetherball pole in the center of the playground. Jermy stooped and pulled off one of Ram's shoes and yanked out the laces. While Jermy was tying Ram's hands together behind his back with the laces, Trey covered him with the Beretta and the other man kept watch.

When Ram got enough breath back to wheeze, Trey leaned in close and warned in a quiet voice, "Not too loud, my brother. There's a jillion little zombies in there. I mean the little, little ones, Pre K and shit. If they hear you they'll come swarming out and let me tell you those little fuckers are hungry. The problem is they're so short they'll start their feast just below the belt. Ya dig?"

As his balls tried to retreat up into his body, Ram nodded. "Yeah, I get it. But you have to believe me, I'm not your enemy. I'm not from Philly; I'm from California."

"You're from Cali? Must be nice," Trey said with a smile. It was an evil smile that Ram in no way trusted. "Was it as nice as that gay-ass country club the *Whites* hang out at?"

"I never went in…it looked nice from the outside. Like a palace, sort of."

The tall, quiet one had finished tying Ram's hands together around the pole; they were already turning the purple of a drowned man. "He be lying. He ain't never been to the *Whites* place," the man said, simply.

Trey blew out with a dismissive sound. "Like I don't know that." He then turned back to his prisoner and sent his fist into Ram's face. Ram's knees buckled and he dropped onto his butt.

"You like that? Huh? Do you?" Trey asked in a hard voice. "Cuz if you don't give me the truth, I got more of that. A whole lot more. Now, look at me." He took Ram's hair and pulled his head back so that he was forced to stare up into Trey's pitiless, black eyes. "We'll start simple. How many men do you *Spics* gots?"

Ram shook his head and steeled himself for the next blow. "Twenty thousand."

Trey gave him a *what can you do* look and then punched Ram again in the face.

"Son of a bitch," Ram seethed. He knew how this was going to go: he would be tortured and then when he was used up he would be fed to the zombie children. "Son of a bitch," he said again, this time more quietly. His life since the apocalypse felt wasted. Everything he had cherished had been destroyed, and now his death would be a waste as well. There would be no getting close to Cassie now…not as a human anyway.

The thought gave him an idea, a very bitter idea. "One more," he said to Trey. "I'm not feeling it. Come on, right in the kisser." With this he bared his teeth, giving his enemy an easy target. Trey smirked and then hit him again. The blow dazed Ram so that he sagged to the side.

Shaking his hand, Trey asked, "Was that better?"

His knuckles were bleeding. Ram saw the blood and the cuts and sneered, "Yeah. Now let Jermy give it a try. I'll tell you who can hit harder. But you got to make it in the same spot so it's fair." The right canine and the front tooth next to it were both loose and he figured he'd lose them with the next punch. It was worth it to infect a couple of Cassie's foot soldiers. He hoped they would go back and turn into stiffs among the rest of them; they'd been the ultimate Trojan horse.

Jermy stepped up, rubbing the knuckles of his right hand, and Ram clenched his teeth. Unfortunately he did so with an expectant smile.

"Wait!" Trey cried, grabbing his friend's arm. He wore a stunned expression as realization set in. "He wants you to hit him."

"No shit," Jermy said, shrugging off the hand.

Trey grabbed him again. "Yeah, but why? Why would he want that? What's the only reason he'd want us to hit him in the mouth?"

The man who'd been keeping watch answered. "Maybe he's infected. Maybe he's trying to get you-all infected. Nigga, let me see your hand."

"No….he's faking," Trey said, pointing with his left hand while his right, he hid behind his back. "He's trying to mess with us. Think about it, Omar. Wouldn't you do the same thing if you were getting jacked up?"

"If I'm faking then Jermy won't mind taking a swing," Ram challenged. When the tall man took a step back instead, Ram hocked up a good loogie and spat it at him, hitting him in the side of the face. He grinned, a bloody grin, as Jermy went into a frantic dance trying to wipe the bloody spit away with his jacket. He then tore off the jacket and flung it away.

In a fury, Jermy came stalking back with gun drawn, however Omar stopped him. "No one fuckin' move," he said with his gun pointed, amazingly enough, at Trey who looked at it with huge eyes. "I need your gun, Trey. You know our laws. We don't let anyone back in who's been bit."

"He's faking it!" Trey cried. 'You know he is." Omar's gun didn't budge an inch.

"I got scratched this morning," Ram said matter-of-factly. "I only have a couple hours left. It's one of the reasons why I volunteered to come here."

Jermy, who was right in front of Ram, looked to Omar for guidance. Omar jerked his head toward Trey. "I guess I need that gun you got," Jermy said.

Trey dropped his chin down to his chest as the gun fell out of his hands. Before he could change his mind, Jermy bent quickly to pick it up. In a second it was unloaded, even the chambered round was jacked out of it. It was then held back out to him.

Trey looked at it and shook his head. "No, I don't need it. He's faking. You'll see."

"Here, take it," Jermy demanded. He forced the gun into Trey's hand and then stuck the single bullet into his front pocket. "Don't puss out, nigga. You know what you need to do...or do you want me to take care of you?"

Trey backed away in something of a daze, holding the gun in a quivering hand. "No. I'm good. I gots this. I gots..." his words trailed off and then he turned and fled as if Jermy was bent on killing him.

"I didn't mean for any of this to happen," Ram called after him. "I'm sorry."

"You can shove that sorry up your ass," Omar said. "It's your kind what started all this, so don't expect me to do you any favors. Come on Jermy. You need to wash yourself better."

"But the ropes," Ram said as they walked away. "You can't leave me here alone. Please."

Omar turned. "You want company? Alright, you got it." He stooped and picked up a stone half the size of an apple and whipped it at the school where it struck an upper floor window. The crash of glass was alarmingly loud. What was worse were the faces that began to appear in the windows.

They were little kid faces, only they had been warped by death and disease and now they were feral, sharp-toothed little beasts, and they were very hungry. They came to feast.

Chapter 8

Jillybean

Philadelphia, Pennsylvania

A minute after the glass came crashing down, interrupting the still afternoon, the first magic marble left her hand, over the objections of the zebra.

Ever since she had heard the car pass overhead, Jillybean had been in a state of the rawest excitement. First there had been smoke, and smoke meant people. Then, came the car, and cars definitely meant people. And, lastly, there were voices drifting down the drain pipes! Voices *only* came from people.

You should be careful, Ipes cautioned. *Just don't go running up there.*

What a nervous-nelly, she thought to herself. Aloud she said, "I'll be careful of the monsters, but not people. That's just silly." It turned out that there wasn't a chance to just go running up anywhere. The two of them couldn't a find a way up to the street that wasn't blocked. In the black beneath the earth the pair went in circles until Jillybean had enough and turned on the heavy flashlight—again over Ipes' objections. The light helped greatly and the two found a feeder tunnel.

"Which way?" she asked from between two rusting relics that had once been cars.

Ipes made a *humph* noise as he was wont to do when he felt put upon. *If I tell you, will you even listen?* he asked. She promised she would. He led her carefully along until they came to a two-story school with a large, cluttered playground. And that was when he was proved sadly right about the necessity of being careful around humans. *We should go*, he said as Ram took another punch to the face by Trey.

"But they're hitting that man," she replied.

And what would you do about it? Are you a gun fighter or a ninja? No. You're a little girl and little girls do not fight. Now come on. I never thought I would yearn for a sewer like some sort of abysmal rat, but it is what it is.

The little girl refused to budge. "We can't just leave him. He might need our help somehow," she argued. In this she was proven right not two minutes later. The three black men left, but not before one threw a rock in a high rainbow arc at the school. Jillybean cringed at the sound, however the cringe turned into a look of horror as small monsters came hurrying down out of the building.

"Ipes! They're kid monsters," she cried in horror. "Oh no. Look at them. Look at them, they're so gross." She was so terrified by the sight of them that she froze, hunkered down behind a silver Honda Accord. Jillybean became Jilly-the-Rabbit, timidly looking out from her hiding spot, still as stone.

It was the cautious zebra that focused her once again. *They are indeed. Now we should get going.*

Her first thought was: Where to? She had no clue where she was, only a vague idea of where she had been, and was afraid to think of where she was going, especially alone as she was.

She replied to the zebra with a simple: "No." And then she fished out a magic marble and kissed it. The little zombies, fourteen in all, had exited a side door and were just nearing the corner of the building and would see the man, who was alone and standing against a pole, in a second if she didn't do something.

With a grunt, she threw the marble at the school with the full intention of having the monsters turn in her direction—which was exactly what they did. Like a gaggle of BFFs the zombies changed direction in midstride as though part of a gruesome clique and followed the sound of the marble, eagerly.

They came dangerously close to the hiding girl and now

she took a wild chance and chucked another marble, this time down the very street she crouched upon. Thankfully the monsters went after the retreating marble without looking once in her direction. The little girl slunk to the far end of silver Accord and watched them go through two sets of aged and dirty glass.

Now's our chance, Ipes said, however Jillybean stopped suddenly. She'd had a queasy feeling in her tummy that had been growing for most of the afternoon and now it doubled her over. She gasped in pain. *Are you alright?* the zebra asked. *You're white as a ghost.*

The feeling passed as quickly as it came and she assured her friend that she was ok. She then ran around the end of the building with her backpack flouncing on her back and her brown hair whipping about crazily from a new wind.

Surprisingly, the man glared at her, and as she came up he lashed out with his long legs trying to kick her. *Careful, he might be crazy*, Ipes warned.

"You think so?"she wondered. With the zebra clutched protectively in her skinny arms, she kept just out of reach of the man's legs.

It sure seemed that the man was nutty, especially when he asked the strangest question: "You can talk?"

Ipes was perplexed at the question. *Does he mean me or you?*

Jillybean shrugged and said, "I don't know. Who are you talking to, Mister?"

Where before the man had ogled Jilly with wide-eyed bewilderment, now he blinked slowly as if in partial understanding, and then he lifted his head and stared over her. "For a moment I thought you were one of those zombies," he intoned with a voice that was dry and empty as a corn husk. He dropped his gaze back to the girl and added, "You should get out of here. They'll come back soon."

"I could untie you," she said and then skirted around him, keeping her distance out of fear of his feet until she was straight on to his back. She then went at the knots with her tiny fingers, however they proved ineffectual compared to the strength of the bindings.

When she made a noise of frustration the man turned around the pole and she stepped back timidly. His face scared her. It was swollen and misshapen on one side, and there was blood, and the eyes were mostly empty of thinkings so that he appeared to her to be half a monster on the way to becoming a full one.

"You tried, now get out of here before they come back. I heard them on the other side of the school."

With a flutter of fear growing in her chest, she looked past the man at the building, while her feet took involuntary steps away. However it was then that Ipes spoke up, as contradictory as ever. *Since we're here, we might as well save him. Those are only shoelaces he's tied with. Find some sharp glass and we can cut him free.*

The schoolyard looked more like a junkyard and so Jillybean went about searching for a large enough piece of glass. She'd look down for three seconds and then look up for two, afraid she would see the little kid monsters charging at her. Down her head would hang and then up quick—down and then up, repeated over and over.

The man hissed continually for her to leave, however she ignored him and continued her hunt until her greatest fear came into reality. There, on the short side of the building, were the little kid monsters and they were horrible.

Stay perfectly still, Ipes warned her. *When they start eating the man we'll slip away and get back to the sewers.*

"No," she said in a stern whisper. It was true the kid monsters were wicked and loathsome in her eyes, and it was also true that they struck fear into her by their very presence. Yet, despite her age, she was able to comprehend the nature of the fear within her. It was a gut reaction to the *possibility* of becoming one of them.

It was this understanding that allowed her to face her

fear and once she did, it became less and the monsters became less frightening. For the most part they were small and even skinnier than Jillybean. She saw that many were missing hands and some even arms, while most limped.

And they were not particularly bright. With their focus on the pole and the man they did not see her at first. It wasn't until she purposely drew their attention, going from *still rabbit* to *flying deer* that they even saw her. Then their jackal-like instincts took over. Instead of indulging in the easy meal of a bound man, they gave chase as Jillybean dropped her backpack and booked it in a dead sprint for the school, hoping to lead them away.

Why on earth did you bring me? Ipes cried from the crook of her arm.

She couldn't spare the breath to answer him. With the pack hot on her heels she made straight for the only door in the building that sat ajar. Someone had stuck a plastic-backed chair in the gap to hold it open and Jillybean leapt on it as agile as a monkey and then another leap took her inside the decaying school. It was surprisingly and unnervingly dark.

There could be more of them in here, Ipes said. The warning was wasted. With the pack clawing their way over and around the chair she had nowhere else to go. With echoing steps she ran down the main hall looking into every room she passed. They were empty, each promising to trap her.

Then she ran out of hall. It ended at a set of double doors and her mind guessed: Gymnasium. She was correct. The doors opened into a dark that was as intense as the sewers had been. It was like dashing into a pool of ink and yet, with the pack of kid monsters coming she had no choice but to head in.

Almost immediately she fell forward as her foot struck something. Thankfully it was the beginning of a soft mat, the kind she used to tumble on when she took gymnastics. By feel she knew it.

Get up! Ipes screamed. The gym doors had shut with a reverberating crash which seemed to have woken something in the dark. A moan drifted along the black. It wasn't the high, squeaking moan of a kid monster, it was something more. It was something big.

Its footfalls were heavy thumps that she could feel coming up through the padded mat and when it knocked into things in the dark there were booms and thundering bangs. An all-encompassing fright seized the little girl. She leapt up and dashed in the direction she thought was the way out, however the walls and the double doors wouldn't come to her outstretched hands. Her wildly waving hands felt nothing but air, while behind, the huge monster came steadily on.

It too was hampered by the lack of light, yet it tracked her, not from the patter of her tiny feet, which made barely a sound—it was her ragged breathing that drew it on. With her overwhelming fear and the dregs of her sprint still on her, Jillybean huffed air like an asthmatic.

Ipes diagnosed the problem, *You're breathing too loud!*

Of course, knowing what the problem was and being able to do anything about it were two different things. She couldn't run from the monster and breathe lightly at the same time. No matter how hard she tried, it still heard her and closed the distance between them with each passing second.

Get out a magic marble, Ipes said, though in the dark his voice sounded so much like her father's that she didn't question what she thought was a useless demand. What good would a marble do? Given the choice between following a bouncing marble and a huffing and puffing girl, a zombie would go for the girl every time.

She ran on with shuffled steps, digging a marble out of her pockets. *Listen carefully, Jillybean,"* Ipes ordered. *I want you to toss that marble gently ahead of us. When it lands I want you to take a deep breath and hold it, and then juke to the right.*

The word "juke" wasn't in her mental dictionary, at least not in her conscious dictionary. Her subconscious dictionary was a different story and held thousands of words that she had never uttered, but which held memories attached from which she could draw meaning:

Sitting on her father's lap in front of the TV, while he swigged beer that made his breath funny. She had been small, smaller even than now, small enough that when he jiggled her up and down on his knee, it was like trying to stay upright on a bucking bronco. It made her giggle and she loved him for it, but he was only half paying attention to her. He was such a good dad that he could parent with half his brain tied behind his back. Most of his mind was on the "the game". Football. It was an unfathomable activity to a four-year-old.

He laughed in joy and hugged her around the middle. "You see that? Mareno just juked that linebacker out of his shoes."

Someone losing their shoes could be funny and so she turned to "the game", only everyone had their shoes on that she could see. A man did catch her attention long enough to affiliate the word juke with this memory. He was cheetah fast, and when confronted by an enormous, hulking man, he dodged to the side making the bigger man stumble and fall.

Juke: The process of changing direction in midstride to avoid a collision with another.

The marble left her hand, gently as ordered, and as it did, she sucked in a huge breath and juked to the right. The marble went clack, clack. The huge beast went stomp, stomp. And Jillybean trembled in fear with her lungs burning and her stomach beginning to pain her once more. The monster brushed by, its slow mind focusing on the only noise left to it. Second after second slipped away until ten had passed and the giant thing was well away.

Slowly, Jillybean let out her breath and, with a feeling

akin to triumph, she sucked in air covering her mouth to muffle the noise. She had done it. The monster was at the far end of the gym scrambling around after a silly marble and, if she was to knock into something else, she had more marbles to confuse him.

Going slow and careful—in her mind like a blind, three-toed sloth—she walked directly away from the creature until she came to the wall of the gym and then she hurried despite the danger. The wall, if followed far enough, would lead to an exit. There would be two if not three in a gym of this size.

And there it was! Jillybean's face lit up as her hands felt the smooth, cool metal of the door; and there were the handles…and something else. Hard as steel, with consecutive roundish loops. Jilly's heart sunk. It was a chain, and next her hand felt what could only be a padlock. There was no getting through this door, and if this one was chained that meant they all were.

There was only one way out: the way she came in. Almost at that second, the little kid monsters, who had been for all this time struggling to open the gym door with their near useless brains had stumbled on the concept of pull instead of push and the gym door swung open. The school hall had seemed dark before, but compared to the pitch of the gym it was practically aglow and enough light fell inwards to show Jillybean standing there looking tiny and vulnerable.

It also showed the giant monster at the far end of the gym. It was huge, over six and half feet tall, and wide as one those football players her daddy had liked to watch. Yes, it was big and scary, but it was the strange fact that the monster was completely naked that sickened Jillybean. It was a subconscious revulsion that manifested itself with another sharp pain deep in her intestines, which brought a groan from her lips.

You gotta suck it up, Jillybean, Ipes told her.

Tears welled and threatened, but Jilly didn't seem to

notice, her fear was too great. "I can't," she whispered in the single second left before the monsters charged and she fell to her knees in surrender.

Chapter 9

Jillybean

Philadelphia, Pennsylvania

The pain in her tummy sent a shiver running along her limbs and a moan that was somewhat zombie-like escaped her lips.

Please Jillybean, Ipes begged her. *Get up. They're coming! They're coming!*

Across the gym from her the kid zombies stormed through the double doors, while the giant monster at the other end of the rectangular room let out a low bellow of a moan, and charged, shaking the floor as he came.

"I can't," she whispered. Her muscles had gone limp and sweat beaded under the wisps of brown hair at her forehead. She felt like crying and she did. The monsters were going to eat her no matter what, and crying felt like the best thing to do at the moment.

In his terrific anxiety Ipes was squirming like mad against her chest. *At least throw a magic marble, please.*

It was all she had the strength and will to do. The marble flew through the air, landing at the feet of the nearest child monster and released its magic. Just as it clacked on the wood the last of the kid monsters came through the gym doors, which shut behind it, halting the stream of light. The dark was so complete, it was as if she had blinked and forgot to open her eyes again.

After the sewers, the dark no longer frightened her, and it wouldn't be a stretch to say she gained strength in the comforting safety of it. The monsters were as blind as she and their headlong rush became a jumble as monster ran into monster. When this occurred, there would be a savage thrashing noise intermixed with growls, and then just as quickly the two would part again, only to run into another of their kind, seconds later.

Now will you go? Ipes begged.

The very idea of crossing forty yards of open floor with monsters flying all about had her sagging again. It would be a deadly game of blind man's bluff and she couldn't see herself coming out the winner. And yet she had no choice and so she stood, leaning against the chained door trying to force herself to leave the meager safety of it.

Her magic marbles had been so effective that before making the dash across the gym she chucked one to the far end of the gym where she had last seen the big monster. If there was magic in this marble it wasn't apparent. Above the roaring and the moaning, and the constant crashes that shook the walls, the sound of the marble was a little thing and if any of the monsters were distracted there was no way to tell.

We don't have a choice, Ipes told her. *You have to make a run for it. Just don't drop me, whatever you do.*

With a deep breath, Jillybean plunged into the chaos. After barely two steps she plowed directly into something huge and fleshy, and bounced off again, losing her footing in the process and thumping to the hard wood floor.

It was the giant. Above her the air roiled with its stink and swished with the passing of his clawed hands as it swept at the dark, hunting for its meal. Madly she kicked away from it only to have another of the monsters trip over her in the dark. She could hear its nails scraping at the wood as it tried to right itself in time to get her, however fear had a good hold of Jillybean's mind and she jumped up and began running with her hands outstretched, going in the wrong direction, but thinking that at any moment she would find the right doors.

Instead her foot struck something hard and unyielding. Whatever it was had an awkward shape like strange stairs, only there weren't any stairs in the gym.

They're bleachers, Ipes said. *You went the wrong way!*
She turned to her right feeling the old wood with her left hand, running her fingers over carved letters and splintered

boards; though it was only for a few steps and then Ipes was pounding his soft hoof onto her arm and saying, *No, the other way. Go back the other way.*

Making sure to keep at least one hand on the bleachers, she turned but was forced to pause as there came a violent shaking along the wood. The vibrations grew in intensity, coming closer, and all she could do was cringe, but then they stopped altogether and Ipes urged her forward. She ran in a shuffle until the bleachers became air beneath her trailing fingers.

To the right, Ipes said with excitement.

She did as she was told, moving right until she hit the wall, where she splayed her fingers and swept her small hands all around. Seconds later the metal of the door was against her palm, and there was the bar, that when depressed would...

Yes! Ipes cried in joy as the light struck them full force. At that moment the chaos behind them ceased as though a switch had been thrown. *Run and don't look back,* Ipes ordered.

Running wasn't going to be a problem. Jillybean stretched out her skinny legs and bolted. Behind her the door closed, but not a moment later it thumped and then shuddered under the fists of the giant. This only spurred her on until she found the door to the outside; she leapt over the plastic-backed chair and then paused as a new wind struck her in the face. It was brisk and bewildering, having brought with it dark clouds.

How long was I in there? she wondered. It couldn't have been long because there was the same man tied to the pole. At the sight of him she stopped, remembering she had been looking for glass before the monsters had come back. She bent over the trash strewn grounds once again; unfortunately the only glass she could find was from the school windows, which had shattered into thousands of little cube-like pieces that reminded her of diamonds.

Forget the glass, Ipes suggested. *Look for scissors or a knife. But hurry, they'll figure out how to get out of the gym soon.*

With her head wagging from side to side, Jillybean searched the playground, dashing from pile of refuse to pile of crap. At the bottom of a blue, plastic cube that looked like the sort of crate that milk was delivered in, she found a pair of scissors. They were safety scissors and were small enough to fit her hand.

"I've got some scissors," she told the man. She held them up for him to see as she ran to him and tried to smile encouragingly, hiding her doubt. In her experience safety scissors were too safe. Most of the time they could barely cut construction paper and now she was going to have to try to scissor through thick laces.

He started to shake his head, but after a quick glance at the school he changed his mind. "Ok...ok, give it a shot, but hurry. And if the stiffs come back, promise me you'll leave. You run away and don't look back." Sweat gleamed on his misshapen face and there was such a wild cast to his eyes that Jillybean couldn't find words to answer him, though she did nod in a small way before skirting around to his back. He spun on the pole and demanded, "Promise me that you'll leave."

"I promise," she said in a voice as small as she was. Satisfied, he turned and she began a vain struggle with the plastic-handled scissors. Even if they had been sharp, which Jillybean doubted very much they had ever been, her hands were far too weak for the job and not one thread parted from the rest. She even tried sawing with the blunt metal. Back and forth her hands went in a blur until she slipped and fumbled the scissors.

"Stop," the man told her. He spun, shuffling his feet so that he had turned halfway. "It's not working. Just go. Get out of here, before..." A sadness swept him, stopping his words and now his head hung so that his brown eyes stared only at the cracked asphalt.

Take his advice, Jillybean, Ipes said with a sigh. *There's just no getting him off that pole, not unless that giant comes out and lifts him off.*

"I guess, but..." she started to say, however the image of the naked monster grabbing the man and pulling him off the pole and then eating him, stopped her. It was a horrible vision, nevertheless it spawned an idea. "What if we lift him off?" she mumbled to Ipes. "Or what if we get some stuff for him to stand on and he can, you know, climb off?"

Thinking she was speaking to him, the man asked, "What are you talking about?"

"Getting you off the pole," Jillybean replied, scanning the rubbish for something sturdy enough for the man to stand on. There were a couple of chairs that were too short, and a teacher's desk that was too big for her to lug over. There were also a number of weak plastic bins of the sort that Jillybean had used as a kindergartener. They held pencils and crayons, and her shoes or her lunch, and it fit snuggly into her cubby—one of these could support her weight, but certainly not the man's, he was just too big.

The man got excited when he first saw the trash she had brought over, but hope faded as he turned in a slow circle and saw little in the refuse that could help him. "Just go," he said again, and now he slunk down to an awkward sitting position.

Jillybean wouldn't be defeated without a try and so she put Ipes on the ground next to the man and then ran for one of the chairs. Seconds later she scraped it back to him making more noise than she wished. She stood it next to him against the pole and said, "Try this."

He made a face after glancing at it and then the height of the pole. "It's too short. Please, you said you would go. You promised."

"The monsters aren't here yet," she reminded him, and then went for a second chair and after she pulled it over she stood there staring, as her brain tried to work out some configuration of the two that would get him high up enough to allow him to slip his arms over the top of the pole.

In a moment she made a noise of desperation. She couldn't see how it would work. "Help me, Ipes, please. We have to get him up high enough so he can get over the top."

As the man looked at her in a funny way, Ipes considered things. *We need to make a stair for him that is at least, let's see...he's about six foot, and the pole is seven. With his hands behind his back, I'd say the stair needs to be four feet tall at a minimum.*

"Stairs? We don't have time to make stairs," Jillybean said. "And asides he can't leave the pole to go walking up stairs."

"What?" the man asked. "What stairs? What are you talking about?"

She waved him to be quiet as Ipes answered her: *We have to build a crude set of steps, because he can't magically hop four feet straight up while tied to a pole. And the stairs will have to go around the pole, like a spiral staircase. Now hurry and get all the books you can find. And those crates, and those little, bin things.*

As the man continued to sputter out questions, she dashed off, going from pile to pile, picking up books and plastic bins and sticking them in one of the plastic containers. When she got back she was short of breath and sweating up a storm.

"Can you get up, Mister?" she asked.

"What?"

"Stand up," Jillybean said. "We gotta build stairs so you can get up off that pole." She didn't wait and began stacking books next to him, however Ipes stopped her.

No, the crate first, Ipes ordered. *He's going to go up sort of to the side and back. It won't be easy so the first step should be sturdy. Now push the chair over here. Turn it around so the back is to the pole. Great. We'll need the books in order to...*

He stopped as their came a series of metallic bangs coming from the school. It was the sound of a door being knocked against a wall repeatedly. It was the sound of the monsters escaping from the school in a manic rush.

"Hurry," the man whispered, afraid. He had stood and watched her construct the rude stairs with a touch of hope, but now his brown eyes were big in his face as he stared over the playground at the school. "You can hear them coming!" It was true. They were coming around the school, thankfully they were taking the long way, which would give them maybe thirty seconds.

Thirty seconds was not much time. Still it was enough time for one attempt. The man tried to step up onto the crate, but his foot upended it.

Guide his feet. Ipes commanded in a rush. *He can't see where he's going.*

Jillybean returned the crate to its position. "Lift your foots. I'll put them on the crate." Half their time was spent getting him from the ground to the crate to the chair.

Now the books! Ipes cried, waving his stubby hooves in the air. *Make four stacks that are as even as you can get them. Then we'll put the next chair on top of those.*

She dropped to her knees and stacked all the books she had into four piles.

It's not enough, Ipes said. *And you don't have time to go get more. We should go. Tell him sorry and let's go!* The moans and the running, slapping feet were louder now. The monsters would be around the corner in seconds.

"What about the bins?" she asked.

The man tore his eyes from the sound of his coming doom and took in the situation. "They'll crack under the weight of the chair. They're too flimsy." He sighed in resignation and she was sure he would remind her of her promise again, however Ipes interrupted.

Not if they are stacked as well! Ipes cried. *See how they fit one into the other?* Jillybean grabbed one and saw that he was right. *Hurry!* Ipes practically screamed. *Just do four. And now make sure the stacks are even.*

Obediently, she did as she was told: stacking the bins, lining up the books, and then struggling the chair up onto them. And all the while she could picture the monsters coming closer to the corner of the building and she could image that she could hear a clock ticking.

"They're here," the man whispered and strangely, where before his face had held a growing fear, now his voice was rough and he sounded more angry than anything else. "You have to go, now!"

"There's only one more step," Jillybean said, after a glance at the little kid monsters. Between them was forty yards of trashed playground. Forty yards wasn't much and had she been alone she would've run screaming away, however this man was a grode up. Compared to the little kid monsters he was really big—yes, he was beaten up, and yes, he had his hands tied behind his back, but still he was a grode up and that meant he would protect her...somehow. But first he had to get off the pole.

"Let me have your foots," she commanded, tugging at the hem of his jeans.

The monsters charged and, guided by Jillybean, the man put one foot on the chair and stepped up with a grunt. Under him the chair began to slide on the slick surface of the plastic bins. Jillybean tried to hold the chair in place, however it shot at her violently as the man made a desperate and graceless hop to clear his hands from the top of the pole.

He came crashing down, landing on one foot, before falling to the asphalt face first. At least he was free of the pole but, with his hands still tied behind his back, getting up was a struggle. Jillybean ran to help him.

"Hurry! Hurry!" she cried over-and-over as she hauled on his arm. Finally he got to his knees and then to his feet and then they started running directly away from the monsters.

Don't leave me! wailed Ipes at the top of his lungs. Without regard to her own safety, Jillybean dashed back. Ipes was more important to her than a leg or an arm. She grabbed the little zebra and paused to stare at the onrushing monsters. The big one had joined in the chase and now, in the light, its nudity was more apparent and more obscene in her mind. Along with horrific lesions and running sores that leaked yellow puss onto its grey hide, its man parts had been partially eaten away, while what remained were blackened shreds that swung in rhythm with its stomping gait.

Run away, Jillybean, Ipes said in her daddy's calm voice. She didn't hesitate. Spinning on her heel, she raced after the man she had freed and saw he was already in need of her help again. He had run the short distance to a chain link fence which separated the school yard from a little alley that smelled of pee, and he had managed to get stuck in a hole in the wiring.

He was grunting and twisting himself to no avail. As she came up to him, with the monsters not twenty feet behind, she saw the problem: his coat was hooked at the collar.

He needs to take one step back and then hunch lower, Ipes said. With so little time for explanations, Jillybean grabbed him by his bound wrists and pulled him back with all the force of her forty-seven pounds and cried, "Duck down lower!"

The effect was immediate and the man came loose and was free on the right side of the fence in a wink. This was not true for Jillybean. The monsters were within arm's reach when she threw herself through the opening, landing on the cement floor of the alley with pebbles digging into her palms. She tried to climb to her feet but something had a hold of her. Grey, scabby hands had her by the loose jeans, and unbelievably one of the monsters had her sneakered foot in its mouth. A scream ripped from her lungs, but then the man was there, stomping on the little monsters who had found the hole in the fence even less manageable than he had.

There was a lip at the bottom of the opening which the first of them had tripped over. The second tripped over the first and so on until four were lying one atop the other, half in the alley and half out, each trying to get at poor Jillybean.

"Get up," the man ordered while continuing his mad stomps. A second later he stepped back, aghast. The giant had come. The monster threw its weight at the fence which sagged and bent inwards. A second blow by the beast snapped a steel ring holding part of the fence to the support pole.

"We have to get out of here," the man said in a horrified whisper.

Jillybean hopped up quick and asked, "To where?" as she backed away from the monsters scrambling to get through the fence at them.

The building that made up one side of the alley had been an apartment complex and now every door hung askew and every window was smashed in. The man shrugged, a move barely discernible from a twitch. "In there somewhere, I guess."

Neither she nor Ipes had a better idea so they hurried into the complex, only to stop short after the first building. All the ruckus had stirred things up on this side of the fence as well. There was a pair of monsters lurching their way toward them.

"I'll draw them to me," the man said between clenched teeth. "You run. Go find your parents."

He started to move away from the side of the building in which they had ducked, however Jillybean grabbed him. "There are places here we can both hide in. We just have to find them."

We don't have time, Ipes warned.

The man shook his head at her and said the same thing,

"There's no time and look, not a door around here is sturdy enough to keep out that giant."

"What about that one?" Jillybean asked, pointing at an iron door around the side of the buildings. The sign on it was beyond her ability to read, all save for the top word: Danger.

The man's eyes went wide. "Maybe it'll work. If it's not locked."

It wasn't, however it was so heavy that the little girl barely had the strength to pull it back. "You can do it! Pull!" the man urged. His head went back and forth from cheering on Jillybean to gaping at the monsters that had seen them and were now rushing to feast. It was a race that Jillybean won with two seconds to spare.

Once she had the door opened enough, the pair of them, and Ipes, dashed into the room and slammed the door shut behind them and then sat against it breathing in gasps and trying to ignore the sound of the monsters smashing into it.

The room itself was fairly well lit by a small rectangular window set high in one wall. "What is all this stuff? Do you know?" Jillybean asked. There were six large cylinders set in two rows. From them sprouted a multitude of pipes.

"It's a boiler room," the man said. "Or it was. See if you can find anything that'll cut these laces. Something sharp or even jagged will work." She was so tired and not at all feeling well, despite this Jillybean took a deep breath and stood on wobbling legs. The man saw this and asked in concern, "Are you all right?"

"My tummy hurts and my head does too."

At her answer a long, weary breath escaped him. "Have you been bitten or scratched by one of them? Let me see your arms."

"I don't think so," she answered, hiking up the Eagles sweatshirt. The evidence suggested otherwise. Her arms were covered in scratches and bruises, but where they all came from she didn't know. "Oh, maybe I was scratched a little. Is that bad?"

"Yes, very bad." He didn't explain further and now he refused to look into her eyes.

Ask him why it's bad, Ipes asked nervously.

She didn't want to, because she was suddenly very afraid of the answer. Regardless, she whispered: "Why is it bad?"

"It means you'll turn into one of them."

Shock widened her blue eyes and she whispered, "I don't want to be one of them. I want to be a girl still." She felt like crying. She could feel her eyes well up and his did, also.

"But that's not going to happen," he said. His words and his voice seemed empty or blank as if he didn't care about her or anything really. "You won't stay a girl and I won't stay a man. I was scratched as well, and now I'm sick and in a few hours I'll turn into one of them."

"You're going to be a monster too?"

He started to nod and then stopped and said, "Unless you turn first." This struck him as funny and he laughed crazily in hard misery and turned a little to his side so that his ugly purpled hands were visible to Jillybean.

He laughed and he cried at once, which scared her.

"What are you laughing at?" she asked at last.

The man turned to her and his face, sweaty and pale, was as crazy as his laughter had been. "I just don't want to get eaten," he said. "And I don't want to eat anyone. Just thinking about it is making me want to puke."

She had the same feeling. It made her head light and her breathing heavy. "If we stay in here we should be fine," she said hoping to cheer them both up. Outside, the monsters moaned and the door shimmied beneath the blows of the giant, but it seemed solid enough to resist his power. "We'll be monsters but we won't be eating anyone. So there's that."

"I'm sorry, but you're wrong. One of us will eat and one of us will get eaten," he told her in a whisper. She started to shake her head, but he cut her off, "Yeah it's going to happen. Whichever one of us turns first will eat the other; that's the way it works."

Chapter 10

Cassie

Philadelphia, Pennsylvania

In sleep, Cassandra Mason possessed an elemental beauty few could match. Her dark features, stylized and large, were a sculptor's dream. They bespoke of a regal nature that, once hidden, had now come into fruition. Though not in name, Cassie ruled with all the power and severity of a queen. She was loved, and feared by all.

It was in consciousness that her beauty faded. The classic plains of her face seemed hard and angry; her full lips were quick to twist into a sneer when she was displeased, but it was in her eyes, those large, brown doe-eyes, where a person's true fear originated. Her eyes, huge and luminous and dark, held such a surety of power, such a presence of personality that few, even the toughest of men, could hold her gaze for long.

Standing in her room, the largest in the brick, fortress-like warehouse, those eyes took in her personal map of Philadelphia and what they saw brought a smile to her full lips. The fact of her power was illustrated on that map. It showed, in shaded grey, the areas controlled by the people she led: the *Blacks*. From a little square in the south of the city, the shade had bloomed to take over so much.

"But not everything," she purred. There were still the dregs of the *Spics* hiding and running for their lives in Camden, just across the Delaware, while the *Whites* who were holed up in their odd bastion in the suburbs. "It'll happen," she assured herself. It was just a matter of time.

Time had matured her, and despite that, time had come easily for her. Everything had come easily. So easily that some whispered she had made a deal with the devil. This wasn't idle chat, either. The devil had gained quite a world-wide following during the apocalypse and Cassie wore the mantle of Devil's Disciple without a qualm. She rather enjoyed it if the truth were known.

She despised the Christian God and always had. Was he not everything she hated? A white man; a patriarchal figure, with his white beard and his white robes, sitting up in his heavenly plantation making all the rules?

And was not the devil depicted as a dark being, cloaked in black? And was he not forced by the white man's God to dwell in the ghetto of hell? And was he not after power without excuse, just as she was?

Cassie was just fine with the devil as her patron; what's more she was happy making sacrifices to him. Anytime someone got in her way and died as a result, she would think of the devil and smirk. It had started with the killing of Julia. Far from sending her into a weepy depression, Cassie had exalted at finally striking back at her enemy. It was something she couldn't exactly thank God for, so instead she had pictured the devil and smirked, knowing he would have appreciated the way the axe had sunk, *cachuck*, right into that stupid red head of hers.

Her enemy...that was how she viewed all white people, and to a lesser extent, the other races as well, as her enemies. This would not be considered much of a surprise if one knew her background.

Her mother, Dee Mason, was not simply a racist who saw only good within the black community, she was also a conspiracy buff...though conspiracy nut would be far closer to the truth. Dee had one criteria for belief in a conspiracy: it had to further her view that every problem in the black community was the white man's fault.

This view held firm despite *any* evidence to the contrary. If there was a crime in which a black person was convicted it simply meant that evidence had been planted. Not even a taped confession meant a thing to her. As she stated on many occasions: *"If they can fake going to the moon, they can fake this."*

It was into this world that Cassie was born and raised, though to be sure Cassie was far more sane than her mother.

Cassie allowed that a number of the conspiracies weren't true; obviously not true, and yet she did not once refute them. To the contrary she championed each and every one, because to her, hate overrode logic.

Not much had changed since coming to Philadelphia. In fact just one thing had: she had discovered that hate—a real, true passionate hate equaled power. When she had come to the city after two months of enduring a hard, cold beginning to the winter alone, she had discovered, much to her annoyance, that the blacks in Philly didn't hate their neighbors.

After surviving the horrors of the "Grey Plague," the black people of the city had no stomach for strife, even though it was clear to Cassie they had been jailed once again by the *Whites*. They had been allotted the portion of the city between the Schuylkill and the Delaware Rivers, while to the north and east they were hemmed in by the Mexicans and Puerto Ricans.

The *Whites* on the other hand claimed everything west of the Schuylkill River—basically the entirety of America! Pointing this out had done nothing. The blacks were eagerly neutral, a state that Cassie despised and vowed to rectify. It took a subtle and conniving hand to steer them into "asserting their dominance" in other words, into open warfare.

She started with propaganda, spreading rumors among the disenfranchised about the *Whites*. Since it was a time of fear and strife these seeds of hatred took on a life of their own with whispers of racism and white "superiority" and a return of the KKK.

To nurse the hate, Cassie then began to deface the city: hangman's nooses were found dangling from light poles;

scrawled graffiti: *Die Niggers!* was discovered spray painted on store fronts across the south part of the city; even manikins were stumbled upon dressed in white sheets. Without proper KKK robes and hoods they looked ridiculous and childish in Cassie's eyes, and yet the people shook with fear regardless.

And still the so-called *Black Leadership* did nothing!

There were six of them, all men, most with grey in their beards and all with heavy feet which they dragged toward any difficult decision. Each was burdened with the same pacifist mindset. They thought they could trade their way to peace and prosperity.

They literally sickened her. It was this feeling that drove her to attain power. When she had first come to Philadelphia she had thought she was the least qualified person to take on a leadership role among her people. After all she was very young, an outsider, a nobody, lacking even a high-school diploma.

But there was no one else with the guts and the vision. Alone, she saw the dangers of being hemmed in by enemies. Yes, the warehouse was strong in fortification and at the moment well-stocked, but what of next year? What if survivors kept straggling in? Would the food hold out? Would there be room in the brick building? Already it felt crowded and closed in—it felt much like a prison.

Rightly, she saw the six leaders as the roadblock stopping the *Blacks* from attaining their proper position, and rightly, she saw how their deaths could further her aims. She would make them martyrs for the cause. Their deaths at the hands of "racists" and "bigots" would turn the little smoldering flame of hate she had kindled in her people into a bonfire.

As everything else for her had been since her arrival in Philadelphia, arranging the deaths was easy. The six supervised the trades with the other communities and it was nothing to block their route with a few trash cans set in the middle of the road. When they went to clear the way, she shot them like dogs in the street, sawed of their heads and mounted them on a nearby fence.

It didn't matter much to her that the leaders had been on their way to trade with the *Spics* instead of the *Whites*, because now the hearts of her people were inflamed and emotions were never so raw, and no man or woman among them was more vocal than Cassandra Mason. She agitated constantly for revenge, access to new territory, and more than anything: a new beginning. A new kingdom for the black people who had so long been oppressed! She was the perfect choice to step forward and fill the very power vacuum she had created, and in the process she turned Philadelphia, *The City of Brotherly Love*, into a burning cauldron where man murdered his fellow man, while the undead fed on each.

Chapter 11

Neil

The Center for Disease Control, Atlanta, Georgia

The two beasts fought loudly and Neil Martin did the only prudent thing possible: he hid. On tip-toes, he slunk down a dim hall and into a back bedroom, closing the door behind him as soundlessly as possible. There, he practically held his breath, listening as the creatures went at it in a desperate battle.

That *they* would fight was the biggest surprise. He had always thought that they were of one mind and that he was their prey, but that had proved untrue.

"It is what it is," he whispered under his breath as he brought out a pump action, twelve-gauge shotgun that seemed like a monster of a weapon in the hands of such a small man—he topped five foot by only four inches. Out of habit, he checked to see if a shell was chambered. It was...

Just then the bedroom door burst open, which solicited a yelp and a spasmed jerk from Neil. The shotgun dropped to the bed as he sprang up.

"Yes?" he asked in guilty innocence.

"I knew I'd find you here," Sarah Rivers said, coming into the room in a wrath. "You are a part of this, so don't think hiding will help you."

"Of course not," Neil said, eager to please. "I was just, uh, the gun...I wanted to check the uh..."

The appearance of Sadie, suddenly in the doorway with her dark eyes smoldering stopped his attempt at an excuse. "You aren't taking her side are you?" she asked in disbelief. "That's completely unfair."

"No, I wasn't," Neil replied and then pointed vaguely at

the fallen gun which had landed on his and Sarah's bed. "The ammo...I was checking it. And the bedspread...it's on backwards. And the shoe." There was a shoe on the bed next to the gun. He pointed at it for reasons that could not be accounted for.

Sarah turned her denim-blue eyes from him to the shoe and then back again. Her glare, fed by her hormone-twerked mind, was all the more fierce. "What, you have a problem with my shoes now?"

"No, not at all," Neil said shaking his head. "You have great shoes."

"This isn't about shoes," Sadie cried. "It's about you two not being fair at all! I have the right to go with Mark. You can't stop me."

Neil raised his hands to her, palms out in the universal sign of peace...or surrender. "No. Yes. Of course not," he began, trying to placate the two women, who had unfortunately synced their cycles.

"Neil!" Sarah hissed in a low warning tone. He guessed this was the sound an adder made when one's bare foot was only inches from coming down on it. "We talked about this."

Feeling trapped, he backed to the wall and floundered, "Yes, right, we did, but..."

Sadie's eyes widened to their fullest. "You talked? Behind my back? What happened to us being open and honest? When did that go out the window?"

"Please, calm down," Neil said, forgetting how that simple phrase had nearly gotten him pegged with a teacup only the month before. "We're fine with you dating Mark. That's not the issue here. We both think he's a fine young man, from what we know of him that is."

"Then I can go?" she asked. "Alone?"

Sarah and Neil locked eyes for a brief moment before Neil answered with a simple, "No." He then gritted his teeth, waiting for the inevitable explosion, hoping for it really, since the alternative was worse.

"You know you can't tell me what to do," Sadie said, her words were ice cold and cutting. "You're not my real parents; in case you forgot."

There was no way he could have—she reminded them every time an argument came up. Her parents were dead, just like everyone else's parents were. Still they were a family. The three of them, four if they counted little Eve, had adopted themselves. They had come together in the midst of the horror surrounding them, and somehow had created a family out of the thinnest of bonds.

"We've never told you what to do," Sarah said, cooling slightly. "We have never ordered you about, have we?"

"You are now!"

Sarah's brief attempt at calm failed. "Neil, she isn't listening!" All the commotion woke Eve from her nap and she began a plaintive bleating that could hardly be heard. The baby had never been loud to begin with and now, after six months of selective training, she was even quieter. The same could not be said for Sarah and Sadie when they were in a mood.

"See what you did?" they cried in unison, each raking the other with their eyes and pointing accusingly.

Neil dropped onto the bed. With all three of the women in his life upset at the same time he lacked the strength to stand. "Sarah, can you please go check on Eve?"

She stiffened and looked within an ace of exploding, however she only flared her nostrils and said, "You better not give in." She walked out of the room leaving only a frosty Sadie for him to deal with.

Just a few more days, he thought to himself. As the quintessential lonesome loser before the apocalypse, he had not been prepared in the least for the fact of PMS. Without basis he had always thought of it as either an excuse some women made when their vaunted restraint lapsed, or as a pretext for men to ridicule the least demonstration of emotion a woman might indulge in.

Now he knew it was a real thing.

And when two women were simultaneously ripping into him for not being supportive, or rendering the meaning of innocuous words to suggest he had called them fat, he didn't know how to proceed, except to tiptoe through the "week" as if he were working his way through a minefield.

"Why is she always like that?" Sadie asked through gritted teeth.

"She isn't always like that, and you know it," Neil said, pulling her down next to him on the bed. "This isn't about us telling you what to do, and it's not about either of us thinking we're smarter than you, or better in any way. It's about us loving you."

Sadie's glare, which had been building in ire, disappeared. Her mouth came open: "But..." she said, her anger faltering.

Neil relaxed a touch. Sadie could be counted on not to know how to deal with it when someone told her they loved her. Growing up in a household with what were essentially two absentee parents, the word love had rarely been used in her home.

"We love you and that's why we care so much about your safety," Neil went on. "Yes, this is about safety. Leaving the base with a boy we barely know is dangerous."

He was proud that she wanted to forage. Without any special skills to trade for food or necessities, it was the only way for the family to survive, at least for now. Neil viewed foraging as a short run solution and was already considering ways to become independent of the constant, deadly scavenging.

"I can take care of myself," she replied. "You know I can."

He patted her leg—it was a leg of hard muscle that could easily outrun not only Neil, but every zombie ever made. "Yes, you can take care of yourself against the zombies, but what about Mark? I'm not suggesting he's some sort of rapist, but what if he's a drinker? Things can get out of hand. Or what if he tries to prove how brave he is? Remember that kid, Albert? The kid who tried to wrestle one of the stiffs to show off for a girl and got bit. It's a fact; boys do crazy things around girls."

"Yeah, well, you're not looking at it from my point of view," Sadie countered. "You're gonna make me look like a child. It will look like you're babysitting me."

"Yes, I'm sure it will. But think about when Eve turns seventeen and she starts asking to leave the base. What do you think your response will be?"

Sadie's eyes shifted down as they saw a possible future where her role would be reversed. Though it was clear she understood the analogy, the teenager held onto the last vestige of her argument, "Still, it's not fair..."

"That's what she's going to say. This is not about being fair. You love her and you'll risk her getting mad at you in order to protect her. Sarah and I are willing to risk that as well." Neil sat back and watched his adopted daughter for signs of thawing—she warmed only slightly, so he added, "We're not saying you can't go with him. We're just saying one of us has to come, too. Besides, we're a great team me and you."

"Who says I'll pick you? Maybe I want Sarah to come along," she said reverting back to her usual, impish personality.

"I meant one of us, other than her," Neil countered. "She's got Eve to worry about and besides, she's not the best with zombies."

"And you are?" she asked. At his hurt look—as small and skinny as he was, he was nobody's idea of a hero—she added, "I didn't mean that. It's just that Mark is really good. You've seen him. He's so big and strong and burly."

At this, Neil smiled with all the humanity of an erector set. It clinked into place one muscle at a time. "I'm sure he's great. How old is he?"

"Only twenty-three," she gushed. "And he is strong. Really strong. You can trust him to take care of me."

Neil wished he could, only he had been twenty-three once and knew better. "I'm still coming. And I'm bringing our two-man tent." At her look of dismay, he could only shrug. "Maybe you'll thank me one day."

"Not likely."

Chapter 12

Neil

Stockbridge, Georgia

Mark's Range Rover bucked and bounced as it plowed through and over a street full of zombies. They made for sickening speed bumps and despite the smile he kept wedged onto his face, Neil felt ready to hurl up his breakfast. After all, running over a zombie was very much like running over a person.

"That's what they get for jay-walking," Mark said, flashing a set of white teeth.

From the back seat Sadie snorted with laughter. "Jay-walking! That's funny. You see, Neil? I told you he was funny."

Neil's smile was so tight that his jaw was beginning to hurt. "You did mention that on a number of…"

Just then a spray of black blood shot across the windshield. It was all Neil could do not to gag and of course Mark found a way to make things worse: he turned on the windshield wipers, making a hell of a mess.

Here it comes, Neil said to himself as his stomach flipped over. In desperation he opened his window, letting in a warm spring breeze that carried a pleasant fragrance. It focused him. He breathed it in, taking big gulps and after a minute managed to say, "Look, Sadie. The cherry trees are in bloom."

Down a side street there were two great banks of the trees; their petals floated on the wind like a warm snow. It was as pretty a scene as he could have wished for. There wasn't even a zombie along the tree-lined lane to mar the view.

"Wow," Sadie said in a whisper, her dark eyes looking even darker than normal with her Goth make-up applied so heavily. "Let's go there. Can we?"

"What for?" Mark asked after a quick glance. "We're supposed to be scouting and scavenging, not gathering flowers for fuck's sake." So far they had done little of either. All the neighborhoods south of the city were either picked-over already or infested to a dangerous degree. So far, they had wasted the better part of a day driving slowly through them.

Sadie looked disappointed. "I guess you're right."

Neil, who wanted to stop as well in order to settle his stomach, gave Mark a look and said, "Maybe she wants to stretch her legs. It sucks to be cramped up in the back seat for so long."

"I suppose it won't hurt," he replied.

They pulled over halfway down the block. Sadie was the first out; she breathed the fresh air and smiled largely as she leapt here and there trying to catch the spinning flower petals before they hit the ground. There were too many for a thousand eager girls to catch them all. In seconds her hair was full of them. Not for the first time Neil wished his pretty Apocalypse daughter would give up the Goth look and start wearing dresses but experience in this area had made him wise and he made sure not to mention it…again.

"Either of you want to race?" she asked. The light exercise had wetted her appetite for more.

Neil had gotten out of the Rover and was stretching— mostly this entailed kneading his knuckles into the small of his back rather than anything athletic. He laughed out a *No* at the suggestion.

"You kidding?" Mark asked. He hadn't done any stretching. Instead he had assumed the role of protector and stood guard with a fat hunk of grey metal in his hands that could spit a huge ball of lead. "I used to play safety on the football team in high-school. I'd wipe the floor with you."

"Care to bet on it?" she asked, ignoring the fact that Neil had rolled his eyes. They were each showing off for the other and it is a universal truism that puppy love was nauseating for everyone on the outside looking in.

"Maybe you should stick to racing Neil," Mark replied. "He looks like he's more your speed."

"Thanks," Neil said, sharply. In truth he wished he was as fast as Sadie, but Mark clearly didn't know what he was getting into and thus his comment was meant to be a put-down. Subtle remarks like these had gone on most of the day and Neil was just about sick of them.

Before he could say anything more Sadie put a finger to her lips to quiet him. She knew Mark could be a jackass, but as she explained he was just trying to prove to Neil how tough he was. He was proving only tough to be around.

"Here's the bet. We race down to that blue car." She pointed at a car that was somewhere in the range of eighty yards away. "If I win then I get to drive for the rest of the trip. And if I lose…" Here she paused and gave a glance to Neil before she whispered something in Mark's ear.

"Hell yeah!" Mark agreed to the bet on the spot.

"What?" Neil demanded, pulling Sadie by the elbow. "What did you offer?"

"Does it matter?" she asked. "High school was a long time ago for him. Five years? Right, Mark?" In a lower voice she added to Neil, "You know I'll win."

Supremely confident, Mark scoffed, "It wasn't that long ago. Here, Neil. Take my gun, but be careful you don't pull the trigger. It's a beast."

"You act like you're the only one who's ever shot a gun before," Neil said, irritably. Despite his anger, he was extremely curious as to the size of the bullets in it. The handgun was so heavy he could use it to exercise with, and it possessed a bore of such width that he could put his thumb in easily. He turned away thinking he would inspect the gun while they were doing their silly race.

Sadie stopped him. "Wait, Neil. You have to officiate."

The word officiate, especially after the secretive nature

of their bet set off bells in his head that seemed suspiciously like wedding bells. "Officiate?"

She laughed at him—it never bothered him for a moment when Sadie laughed at him—and said, "You know: *On your mark, get set, go*? You act like you never ran a race before."

It had been a while. Somewhere around twenty years since he had raced, and those had not exactly been races in the strictest sense. Rather they were desperate sprints, running from bullies, a daily occurrence in high school for Neil.

"Fine. If you're ready?" he asked.

Sadie had one foot on the high hood of the Rover and was in the middle of stretching her leg with her chin pressed to her knee. Her flexibility was admirable…and worrisome to Mark who was doing little besides deep knee bends that weren't at all impressive.

They finished and came together in the middle of the street. With little fanfare, Neil counted off: "On your mark…get set…Go!"

At the word go the pair took off, and Mark did indeed prove very fast. He was tall and strong and still in the prime of his youth. It was to his credit that he only lost by ten feet or so.

"Son of a bitch!" he cursed as he came to a spluttering halt and stood bent over at the waist, breathing heavily. Sadie on the other hand came jogging back with a bright smile and just the lightest glint of sweat on her face.

"You've gotten slow," Neil joked. She laughed and then went into more stretches, waiting for the inevitable. She didn't have to wait long. "What do you see in Mark?" Neil asked after less than a minute. "He barely respects you and he doesn't respect me at all. You won't be happy with him."

Despite that she had prepared for this, she still sighed, loudly. "You don't know him like I do. He's much nicer in private. I know you won't believe me but he likes you. His jokes are just him being a guy."

Well that would explain why Neil wasn't getting the "jokes". He had never been much of a man's man. He was small and somewhat effeminate, and spent most of his life detesting the frat boy, slap-on-the-back, hearty-handshake types. As well he disliked the dirt-under-the-nails, grease half-way up your arms, plumbers-crack fellows either. And he disliked gay guys as well. Almost everyone, especially women, assumed he was gay, which bothered him to no end.

Things had not gotten much better with the apocalypse. He still didn't fit in. The frat boys were natural soldiers and heroes, while the mechanical types possessed skills that were highly sought after. And what did Neil have to offer?

Not much.

He could not imagine a more impractical education for the demands of the new world, than the one he had received. What possible good was his degree in finance now? How would his knowledge of *nonrecurring impairment charges*, or *currency fluctuations* come in handy in the face of a horde of zombies? So far it hadn't.

"Just give him a chance," Sadie said in a low voice. Mark was finally coming back, still grumbling under his breath. Louder, she said: "The keys if you don't mind."

He tossed them to her and declared, "I want a rematch. When I'm not wearing jeans! And these sneakers, they don't have any traction."

Neil handed over the pistol and was only too glad to do so. He could've hammered fence posts into frozen ground with the thing. Besides, he had his Beretta and his trusty axe, while Sadie had her little Glock. She had painted the flat parts in a glossy pink. It was an ugly weapon, like frosted death.

"Excuses, excuses," Sadie said lightly. "So should we try one of these houses?"

They took in the neighborhood and Mark's sour look deepened. Though the street was pretty with its cherry trees in bloom, the houses were of the two usual varieties and neither was good. There was the zombie-home-invasion type in which the house looked like a bomb had gone off within it, and the second type: the subtle human-scavenged house in which a door might have been shouldered in, or a single window smashed but was otherwise intact.

When they were mixed like this it was a bad sign. Someone had scavenged the area and it was sure thing that they didn't skip the zombie trashed houses.

"There aren't even any lurkers," Mark said in disgust. "It means someone's been down here and killed them all."

"Finding the right house is like panning for gold," Sadie griped. "There should be like a central map back at the CDC so that everyone knows what areas have been hit already."

It sounded like an excellent idea except that humans would be involved. "It wouldn't work," Neil said. "People would lie. They'd say they hit all sorts of neighborhoods so that those houses would sit like gems that they could come back to at any time. Then again, people may be already doing that. Remember all those streets with the orange Xs spray painted on the doors? We just assumed those houses had been picked over. It doesn't mean they were."

"So what does that mean for us?" Sadie asked.

The answer was as clear as it was undesired. "We have to go further out," Neil replied.

Further out meant all sorts of possible trouble and, worse, it meant they would be further away from any sort of safety.

Chapter 13

Sarah

The Center for Disease Control, Atlanta, Georgia

Eve's pudgy, dimpled knees locked, then unlocked. They locked again with a snap, like a tiny, soft robot coming awake suddenly. They then wavered, jiggled, and finally trembled with the strain of holding up her seventeen pounds. In the end she plopped onto her diapered butt.

Undeterred, she again reached for the end of the coffee table. This attempt, her third, ended with her chin clipping the table and her eyes filling with tears.

Sarah waited to say anything. She paused in mid-crouch, fighting the normal motherly instinct to pick her baby up and clutch her to her bosom and soothe. As always, it was a struggle to remain cold and calculating. No matter the extent of Eve's "injuries" Sarah forced herself to barely react.

She waited as her tiny daughter made little pouty sounds. Ten seconds elapsed before Eve reached for the corner of the table once more.

"I'm doing the right thing," Sarah told herself, despite that it did not feel right in the least. Rather it felt like the "man" thing. It was how her ex-husband had always done things with regard to Brittany, Sarah's first child.

"*She'll be fine.*" This had been a veritable catch-phrase of his for Brit's first three years.

"Sometimes she wasn't fine, Stew," Sarah said to the room, still feeling the anger even after all the years that had passed.

Eve looked back at her, fat tears, near perfect in their symmetry sat on her lashes; one for each eye. "What a big girl you are," Sarah told her new daughter, in hushed tones. The new world with its new rules dictated that she not be overly effusive.

Sarah hated it. She hated that Eve wasn't allowed to cry. A few tears were ok; whimpering was alright, depending on the situation, but crying was just plain wrong. And bawling? Bawling was strictly forbidden. Sadly, so was laughter. Sarah could envision the playground of the future: a perfectly oiled merry-go-round whispering by as the children, sitting upright in the saddles of their garishly painted ponies, did little more than grin at their parents or wave with a shy hand. If there was laughter, it would be a soft heh-heh.

There'd be no more peals of laughter. No more excited whoops! Definitely screeching with the sheer joy of life wouldn't be allowed, and if there was ever a skinned knee, the poor child would just have to deal with it—quietly.

"You're a tough little soldier, aren't you Eve," Sarah said with a grim smile. Just like all of it, she hated using those words, despite that they were necessary words. It was a dangerous time to be a baby, or to even have a baby. Even behind guarded walls it was dangerous, because who knew what the future held? Stronger walls had fallen already and better soldiers had been overcome. Eve had to be ready for anything.

Since they were pioneers of sorts, she and Neil had carefully thought out their parenting strategy. They were setting the standard for all other parents to emulate—not that there were many. Of the twenty-one hundred souls left at the CDC there were eight children below the age of thirteen, with Eve being the only one below the age of seven. Nor were there many babies on the way; a mere handful. Women were rightly afraid to get pregnant—for themselves and their future babies.

No one understood this better than Sarah. She dreaded the idea of stepping a single foot beyond the walls and slept horribly whenever Neil and Sadie ventured out.

"They're going to be fine," she said, partly to Eve, but mostly to herself. "Daddy and big sis are going to be just fine." She hoped. Sarah didn't think she could raise Eve alone. It was labor-intensive being so attentive, striving for the perfect mix of love, freedom, and safety. It was also a joy, even compared to raising Brit.

Back in the old days it was considered normal to hand your two-month old baby to a nanny or some local lady with a houseful of brats. At the most, people kept a child until pre-school and sometimes pre-pre-school if there was a government program in place—Head Start or some such that did little besides destroying the concept of motherhood.

Sarah hadn't looked at it like that, not back then. Instead she had some fool notion that it was *so* important to work outside the home, as if the world wouldn't continue to turn with one less pharmaceutical rep in high-heels and a short skirt pushing her pills. She now knew the truth. She was a fool no longer. The truth was that she had one overriding purpose and that was to parent her child, to be a mom. Everything else in her life was secondary.

"Oh, Brit," she whispered, picturing her beautiful daughter. At the sound of Sarah's voice, Eve looked back at her. She had one little fist shoved knuckle deep in her mouth; her chin was aglaze with drool. "Yeah, Sweetums, Mommy messed up with your big sister. I wasn't a good mom. That's the truth. I was a part-time mom—nights and weekends only."

Nights, when Brit was asleep and weekends, when she was off with friends.

"And that's why she's dead," Sarah went on, feeling depression begin to creep over her mind. "Brittany's dead because I was only around when she wasn't. What kind of mother is that?"

At the question, Eve jiggled head to toe, sat down with a light thump and then released gas like a conversational duck: *quack, quack, quack*. Just like that the spell of gloom departed from Sarah and she smiled. Eve smiled back, but just for a second. She then took on a faraway look, as if she were considering the geo-political ramifications of zombie migratory patterns. Her face slowly turned red until she lit up her diaper with an eye-watering stink.

"Are you saying I was a shitty mother?" Sarah asked with a shake of her head, and a little laugh.

Eve replied: "Da-da." Her only real word.

"He'll be back in a few days and as much as I'd like for him to change that toxic-waste-filled-diaper of yours, I'd certainly be a bad mom…again, if I did. Wait here." Before dashing back to the master bedroom, where the extra diapers were kept, Sarah gave a last glance at the living room to make sure there wasn't anything Eve could stuff into her mouth and choke on.

"I hope you're almost ready for a nap Evey-poo," Sarah said from the hall. "Because mommy is…"

She stopped in mid-stride as a wailing sound started up from outside the apartment. It was a confusing sound, mainly because it was a new sound, or rather, it was an old sound from the old days, and one she hadn't heard in years and hadn't expected to ever hear again. It was an air raid warning. Any alarm, by definition, was supposed to be alarming and yet this one was doubly so. Up and down it went with growing urgency in its mechanical voice.

Turning on the spot, Sarah raced back to the living room to stare with wide, worried eyes out the window. The sky was a perfect robin's egg blue, unblemished by a single contrail—the telltale sign of an inbound jet. And this was perfectly normal; exactly what any sane person would expect. After all this wasn't London during the Blitz. There weren't German Heinkels overhead dropping bombs.

Then what was the siren all about?

"Could be an accident," she commented. "Or a prank." She turned back to the task at hand, changing a diaper, though she did so with a troubled heart. This time she decided to keep Eve close and so scooped her up and took her to the bedroom. There she put the baby on the bed where Eve immediately grabbed her own toes—she knew what was coming.

"Da-da. Ba-dah, ba, ba," she babbled, her blue eyes going round in her head with the warble of the siren.

Sarah sped through the re-diapering without answering her daughter; she was too preoccupied with the siren and her growing fear. Why hadn't it stopped? Why did they let it go on and on? It had been over three minutes now and was driving her bonkers...

"Hey," Sarah exclaimed, relieved. Finally, the siren had stopped. "That's a whole lot better." She straightened Eve's pink dress and was just about to pick her up when she caught the sound of a more distant, or perhaps a more muffled alarm that had been buried by the siren. It was a repetitious: *meep, meep, meep.*

"Come on, Sweetie," Sarah said, buckling her holstered Berretta around her waist and then hitching Eve to her hip. The gun was reassuring, as was the view from her window: clear blue skies, the football field of Emory University that sat across the road properly empty, and the distant grey/green haze of Georgia in the spring. There wasn't a zombie in sight. So what was with this new alarm?

In just under two minutes, Sarah zipped down to street level and found the main avenue of the CDC compound clogged with people. Judging by the numbers she was the last one to see what the fuss was about.

"Sarah!" A woman pushed her way through the crowd. It was Shondra Davis. She was new to the CDC and like most people, very much alone in the world. After spending the winter holed up in Birmingham, starving and watching as her family and friends were killed one after another by endless zombie attacks, she had finally decided to make a run for her life. Only by luck had she come east to the CDC.

During her ordeal, she not only lost every person she had ever cared about, she had also lost over a hundred and fifty pounds. Her skin was the color of bark and had the consistency of a bloodhound's cheeks.

Shondra threw her flappy arms about Sarah and hugged both her and Eve. "Oh, it's bad. It's bad, isn't it?" she asked, her brown jowls all aquiver. The same sort of worried question riddled the crowd.

"I don't know," Sarah replied, trying to see over the taller woman. "I don't even know what's happening." As far as she could tell, nothing was happening. The alarm seemed to be drifting up out of the depths of the main CDC lab, from which people scurried, looking back as they did, as if something was after them.

"I guess no one does," Shondra said. She hadn't moved to relinquish her hold on Sarah.

A man in front turned around and said in a thick Alabama accent, "They may-could have stiffs up in there. You know, to do speariments on. I betcha some got out and are eatin' everyone in sight."

"Would they make this much ruckus over a few stiffs?" another asked. He was a tall stick of a fellow with radar dish ears and a web of wrinkles around his eyes. He answered his own question, "I really doubt it."

The man from Alabama gave him a sneer and asked, "Since y'all so smart, Ein-stein, what do y'all figger it is?"

"Germs," he answered, hushing the crowd with his one word answer. "That there is the CDC. It's where they keep all the germs. My guess it wasn't no zombies what got out. It's the germs what got out."

Chapter 14

Neil

Ola, Georgia

"Nothing! Only more dead ends," Mark grumbled, kicking open the screen door with a bang and stepping out of the house. As Sadie had mentioned, on *many* occasions, he was a strapping young man; beneath his weight the weathered boards of the wraparound porch groaned.

Irritated by the noise and the whining, Neil followed him out, rolling his eyes behind Mark's back. "At least it wasn't picked over," Neil said. "It should give us some hope that we'll find a good house around here somewhere."

The bigger man turned just as he was about to go down the steps and shook his head so that his brown hair swung in his eyes; his hair was long even by apocalypse standards— another strike against him in Neil's mind. "That's completely fuckery!" Mark exclaimed, flipping his hair back to clear his eyes. "The truth is the exact opposite. The fact that the house *wasn't* picked over and was still useless means…I don't know what. But it's all fucked. I mean, where's the damned food?"

"Eaten," Neil said, simply. He was too tired to be as animated as Mark over things he couldn't change. "Whoever lived here ate all of it, down to the last Saltine. But that doesn't mean there weren't homes that were broken into by the stiffs. Those homes might be packed with all sorts of stuff."

"And they might not. Shit! We're wasting our time."

"Mark, calm down, please," Sadie said. She had been on guard outside and she pointed to a few zombies headed their way. They were on a somewhat secluded street, in a small town that was midway between the rural life of the country and the last vestiges of suburbia. The homes were large and further apart, but there were still plenty of them.

More than enough to house zombies in numbers that they didn't want to tussle with.

Mark glanced at the stiffs and then snorted in derision.

Neil looked them over with an experienced eye, judging the difficulty of killing them without getting bitten or scratched. They were whole and healthy, and walked quicker than the average, which wasn't good. "Sadie, come on up here. The porch steps will stymie them long enough for us to put them out of their misery."

"I swear I don't get you, Neil," Mark said with a bit of a smile, relaxing somewhat. "Whoever uses a word like *stymie*? And what misery? Those fuckers are the ones causing all the misery."

Not for the first time, Neil glanced to Sadie, wearing a look that made it clear he couldn't understand what she saw in Mark. She caught the look, smiled thinly and came up the steps to wait for the zombies to arrive.

Neil killed them one after another—the steps did indeed flummox them so that their deaths were not particularly difficult to achieve although he did get some black blood on his sleeve. "There's probably a better way to do this," he said, wiping his light jacket on the long grass of the front yard.

"There is," Mark said. "It's called using a fucking gun."

"I said a *better* way, Mark. Not a way to have every zombie in a five mile radius coming down on us."

Sadie skipped down the stairs, intentionally ignoring the corpses as she always did. "Maybe you can use my baseball bat. There'd be less blood. I hate the blood the most. It's so gross."

"A bat is not such a sure thing when it comes to killing them," Neil replied. "Some have heads like granite." *And it hurts my hands*, he didn't add, not wanting to appear wimpy around Mark.

With his bloody axe resting on his shoulder, he stood thinking about the business of killing zombies. He hated all of it, but it was the blood that was the worst. After every killing he would fastidiously inspect his skin and clothes to make sure he hadn't been splattered.

Just then, however it was not the blood that had him thinking, it was the danger in killing.

Slaying zombies quietly in close-quarter combat was a fairly hazardous undertaking. One slip of the hands or one accidental trip could mean a very bad death. Neil had tried using a bow and arrow with very poor results. Part of this was due to his lack of skill, however the way a zombie lurched in an unpredictable manner meant a head shot—a real, killing headshot—wasn't going to be easy for anyone using a bow.

"Let's see, you don't like guns or axes or bats," Mark said, counting on his fingers with the mention of each different weapon. "I would suggest a spear, only I'm thinking that would be too icky for you as well. Maybe you should try putting them in *time-out*."

This actually triggered a thought in Neil, despite the flippancy of the remark. However, the thought went out the window when Mark continued in falsetto: "*You naughty, naughty zombie. If you won't eat all your brains, it'll be the corner for you! And this time I mean it.*"

Sadie forced out an uncomfortable laugh and tried to change the subject, "So, where are we going to spend the night? Not here I hope. That front door looks rickety as hell."

Neil thought for sure Mark would make some braggadocious comment, however the younger man simply agreed that the house wasn't suitable.

They moved on. It was late in the afternoon and the sun was dropping out of the sky when they found a place to encamp. It was a rectangle of a home hidden from the world by great, moping willows. Compared to the elegant estates of south Atlanta, it was hardly more formal in its architecture than a doghouse and yet it appealed immediately.

The previous owners had gone to great lengths to preserve its integrity. The windows and doors were fortified, boarded over with inch-thick plywood and barred with steel to keep out the undead. Still, their hard work had not saved them.

The little group found the bodies of an elderly couple in an upstairs bedroom. They were wizened like old apples and not just from the length of their internment.

"I think they starved to death," Neil said after inspecting the kitchen. Though there were a few spices, everything else had been eaten, up to and including a large bag of dog food. Of the dog there was no sign and Neil had the uncomfortable thought that it had been eaten as well.

Sadie looked pained at the idea of the pair dying of starvation and said, "But they have a pond just out back. I saw like three fish jump in the last minute."

"Yeah, and did you see the woods all around?" Mark asked. He had grown quieter as the murk of evening settled in. "You might have seen three fish but I saw about fifty stiffs. They're prowling all up in the woods."

The night passed without incident, though it was a hard burden to have to listen to the fish jump and splash in the pond throughout the evening hours. Neil dreamt of fish—of catching them, of cooking them, of eating them. The thought of fish filled his mind almost straight through the night. In the morning he stood at the back window, watching the fish do their thing as the pale dawn ate up the mists.

"I'm going to catch one," he vowed. They had fishing poles, which was good, and lures, which wasn't. At best Neil was a subpar fisherman and with lures he was worse than that. His only success had been with bait. The problem was that they didn't have any—though he knew where to find some.

"Can you get a fire going, Sadie," he asked, "And Mark, if you'll cover me?"

Mark looked at him skeptically. "You're going out

there?" The morning was so new that the zombies hadn't yet retreated into the dim of the forests.

"Yes. Just for a little while. All you have to do is keep them off of me for a couple short minutes."

They were some of the longest minutes of his life. With a plastic container in one hand, a trowel in the other, and Mark just behind him, Neil darted out the back door and ran to where a canoe sat with a goodly amount of brackish water floating in the bottom. He upended the thing, grunting as he did so, and then scrambled about after the insects retreating from the light.

He grabbed three black beetles, a centipede as long as his pinky, and two huge worms that stretched as he pulled— one snapped in half; he kept it anyway. Next he went to a flat rock, however, before he could flip it over an explosion broke the still air and echoed like rolling thunder.

"Jeeze!" Neil cried. A single zombie had come shuffling from around the house and now it lay on the ground with half its head gone.

"You wanted me to cover you," Mark said with a shrug. "What did you expect?"

"I expected you to kill them quietly, if you could," Neil answered. As evidenced by the swaying trees and crashing footfalls from the nearby forest, the time for quiet was past. Neil flipped the rock, grabbed all the bugs he could and then ran for the house, holding his left ear against the drum-shattering explosions of Mark's 50-caliber handgun, a Taurus *Raging Bull 500*.

"Did you see that fucker's head come apart?" Mark asked giddily once they were inside. "It was awesome!"

"Yeah, it was great," Neil said, poking beetles back into the bucket. "I hope this is enough."

Sadie, who had been watching from the door instead of starting the fire, glanced in the bucket and asked, "Enough for what? You can't go back out there, especially not to go fishing. I saw like a hundred of them. They're all over the place."

"I'll be fine. It's Mark you should worry about."

Mark stopped in the middle of topping off the load in his hand-cannon. "If you think I'm going to go fishing with all those fuckers out there, you're crazy."

"No, I'm going to be the one fishing," Neil said, checking his pole, making sure the bobber was set a good two feet above the weighted hook. "I just need you to back the Rover down to the pond. I'm going to fish from on top of the roof. I'll be fine. No zombie can climb up there, not with the big tires you got on her."

"What about me?" Mark asked. "There were some big stiffs out there. The glass won't hold." Car windows were strong enough to repel the smaller weaker zombies, but against the larger ones, it was just a matter of time before they broke through. "Did you think of that, Smart-Guy?"

"I did. You'll sit very still and drape yourself in a sheet…"

"What? That won't fool them!"

Neil fished out one of the beetles. "They won't even notice you. They're going to be looking at me like I'm the cherry on top of an ice-cream sundae. Just don't move around a lot and stay hidden; you'll be fine."

The plan worked like a charm. The pond brimmed with so many stocked fish that Neil hauled in three bass and two good sized sunnies before he ran out of bait. Not that it was easy. Standing atop the Range Rover, exposed for all to see, he felt vulnerable, like a piece of bait himself. After a while, though, Neil noticed the surrounding throngs of zombies stretching out their arms to him; they moaned and swayed as if to an unheard beat. The whole thing made him feel like a rock-star in hell.

With plenty of fish in his bucket, Neil tapped on the roof and Mark nearly sent him tumbling among his hungry fans by flooring the Rover. He just managed to hold on for the short trip around to the front of the house where they ran for the door before the stiffs could catch up.

The three of them ate till their stomachs were stretched and uncomfortable. "I wish I knew the first thing about how to smoke fish," Neil said, picking his teeth with a bass-bone. "I know Sarah likes fish a lot."

"It can't be that hard," Sadie said, but didn't offer any more thoughts on the subject. Her eyes were glassy from the big meal.

Despite the desire to nap, the three forced themselves up and, after a sprint to the Rover, they went on looking for the right homes to ransack. It was a long, dangerous day investigating them. The zombies were like ants at a picnic—every time they stopped, out they would come. Sometimes they came in ones or twos, while at other times they seemed to form marching lines. Once the three sat trapped in an upstairs bathroom of a trashy, redneck bi-level for two hours until the horde broke up.

And just like the day before Mark followed a similar pattern. In the morning he made rude jokes, mostly jibes at Neil; in the afternoon he grew restless and agitated and just as dark threatened he'd become quiet and somewhat withdrawn. The third day was much the same. They had only planned for a three-day trip, however they were on such a bad streak that they had barely filled two boxes with canned goods and a third with other essentials: candles, spices, bottled water. They decided that a fourth day was in order despite knowing that Sarah would be worried sick.

In the old days it would've been only a couple hour trip back, now it was a whole other story. Not only were many of the roads and bridges impassible, they couldn't afford the gas to go back to the CDC; fuel was another essential that they were struggling to locate.

That fourth day started with another attempt at fishing, unfortunately Sadie insisted on getting a turn and through her inexperience, the girl from Hoboken managed to waste all the bait and lose three hooks. Two strange-looking and even stranger tasting fish were all she had to show for two hours of sitting on top of the Rover.

For once Mark needled her instead of Neil. She accepted the jokes in an embarrassed silence while Neil glowered. He was somewhat used to being made fun of, but he'd never had a loved one made fun of before and it made him far more angry than he thought it could have. It wasn't something he could laugh away or let roll off his back. Breakfast that morning was a hushed, angry affair because of it.

Luckily, success smoothed over any tensions as they happened upon a jackpot of a home. Jackpot being a relative term, they managed to fill half the Rover with four boxes of canned goods, two scoped rifles with three hundred rounds of ammo, fourteen gallons of gas, and finally the greatest prize: two bags of flour and another of sugar.

"Bread," Sadie exalted holding up one of the bags of flour as if it was the Super Bowl trophy. "We can make bread!"

They stood around the flour for a few minutes and talked about all the different types of food they missed the most, until Neil got them going again. From then on Mark was different. He laughed the most, worked the hardest, and finally Neil saw why Sadie was attracted to him. Even the afternoon irritability wasn't so bad.

Two hours after lunch they were traveling down a sunken road when they spied another house that drew their attention.

It was little more than a cabin in the woods and yet it yielded another trove, though not nearly as exciting as the last. It was clearly a Man Cave as demonstrated by the cans of beans, and the cans of chili with beans, and the cans of franks and beans...and the porn. There were other essentials as well and everything, minus the porn, was stowed in boxes, piled on the baggage carrier atop the Range Rover, and lashed down.

Tired now, the three argued whether to go on, spend the night, or try to make it back to the CDC. It was after four at that point and Mark had grown sullen and wanted to stay since there weren't any zombies in evidence. Neil wanted to go back, but was quickly voted down by the other two.

"It'll be dark soon," Sadie complained. "We shouldn't travel in the dark. I say we go on for a little longer. We're on a hot streak, let's not spoil it."

Her logic won out over Neil's pining for Sarah and Mark's desire to get under cover sooner than was needed. They bid farewell to the cabin and decided to go on along the sunken road to see where it led. Strangely it petered out after a mile or so. The road, dirt to begin with, turned into a rutted track and ever so slowly the ruts faded until the Rover sat in deep heather.

"This doesn't seem to be going anywhere," Mark said, in a voice slightly higher than normal. The forest edged in too closely for his tastes.

"We can turn around," Sadie said, doing so without any debate. "There were a few houses back on the..." She stopped the Rover in mid-turn as something caught her eye. "I think I see where this leads."

She pointed to a barn not more than a half mile distant. It had been obscured by an arm of the forest. Even from a distance they could see that the roof was shabby and weathered, and that the red painted siding had faded to a rusty grey.

"Do we bother?" Neil asked, still wanting to go back home and looking for any excuse.

Sadie shrugged with a single shoulder. "I say yes. There could be an even bigger stash in there. Who knows? They might even have more porn!"

Neil laughed at her joke, but Mark only squinted at the barn and then back the way they had come. With the trail slunk lower than the surrounding forests and overgrown with shadows it didn't look all that appealing. "I say we go on, too," he said. "Even if there's nothing, I bet that barn has a loft we could spend the night in."

With the decision settled, and the trail apparently consumed by nature, Sadie took the Rover across country, heading directly for the barn. It was slow going despite the SUV's four-wheel drive. The ground was pitted with strange depressions and when they weren't thumping into one, they were bouncing over mossy tree trunks that were practically invisible in the tall grass.

Eventually as they came within a few hundred yards of the barn the land evened out. Here it had been properly tilled and cultivated the year before but, oddly, not harvested. There were still towering corn stalks—all yellowed and dry as bones. Rows upon rows of it. The ride became gentle, but slightly unnerving since visibility dropped to only a few feet in any direction.

About fifty yards from the barn the old corn played out so that there was a wide circle surrounding the building where they could see all around. Sadie stopped the Rover on the edge—half in the corn, half out of it. "Here's where I get out," she said.

She wanted to show off some more. Neil knew better than to argue. Mark did not. "What? Why?"

"I want to stretch out my legs with a little run," she said, turning off the engine and sliding out of the Rover. "Besides it's a good way to flush out any zombies hiding around here. Cars confuse them sometimes, but a choice piece of meat like me will have them rushing out for dinner."

"That's what I'm worried about," Mark retorted.

"I'll be fine. There ain't a zombie alive that can catch me. Besides, I have my *Tomb Raider* special, just in case." She held up her ugly pink and black Glock.

With a wave she began to jog in the general direction of the barn and she seemed so confident that both men settled in to observe. Sadie was a joy to watch when she stretched out her slim legs in a wild sprint, however she didn't this time. Instead she only jogged or skipped, warming up, until she came abreast of the barn. Then she peeked in and immediately hopped back.

More slowly, she took a second look. When she turned back to them it was with a look of defeat. She held up both hands with fingers splayed.

Neil interpreted, "There at least ten zombies in the barn. We'll have to find a better place to..."

He stopped as he saw the cornstalks part all along the rows behind Sadie. Jumping out of the Rover, he pointed and shouted, "Look out behind you!" She turned for only a split second and then urgently she pointed back at him.

Confused, Neil glanced at Mark and asked, "What the hell is she..." Just then a zombie stepped out of the corn right next to Mark's window and stared in with unblinking, yellowed eyes. And now the corn all around Neil whispered with the coming of zombies—by the hundreds.

Neil could see them through the yellow stalks. They were just feet away. He did the only prudent thing for a man to do; he let out a yelp and then hopped back into the Range Rover, shutting the door against grey arms that reached out for him.

"What are we going to do?" Mark asked, shying back as the zombie at his window began to thump the glass with a heavy fist.

"Drive!" Neil ordered from the back seat. "Move over and drive! We have to get to Sadie." The girl had not budged save to spin slowly as the corn gave up the dead. She was surrounded by what appeared to be hundreds of them. They were closing in on her, but Neil saw there was still time to save her.

Mark, his face contorted and no longer handsome in the least, slid over to the driver's seat and then fumbled around groping beneath the dashboard as though he were a blind man. "The keys...they're gone! She has them. Sadie took them!"

Both men snapped their heads around to look at the girl in black; with so many zombies advancing on her she was barely visible.

For Neil Martin, time slowed nearly to a stop for the span of two long breaths. He drew air drew into his lungs, ever so slowly and breathed out in the same manner while his mind went into overdrive as he analyzed the situation:

Question: *Was there time to hot-wire the car?* Answer: No. Even if I knew how, it would take upwards of a minute to accomplish.

Question: *How much time did Sadie have?* Answer: assuming she shot the closest zombie at any one time, and did not miss, she would be overwhelmed in eighteen seconds plus-or-minus two seconds.

Question: *Can she escape the encircling zombies by running or fighting her way out?* Answer: No. There are far too many and she is not that capable with her Glock.

Question: *What are my options?* Answer: Only one. Kill as many of them as I can and then die by her side.

Question: *Why can't I hide here in the Range Rover instead?* Answer: That is not an option.

Question: *Why not?* Answer: It is not an option.

Question: *Why isn't it an option?* Answer: She chose to be your little girl and you chose to be her father. You love her and you won't watch her die and do nothing.

Question: *But I'm afraid.* Answer: Yes. Get out of the car.

Just like that, time snapped back into place and Neil knew all that he needed to know. "Come on!" he screamed to Mark. His fear for Sadie was a black hunk of ice in his chest that made the rest of his body numb. He grabbed his gun and slammed open the Rover's door, smashing it into a zombie that had been right there. The creature was knocked to the ground by the force of the blow, yet the tactile sensation of it did not register on Neil's brain.

The same was true with his Beretta. When it went off,

seemingly by its own volition, it did not buck, while its report was muted. It seemed like a weak thing in his hands—like a gun from bad dream. Since the advent of the apocalypse he had many such dreams, the kind where his feet seemed to run in deep molasses, or where his arms were so weak they were all but useless, or dreams that his gun shot BBs or pellets and the zombies came on grinning, undeterred.

It was like that now, except the zombies did fall as he shot his way through them, only so many more sprang up to take their places that the world retained its nightmare quality all the way until he reached Sadie.

"Neil! Why?" she asked before shooting a closing zombie. It made a noise like a bullfrog croaking and then fell at her feet.

He had neither the time nor the breath to answer. His sprint, a mere forty yards of winding through, and sometimes plowing over, an army of undead, had tired him. Instead of answering, he turned a tight circle, shooting those beasts nearest and searching for the part of the deadly ring that was thinnest.

It was only then that he discovered Mark hadn't joined him in his mad dash. It was a catastrophic let down; with his size and his skill with guns, Mark might have made all the difference. Neil couldn't spare a second to worry about that now. His notion that Sadie had eighteen seconds left before she was overwhelmed hadn't been correct. From the moment Neil got to her the pair were shooting nonstop, generally with great accuracy since the zombies were now within feet of them.

"This way!" Sadie cried, grabbing Neil's hand and turning him ninety degrees. She had caught sight of where the ranks of the zombies were only two deep instead of five or more. They shot their guns dry and made a hole big enough for them to run through.

A second later they were in the corn, sprinting past

skeletal stalks with little to cover their frames but a few old, yellowed leaves. They had escaped the initial wave, however their salvation was short lived. The corn was rife with the creatures and everywhere they turned grasping hands reached through the stalks for them.

With no other option they ran, though they did so without aim or direction, fleeing *from* constant danger instead of *toward* some place of safety.

Somehow, in the maze of corn, they got turned back to the barn clearing where a wall of zombies stretched across the view greeted them. "No, go...back," Neil gasped, grabbing Sadie's shirt and pulling. She spun to the left and led them, zigging and zagging around the zombies. Neil benefitted from the confusion she wrought. With their limited brain power, the zombies fixated on the human in front and, for the most part, didn't even seem to notice him. Sometimes he found himself running next to zombies or just behind them. After five minutes he was so exhausted that he could barely muster the energy to care.

The headlong escape could not last forever. Neil was flagging and dizzy, stumbling like a zombie himself, while Sadie was breathing deeply and sweating up a storm.

"Go...on," he wheezed. His legs were as stone and his feet unresponsive. He had not trained in years and the torrid pace threatened to explode his heart which whomped in his chest, shaking the phlegm building in his lungs.

Sadie didn't bother to dignify the request. Instead she used her empty Glock to smash in the temple of a zombie charging from their left. The creatures seemed unfazed by the nonstop running, however all the changes in direction had left them going every which way.

"Look!" Sadie said with some excitement. At first he didn't see what had her smiling. The corn ran to the edge of a neighboring property and all he saw was a sharp drainage ditch that he was sure he lacked the strength to jump across.

"Huh?" he asked, lacking the wind to form words.

She was already pulling him on. "We'll jump it. They won't be able to," she explained. It didn't look like much of an obstacle for anyone but Neil. It was about four feet wide and three feet deep but even that seemed like too much for him. "Go first," she ordered.

He stumbled on while she ran parallel to the ditch waving her arms getting the zombies to come after her once again. It was the only way he would have made it—and, even with the benefit of not having zombies right on his tail, he didn't quite make the leap. The further wall of the ditch was wet with mud and he smacked square into it. However he was no mindless thing and so grabbed a nearby root and pull himself up. Seeing him somewhat safe on the other side, Sadie leapt the ditch with the grace of a gazelle, and jogged over to him.

Neil was only then getting to his feet, while behind Sadie the ditch was filling with the grey bodies of the living dead. There were hundreds of them, maybe upwards of a thousand. They simply charged into the ditch as if it wasn't even there, squashing those who had landed in the pit ahead of them. The long ditch was alive with roiling corpses.

"It won't hold them forever," Sadie said. "Come on."

Flush with victory she turned, took one step—into a hidden gopher hole—and went down with a cry of pain.

"My ankle! Oh jeeze, oh jeeze," she moaned, over-and-over again as she rolled on the ground. "My ankle. I broke it...I think I broke it."

He dropped to one knee and tried to take a look at her leg, but couldn't because she wouldn't stop rolling in agony. It was only when she went suddenly still and pointed behind him that he had the chance to see the extent of her injury, but by then it was too late.

"Neil!" He followed her pointing finger and fear-stricken gaze which swept the entire ditch; the one thing holding the zombies back. "Shit," Neil whispered. The zombies were climbing out.

Chapter 15

Sarah

The Center for Disease Control, Atlanta, Georgia

It's the germs what got out.

Sarah's mouth fell open at these words and then as a sudden false notion struck her—that germs are worse if they land on your tongue—she shut it with a snap. She wasn't the only one who listened and worried over the words of the tall, jug-eared man. All around her people were backing away from the main CDC lab, pressing in close to the late comers such as Sarah and Shondra.

"Now don't y'all be a panickin," the one with the 'Bama drawl said, raising his hands. "That there's the CDC, alright. The "C" stands for *control*. They control diseases up in there. It's where they cure 'em."

At this proclamation the crowd breathed out a sigh of relief as if they were a single organism with a thousand mouths.

"Do what you want and think what you want, but this redneck don't know shit," the jug-cared man who had first mentioned germs said, pushing his way through the crowd, clearly leaving. "If you don't believe me, why don't you ask him how them science geeks make the cures."

If the man with the drawl knew, he kept it to himself. He only shrugged and was seen to mumble something.

"You see?" Jug-ears exclaimed. "Let me tell you. They need the germs in order to make a cure. Them science boys take a germ, like the plague or the measles or this zombie shit, and they monkey around with it until it starts killing the other germs."

Sarah was somewhat certain that the man had his

science wrong, except for the very important fact that there were indeed germs and viruses and deadly bacteria housed at the CDC. She had always known that but, with the zombie apocalypse occurring, she had assumed the scientists had put all that away so as to concentrate on what was really important.

"Then what's with the alarm?" she asked. "I can't imagine them working on anything but the zombie virus and it's not airborne. We can't just breathe it in, right? *We* shouldn't be worried, right?"

"It ain't *supposed* to be in the air," Bama said, slowly, as if remembering something important. "But I seen me all them National Guard boys runnin' round with them gas masks on back when this all first started."

"Then just like you, they didn't know any better," Jug-ears shot back from the edge of the crowd. He stood very close to Sarah and because of that proximity she felt the need for a gasmask herself. He sweated out a bitter aroma of acid and garlic. Even little Eve seemed affected by the pungent body odor; she turned her button nose around to face into Sarah's bosom.

"And besides, them gas masks is for chemicals," Jug-ears added.

This meant little to Sarah who turned to Shondra and said in a whisper, "I don't know what difference that makes. They both kill you just the same."

The jug-eared man with the bad body odor heard, but didn't take offence. He looked Sarah up and down with a hungry male eye. "I'm gettin' outta here," he said, edging closer. "You should be smart and join me. That alarm is a wakeup call. They got germs up in there and they're still playin' with them. And *they* can't be trusted."

"Then y'all just git going," Bama said aggressively. "Run away, now. Go on! It prolly weren't nothin' but a bleach spill. And for me, them zombies what be worse than any germ. Ain't no germ eat your face off."

Jug-ears walked away with an exaggerated shrug that implied to the crowd: *I tried to warn you.*

It was a warning that settled into the bones of everyone present. The crowd nudged further back from the main lab. They milled about just down the block and worried over any breeze that came from its direction. Eventually, men in full Bio-suits went back inside the lab and minutes later the alarm ceased its nerve-rending *meep, meep, meep.*

Again the crowd breathed out as one.

Then everyone went home to the apartments and the offices converted into apartments that surrounded the building where all the germs were kept. Those people with windows that looked down upon the lab sat in them and watched in a vigil that went on without let up. Anyone walking the streets, and there were very few of those that day, found the view strange—in every window was a face if not two and all wore a matching look of fear.

Sarah's windows faced the opposite direction, which in a way was worse. She felt painfully alone. It was true, she could have accepted one of Shondra's continual invitations to visit which had not declined in enthusiasm in the face of Sarah's clear indifference. She had visited once and it had been worse than being stuck alone in her apartment.

Shondra was a physically active worrier. Even with a guest present, she paced and sweated, going back and forth from every window in her apartment as if the view was apt to change in some meaningful way with the passage of a few seconds.

Her anxiety also seeped into her voice which went from slow and sugary to squeaky. "The germs got out didn't they? I just know they did. We're breathing them in right this second! I woke up with a cough. Eh-Eh. And there! It's back. Oh, my goodness what are we going to do?"

"You can leave," Sarah suggested. "I know lots of others are."

The black lady looked shocked at this suggestion. "And

get eaten by zombies? No way. I saw too many people get eaten alive."

So instead of visiting or going about the increasingly empty streets, Sarah stuck to mothering her daughter and counting food. Both were obsessions with her. Clearly, mothering was understandable, but her compulsion to count and recount, and calculate consumption rates, and then recalculate them over-and-over again throwing in insane variables, was not.

Because of their previous incarceration, Sarah's four-person family was easily the poorest at the CDC. Even Shondra had managed to show up in a Ford F-250 with its bed overflowing with scavenged goods, though she was the first to explain it had all been luck, having come upon the vehicle abandoned and already filled.

Most everyone else had their one or two person apartments stacked from floor to ceiling with boxes of goods. Without currency, trading was how certain unscavengable essentials were gotten a hold of. Clean water being the most important of these essentials.

The day after the alarm, Sarah picked out a can of yams, hitched Eve to her back, checked the load in her Beretta, and went out to trade for two gallons of distilled water. She needed and wanted so much more. One of the gallons was for drinking and making formula, the other was for bathing Eve and herself—the dregs of which would then be used to flush the toilet which was a once a day occurrence when she was alone. Weekly she treated herself to a three gallon "full" bath—she never really felt clean like she used to.

As usual, she and Shondra met by the trading stands. Normally they both liked to linger in the sun and chat an hour or two while they nosed over what was being offered. What was different that day and for the next two, was that Shondra was in a hurry to make her trades and go. It was clear she was under the impression that the air in her apartment was cleaner in some way than the air on the street.

Getting water quickly wasn't an issue on that day; the usual crowds were half what they normally were. Most of the traders were there, but the people weren't. It was unnerving.

The day after that the crowds were sparse, and the day after that the word *crowd* was a gross exaggeration.

"Where is everyone?" Sarah asked her friend.

Shondra was a tall lady and so when she whispered she felt the need to bend down. "Some just up and left for good," she said in such a breathy whisper that Eve giggled, thinking it was a game. "But most say they're taking a vacation. Like for a few weeks or a month, you know? Just to see what's going to happen."

"What do they think is going to happen? Do they really think the air is full of germs?"

The woman scanned the people around as if checking for spies. "Maybe," she said in a way that suggested her answer was really *yes*. Again Shondra was quick to leave and Sarah hurried to her apartment. There she made the foolish gesture to her growing fear by putting towels down at the crack where the front door met the sill, just in case.

The following day, the fourth since the alarm went off, and two days after Neil said he would be back from his scavenging trip, Sarah woke very early; even before Eve began to stir. She lay in the king-sized bed and felt every square inch of its emptiness. The area next to her was a barren expanse, a forbidden zone, so forlorn that she dared not enter it lest its extreme lonesomeness overcome her.

He should've been there...or more accurately, since Neil was an early riser, that side of the bed should've been mussed and warm, and his aroma still strong on his pillow. Instead, the sheets were cold and still neatly folded, like a sterile hospital bed.

"It's early yet," she said, without making any pretence at being quiet. She needed company and no one could fill a room with their presence like Eve. The baby smacked her lips, waking. Sarah waited for Eve to make the quizzical noises that she used in lieu of actual words.

"Ooh?" By this, Eve meant: Is anyone there? Is it time to get up?

"Yes, my sweetums," Sarah cooed, going to the bassinet that sat at the foot of the bed. In it, Eve was blinking her big eyes and trying to crane her head around to see her mommy. When she saw Sarah, her tiny features lit up in a big smile— it was this smile that made all the work and the fear of the future worth it.

And it kept the loneliness at bay, but not the anxiety.

This was the fifth day. Where were they? Had something happened to Sadie or to Neil? The thought of either being hurt was like broken glass churning in her guts.

"It's neither," she told Eve, forcing a smile onto a resisting face.

"Da-da," Eve told her. The smile bent on Sarah's face and she didn't notice. All day it sat like a crooked picture on the wall, though very few people saw it. Bob, the water guy, wore a matching one, while the people at the stands barely looked up from their wares to acknowledge either her or Eve. And Shondra never showed up for their normal meeting.

"She's probably still in bed," Sarah told Eve, needing to hear some sort of explanation even if it came from her own mouth.

The day progressed at a snail's pace. Most of it was spent staring at the door or trying to listen past it into the hall beyond, hoping to catch the familiar voices. The hall stayed eerily quiet all day. The entire building did as well; it was as though she and Eve were the only ones left in it. The thought was unbearable and yet no proof came forth to counter the idea that they were very much alone.

It wasn't until just after their meager supper that a sound did come to her: *meep, meep, meep*. The alarm!

"Da-da?" Eve asked.

"No, it's not Da-da," Sarah said, rushing first to the window which showed little besides the drawing of the day, and then to the front door. Here, she finally discovered proof that she wasn't alone. Tentatively, opening the door, she glanced out. Up and down the hall heads poked out of doors and the people began to babble nonsensical questions to each other:

"Is that the same alarm?"

"What's it mean?"

"Is it for real this time? A real emergency?"

There were many questions but no answers. Sarah forced herself to ignore the alarm and her growing fears. She shut the door on the babbling; if she wanted to hear a bunch of incoherent rambling she had Eve for that.

After a large, steadying breath she managed to turn her attention back to her daughter: "Let's finish these mushed up peas. What do you say?" Eve made a face. Peas were not her favorite—still, she ate them; she was trained to.

"Open wide," Sarah said, demonstrating by opening her own mouth in a round "O" and lifting her chin slightly. Eve followed suit and Sarah brought a tiny spoonful of mashed peas to her mouth. The peas and the spoon and her hand shook as she did so.

Sarah tried to laugh it off, but the shaking not only persisted it grew worse as more noises were added to the muted alarm. These weren't just hall noises. In the apartment above her, there were thumps and rattles, and the sound of rolling wheels, and frequently something large was dropped.

Next door, the walls vibrated every once in a while. There was the clink of plates being stacked and a good deal of scraping of what Sarah began to suspect were boxes being slid across the floor.

They were the sounds of people leaving.

When the peas were done and Eve had her mouth tight around the business end of a bottle, Sarah got up and listened at the front door and heard hurrying footsteps going back and forth, and the grunt and heavy breathing of people carrying cumbersome loads. She ran once again to the window. No longer was the sight calming for her.

Four stories below, trucks and SUVs were being packed as fast people could shove their belongings into them.

"Is it for real this time?" Sarah asked the glass. If it was, she was a fool to just stand there. "Come on sweetums, we have to find out if...no. You can't come. Mommy has to go out and you can't come. It might be dangerous. There could be germs." Here she paused, fearing what she had to do. "You have to stay here. It'll be ok. I'll be right back."

Eve cocked her head as Sarah backed away. Though her little features began to grow dark, Sarah knew she wouldn't cry...this was something she had been trained on as well.

"I'll be right back," Sarah repeated, one more time and then slipped into the hall. Her insides squirmed with nasty questions. Would the germs kill her in an instant? Or would she linger in pain? If she died quick, what would happen to Eve? Would one of her neighbors take her? She knew that there were some who were jealous and coveted the baby.

Sarah locked the door behind her. "There are no germs. It's just another false alarm, like last time," she said to herself.

Vince from two doors down pushed past her with boxes in his arms. "Vince? What's going on?" she called out.

"Me and Gwen are getting outta here. Can you get that door?"

With his chin he indicated the stairwell door and Sarah dutifully held it open for him. "Has there been a leak or something? Or is this another false alarm?"

"It's germs of course," Vince said, puffing as he went down the stairs. "Why else would the alarms go off?"

There were other reasons. Simple ones like a short in the wiring of the alarm system or a misreading by the sensors, or maybe it was just human error...Sarah started down the stairs with the realization that "human error" could also encompass accidentally releasing deadly germs.

"No," Sarah said, firmly as she hit the evening air. "If the germs were released it had to have been done on purpose. They had to have a zillion safeguards to prevent an accident."

Just in front of her, Vince glanced back to see who she was talking to. Sarah ignored him and his look and continued on around the side of the building. There, she stopped and watched in horror as people fled in every direction and from every structure, including the main CDC lab. They ran helter-skelter as if escaping from a fire, and didn't look back.

The sight answered her every question: this wasn't an accident. For a full minute she stared, until the last of the lab emptied. Only then did she turn on the spot and run up the four floors to her apartment.

"Eve!" she cried, feeling a terror inside her. "We're leaving."

The baby seemed to understand there was something wrong. With great seriousness, she tipped her bottle back and eyed her mommy as she rushed about gathering clothes and putting them and what food she could carry into two large backpacks. There would be no boxes for Sarah, and no extra trips. There wouldn't even be a car; they owned a Honda but Neil had siphoned the last of its gas to use on his scavenging trip.

Now, with killer germs in the air, there was only one thing for Sarah to do: run away.

But to where? And what about Neil and Sadie? What if they came back? Sarah paused, thinking about the death-trap they would be unwittingly coming home to. "But what if they don't come back? What if they were already dead?"

So many questions, without answers spun her head. She found she could only focus on one thing: Eve. Protecting her baby came first above all else. Sarah set Eve in her baby-sling that snuggled to her chest, she then set the heavier pack on her back counterbalancing the baby and, finally shouldered the second pack, offsetting her balance once again.

It would have to do. She then left, never seeing the little apartment again.

Chapter 16

Neil

New Eden, Georgia

The ditch, their last chance for salvation, was being filled with successive waves of the undead. Grey, scabby bodies writhed and scrambled over each other in their mindless desire to get at the pair. Neil choked at the sight.

"Can you stand?" he asked Sadie. It should've been a question for himself as well; his lungs were fiery billows, while his leg muscles trembled in exhaustion.

Sadie tried and collapsed, tried again with Neil's help and was able to stand, barely and only as long as he held her upright. Running was out of the question; limping was all she could hope for and they both knew what that would mean. In misery at what was surely to be her fate, she began to shake her head and her mouth came open but Neil didn't want to hear whatever she was going to say.

"No!" he barked, cutting her off before she began. "We're going to make it. Here bend over." Reluctantly, Sadie bent at the waist and he went up under, picking her up fireman style. She was surprisingly light. At first.

Turning from the ditch and the dead, he saw his goal, a single tree casting its shade over a field of turned dirt. It was two hundred yards away across open land. If Neil had been fresh and strong, running unburdened, he would've still lost the race. Maybe he would have made it to the tree just ahead of the zombies, but there was still the trunk to climb and as he was no longer twelve-years old, he wasn't much of a tree climbing specialist.

But all that was moot; he was not unburdened and he was far from fresh. With the late afternoon sun blazing to his right, looking prettier than it had any right to look, Neil took off in a weary shamble with the girl across his back. It didn't take long before Sadie went from surprisingly light to monstrously heavy.

The ground he was running on only made things worse; a tractor from the summer before had cut it up in rows three feet apart, preparing it for cultivation that would never happen. The dirt was loose and the humped intervals frequently caught his feet as he stepped over them.

"They're coming," Sadie whispered. Her words, flavored with resignation, were flat and emotionless. Neil took a glance back. The first of many zombies had climbed over his brothers and came charging. Neil had a twenty six foot head start. It could've been a hundred yards and it wouldn't have mattered. "Drop me," she said. "Please, Neil."

"No," he gasped. Step, step, step, big step. Step, step, step, big step. It became a rhythm that he made his body dance to and he vowed he would continue to do it until he was pulled down from behind.

"Please," she begged, her words going up and down as he jostled her. "If you don't, we'll both die…and if you die it will be my fault. Don't make me a murderer."

Step, step, step, big step, big breath. "Your life…will be…my fault." Just saying those words slowed him down and he nearly tripped going over the next ten inch tall hump of dirt. He forced himself on as sweat ran like acid into his eyes and his breath burned. It was as though his chest cavity was on fire; and it wasn't just his chest; everything hurt. Neil went on until he began to think that death would be a relief from the pain.

Soon he began to stagger and each of the humps became momentous hurdles that had to be considered and climbed rather than simply stepped over.

"Neil…" Sadie began again.

He cut her off with a rasped out angry, "No!"

Surprisingly, she didn't argue. "Keep going," she urged and now there was, if not excitement in her voice, at least a modicum of hope.

"Huh?" He turned to look back and exhausted as he was, the effort unbalanced him and sent him sprawling. Still the brief glimpse gave him hope and that hope gave him the strength to at least try to stand again. The zombies, with their diminished spatial capacity and poor depth-perception were having just as hard a time navigating the tilled field as he was. They didn't trip over every hump, nor even every third hump, but every fourth or so they would stumble and fall in a heap of flailing body parts. And when one went down it was certain to trip up those just behind.

It was like watching an army of extremely drunk men and women attempting to march and, from a place of safety, the ludicrous view would've been comical. Still the creatures gained quickly with the pair of humans on the ground, staring.

"Come on, Neil!" Sadie cried. She rolled off of him and then held out her arms. "Just support me. Like a three-legged race."

When they were both standing, she slung an arm over his shoulder, while he grabbed her around the waist, taking a firm hold of her jeans and then they started off in an ungainly hop/walk. At first they barely kept out of reach of the lead zombies, but eventually one went face first into the dirt and the others followed like dominos. This gave the pair breathing room in which to form a cadence that carried them on to the tree where another surprise was waiting for them.

From further away, the tree's trunk, which was shorn of low jutting limbs, looked too wide to shimmy up and Neil had feared that he would have to sacrifice himself to boost Sadie up high enough to make it to safety. Now, he saw that not only had someone nailed a ladder of wood planks onto the trunk, they had also made a platform of sorts in the branches higher up. It was like an unfinished tree-fort. Despite its rough nature it was a thing of beauty to them.

"Go first," Neil ordered in a voice that could not be argued with. He pushed her at the ladder and, disregarding her gender completely, shoved his hand into the crack of her ass and heaved upwards, lifting her in a display of strength that was quite unlike him. With only one leg to assist her, she was a slow climber. Agonizingly slow. Even with his continual help she had barely cleared ten feet before the first of the zombies arrived.

Neil didn't wait to be eaten. He climbed up as high as he could and it was again an awkward thing; she practically sat on top of his head as she adjusted her hands.

"Sorry," she said every time. Save for the kink in his neck, he didn't care—he was saving his adopted daughter and for that he would've accepted far more pain.

Finally, they made it to the platform and both simply threw themselves on the planks and stared up at the greening spring canopy as they gasped for air.

"I love you," Sadie said after a time. Having been carried half way across, what felt like a battlefield, she had the strength to speak. Neil did not. He could only nod a little. She laughed as she always did when danger had been narrowly averted. "And you love me," she went on. "Like a dad, a real dad…or more than like a real dad. My own dad wouldn't have done that. He left me once before and there wasn't even a zombie army after him as an excuse."

"I'm sure…" Here Neil swallowed what felt like an even mixture of dirt and saliva…"I'm sure he would have stayed."

"No. He was a bare minimum kind of guy when he was around. He only acknowledged my existence on my birthday or Christmas. Or if I did something he didn't approve of, like this haircut."

Neil smiled. "I don't approve of your haircut. Girls should have long hair." He sobered suddenly as he remembered something else he didn't like. "And your choice of boyfriends…" he left off with a look.

Sadie caught her breath suddenly. "What? Is Mark ok? Did something happen to him?"

"No…at least, I don't think so. We saw all the zombies

and saw that you were trapped. I yelled something like *come on*, but I don't think he did. He stayed in the car." Neil could tell this news pained her worse than her ankle. And quickly he added, "Maybe there were too many of them on his side. That was probably what happened. I just had a few so it was no big deal. He's probably trapped right now."

In his mind he could picture Mark cowering under a sheet, safe and sound. Perhaps he was even then nibbling on the cookies they had found at the last place or drinking some of their water. Just thinking about that, when he was so thirsty from his efforts, made Neil angry but, for her sake, he forced it away.

"I'm sure he's fine," he said. "Probably he's worried sick."

"Or he thinks we're dead," Sadie moaned. "I can't imagine what he's going through."

Again, Neil pictured Mark under a sheet, hiding, drinking, and relaxing until the stiffs all wandered back into the corn. "Yeah, the poor guy."

Sadie missed the veiled sarcasm. She rolled to her stomach, inched her way to the edge of the platform, and peeked down at the zombies before pulling back. In a whisper she said, "They're all over the place, damn it."

Neil took his own look. A few hundred zombies were in the field, still tripping over the mounded dirt, though now they had begun to wander mindlessly. Another fifty or sixty were beneath the shading tree and would likely stay as long as they kept hearing human voices.

"If we keep quiet they'll leave soon," Neil said, pitching his voice so low he had to practically speak into Sadie's ear.

"Then you'll go rescue Mark?" she asked.

With an effort Neil kept a straight face, and nodded. He would make an attempt to get back to the Range Rover, not for Mark, but because the two of them would likely die if he didn't. They had no food or water, nor any shelter; they didn't even have coats, and the spring nights could still get cold enough to kill.

The pair settled back down on the platform and waited a long, dreary hour until the night was upon them and the zombies moaned their way elsewhere.

Neil turned onto his stomach and stared down, looking for any sign of the monsters. When he was satisfied, he whispered to Sadie, "When you see my headlights, start coming down. Take it slow, but not too slow. I want to be able to pull right up, get you in and then go. You understand?"

"Yeah. Don't forget these," she said and then pushed the keys to the Range Rover into his hand. He grinned at them and she did as well, but suddenly she grew serious. "Good luck."

He would need all the good luck he could get. There was no telling what the zombies were doing in the corn. Were they just standing there, waiting patiently for the next human to happen by? Were they wandering through it in their mindless way? Or were they chasing each other thinking that each was a human meal? No matter what, each scenario made it highly unlikely that Neil would be able to get to the Rover unnoticed.

What scared him the most, and there was a whole list of things that scared him, was getting lost in the corn. It could go for miles for all he knew and once he was in it, everything would look the same.

"I'll be back," he said, pocketing the keys. After taking a shaky breath, Neil gave Sadie a toothy, fake smile and then slid over the edge of the platform. Down the ladder he went, gripping the boards with sweaty, desperate hands.

It was a dark night, but in this case it worked in his favor. He was just a shadow moving slowly through other shadows. He was invisible—or so he told himself so that he wouldn't shake to pieces with his fear.

While in the field he decided to go at a cautious walk, conserving his strength and limiting his chances at turning an ankle. For some reason he kept his hands pulled into his chest as he went. It was as if he was afraid that there were zombies only feet away that would take a nip if he wasn't careful.

This was, of course, absurd while he was in the tilled field. With the bright stars overhead, he could see well enough to know he was alone. In the corn it was another story.

An old corn field, especially one that was improperly set fallow, was as dry and dusty as a pharaoh's tomb and like one had a long dead smell. This particular field was different in that the dead smell wasn't old. It was ripe and sickly, like maggot-covered road kill on a summer day. Neil hadn't noticed the stench on his race through the corn earlier. Now it could not be overlooked.

As bad as the smell was, it wasn't the worst sensation to grip him. The shadows that slunk up and down every row captured his imagination and filled him with stark terror. In the dark the zombies had become nightmare creatures hunting him—and that wasn't the worst either.

It was the sound that filled the corn field which had him frozen in place not twenty feet in.

The air was thick with the moans of the dead. It was the haunting melody of ultimate misery. It was the song of a thousand tortured souls in hell. And it came from all around him.

What little strength he had, left him and he cowered, afraid to move forward and even more afraid to go back. Somehow he was sure that a wild flight across the open field behind him wouldn't end as well as it had earlier. *They* would catch him this time. In his mind the zombies had grown into shadow-creatures that were far stronger and faster.

A new sound that was worse than all the moaning grew in the dark night. Angled on his left, something moved closer to him. It crunched the old husks beneath its feet and whispered past the crow-pitted ears. It was large enough to fill the space between the rows and that meant it was far larger than Neil.

Closer…closer.

Neil became very aware of his bladder. He couldn't remember the last time he had relieved himself, but he knew when the next time was going to be—any second. It was a pain in his gut that expanded with each of the slow steps that approached. If he knew where he could run that would be safe, he would have booked it right then, only nowhere was safe. Now, more steps approached, crackling the ground on his right. Behind him the corn parted with the snapping of the short-armed stalks.

The moaning became louder, excited, and the smell was suffocating.

Panic had a good hold of him, torquing his mind and his senses so that when the first of the zombies wandered up to him, he didn't see that it was missing an arm and was as thin as the corn stalks it was having trouble pushing through. To Neil it was nothing less than a demon.

He fled mindlessly. Direction and intent went out the window, only speed mattered. His feet took him at right angles to where he really needed to go and so with every passing second he went further from the barn and the Range Rover, and closer to death.

By ill-luck he managed to flee from a somewhat harmless zombie into the arms of one that was truly dangerous. Right in Neil's path it stood. It had been a soldier once and with the helmet on its head, the zombie stood six and half feet tall. Across its back, the tattered remains of a poncho flared in the light wind so that it seemed just as wide.

Too late Neil saw it. They came together in a crash and as the lighter of the two, Neil ping-ponged away.

"Oh, God!" he cried. Turning on a dime he headed straight back the way he had come, with the hulking beast charging right down on top of him. It was well fed for its kind and dreadfully fast. What's more, the earth was parade-ground flat between the rows of corn, which meant the beast would not slow and would not fall.

Neil ended up doing both.

After the day he'd had, his stamina began to fail him quickly. His legs tired and within thirty seconds the zombie's long arms were within inches of him. A scream built within Neil's lungs and only needed a catalyst to release it. In midstride the man turned to see the zombie grinning in anticipation of its coming meal. That was enough.

The scream had the all the manliness and machismo of a six-year-old girl's scream. It ripped the night air and would have gone on-and-on until the zombie tore out his throat had not Neil tripped over his own feet. With hands extended he went down in a rolling heap.

Now, the zombie, regardless of its size and speed was still mindless. Its reaction time was measured in seconds rather than fractions of a second and thus it tripped square over Neil, going face first into the dirt. This gave Neil just enough time to hop up and stumble into the corn where he was swallowed up by the night and the forest of stalks. There he wandered, panting like a dog, not realizing he was close to his destination until he stumbled out into the barren dirt yard that surrounded the barn.

Where once the corn held every fear he could imagine, now the open air was worse. It seemed like a hundred eyes were full on him; in a flash he ducked back into the screen of corn and crouched, listening. Below the endless wailing of the dead he heard movement, but the sounds seemed to be going away from him.

"Thank God," he whispered. Trying for stealth, he circled around to the Range Rover and once there, felt his relief turn to anger. It was just as he pictured it: Mark was just a dim lump beneath one of their sheets. He was even snoring!

Despite the rage that began to boil his insides, Neil slipped into the car quietly, and with a yank, ripped the sheet from Mark's face.

It was somewhat comical to watch the big man come awake spluttering in incoherent fear. Neil wasn't in the mood for comedy however. He yanked the Taurus *Raging Bull* from Mark's hand before the man was fully alert and pointed the heavy pistol square into his face.

"What the hell happened to you?" Neil demanded. "You left us out there to die!"

"Huh? What? Neil...It's you," Mark said finally when he could think clearly.

"Yes it's me. Who'd you think it would be?"

"I dunno. I thought you were dead. What about Sadie? Is she...?"

"As far as you're concerned she's dead," Neil spat, feeling suddenly savage. "You can make any excuse you want, but you two are over. I won't have a coward dating my daughter. In fact I have half a mind to kick you out and let you see how it feels to get chased by a thousand zombies."

Mark's face went white. "No, please don't. I'll end it, I swear. Just...don't make me go out there."

The man was so genuinely afraid that Neil's anger went from boil to simmer. "I won't. It would be murder, and I'm not a murderer. But you...I need, no I demand an explanation. We almost died out there and you could've helped. What was it? You wanted all this stuff to yourself? Or were you getting tired of Sadie and thought it would be an easy way out for you?"

"No, it's none of that," Mark said quietly. "It's just...I can't..."

There was something in the man's voice that had Neil looking at him closer. In the dim light of the stars there was a glint to his cheeks. "Are you crying?" Neil asked in disbelief. "What the hell do you got to be crying about? Because you can't date Sadie? Because you are a goddamned coward?" Neil was about to go on but Mark sniffled and nodded.

"Huh?" Neil asked, not at all expecting the tiny bob of the man's head. "Well, which is it? Are you a coward or is it Sadie?"

"It's not Sadie."

Neil let the heavy pistol drop into his lap and sat back in disbelief. Mark wasn't the kind of guy to admit being afraid, let alone being a straight-up coward. Neil knew he was that kind of guy, but not Mark.

"Perhaps it was a onetime thing," Neil said, softening. "I mean there was a freaking gob of them out there, right? If it was anyone but Sadie I don't know if I would have gone out to…" He stopped. Mark was shaking his head. "What are you saying?" Neil asked. "It wasn't a onetime thing? Please, you can't be that much of a coward. No one who's made it this far in a zombie apocalypse could possibly be all coward."

The tears were heavy now and the sniffling so constant that it turned Neil's stomach a bit. "I am that much of a coward," Mark choked out. "I'm not like you. I've never killed a zombie without a gun. Or went out hunting them with only a rock or any of that stuff Sadie says you did. I can't even go out at night. I can't. My heart starts going crazy and my chest hurts so much I can barely breathe."

He was almost hyperventilating right there in the car.

"Hey, calm down," Neil said. "I'm not anyone's hero. I'm just as afraid as the next guy. Hell, when all this started I couldn't leave my house. I was too afraid."

"Oh, yeah?" Mark said. He smiled bitterly then. His face was a picture of misery. "I couldn't leave my house not even to save my mom. She died ten feet from my front door and I didn't do anything but hide in the closet. What do you think about that? What kind of man lets his mom die without lifting a finger?"

The best answer Neil could give was to lift his

shoulders in the tiniest shrug.

"Someone who's not a man at all," Mark said, answering his own question. He wiped his eyes aggressively as if he were trying to scrape them away. "I put on this show as a tough guy, but it's all an act. That's why I didn't help save Sadie. I wanted to so bad. And I almost did. I even had my hand on the door handle, but I couldn't bring myself to open it. Then it was too late. Stiffs were everywhere and you and Sadie were gone and then there weren't any more gun shots."

Neil got a chill remembering how close they had come to being eaten alive. "But that's all over with," he said trying to make the situation better. "The good news is we got away. So, no harm, no foul."

Mark looked out the window at the stars and asked, "What are you going to tell Sadie? About me?"

"Honestly, I don't know," Neil confessed. "If we were in the old world I wouldn't say anything. Courage was very over-rated back then. It tended to get you in trouble. But now? She has to know. Not knowing can get her hurt."

"She'll hate me," Mark said. "Especially when she compares me to you."

It was almost laughable to Neil that someone considered him to be anything more than a chicken. Every day since the apocalypse began he had lived in a constant state of fear—hardly the mind-set of someone courageous.

"She won't hate you," Neil replied. "She'll understand. It's just a phobia is all. Something she'll want to help you get over. And we'll start now. Let's go rescue her."

Mark turned instantly grey. "Rescue?"

"Yeah. It'll be nothing. She's up in a tree about a half-mile away. We ride over—you hop out and help her down, while I cover you. Mark! Don't give me that look. It'll be fine. I won't let them near you."

"Why does anyone have to get out?" he asked in a whine.

"Because she turned her ankle and can't walk on it. Now take a deep breath and let's do this. It'll be your first step in kicking this phobia. Step one is to face your fears."

Mark looked green and five minutes later Neil did as well.

When they came roaring up, Sadie didn't climb down as she was supposed to. Neil cranked down his window. "Sadie? Come on!" Though he hissed these words quietly they were plenty loud enough to be heard, but there wasn't an answer. "Mark, get out. Go up there and see what's going on."

Besides a heavy panting, Mark didn't budge.

"Damn it!" Neil seethed. Jabbing the *Raging Bull* down the front of his jeans, he got out and raced around to the other side of the Rover. "Sadie?" he called as he began to mount the planks nailed into the tree. There was no answer and when he got to the platform a cold wave went down his back—it was empty. He had known it would be, but the sight chilled him nonetheless.

"Sadie!" he cried out at the top of his lungs. He then paused trying to listen for any response but all he heard were the low moans of the advancing zombies. The tilled field was alive with them once again.

Chapter 17

Ram

Philadelphia, Pennsylvania

Ram watched the little girl's eyes fill with tears. "Don't eat me," she pleaded. "I don't want to be eated. Ipes says I'm too skinny to eat and he should know."

"I don't know if I would have a choice," he told her. The idea of eating human flesh started to do a number on his already weak stomach. Nausea built in him so fast that he barely had time to warn her. "I...uh...I think, I'm going to be sick. Don't look." With his hands tied behind his back and his stomach heaving violently, Ram lacked the strength to even attempt to stand. Instead he turned on his side and vomited onto the cement floor of the boiler room.

Despite his warning, the girl watched and as she did she went from pale white to a light green. "Scuze me," she said before hurrying behind the furthest boiler where she too vomited. She then sat back in the darkest corner and cried.

"What's your name?" Ram asked after a while when his stomach had settled. Vomiting had helped and he felt the slightest bit better. Though having the hot stinking mess right next to him wasn't helping; he rolled away from it and then fought himself into a sitting position.

"Jillybean," she answered. She came forward so that she wasn't just an outline in the gloom. "And this is Ipes." In her hand was a stuffed animal: a zebra. It wore dark blue shorts and a lighter blue shirt.

Despite his sickness and his coming death, he couldn't help but smile at the little girl. She was innocent and sweet and button-cute. "My name is Ram. I'd shake your hand if I could but I'm sort of tied up. I'm sorry about all of this."

She came closer making sure not to cast her eyes anywhere near where he had thrown up. She also made sure to stand just out of reach of him. "It's nice to meet you, Mister Ram. Ipes thinks it's nice to meet you, too, except he isn't saying it because he doesn't trust you."

This brought out a laugh. "That's one smart zebra. I'm going to turn into a monster. It's wise to never fully trust a monster."

Jillybean cocked her head for a moment and then said, "No, uh-uh. He thinks we shouldn't trust you on account of you being tied up and punched on the head. What did you do to those men? It must have been awful bad."

"What I did?" Ram asked in disbelief. Explaining war to a six-year-old was hard enough but a race war was so foolish even to him that he found he lacked the energy to even try. "It doesn't matter now what I did or didn't do. But I can promise you, I have never hurt a little girl or a zebra before. You're safe for now."

"Until you turn into a monster," she said.

"Or until you turn into a monster," he countered. "But I hope it's me. With my hands tied up, I doubt I'll be able to get to my feet. Zombies are real klutzy."

"Klutzy?" she asked and again cocked her head as if listening. She then added, "Ooh. You mean they trip and fall a lot. There was this one monster, Mrs. Bennet. She used to be this mean ole lady before she turned into a mean ole monster—Ipes says there wasn't all that much to change with her…"

Jillybean began a string of sentences that was as long as a freight train. Seemingly, she spoke without taking a breath or any real pause. Ram secretly delighted in the sound of her little voice and the way her features grew animated and how she looked to her zebra to fill in any half-forgotten memory. He reveled in this moment of sweetness, figuring it would be his last good memory before he died.

Finally, she ended her monologue, though not because she had run out of words, these she seemed to have an endless supply of, instead it was because there came a sudden silence from outside the metal door. No longer did the giant zombie smash his fists into it trying to break it down. As well the moans of the other zombies had retreated.

In place of these noises, which had been the background of their short conversation, was a thumping sound coming from further away. After a minute, this too ceased.

"Hide," Ram told Jillybean. He had a gut feeling that the zombies had been drawn off purposefully. "Go! If anyone comes, stay hidden unless I call you."

She began to scurry away, but then she paused again with her head cocked. Turning back, she gave him a suspicious look. "What if someone is coming to free me? You never didn't tell me what you did."

"Now's not the time, Jillybean!" he hissed, pointing with his chin at the boilers. "Please hide."

"What did you do?" she insisted.

Again he was stuck: how do you explain a race war to a little girl, when he could hardly explain it to an adult. He decided to skip the race aspect—it made things only slightly easier. "Do you know what a war is?"

"Kinda. Like with soldiers and jets, right?"

"Yeah," Ram said. "It's when people fight. For some reason people here in Philadelphia are fighting each other and they think I'm their enemy."

"And you aren't?" she asked with a quick eye, ready to judge the honesty of his answer.

"No, I'm not. I used to be a cop, back in the old days. You know what cops did, right? They get the bad guys. Unfortunately, the leader of one of the groups here in Philadelphia is a murderer. She killed someone I loved. That's why I'm here. I want to stop her from hurting anyone else."

Jillybean nodded in a slow manner as she considered his words. Finally, she said, "We believe you. But what are you…"

It was then that Ram's gut instinct proved true. The

doorknob began to turn and Jillybean shot away out of sight.

In a second a seething black man stood framed in the doorway. It was Trey. He took in the room; the vomit, the bound man, and the boilers in a single sweeping glance. "Where's the kid? I saw a boy save you."

"I told, uh, him to lock me in and run away," Ram lied. "So who knows where he is? What do you want? Are you here to watch me turn into one of them? That's pretty sick."

In Trey's right hand was his pistol and in his left was a long knife that looked razor sharp. He dropped down to his knees in front of Ram and held the knife up so that the steel of it glinted. "I need to know for real," he asked. "Are you sick?"

"Yeah," Ram replied.

For some reason this infuriated the black man. Dropping the pistol he grabbed Ram by the shirt with a shaking hand and screamed into his face, "Don't fuck with me! Are you really sick?" Now he brought the knife up so the point was just under Ram's eye where it dimpled the skin.

"I'm not lying," Ram answered. Despite the proximity of the knife he forced himself to speak in a calm, easy voice, hoping Jillybean would hear and not be afraid "I was scratched this morning and have been getting sicker ever since." He then lowered his voice to a whisper and added, "So if you want to use that knife to kill me, you'd be doing me a hell of a favor. Just make it quick."

Trey ignored the request.

"But I feel fine. I feel good," he said, even though there was sweat glistening across his forehead and a twitch next to his mouth that kept forcing him into a half smile/half-grimace. "And look at these scratches," he cried, turning his hand around suddenly, nearly taking out Ram's right eye with the knife. "They're barely scratches. Maybe the virus didn't take. I hear that sometimes it doesn't. You ever hear that?"

Ram had never heard of it before, but if it was a possibility he didn't think Trey was going to be the one to get lucky. The cuts on his knuckles made by contact with Ram's teeth were deep. Ram ran his tongue over his sore teeth, remembering how viciously Trey had attacked him.

"I think you're screwed," Ram told him. "The scratches I got this morning barely broke the skin, *and* I washed them with rubbing alcohol within a minute. It didn't matter a hill of beans. Sorry, but you're screwed." He wasn't really sorry at all. He had done nothing to deserve the beating he had received. His apology was clearly less than heartfelt.

"Sorry?" Trey cried in outrage as spittle flew. "You kill me with your dirty mouth and all you say is sorry? I'll show you just how sorry you're gonna be. You're gonna be the sorriest zombie ever, by the time I get through with you."

The knife, a slice of glittering steel in the otherwise dim room, came up again, and it was so close to Ram's face that it filled his vision. He didn't see Jillybean come out of her hiding spot until it was too late.

"Please don't hurt Mister Ram," she said in a squeaky voice that shook as much as she did. Her face had the green tinge once again, but whether it was from fear or sickness, he didn't know. Trey jumped at the sound of her voice and spun about holding the blade out, looking afraid and rather ridiculous cowering before such a tiny girl.

"You're a girl," he told her. He seemed confused by either the concept of her sex or the fact that she was there at all, or maybe it was the bewildering turn his life had just taken.

Her lips barely parted for her to say, "Yes."

Trey tried to glare at her, however his odd confusion wouldn't allow it. He turned back to Ram, and asked, "Why would you bring a kid out here? Especially, one of *them*? You had to know what would happen if a white girl got caught."

Again Ram forced calm into his voice: "I didn't bring

her out at all. You saw me; I came alone. I don't know how she came to be here."

"I came through the tunnels," Jillybean explained before correcting herself. "I mean I came through the storm sewers. It was very dark. I think I'm gonna be sick again." With that announcement she went back behind the boilers and vomited. For some reason when she vomited it had a sad sound to it. When Ram vomited it was harsh and noisy, like he was trying to bring up his spleen.

Trey's confusion increased, but then something clicked. "Is she alright?" he asked. Ram gave him a significant look and shook his head, which Trey interpreted correctly. "Bit?" he whispered.

"Scratched," Ram said with a shrug, as if one answer was as good as another. "We don't know which one of us is going to turn first."

"It ain't gonna be me, that's for certain," Trey said in a whiny tone. "But I can't tell if that's a good or a bad thing. Do I watch you guys turn? Or do I just get it over with and pull the trigger on myself? What would you do if you had a gun?"

Ram had planned on shooting himself, but that was before he found himself with two "companions" both of whom were going to turn. "I'd do the merciful thing," he answered truthfully. "When the delirium commenced I'd use a properly weighted instrument to render the individual unconscious or use it to cause a cessation of breathing or brain functioning. If you understand me."

"Huh?" Trey asked. "What's with the five-dollah words?"

Again Ram jutted his chin to the back of the room where Jillybean was making a sound like a bullfrog as her stomach heaved up only air. "She doesn't need to know what's going to happen," Ram whispered.

The black man, looking suddenly weary, sat next to Ram. Leaning in he asked in a low voice, "You want me to kill her? Really?"

"Not just yet, but when things start to get bad," Ram said. "You've seen what happens to people. We all have. It would be a mercy."

"That's some pretty messed up shit, killing a little girl. I don't think I can do it," Trey confessed. "Can you?"

Just then Jillybean came back. From one hand Ipes dangled; the other she held to her stomach. She was sweaty, trembling, and so pale that her skin was almost translucent. He could see tiny blue-green rivers of blood standing out beneath it. She didn't have long. "I can do it," Ram told him. "You'll have to cut my hands free...what? I can't very well take care of her like this."

Trey sat back from him, and stared, trying to fathom if Ram was being honest. It was quiet in the room until Jillybean said, "I have to go bathroom real bad. Number two!"

"This guy will help you," Trey told her. He pushed Ram onto his side to expose his bound hands. He began to saw at the shoe laces with his knife and whispered, "You said you wanted to take care of her. Let's see if you can handle this first."

A groan escaped Ram as his hands came free. He swung them about trying to regain circulation but Jillybean's potty-dance was too insistent. "Follow me," he told her, before opening the metal door and darting out into the darkening afternoon. The clouds hung low and heavy. When they finally broke, Ram guessed it would be a doozy of a storm.

Ram took the little girl up two flights of stairs until they found an apartment that was quiet. "Hold Ipes, will you?" she asked and did not wait for an answer. She shoved the zebra into his arms and then went into the bathroom. After a minute of pitiful groaning she called to him, "Mister Ram? I don't have any toilet paper. What am I supposed to do?"

He had already given this some thought and had searched about, finding a box of tissues. "Here you go,

Honey," he said tossing the box into the bathroom without looking.

"My Mommy used to call me honey before she died," the little girl said, coming out and shutting the door behind her. She then held out a hand to him. Ram blinked at it for a second and took her little one in his big paw. "No, silly," she said with a smile. "Ipes? My zebra? He doesn't know you very well and can be very ascared, especially of big people."

Ram had forgotten that he was even holding the stuffed animal. "Well you have nothing to worry about," he explained, handing over the zebra. "Me and Ipes became good friends while you were in there."

"Really?"

"Oh yes. And we both agree that you need to take some of this." Ram produced a big bottle of Pepto-Bismal and set it on the kitchen table. He had found it in the second bathroom while looking for toilet paper.

The very presence of the bottle seemed to pain Jillybean. "Not the pink stuff. Please, I hate the pink stuff. And I feel better now, really. My tummy's ok, it really is."

"I'm sorry Jillybean," Ram said unscrewing the lid. "You need to take this and Ipes agrees. He told me so. And he is very smart for a zebra."

Jillybean dropped her face and said in a small voice said, "He says: Thank you. And he says I have to take the medicine, too. It's apose to help my tummy. But I don't like it."

"I don't like it either," Ram told her. "But I have to take it too. Do you want me to go first?"

After a moment to think she said, "Ipes says I should get it over with." The little girl held out a shaking hand.

Ram touched her brown hair, stroking it gently as she held the bottle and looked at it as if it were poison instead of medicine. "It'll be ok," he said softly.

Trey came in and, after tossing Ram the shoe he had abandoned in the playground, he leaned against the door frame to the kitchen, shaking his head. He spoke out of the side of his mouth to Ram: "You ain't gonna be able to do it. Admit it."

Could he kill this girl? This precious little thing with the big blue eyes and the nub of a nose; this tiny human who had already displayed such courage?

"For her sake, I have to."

Chapter 18

Jillybean

Philadelphia, Pennsylvania

The pink stuff sat in front of her smelling like fakery as it always did. It looked nice, being pink and all, but it tasted icky.

"What do you have to do?" she asked Ram.

At this he laughed nervously and then pushed the bottle of Pepto closer to her. "Never mind that, Jillybean. Take your medicine. The quicker you take it the quicker you'll start to feel better."

He's right, Ipes said. *For a human he's also pretty smart. Now bottom's up. Take a big chug and just get it over with.*

"Fine," she grumbled and then, going against the prudent advice of her friend, she took a little sip. It wasn't that bad! In fact it was good. Except for the tangy meat she'd had that morning, the Pepto tasted better than anything she'd eaten in weeks. It sure beat the hell out of pine needle stew.

"Slow down," Ram said as she began to chug the pink liquid. "Too much medicine is bad for...never mind. Save me a swallow. You can have the rest."

After drinking half the bottle and smacking her lips, something that Trey found hilarious, she passed the rest to Ram, secretly hoping that he would only want a little. He took two big, man-sized swigs, made a noise that she interpreted as: *not bad*, and gave her the bottle back.

"That's better than I remember. And it sure hits the spot," he added rubbing his stomach. He then looked to Trey, who stood with one hand on the butt of a gun that stuck out of his pocket, and then to Jillybean who held the bottle of Pepto the way a wino would grip his last bottle of Maddog 20/20 rotgut.

"So what are we going to do?" Ram asked.

Jillybean shrugged, and Ipes was equally clueless. They had been focused on survival for so long they didn't know what else to do with themselves. Scrounging no longer mattered; nor was it important to worry over keeping her pine needle soup in the sun; or changing out the water containers in the face of the big rain that was coming.

Trey slapped his blue-jean-covered thigh. "I don't know what you guys are going to do, but I ain't gonna sit here waiting for it to happen. I have to do something."

"Is he like us?" she asked Ram. "Is he going to turn into a monster?" Ram flicked his eyes to Trey and then nodded. "Sorry, Mister," she said with sweet sincerity. "At least we'll be monsters together." For her this was something to hang her hat on—being all alone was a far greater fear than being a monster.

"Call me Trey, not Mister Trey. And yeah, we'll be monsters together."

Ram, who had been re-stringing his shoe with a lace acquired from somewhere in a bedroom closet, said, "I have an idea of what we can do. We can try to broker a peace. I wasn't lying before. The *Whites* want peace."

Trey rolled his eyes. "You is such a dumb Mother-fuc…" he paused and glanced guiltily toward Jillybean before resuming in a more subdued tone. "Listen, it don't matter what the *Whites* or the *Spics* want. The Boss-lady wants war. She wants her some vengeance. She wants the black people to rise up and take their rightful places. And ain't nobody says dick to her. Oh, sorry, little girl."

"Jillybean. My name is Jillybean."

"Really? Your name is Jillybean?" This seemed funny to him and he cackled. Jillybean only nodded, not quite understanding the joke. Smirking, he went on, "White folks be crazy sometimes. No offence."

That means he doesn't want you to be mad at what he said, Ipes explained.

"Oh, I'm not mad, Mister…I mean, just Trey. Can I ask a question? Why does someone want war? Do you want war?"

"No, not anymore," Trey said quietly. "I never really did. Nobody did. But Cassie gave us something that we really wanted: leadership. We wanted someone to take control, to give us a direction. We were just surviving and she had this vision for us to be doing so much better. And look where I am now."

"You should do something about it," Ram said with eyebrows raised.

Perhaps out of habit, Trey went to the refrigerator and looked in, ignoring the stench that came wafting out. "You don't stop do you?" he asked Ram. "And that's because you don't know what's what. They'll kill me if I try to go back now. Same as if Jelly bean here tried to go back to the *Whites* or…"

"It's *Jillybean*," she corrected. "Jill-y-Bean."

He grunted out a laugh and shut the fridge, which was a good thing. With the Pepto doing its job, Ram's stomach had just been settling down, but the smell from the fridge was threatening to bring up a big pink wave of puke.

"Jillybean, sorry," Trey acknowledged with a nod of his head. "Either way she can't go back to the *Whites*, not when she got the virus all up in her. Same with me. If I go back to my people they'll shoot me on sight. And if you try dude, they'll tie you up until you turn grey and then they'll set you free, up with the rest of the *Spics*. That's the way Cassie likes it. She calls it psychological warfare."

The kitchen went quiet at this admission. Jillybean understood enough to know the three of them couldn't go be with other people.

"You can come back to my house," she volunteered. "I have pine-needle soup that's almost ready."

"Did you say *pine needle soup?*" Trey accented each word in disbelief. "That's soup made out of Pine needles?"

Jillybean's head went up and down very fast and she began to jabber: "Yeah, it's not so bad. What you gotta do is put a bunch of pine needles in water and let it sit in the sun all day, or maybe two days, you know. Kinda like sun tea, only it's sorta bitter. And I got a place for us to sleep in the attic and its very safe and all, 'cept you have to watch out for ole Mrs. Bennet."

A derisive breath of air snuck out of Trey. "You can count me out. Having pine soup with a bunch of white folk sounds crazy to me."

"No one lives there but me and Ipes," Jillybean explained. "Mrs. Bennet isn't a person, she's a monster. She's not allowed in the house."

Even with this "explanation" Trey still didn't want to humor the girl. "I'll take you home," Ram said. "Do you know the way?"

"Ipes does. He has smart retentions about his memory. That's what he says at least. I'm not sure what that means. 'Cept he can amember all sorts of stuff that I don't. Like he knows how many of the little tunnels we passed and I don't."

"You're going back through the sewers?" Trey asked, again with disbelief coloring his voice.

"I don't think we have a choice," Ram replied. "Unarmed, it's the only way we can travel through the city."

Trey pulled back one of the kitchen chairs and dropped onto it, making it wobble dangerously; one of its legs was bound together with duct tape. "I can't see why you just don't stay here." He glanced around at the spare apartment. It had not been much before the apocalypse; now it was little better than a trash heap.

"Remember what you were saying about not being able to sit still?" Ram asked. "That's me right now. The fever should be kicking in any time and I feel like I should be doing something. Anything, really. I'm just glad my stomach has settled down. What about you, Jillybean? How are you feeling?"

She had to pause and actually think about it before she answered, which he took as a good sign. "It's better now that I pooped and we gots this medicine..."*Now that we have this medicine*, Ipes corrected..."I mean, now that we *have* this medicine. I feel a little better."

Ram stood and turned his swollen face to the person who had beaten him. "I say we get going. Are you coming, Trey?"

"The sewers? Really? I don't think so."

"In that case, good luck."

Trey tapped his foot for a moment and then grudgingly said, "You too."

There was an awkward moment between them, which passed in silence until Jillybean patted the black man's hand. "Bye Mister Trey," she said in her small voice.

Then the two of them, Jilly and Ram, left, stepping out into a quickening wind that was already cycloning debris around the apartment buildings. A few zombies were in evidence, shuffling quickly around a car; they were after a mangy cat that sat on its hood; they didn't notice the man and the girl.

Ram stayed low, moving in spurts. Before heading for the sewers, they went back to his Humvee and took the only thing in it of any value: a tire iron.

With it he jacked up the manhole cover atop the storm drain that Jillybean had exited from. "Are you sure this is the one?" he asked for the second time as he scraped back the heavy metal disc.

He doesn't listen very well, Ipes remarked.

Jilly shushed him and then addressed Ram, "Ipes says it is the right one. You'll see. He amembers all sorts." She gave a glance down into the hole where the black was thicker than soup and then after giving Ram a reassuring smile she began to climb down with Ipes clamped between her teeth.

"Wait!" a voice called out, stopping her while her head

was just at the level of the street. It was Trey, jogging between the carcasses of the automobiles in the street. "Maybe I'll come. I was thinking I didn't have anything better going on and…you really came this way?" Trey asked in disbelief as he stopped next to Ram. His face was tight and he was clearly unnerved at the idea of going down beneath the earth.

We don't have time for this, Ipes warned. *There are monsters coming.*

He was right as usual. Alerted by the running man, the streets were flooding with the beasts. They were swarming towards them like a locust storm. Jillybean gave a grunt of warning and then began to scale down the ladder as fast as she could. Ram saw them as well. He pointed behind Trey and then went down the rungs going so fast that he was close to stepping on Jillybean's fingers in seconds.

When Trey turned and saw the zombies that had followed him, he cried out, "Mother-fucker!" Then he too was on the rungs.

"Don't forget the cover," Ram reminded him.

In a second the cover was in place and in the next second, the zombies were stomping around on it, making odd thunking noises. With the light shut out, Jillybean experienced the totality of dark for the fourth time that day but unlike those other times she went down the ladder smiling.

She had people.

Ipes was a fine companion, but he was still just a wise-cracking, know-it-all zebra. People needed people; it was a law, she was sure.

"I'm down," she said as her lower foot struck the cement of the feeder line. She made sure to step lively out of the way. Ram was coming down, grunting and breathing heavily like a bull. Above him, Trey seemed frozen on the first few rungs.

"How is this better? Why did we come this way? It's so

fucking dark I can't see jack shit."

"Watch your language," Ram warned.

"My fucking language? Are you fucking kidding me? We're all going to be dead by morning! Oh shit! I almost fell. I can't see anything. How did you come through here little girl? Was it this dark before?"

Jillybean looked around trying to assess the level of darkness. It proved an impossible task. "Um…I think so. It feels just as dark. Oh, sorry, Mister Ram." She had gotten turned around and had walked right into him. She felt his large hands touch, first her shoulder, then the back of her head, and then her face. She giggled into his palm.

Above them, but not so high as before, Trey cursed some more and then after a few seconds he clunked onto the cement. "Oh, hey. I'm down."

"We should probably be quiet now," Jillybean said, feeling on the walls down low for the small tunnel that would lead to the larger trunk line. "If there are monsters about we'll hear them first if we don't make any peeps."

She found the tunnel and started through it on hands and knees. When Ram found it he gave out a whistle of surprise and a grunt of effort. And then more grunts. He was the larger of the two men. Jillybean could imagine him getting stuck like a cork in a bottle.

"Oh this is unreal," Trey said in a whisper. "Ram? Can you fit? You're not getting stuck at all, are you? Ram? Are you stuck? Ram?"

Finally Ram answered. "The girl said to be quiet. So please zip it. And no, I'm not stuck."

Despite the racket, they made it into the larger tunnel without attracting any monsters. Jillybean made a noise, "Hmm." The tunnel was ankle deep in running water. It hadn't been like that before. "This way," she whispered to Ram who was on all fours like a very large dog.

Bent over in a slouchy way, she started walking into the stream and found that she couldn't do so with her usual level of stealth. Her feet splashed no matter how she went. It didn't matter if she lifted her feet high or shuffled along, she still made noise.

Don't worry, Ipes said, calming her. *You have two strong men with you. And me, of course.*

After only a few minutes, it hardly mattered how much noise she made. The water speeding past rushed loud, so that they had to raise their voices to be heard.

"I don't like this," Ram said. They had barely gone more than a hundred yards and already the water level had quadrupled. It was over a foot deep and now was a drag to their forward momentum. But at least it tasted good.

"What don't you like?" Jillybean asked and then cupped her hand for another drink. Whenever she paused, she drank. Like a camel, she had gone nearly the entire day without a single drop, and now she was filling her hump, so to speak, though in this case it was her stomach, which felt swollen like a swinging bag.

"The water level," Ram answered. "There are things called flash floods in the desert. When it rains all the water is channeled into a few rivers and these become swollen and are very dangerous."

But it isn't even raining, Ipes replied.

Trey must have heard because he said, "But it isn't even raining. This is probably from way up in the city."

"That only makes it worse," Ram said. "If it does begin to rain here we could be trapped. We should go back, now."

"Shit!" Trey cried. He could be heard thumping into the walls of the tunnel as he turned in a panic. His splashing retreated in the dark. Ram laughed quietly while Jillybean took another drink and noted that now she didn't have to stoop at all; the water was at her knees.

Ram may have point, Ipes said. *Not to mention, I'm starting to get wet. Hold me up higher, will you?* She did, tucking the zebra into the top of her sweatshirt so that only his nose and beady eyes stuck out.

Ram led the two of them back and it became as easy as sitting down; once the water got a hold of her it just swooshed her along. It was fun, except once she bonked her head which smarted enough for her eyes to tear up. Ahead of them Trey was cursing, however the water had begun to rush with such vigor that they couldn't quite figure out what he was on about until they came closer.

Trey was screaming, "There's too much water! There's too much water!" He was certainly right. Above them the storm had finally broken out, unleashing millions of gallons of rain water. Down in the sewers the sound of the water had grown to a roar. From behind it pushed Jillybean with so much force that she was plastered up against Ram like a leaf on a windshield.

"We can't go this way," Trey yelled. "Go back." Jillybean reached past Ram and felt the now slick walls of the tunnel and then she found the feeder tube. The power of the water rushing from it peeled her hand back and it hit something soft; some part of Ram's face.

"We have to go back!" Trey screamed. "We're fucking trapped." The intense dark and the rising water had worked on his mind. He tried to climb over Ram and Jillybean.

Right in front of her, there was a scuffle and hollering. She tried to back away but the water pushed her into the tangle of flailing fists. One struck her on the side of the head and ghost-light shot across her vision leaving her blinking.

Ram was the stronger and somehow managed to hold Trey pinned on the tunnel wall. "Calm down!" he shouted in a bellow. "We can't go back. It'll be too much of a slog if we go back. It'll take too much time. I say we let the water take us. It's got to empty soon. A few miles at the most."

"You don't understand, I can't fucking swim!" Trey cried. "I'll drown."

"Just turn around and face down stream and keep your head up. Can't you tell how fast the water's going? We can be at the ocean in five minutes! Go, or it will be too late." If

Trey took Ram's advice, there was no way for Jillybean to know. The water had become a fury. "Get in front of me!" Ram yelled to her. He reached around with blind, fumbling hands and brought her to sit in his lap—but not before she bonked her head once more.

Before she could even blink away the pain, wind rushed past and water began to spray into her face. She reached out and the wall zinged against her fingertips. They were speeding down a black pipe and where it went was anyone's guess. Periodically they were knocked to the side as they passed feeder tubes gushing with water and once they almost found themselves upended by the force. Minutes later they crashed straight into Trey. He yelled something but whatever it was became lost in the din and then he seemed to just evaporate in the impenetrable blackness.

At the next feeder tube a geyser struck Jillybean square in the face. She sucked in a mouthful of water, began choking, and instantaneously fear seared her heart. She began to panic, thrashing around, smacking her head again on the top of the pipe. A mindless berserk flailing overtook her limbs, and she slipped lower in the water.

Ram saved her. He took hold of her and cradled her in his arms, keeping her above the water until before them the black of the tunnel gave way suddenly to a grey light and in a moment they had to blink away the dim light of a raining evening.

Then they smashed square into Trey's lifeless body.

Chapter 19

Ram

Philadelphia, Pennsylvania

Grey rain water roared down the trunk line with such force that the unmoving body of Trey was pinned against the grating that separated the tunnel from freedom, and Ram was jammed against him with Jillybean in between. With the weight and the power of the water, it took all his strength to keep her from being crushed.

Desperately the little girl squirmed to keep her head up out of the water. She spluttered and coughed and Ram could see her mouth moving, forming words, but the noise was tremendous, so he shook his head to let her know he couldn't hear her. With gritted teeth, she squirmed harder, clawing at Trey and kicking off Ram until she had climbed to the top of the tunnel near the grating.

Then she disappeared.

There was a small space at the top of the grate that her skinny torso and thin hips fit through just as neat as you please. If Ram had not been fighting for his life he would have been happy that she had got away. Instead, he barely gave her a second thought as he hacked and choked and retched out rain water, all the while straining to climb higher up the grating as the tunnel filled.

There were only inches left at the top of the tunnel when he felt a vibration through the grating. *Chung! Chung! Chung!*

Jillybean was doing something. The ringing noise was the sound of metal striking metal. It went on-and-on, longer than Ram thought her skinny arms could bear. She proved more resilient than he knew; one second he was crushed against a grating unable to move any longer from the sheer volume of water striking him, and the next the grate swung

[177]

open, and he shot out into a river.

"Get Trey!" she cried, before Ram even knew which way land was. She was high up over the river, standing on the storm drain and pointing at the black man with one trembling hand. Trey was face down and unmoving not far from Ram.

"Damn," Ram whispered, guilt seeping into his waterlogged pores. With his draining strength he began to swim to Trey, but then stopped in mid-stroke as he realized that he was now swimming toward a zombie. Trey had been infected. He would 'turn'. The only question was when.

Ram began the swim back to the shore. Fully clothed it was an ordeal.

"What are you doing?" Jillybean asked. She had climbed down from the pipe and now stood on the sand, holding herself as the rain struck her sideways. "You have to help Mister Trey."

Ram thought saying "no" to her was a difficult thing. For one, she had saved him—twice now. And for two, she looked so pathetic: a wretched orphan, bedraggled after a harrowing journey beneath the earth, and shivering in a cold downpour.

"It's better if I don't," he said. Beneath his feet he felt the river bottom; it was muck and mud. He staggered through it to lie on the shore.

Jillybean came to stand over him. "I guess...I know," she said, speaking to the lump beneath her shirt. "Ipes says Mister Trey is gonna be a monster soon and we should leave him alone. What about us? Do you know when we're going to become monsters?"

"I don't. Hopefully not just yet."

"I hope it's after dinner. I'm hungry and I don't want to eat what the monsters eat. That's grotey...no, I don't think so Ipes. Ipes says I'll like eating people when I'm a monster. What do you think, Mister Ram? Would you like to eat a person?"

He struggled to sit up and needed Jillybean's feeble strength to help him stand. "I don't know," he answered. "Maybe." His mind was on their more immediate needs: shelter, warmth, and real food. Around them the city had effectively ended. They were on the edge of the shipyards, a dirty industrial area that had as its only redeeming quality a lack of zombies.

"Come on, Jilly," he said, holding out his hand. She took it without hesitation as if it were the most natural thing in the world. They tromped along the edge of the water, heading to a bridge. It was a major overpass; all concrete and painted steel. As they closed on it, Jillybean shied back.

"That's not safe," she said. "It's too open. Ipes says we can't be in the open. We saw a show once about animals and there were mice and birds with big pointy fingers on their feet. And the birds would eat the mice if they came out of their…camel…camel-flodge."

Ram chuckled. "You mean camouflage. And you're probably right. But we have to get across somehow."

"Ipes doesn't think so. He says you are reacting to your environment. Whatever that means…oh. He says that you see a bridge and your mind thinks it has to cross it. But you don't ask why. You don't ask: what's over there that's better than over here? Ipes sure does talk a lot. He's always going on…yes, you do...you do too!"

"You're being loud, little mouse," Ram warned. The fact that she carried on conversations with her stuffed zebra didn't bother him in the least. It was a coping mechanism and one that she clearly benefitted from. And besides, her time was nearly up. She was wan and shivered. Her eyes were bright as pearls compared to the dark circles beneath them.

"Look there's some stores," he said pointing across the highway. "Maybe we can find one with something to eat."

The pair crept up to the embankment just off the run of asphalt and paused only long enough to look both ways. Not for oncoming traffic, but for zombies. The road was clear so they darted across, holding hands.

The stores were a disappointment. It was nothing but a dinky stripmall: a few vacant spots, a looted convenience store, a drycleaners with a smashed in window, a Chinese restaurant that was blackened from an old fire, a florist's shop where the tiled floor was blanketed in broken glass and dried petals, and finally a carpet store.

Jillybean stuck her nose to the window and cupped her hands to see in. "It's only a carpet-selling place," she said, dejectedly. "We should try in the asia place. They eat with sticks."

The restaurant had been ransacked down to the last fortune cookie.

"How about we at least get some dry clothes," Ram said. Though the window of the dry cleaners had been shattered, nobody had bothered to mess with the clothes. These still hung overhead in compressed rows. "Here, I don't want you to get cut," he said, lifting her through the front window—she weighed next to nothing and her ribs were like a row of twigs he could snap without a thought.

"They won't have little kid clothes here," she said, her face drooping.

Ram set her on the counter and lifted her chin so he could look into her eyes. "You don't know that. Ask Ipes, he'll tell you that little girls sometimes bring in fancy dresses to a place like this." She gave a glance to the spongy zebra— it looked as sad as she did. "I'll be right back with a dress," Ram said.

There wasn't a single dress in all the hundreds of clothes hanging from the conveyored racks. The best he found was a suit that had been sized for a boy, and even it would have to be tailored in some way in order to fit Jillybean. With that in mind he poked his nose into a side room where he saw the glint of a white sewing machine.

There were clothes on a rack, needing to be hemmed or

brought in or even lengthened. Among them was a white gown made for a very small person. It conjured the image of a wedding in Ram's mind; an outdoor wedding on a bright summer day, with pretty bridesmaids and a very young ring bearer with her brown hair in a bun and her bright blue eyes, smiling.

Excitedly he pulled down the dress and rushed back to Jillybean. With a flourishing bow, he presented it to her. "Your Ladyship," he said. "I have your gown for the ball." Her face lit with such joy and emotion that, unbelievably, Ram felt himself close to tears.

He blinked them back, reminding himself that he was the original badass. He was a warrior, a hard man, a slayer of zombies uncounted…and yet his eyes were hot…and so was his head.

That explained his raw emotions: the fever had finally kicked in.

"Go try it on," he urged.

"I have to go the bathroom, too," she said. "Can you watch Ipes and maybe stay near the door. I'm just a little ascared."

He said he understood and that he would stand guard. The sun had set on a nasty day and there was very little in the way of light left in the sky for them to see by. Ram sat with one butt-cheek next to the sewing machine and felt sorry for the girl. Her guts were churning with the virus, so that she cried out in pain as they cramped.

"It'll be ok," he said, knowing that it wouldn't. His own stomach rebelled as well, but he clamped his lips shut against any outward expression of pain.

A few minutes later she came out of the bathroom in the dress. Despite that it was all satin and pearls, and that it fit her as if she was born to wear it, Ram had to force himself to smile. Her skin was ashen and her pain drew down her pretty features: she looked more than half-zombie already.

"You are a princess," he told her.

"I don't feel like one." She had to hold the wall to keep herself upright. "Is it almost time, do you think? Becoming monsters, I mean?" When he hesitated telling her the truth she grew teary-eyed. "Don't let me be a monster alone, please. I'm ascared to be alone."

Ram dropped to one knee, opening his arms. She flung her skinny body into him and again he had to remind himself what a tough motherfucker he was, how he was a rock, how he didn't cry just because a little girl was getting screwed over by the vagaries of life. Shit happened, right?

"I won't leave you alone. We'll be monsters together. You and me. Now, let me see you properly. Spin around for me. Give me a proper twirl."

She spun and let the dress lift, showing off her coltish legs, and as she did she smiled. The smile gave her life; it brightened her face and the room, and Ram's heart. If there was anyone he would be a monster with, it would be this little girl.

"Oh, hey. You have a tag," he said, pointing at the back of her neck. "I'll just snip that off." He dug through the drawers of the sewing table and found that the second one down held more than just scissors.

"Holy cow!" he cried. "Look what I found." He brought up a handful of fortune cookies from the drawer—it was filled with them.

"I had those once," Jillybean said in awe. "They have words in them on little pieces of paper. What, Ipes? Oh...he says they tell the future!"

"Sometimes they do," Ram said handing her one. "Sometimes it's just a goofy saying, or lucky numbers."

"Oh. I hope mine is all three." She cracked her cookie, stuck half of it in her mouth and then tried to read the tiny letters, squinting mightily.

"If you're going to try to read that, we need fire," Ram said. "Wait here. I'll see if I can find some wood or something to burn."

In the flower shop, he found plenty of dried kindling. In the Chinese restaurant he found splintered boards, what once had been a table. In the carpet store he found six Persian rugs; they were three-by-five, but when rolled would make long-burning logs. And finally in the convenience store, among the trash behind the counter he found a lighter.

Finally the dry-cleaners provided a steel tub to act as his fireplace. In minutes they had a fire going in the sewing room. It was smoky as hell, but it was warm, bright and comforting. They sat huddled in a comforter that someone had left to be dry-cleaned. It was gigantic, big enough for both of them, and Ipes, to fit comfortably.

"Now my little princess, what does your fortune say?" When he saw her puzzling over the letters he asked, "Do you know how to read?"

Jillybean nodded in a tentative manner. "Some stuff I can read and some stuff Ipes has to help me with. Mine says: Love. Is. Like. Wild...flo...flo...worse?"

"Flowers," Ram prompted. "Love is like wild flowers. That's nice."

"There's more," Jillybean told him, holding up the piece of paper as her proof. "Love is like wildflowers...It. Is. Often. Found. In. The most...un—like—ly...unlikely places." She read it again to herself, her lips moving silently over the words. "Is that the future? I don't get it and neither does Ipes. He thinks it's a poem but it doesn't even rhyme."

Ram was precluded from answering by a sharp pain in his stomach which had doubled him over and left him gasping. Jillybean saw and could do nothing to help. She only nibbled on the end of her cookie, with a fearful look on her face.

"It's...it's just a saying," Ram managed to say after a minute of struggling against the pain. "It's a nice saying. I think it means that love can be found anywhere, even in places you don't expect to find it."

"That is nice," Jillybean said, casting quick glances at

his face.

"What?"

"You're all sweaty," she said, nervously. "And your face is not so good. Are you feeling much like a monster?"

Ram touched his head. He felt very hot. Throwing off the comforter, he reasoned, "It's the fire. That's all. Here, read my fortune, will you? I'm not feeling well."

She looked at the strip of paper for a long time with her mouth open, her lips very red compared to the awful white of her skin. "It says: The time is right to make new friends." Her hands dropped into her lap as if overburdened by the weight of the fortune. "I don't think we have time to make friends."

"Probably not," Ram agreed. He felt a little better with the comforter off of him. "Do you want another cookie?" Although she'd only had the one, she shook her head. In the last few minutes she had turned ghostly pale. "Maybe there's something else in that drawer. I could use some candy or something else. What about you?"

"I don't think so. I think I might throw up again," she said listlessly. "I wish I knew what I did with the pink medicine. I think I dropped it somewhere in the tunnel."

Ram did not like the way she had suddenly gone lethargic or how she had broken out in a sweat; it plastered her hair down and turned her face shiny. "It's too hot in here now," he said, getting to his feet. "Let's get this door open a little bit. That's better. And let's see what's in these drawers, maybe there's something good." Despite his ebbing energy he tipped her a wink to try to rally her spirits; she only continued to look upon him dully, her eyes glazed and her mouth hanging slack.

He knelt beside the sewing table and opened the bottom drawer, praying to find another bottle of Pepto, or anything that would help her to feel better. Instead he unearthed a hoard of chopsticks, enough to build a doghouse with, and a supply of soy sauce packets, enough to drown in, and beneath all that was a confused rash of buttons. They were of every color and caliber. He took a handful and let them sift through his fingers, enjoying the simple tactile experience.

Jillybean looked over at the sound of them skittering back down among the rest. Ram gave her a smile which she returned tepidly. "Hey, I found a walrus in here," he told her.

"You did? Like Ipes kind of walrus?"

"No, much bigger." Ram turned away, took a pair of chopsticks from the drawer, and stuck them up under his upper lip making long "tusks" out of them even though just doing so made him want to gag. He had to take a deep breath to steady his stomach before he turned back to her.

"Hi. I'm Wally the walrus," he said around the wooden tusks. Just this little act took up much of his remaining energy. He had hoped for a giggle for his effort, but she could only smile briefly. Her face was cherry-red and fever-bright and that meant she was getting close. First was the fever. Then came the delirium, ranting and raving, then she would slip into a coma. Then she would come awake as one of *them*.

She swallowed thickly and said with an effort, "Ipes says my dad used to do that, too, but I don't amember."

"Oh yeah?" Having anything in his mouth almost had him barfing; quickly he pulled them out. "Do you want some buttons? There's a million in here. There's also some soy-sauce." He held up one of the packets.

"No thank you," she said in a little voice, and then laid back into the comforter, unable to summon the energy to do anything but stare up at the ceiling, which was turning black from the fire. "Isn't that what you put on your food this morning?"

Ram dropped the soy sauce and gazed at the girl in confusion. "What? No, it was teriyaki sauce. But...how did you know?"

"I saw you this morning after breakfast," Jillybean answered after a sigh. "You almost ran over Ipes and you made some sort of meat and you put that terriblyaki sauce on it. I ate your leftovers; I liked it this morning, but now I couldn't eat it at all. I think that it'll make me more sickerer. I can't even think about it."

She had seen him at breakfast? How was that possible? He had been way on the other side of the city...no, further than that, he had been in the suburbs. Wasn't that miles from here? As he struggled to remember, a burning drop of sweat stung his eye; without thinking he ran his sleeve across his face, then he drug his hand through his thick hair and stared down at Jillybean without really seeing her, his train of thought completely derailed.

"Man it's hot," he said, more to himself than to her. Nevertheless she nodded slowly as if the effort was nearly too much.

"I'm burning up, Mister Ram."

"Yeah," he said in a whisper. "What were we talking about?" His mind had been on something...breakfast, and Jillybean and something about miles. With his growing fever his mind felt torpid and his thoughts came to him sluggishly out of a grey haze.

"I'll just open the door," he mumbled, forgetting that he had already opened it. With the lacquered hunks of table wood finally catching on fire the sewing room was hot as a furnace, and with the Persian rug belching out black smoke, Ram could barely see the other side of the room

He stood up and felt the floor tilting and the walls spinning.

The next second he found himself on the floor of the sewing room with Jillybean shaking him weakly. Distantly, he heard her say: "Ipes says we have to get out of here. The smoke will kill us."

There was a lag time between her words leaving her lips and his understanding them. They were going to die if they stayed? Maybe it was better if they did.

"Come here, Jillybean," he said, gently pulling her

down and resting her head in the pocket of his shoulder. She didn't resist. "Maybe it would be good if you slept." Lovingly he touched her cheek.

"And you won't leave me?" she whispered. "We'll be monsters together, you promise?"

"I promise."

Chapter 20

Ram

Philadelphia, Pennsylvania

They would be monsters together and monsters forever. That's what fate had in mind for them.

Lying on the ground, the smoke wasn't nearly as bad; it was only a grey haze a foot or so above his face. The air was cooler as well and his head cleared somewhat. But was that a good thing? The minute before he had been ready to accept his oncoming death, but now he felt the loss, and was especially sad about the little girl. Ram kissed Jillybean on the forehead.

"I won't leave you," he told her. "It's the least I can do for a girl who has saved me twice now."

She cracked a bleary eye and said, "Ipes says it's three times. This morning when you were surrounded; this afternoon when you were tied to the pole, and this evening when you almost drownded."

Her words were little whispers against the backdrop of the rain and the fire. Ram wondered if he heard correctly. "That was you this morning?" he asked.

"Yes," she said with an effort. "You were running around this person's front yard, 'cept the person wasn't a person, he was a monster."

Though the smoke was a little less, his head began to spin even faster. There was something in her words that he was missing; some vital piece of information that was on the tip of his brain that he felt for certain would make some sort of difference. It was like a puzzle and a word search combined. It roused him more than the grief of his coming death.

"In the street, that was you?" He went on after a moment when the answer to the puzzle simply didn't reveal itself to him, "How did you follow me all the way from the other house where I had breakfast? And...and what did you do? The zombies were all around me, but you did something to distract them."

"I threw a magic marble," Jillybean answered through lips that barely parted. "I'm tired, Mister Ram. I can't keep my eyes open. Ipes says when I wake up I'll be a monster so I'm trying to stay awake but I can't. I'm too sleepy."

The puzzle would just have to go unsolved he decided. "Then go to sleep, little Jillybean," he said with a smile that she didn't see. "And don't worry about this monster business. Fate has brought us together."

Within seconds, she began to snore a child's snore. The light, trusting sound caused his smile to jitter at the corners, and within seconds the tears finally began. They had been threatening for some time, but now that he was out of time he dropped the last of his manly persona and let them come.

They felt good. His eyes had been burning from the heat and the smoke and from his grief and sadness over the terrible business of fate.

What else but fate would have had him driving all over the city, only to be found time and again by a defenseless girl travelling on foot. And not just found—he had been saved by her. Three times he'd been saved, only to end up dying together. Fate was a cruel bastard.

If only she hadn't followed him. If only she had...what? Sat alone in her home, slowly starving to death? Would that have been her fate if not for Ram? And would it have been a kinder fate? Probably not. She looked completely malnourished and was so stick-thin that it was unsettling to feel her bones beneath her skin.

"It was the goose," Ram said to himself. It was most likely the smell of his cooking breakfast that had driven her out of her home. If so he regretted ever seeing the bird.

It had been sitting all by itself and hadn't stirred a feather when Ram slowed his hummer to a crawl, stopping just beside it. The goose had only gazed blandly until he had pulled the trigger of his pistol. Then it had squawked once, turned a summersault and had just laid there, breathing until Ram whisked off its head with his hunting knife.

"It was the goose that killed you, wasn't it?" he asked Jillybean. She did not stir at the sound of his voice. Panicked he turned slightly and checked to see if she still breathed. Her chest barely rose.

"All for a goose that wasn't even very good," he said.

In his opinion it had been a waste of perfectly good teriyaki sauce. Even with it, the meat had been oddly tangy. It reminded him of this one other time he'd eaten something with that same odd flavor...

"Holy shit!" he cried as his mind picked up a frail thread of memory: February 14th, 2009. It had been Valentine's Day. He remembered the exact date because he had been seeing a girl for all of three weeks. Her name was...Julia? No, that was someone else.

"Jess," he said. Her face was blurry in his mind. She'd been tall with chestnut brown hair but other than that he couldn't recall her. However he could recall being weird about that Valentine's Day. She had hinted quite a bit about a deeper commitment and he recalled that he liked her but certainly didn't love her, not after three weeks. All of which made Valentine's Day an awkward time...

Ram suddenly shook his head to clear it. The memory was going down the wrong route. His feelings weren't important. It was the fact that he had taken her out to dinner to one of the most popular restaurants in L.A. There was a crush of people, a long, long wait, and then slip-shod service, followed up by an odd cut of beef that had an even odder tang to it.

That night and all the next day he'd been sick: nausea, diarrhea, a light fever, and body-aches. Just like what was happening to him, now.

As his heart began to pound, he took stock of himself and suddenly he didn't feel like a man on the verge of becoming a zombie. Yes, the idea of food made him queasy, and there were some dreadful sounds coming from low in his bowels, but where was the fever? He hadn't felt hot until the fire had really begun to bake the room. And where were the cognitive changes: the building delirium that manifested as a mania that bounced between tears and furious ravings?

Where were these symptoms in Jillybean?

Softly he touched her forehead—she was hot from the fire, but not fevered hot. With the gentleness of a father he turned her bare arms and inspected the minor wounds that covered her. They all looked more like rug-burns than lacerations from a zombie's talons.

"What about mine?" he whispered. Delicately, he touched the scratches beneath his shirt, tracing their outlines. In the sewing room with them, a tall mirror took up most of the wall directly across from him. All it took for him to confirm or deny his own mortality was for him to lean over slightly and lift his torso.

He hesitated. What if the scratches were cherry-red? What if the "poison" lines arced out from them as they did in most afflicted victims? What if they had already begun to stink and leak the grey-yellow pus? What if he was just fooling himself with this whole food poisoning nonsense? What if he was just grasping at straws?

A big breath came and went...then another, before Ram worked up the courage to look at his own skin. The scratches were just that, scratches and the smell was that of musty rain water.

He stared for over a minute. "But...I was scratched," he told himself, hardly believing what he was seeing. The he remembered Trey: *What if it doesn't take?*

Was that possible? Did the virus sometimes fail to catch? Or was he just immune? This thought sent a bolt of excitement through him, but it fizzled when he remembered the rubbing alcohol. It was probably a combination of barely being scratched and the fact that he had been able to clean the wound so quickly.

Either way it hardly mattered. He had the symptoms of food poisoning, not of the zombie virus. And so did Jillybean!

"Hey? Jillybean? Wake up," he said giving her a gentle shaking.

She grunted out a: "Huh?" and then turned on her side, exposing a cheek, wet with little kid drool.

"Wake up Jillybean," he said, trying again.

Without opening her eyes, she answered, "I'm sleepy, Daddy."

Ram was only able to say, "I'm not your..." before choking on his words. Clearing his throat, he tried again. "It's me, Ram."

"What is it?" she asked, coming out of sleep quickly. "Is it monsters?"

"No, it's not monsters. I've got good news. Look at my scratches. They aren't infected!"

Jillybean didn't understand his enthusiasm. "What's that mean?"

"It means I'm not going to turn into a zombie!" Though he was all smiles, she did not share in his happiness. Instead she rolled over onto her side and addressed him with a single piercing blue eye.

"But you promised," she accused. "You said we would be monsters together."

Ram laughed. He couldn't help it. The feeling of life was so strong in him that he threw back his head and laughed so hard that the black smoke above them rolled up on itself. "You don't understand. You're not going to turn into a monster either. Look at your arms."

Dutifully she turned her arms this way and that. She even tried to see her elbows. "What am I apposed to see?" she asked.

Again, Ram couldn't help laughing. "Nothing! You have just normal scratches, probably from wandering down in those tunnels. If they were monster scratches they'd be all puffy and smelly."

"They would?" When he nodded, she tentatively gave her arms a small sniff, followed by a larger snuffle. "I don't smell anything."

"Exactly!" he cried.

She began to smile, showing even, white teeth, but suddenly her features twerked and her eyes lost their focus. "I don't get it, Ipes. What does that mean?" she asked of her stuffed animal. Whatever he said wasn't good. Crestfallen, she looked back to Ram. "We're still going to die. Ipes says you are delusioning yourself. In your brain, he means."

Ram scoffed. "Well you tell Ipes that in this case he is..." He stopped in midsentence when he discovered he was addressing a stuffed animal. Clearing his throat he started again, this time making sure to look Jillybean in the face, "I'm not delusional. I was scratched like, eleven hours ago. I've never heard of anyone going eleven hours without developing the fever."

She glanced to Ipes as if for rebuttal and the zebra did not disappoint. "You want me to say that?" she asked the stuffed animal. "Ok. Ipes says that anec-doo-dal. Oh, sorry. *Anecdotal* evidence is not evidence at all. Sciencey speaking that is. That's what he says."

She looked to Ram, but he was too taken aback by the string of unlikely words which had been uttered by the little girl. She suddenly seemed embarrassed as if she had done something wrong.

"My daddy said that once," she said as if, because of his silence, she had to explain. "He was arguing with a man on TV. He said there was a difference between casual observation and...something else. I don't really amember it all and neither does Ipes."

"I suppose he was right, in a manner of speaking," Ram admitted. "But I'm not a casual observer. My evidence isn't anecdotal. I've see many, many people become zombies.

Too many of them. I would even go so far as to call myself an expert on the subject, and it is my expert opinion that you aren't going to turn into a monster."

"But I'm sick, for reals," Jillybean insisted. "I don't feel good at all. I'm starting to feel like I have to throw up again."

"You have food poisoning," Ram told her. "Remember the meat I cooked this morning? We both ate it and we both got sick. The good news is, by tomorrow we'll both be better."

Now, she unfurled a proper smile. "Ok, that is good. Ipes thinks you're smart. He said you weren't before but you're getting better, and that's good. I never wanted to be a monster anyway, you know? Amember those little kid monsters at the school? They were gross. Can you turn down the fire, please? It's awful really hot and it's making me sleepy."

The fire was taking care of itself. It had already consumed the Persian rug and was now working on reducing to ashes the pieces of table from the Chinese restaurant. Already the curtain of smoke had lifted, making it easier to see and breathe.

Settling her head back down onto his shoulder, he whispered, "Sleep is what you need, Jillybean. So close your eyes."

Chapter 21

Jillybean

South of Philadelphia

In the morning, while Ram snored, Jillybean went into mouse-mode and crept over to the restaurant next to the drycleaners. There she used the bathroom. Her stomach felt much better, but she still suffered from diarrhea.

Better out than in, Ipes told her when she came out weak and shaking. He had asked to be left in the main room to keep watch, though she knew that wasn't why he wanted to stay on the counter, he didn't want to get the smell on him.

"I guess," she answered, holding her belly. "I could use some chips and some water. Do you think it's safe to drink out of them puddles?"

The zebra looked outside where everything was damp. The rain had moved on leaving a cold, wet morning behind. *Out of those puddles, and maybe, but why chance it? Mister Ram can help you out. Have him boil some water. That's supposed to make it clean.*

"But it'll be hot."

Ipes snorted—a loud noise with his big nose. *It'll cool and besides look right there.*

He pointed with a flat hoof at a wooden box. It was turned on its side, stuck between the counter and a bench. Jillybean found that it was almost permanently stuck there. It took all of her might to free it, but it was worth the effort.

"Is that...?"

Yes, it's tea, Ipes said, filling in the word that she could only picture in her mind. *And look, they have mandarin orange. Your favorite.*

Taking the box and the zebra she hurried back to where Ram slept. She paused with her hand out to him wondering:

was it alright to wake him up? The sun was up, didn't that mean he should be as well?

Early to bed, early to rise, that's what your daddy always said, Ipes remarked. *Besides the tea looks really good. We could even add some fortune cookie to make it sweeter.*

The idea was a good one and again she put her hand out. Then she remembered how her mom used to like to sleep in, especially when she had been sick—and Mister Ram had been sick.

You were sick and you are up, Ipes noted.

Jillybean refused to answer him. As always he was being greedy for cookies. Instead she waited patiently...as patiently as a six-year-old could, which meant her attention wandered and Ram woke to find her playing with Ipes.

She was on him immediately. "Can you make me this? I found it in the asia place. It's tea."

His eyes had barely begun to focus. "Huh?"

"Tea is something you drink," she explained holding up one of the packets. "You have to put it in really hot water for a little while. I'd do it but I don't know how to make fire. Ipes says you have to rub sticks together but I think he's trying to be a jokester again. So can we?"

Ram squinted at the tea for a moment and then yawned.

He looks like a bear when he does that, Ipes said. He then held his nose. *And smells like one!*

"Stop being naughty to Mister Ram or you won't get any tea, and you can't have cookies without tea. Everyone knows that is the way of things." When Ram went from sleepy to confused, Jillybean explained: "Ipes was being bad. He can be very naughty sometimes."

"I think he's pretty smart," Ram said. "And you are too, Jillybean. How old are you?"

"Six and three-quarters, probably. I don't know if another year went by. Did it? It's real hard to know what day it is anymore."

Ram stood and stretched, looking tall as a giant to the little girl. After popping his back he said, "It is after the New Year, but that doesn't mean you got a year older. It depends on when you were born. What's your birthday?"

Jillybean bit her lip and then stared up at the ceiling. "Uh," she said, tapping her foot. The date wasn't coming to her and for some reason she found it annoying. "Ipes?" she whispered. "When is it?"

Before the zebra could answer, Ram shot her a look with a raised eyebrow and then turned away to the steel wash tub, pretending he hadn't heard the question. After the bonfire from the night before, the tub was mostly black, however along one side it sported a rainbow sheen of oil.

"It doesn't really matter when it is," Ram said before picking up a hunk of the lacquered table and snapping it in two. "We can make up a day if you want."

"I know when it is," she said defensively. "It's just..."

It's in May, Ipes told her. *Remember last year we had a picnic? Mommy picked us up from kindergarten and she said that thing about May showers bringing all the flowers.*

The memory came back to her in a rush. The park was warm and sunny; there had been gifts and food that she couldn't remember. Daddy tried to teach her to throw a Frisbee, but she couldn't make it go straight. It would wing off to the right, every time, where it would immediately go spinning away on the ground. Once a happy dog had chased it and she had chased after the dog and daddy had chased her.

Mommy stayed with the food and sang under her breath. She never sang out loud except when she was alone and so Jillybean only caught snippets as she ran past; it was a love song and it made Jilly want to stop and listen, but she never did. Eventually, she tired of the Frisbee and the dog left to be with its owners. At Daddy's suggestion they walked along a river and picked flowers, making a straggly bouquet that her mommy exclaimed over.

"*They're beautiful, Jillybean, just like you.*" They hugged until Jilly couldn't breathe and then her mommy recited: "*April showers bring May flowers.*"

"My birthday is in May," she told Ram in a small voice. "I'm a May flower. On the seventh, I think. Is that nearly now?"

The man snapped another board, sending splinters flying. "Almost. You'll be seven on the seventh. You know seven is a lucky number?"

"It is?" she asked before consulting a higher power than either Ram or Ipes: the fortune that she had scraped out of the cookie from the night before. She had liked the saying on it and so had laid it out to keep it from being crushed. Now she flipped the little rectangle of paper over to where there were numbers printed.

"You're right!" she exclaimed. "There's a seven right here. Hey, Mister Ram, what is a lucky number? What's it do for you? Does it help you win at cards? I heard that once." As she spoke, her curiosity over the magic of creating fires had her edging close to the wash tub where Ram was now kneeling as if in supplication. He wasn't rubbing sticks together like she thought he would. Instead, he had built a small teepee out of chunks of wood and was using a lighter to set some paper ablaze within it.

He blew gently on the flames and stuck out a hand to her. "That's close enough. You don't want to ruin that fancy dress. Have you seen yourself in the light? There's a mirror. Go take a look while I get this going."

Immediately the idea of fire and lucky numbers left her as completely as if they had never been. Jillybean hurried to the mirror and stared at herself until it seemed as if an unfelt wind began to turn her left and right. The "wind" lifted her knee-length dress slightly with each turn. And then it spun her about completely and the dress flared higher.

She didn't even notice that Ram had created his fire until he came to stand behind her in the mirror. Around a smile, he said, "You're very pretty." This caused her to go red and the twirling ceased. Ram nodded as if this was normal or proper and said, "I'm going to get a kettle from next door. Can't have tea without a kettle, right? While I'm gone, you should go into the front room. I just don't like the idea of you so close to the fire when I'm not around."

Obediently she started for the front, but he stopped her without effort. "Don't forget these," said, holding up her sneakers. "There's broken glass all over the place in there."

It was with reluctance that she took them. They had once been a pretty silver accented by the Nike swoosh and laced in bright pink; now they were mostly grey with mud stains. Also, each was split at the toe where her feet were slowly erupting out of them.

What really bothered her, however, was that they didn't match her dress. It's why she had kicked them off in order to twirl. "Can you get me some new shoes, too, if they have any. White would be good."

"Shoes?" he asked. By the look in his eyes, Jillybean could tell that fashion was a foreign concept to the man. "I don't know if we have time," he added.

Jillybean was long experienced at working a father-figure around her little finger. She toed a button and put her head down. "I guess. It's only these are too small for me. My foots stick right out the front." Here, she held up the shoes and pointed at the holes: Exhibit A. "They really hurt and give me blisters, see." Now she put a foot up to display: Exhibit B. This exhibit wasn't too convincing since there wasn't any evidence of blistering. Undeterred, she went on, "The water must have washed them away. And asides my old shoes don't go with my dress, which I might as well not even wear, even though it's pretty."

Ram scratched his head; her arguments had clearly failed. It was then that Ipes helped out. He whispered, *Please, you meant to say.*

She was quick. "Pleeease, Mister Ram?"

"Fine. I'll check out a few of those houses up the road. Remember, I can't guarantee anything."

"Thank you. Thank you. Try to get them without heels. You know what heels are, right? They make you tall, only I can't walk in them and my mom doesn't think a little girl should wear them. I won't look like a lady and I'll break my ankles. That's what she says." Here she paused only long enough to draw in a big breath. Ram held up one of his brown hands to keep her from going on.

"Stop your singing, Little Bird," he said. "I told you I would try. Now stay away from the fire and keep an eye out for stiffs."

She wondered at the word: *stiffs*.

He means monsters, Ipes informed her. *As if you need any advice about dealing with monsters.*

"Yeah, I can deal with the monsters," Jillybean said to her friend as she watched Ram slip away. They were in the front room standing at the broken window. "Unless it's little kid monsters like at that school." The thought of them, of their greedy mouths and tiny, pointed teeth gave her the shivers.

Ipes was watching the man as well. *What's he up to? Look at him. Look at him go from car to car like that.*

Jillybean shook her head in wonder. "He is going tall."

And he has the nerve to tell us to watch out for monsters! Ipes cried. He crossed his arms in indignation, while his tale bristled like a pipe cleaner. *It's almost as if he's on parade out there. You know what his problem is?*

The little girl shrugged. "No, but he is getting me new shoes. So maybe we shouldn't be so mean."

Ipes ignored her. *His problem is that he still thinks like a man. Like he's still at the top of the food chain. He stalks like a lion when he should be scampering like a squirrel. After yesterday it should be obvious that he is now the prey and not a predator.*

"Maybe," Jillybean replied. She was quite smitten with

Ram and couldn't imagine saying anything negative about him.

If Ipes had eyebrows they would have come smashing down in a glare. Instead he wrinkled his big nose a bit and asked, in a high voice: *Maybe? Maybe nothing! He's barely watching his flanks. And did you see how he crossed that intersection? I could have...*

A rock went skittering across the asphalt of the parking lot, freezing Jillybean in place. It was for a split second only and then she slunk behind a fake plant that was a few feet from the front door. There she filtered the sound of the rock through her mind, fixing it with a likely origin. It wasn't from a monster; there would be moans drifting on the quiet morning air. It wasn't from an animal either. The largest mammal left in Philadelphia was the raccoon and they never sent stones skittering; they were much too careful.

That meant the rock had been kicked by a human.

More sounds: breathing from at least two people. They were mouth breathers, trying and failing to be quiet. Someone crunched glass underfoot, only to be shushed by another. Jillybean's mind now had a firm picture of their number: three, of which at least one was male.

Against the counter across from her, a shadow bobbed and then almost above her a face appeared in the window. The person was black and a man. He had a patchy beard that went halfway down his neck and nostrils that were wide and very deep.

Was he a good guy or a bad guy? Ram had told her of an ongoing war in Philadelphia—was this man apart of it? And, if so, was he like Trey who had turned out to be not so bad?

With the limited information she possessed, she decided to err on the side of caution. Caution was something Jillybean took seriously and she might have been made of stone for all she moved.

The bearded man gestured toward the door where two

seconds later another man appeared. He was tall, though not as tall as Ram, and she could tell he was skinny despite the layers of mismatched clothing he wore. He was black, like his friend, and had the most unique hairstyle Jillybean had ever seen. His afro was tight and thick, four inches tall and flat on top, but what made his hair so truly distinctive was that he was bald down the center of his head. He quite literally had a "U" on his head.

Peering through the leaves of the fake bamboo, it was all she could see. It was as if nothing else mattered; she couldn't stop staring. The man had his head down, searching the floor for a quiet path through the glass and that soft looking "U" went this-way-and-that in a beguiling fashion. Eventually he stepped into the work area of the drycleaners and the spell was broken, at least for the moment.

The man with the "U" carried a big gun that required two hands. The person who came into the dry cleaners next had only a pistol; it was flat, grey and seemed to weigh a lot. The woman who carried it held it in both hands and still the weapon shook. Much like the other man, the woman captivated Jillybean.

She had thick strands of brown yarn for hair and soft mocha skin. Though she wore clothes that were just as mismatched as the first man, she somehow made them look fashionable. She also wore glasses with pink frames and Jilly wanted pink glasses too.

The woman followed the man inside, and finally came the bearded man she had first seen. Though he was smaller than the other two he was clearly the most dangerous of them. His black eyes were sharp, dancing here-and-there, while his feet crept through the glass like a panther might. Jillybean shrunk back.

Drawn by the smoke, the three went towards the sewing room where the lady called out in a soft, nervous voice, "Anyone dere? We doan wanna hurt no one. We jes wanna talk." Her accent was thick and strange. To Jillybean it sounded part southern and part foreign.

After a second of waiting, the man with the U head peeked into the sewing room and then blew out a sigh of relief. "Whoever was here, dey are gone now. Mebe a walh." His relief was so obvious that Jillybean took heart: there was someone in the world more afraid of her than she was of them.

"I don't think so," the bearded man said in a voice untainted by an accent. "The fire is new. No one makes a fire and then just wanders off. But I think you can relax, Donna. They aren't a bunch of bandits. My guess is, it's only a man and a boy. There are only two tracks in the dust; one big, one little. And look at these clothes."

He held up Jillybean's borrowed Eagles sweatshirt and pegged jeans. The woman, Donna, let her gun drop to her side.

"So what do we do?" the man with the "U" on his head asked. "Do we jes wait cheer, an sees if'n dey come back?"

As Jillybean was trying to decipher the words, the bearded man answered, "No. I don't want to spook them. Remember those hillbillies from last week? Too many people are altogether too trigger-happy these days. We'll write them a note. We'll see if they want to meet up on the highway."

The more Jillybean heard these people speak the less afraid she became. In her mind there wasn't a need for a note or a meeting out where the monsters could see them. Boldly, she stood and went to the doorway that led into the work space of the drycleaners.

"Das a soun' plan," Donna said. "I doan wanna…" Movement out of the corner of her eye had her turning. For a split second, the little girl in white and the woman with yarn for hair stared at each other, then in a blink, the girl was snatched out of sight and Donna screamed.

Chapter 22

Ram

South of Philadelphia

By chance, a sparrow whisked low across his field of vision and as he tracked it, he turned just in time to see three strangers enter the drycleaners. That they were human did nothing to calm the sudden spike of fear in his chest. In fact it only made it worse. Zombies were horrible creatures, but, sadly, humans could be worse in their cruelty.

Unarmed and uncaring of that fact, Ram sprinted down the street, racing until he felt that his heart would burst. Although, whether it was from the exertion or out of fear for the little girl, he didn't know. Like Julia before her, his heart had latched onto Jillybean, leaving Ram without recourse—he would die for her.

Julia had said he had a hero complex, but that wasn't entirely correct. Ram knew he wasn't a hero; he was selfish. When Julia died, a part of him had died as well. It was the part of him that had seen a real future in this new world. A future where he could be happy. Where he could have a family and love and security; things he would have been embarrassed to admit back when he was a D.E.A. agent.

Now these intangibles felt to be the most important things in the world. He had come to the conclusion that the world was beautiful *only* because beings as lovely and brave and sweet as Julia and Jillybean existed in it. Without them the world wasn't worth living in.

Without them the only things left for Ram was revenge and death. He had sought both after Julia died but he had found Jillybean instead. Just as with his dead love, he had instantly found her to be precious and something worth living for, and dying for.

It was why he raced past the carpet store and the

Chinese restaurant and stopped in the entrance to the drycleaner's. He could not see the three humans; they were around the corner slightly and out of sight. But Jillybean was right there, steps away, standing in the doorway that headed back to where all the washing machines sat slowly losing their shine.

Ram took one big step, grabbed the little girl around the waist and yanked her back as though she was as light and insubstantial as a kite.

A woman's scream ripped the air and now Ram was sure the hunt would begin. He turned on his heel and charged back the way he had come.

"You do not need to be afraid," Jillybean said with such assurance that Ram gawked at her instead of watching where he was going with the result of nearly tripping over a lip in the sidewalk. He stumbled, and only just caught himself on the doorjamb of the carpet place. Going with his momentum, he ducked into the dark store and stood panting against the wall.

"They don't want to hurt us," Jillybean said, calmly. He had her around the chest, in the exact same position that she held her zebra. "Listen," she commanded. The world had grown so quiet that he could hear the people talking from two doors down.

"Dair was an angel," Donna cried. "Right dair. I saw her wit my own two eyes!"

Jillybean giggled and whispered, "She thinks I'm an angel."

"Quiet, please," Ram said, listening. Someone was crunching glass, slowly moving toward the entrance to the drycleaner. It was the sly sound of a man on a hunt. "We'll go out the back door," Ram whispered, starting toward the rear of the building.

"Mister Ram, I overheard them," Jillybean said. "They only want to talk. They were going to leave a note asking to meet us. We don't have to be afraid."

"They've got guns and we don't," Ram said in a growl.

"Does that mean we're going to be afraid of everyone?" she asked skeptically.

Ram paused at this. "Maybe once we leave the city, we can take some more chances." The words rung false even as he said them. The truth was, that unarmed as he was, he was afraid—afraid for himself, but more afraid for Jillybean. He knew the evil in people better than most.

"I don't think they're from around here," Jillybean said. "They talk really funny. And they were more afraid of me than I was of them. We should at least see what they have to say."

They were at the back door, he glanced up and down the alley; it was free of zombies. "Fine, I'll talk to them. You stay out here. Do not come in."

"But..." was all she had time to say before he shut the door on her.

He would talk...or that was the vague plan. Instead he loped back to the front just as a black man came up to the front door with a pump action shotgun at chest height. Ram stepped behind one of the carpets that were propped up against the wall. As he was bigger, faster, and had the element of surprise, it was nothing for him to take the gun from the unsuspecting man.

"What do you want?" Ram asked two seconds later with the gaping bore of the shotgun pressed to the man's neck. The inquiry was ill-conceived and so without waiting for a response he immediately changed his question to, "Where are you from?" He thought it a more informative question, though the possible answer scared him. What would he do with the fellow if he was from Philadelphia and thus part of the race war? To execute him in a summary manner, Ram deemed was outright sinful. However to disarm the lot of them could leave them in state worse than death.

He was thankful when the man grunted, "Cincinnati, Ohio."

Ram began to relax, but then he remembered how Jillybean had mentioned them speaking in a strange manner. This man didn't have any sort of accent. "Do you have any I.D. on you?" Ram asked.

"Are you serious?"

It did seem like a preposterous question and yet he felt it would go a long way toward his being able to trust the man. "I am serious. Things around here are messed…"

"Steve?" a man called, nervously from the street. "You cool?"

"Tell him you're good," Ram ordered Steve, inadvertently pressing the gun harder into the man's neck. "Then tell him to go away…"

"Why should I?" Steve asked, turning to face Ram. "I didn't do anything to you. There's no need for this."

"Maybe there is from my point of view," Ram said. The words had just slipped from his mouth when the other black man peeked into the store. Upon seeing Ram he immediately began to jabber in some strange language—it seemed French-like, but with a twang. He was answered by a woman and very quickly Ram had two guns pointing his way.

Things devolved quickly. There was a great deal of yelling and cursing and threatening by all involved. Into the midst of this Jillybean walked. Against Ram's instructions, she had run around the building and now stood there with her hands held out in a calming manner, ending the confusion with her very presence, and quieting the room.

"It is dey angel," Donna said, clutching her pistol to her breast.

Being called an angel caused the little girl to giggle again. She had come into the main part of the showroom and now turned to look at Donna. "I like the way you talk. Where are you from?"

"Nah-lins," Donna answered. "What about you, Cherie? Ain't a one of us dat seen childrins in all some time."

Jillybean blinked, trying to understand the heavily

accented words. "My name is Jillybean, not Sherry, and I'm from here, in Philadelphia. And I've never heard of Nah-lins. Is that in another country? I used to know all the states but I think I forgot some. Probably I must have missed a day of school." She didn't pause for Donna to reply to the questions, instead she went on, "And I'm the only kid I know of, unless you count kids who got turned into monsters. And they're not real kids, right, Mister Ram?"

Now she paused for him to answer. "Not anymore, Jillybean."

Ram knew she had expected the answer and had to wonder why she asked it. And her odd queries didn't stop there. "Do you have kids, Mister Steve?" she asked the man at Ram's feet.

"No," he said easily, but there was a warning look in his eyes. It wasn't a dangerous thing, just a suggestion not to continue this line of questions. As an added measure he also flicked his eyes to the man with the odd "U" shaped afro.

Jillybean didn't need to ask. The man volunteered in a slow, sonorous voice: "I had me a son, but never knew how he ended up."

"That is sad," the little girl said, and just like that the spell of violence which had gripped the room dissipated.

Ram let out a long breath. Without people screaming and pointing guns his way it was easier for him to think. It was clear these people weren't from Philadelphia. There wasn't the instant hatred like he had seen in Trey's and Jermy's eyes. These people were just fellow travelers.

"Here," Ram said, putting out a hand to help Steve up. "Sorry about getting so rough, but things aren't good in this city. If I were you I'd detour far around it."

Over mandarin orange tea in the sewing room, he went on to explain about the sad race war and how he and Jillybean had come to be there.

"Oh, Cherie, dat is some fright," Donna said and took Jillybean into her arms. That the little girl was completely relaxed there made Ram suddenly anxious. What if she wanted to go with them? Logically, it made sense for her to travel with them. There were three to his one. They were armed with guns while he had only his fists. Finally, they had a woman, a maternal figure who seemed enthralled with the girl. For some reason the idea losing her made his throat go tight.

"Where are you heading by the way?" Ram asked. Though he spoke to Steve, he was looking at Jillybean, hoping to catch her eye. He wanted her to come sit with him in the comforter, but she was playing with Donna's yarn-like hair and didn't notice.

"New York," Steve answered. "There is a man who has a cure for the virus there. Least, that's what we heard."

Ram nodded. "I heard the same thing. The only problem is that he charges a thousand bullets or an equivalent in canned goods or fuel. Do you have that?"

Steve dropped his eyes to the fire and shook his head. "There are other ways, though. That's what we heard. There are some people who are looking to take on indentured servants. They'll pay for your virus shot, but you'll owe them some time as their servant. It's humbling even thinking about it."

"How much time?" Ram asked. After his close call the day before the idea of being vaccinated against a scratch or a bite really appealed to him.

The black man's eyes flicked from the fire briefly. "Ten years."

It was a lie. Both of Steve's friends had stiffened slightly at his answer. As a D.E.A. agent Ram had been lied to on a daily basis and now he was adept at not just spotting lies, but also hearing the nuance of partial truths. Steve had lied; the length of servitude was shorter than he was letting on. Of course this brought up the obvious question of why would he lie?

Was this his way of making sure that Ram wouldn't try

to tag along? Even after his scare, Ram considered giving up ten years of his life ridiculous. But if it wasn't ten years, how long was it? Four years? Five? Five years seemed like a long time to be basically someone's slave. Then again it took only one scratch to doom a person…unless they got lucky. Ram couldn't count on luck a second time.

Could he do five years?

"Are there rules about this sort of thing?" Ram asked. "Like a contract? I wouldn't want to spend so many years playing step-and-fetch for someone and get screwed in the end."

After a sip of his tea Steve remarked, "Even if there is a contract, it may not be worth all that much. It's not like you can take a guy to court these days. This all may be moot, right now it's only a rumor, so I can't say."

Again, Ram knew Steve was being misleading. The concept of indentured servitude had to be more than a rumor. The vaccine itself certainly wasn't. So, why the lies? Why try to steer him away from going? There had to be a logical explanation to keep an obviously capable man from joining their three person group. Anyone would think that in this time of zombies and race wars, the more friends you had around the better, but it seemed that none of them was keen on him going along.

He didn't think it was about skin color; they weren't a hateful group at all. And it wasn't about personalities clashing; Ram had been genuine in his apology and they had accepted it in the same manner. So why were they threatened by him? Then it clicked in Ram's mind: How many of these servant spots could there realistically be? Just as in the old world, there were likely to be only so many "rich" people.

He was competition, which meant that if Ram wanted to travel to New York, he would have to travel alone. It wasn't something he wanted to contemplate. "Without a binding contract, it's probably not for me," Ram said after a sigh. "I wish you luck in New York."

Steve relaxed immediately. "So what are you going to do?" he asked, nodding slightly to Jillybean who was in an animated one-way discussion with Donna.

Ram hadn't thought at all what he was going to do with her. He couldn't bring her back to her empty home and let her starve, and he didn't like the idea of handing her over to the *Whites* of Philadelphia. Though they hadn't seemed like bad people it didn't mean they would stay that way, or that they would even survive. Cassie was breeding hate in the city. It was a cancer that would likely spread and destroy everyone around her.

That left him with few choices. He had come north with revenge in his heart, but now with a little girl in tow he couldn't exactly start killing people. Killing was exactly what it would take to get at Cassie now that she had turned her people against the world. He would have to hunt and torture and slay.

The idea was depressing.

"I don't know," he confessed. "I haven't even asked her what she wants to do."

"She?" asked Jillybean immediately. "Does 'she' mean me? If so, I want to stay with you Mister Ram. I heard you talking about New York and I don't want to go to New York. Sorry Miss Donna, but they have bums there. Did you know that? We used to have them in Philadelphia, but now they're all monster bums, which is worse. But in New York they had zillions of them. I saw it on TV once. All these bums. And now New York is probably filled with monster bums worse than anything."

Hearing her chatter like a chipmunk was always refreshing to Ram. It was as though her life was an uncontainable fountain that bubbled out of her in words. "I could take you down to the CDC," Ram suggested. "You could be a big sister to a beautiful baby girl down there."

This got her attention. "Is she your baby? Is *Seedeesee* far? Is it like Washington DeeCee? Could we get there today? Do they have food there?"

The questions shot from her lips with bewildering rapidity, but Steve picked up on the last. He glanced his keen eyes around. "Where is all your stuff? Don't you have any food or weapons?"

"We have more tea, if you're thirsty," Jillybean offered. "And there are still some fortune cookies left." Like a proper hostess at a proper tea-party, she had already served two cookies per adult. There weren't many left.

"Das all you have?" Donna asked in surprise. She began to dig in her pack, saying, "Oh, no. Dat will not do. Here, Cherie, take dis, it is shicken and dumplin's. It is very good and will fill you right up. And take dees. It is tuna, like for cats. Dees is beans. Dey's good wit molasses."

Steve looked nervous about how much she was offering, while Ram grew embarrassed. Jilly took it all, her stomach rumbling loudly with each can that was handed to her. "Thank you, Miss Donna," she said politely when the woman had emptied her pack. "Can you explain this one again? What is *shicken*?"

Donna laughed. "Y'all know what a yard-bird is, cept you name it *chicken*," she said, over-pronouncing the word. "Down to Nah-lins we speak our own speaks. We has a mash of English, French, Creole, and Cajun."

"It's a wonder anyone understands anyone else," Steve said. He then stood and hoisted his pack on his shoulders before Donna could give away any more of their belongings. "I'd give you a gun, but we only have the three and very little ammo left. I'm sorry."

Ram understood. It would be easier to give up his left hand than part with a gun. Even Donna didn't volunteer hers and kept it purposely out of sight. Ram clapped Steve on the shoulder and said, "You've been more than generous with the food. If it was just me I would've been happy with a can of tuna, but Jilly, here hasn't eaten a proper meal in weeks."

Steve waved away his words and said his good-byes, as

did the man with the odd afro. Donna offered hugs and kisses. "You keep dat angel safe, y'hear?"

Ram heard and promised he would, but with all promises that had any meaning or consequence, it would prove to be very difficult and ultimately deadly.

Chapter 23

Jillybean

The Mid-Atlantic Seaboard

The rain would not let up, and neither would Ram. When she grew too tired to walk he tossed her across his shoulders and let her snooze, drooping forward over his head. When she complained of being too hungry to go on, he let her eat, while he only nibbled, keeping constant watch as he did so.

They were two days out of Philadelphia and Ram had grown frustrated at their inability to find supplies or any useful transportation. A Volkswagen Jetta, smelling of dead opossum, and with a smidge of rusty gas had got them forty-eight miles into Delaware. A ten-speed bike sporting sagging, semi-flat tires had got them another thirty before the rubber gave out.

The bike ride was exhilarating. Jillybean had ridden on the handlebars as Ram dodged the monsters that would frequently pop up out of nowhere. It was like a wild game version of tag for her.

The rest of the time they walked in the rain. Sadly this meant that Jillybean couldn't wear her new dress. To keep warm, she was forced to wear the hideous *Eagles* sweatshirt and the too-long jeans that she kept pegged at her ankles with safety pins. Over all of this she wore a yellow rain slicker, which at least matched the yellow boots that Ram had found for her. These were perfect for splashing in puddles with, however Ram would look at her wearily when she did, so she kept it to a minimum, like when he was busy searching houses.

Technically, she was supposed to be hiding while he did this, but she had Ipes with her and Ipes claimed that if a lion from the Serengeti couldn't sneak up on him, a monster didn't have a chance of getting close. Besides, like the rabbit, she never strayed far from her hiding spot and she always had an escape plan in mind in case it was compromised.

Ram had taught her that trick. Whenever they stopped to sleep or use the bathroom or simply to hunker down, hiding from the monsters, he always made sure there was a back exit. "Never trap yourself, Jillybean," he told her.

He was very smart that way, and because he was so smart she wasn't nervous at all that he had been gone for over an hour, and that the sun was deep in the west behind dark clouds, and that the house he had left her in was creepy and making weird sounds.

Not nervous at all.

Something moved directly above her and her grip on Ipes became a guillotine choke. *Let go. I can't breathe*, the zebra hissed. *It's not a monster. Mister Ram checked before he left, remember?*

"Then what is it? A ghost?" The shadows in the house had grown with every passing minute and now she was beginning to see scary shapes where before there had only been a coat rack and an overturned chair.

Ipes snorted at her. *What did Daddy say about ghosts? he told you that there aren't any such things. It's probably just a rat.*

She feared rats more than zombies which was why she was suddenly happy for her jeans and boots, and why she did a quick twirling dance that was totally without grace. As she spun, she stared all around the floor afraid to see a jillion rats surging at her. She then jumped up on the living room couch and sat on its tall back with her knees drawn up.

You squeaked," Ipes said, laughing at her. *I was just joking about it being a rat. I don't think there are any left. Just like dogs, they're all dead. If I had to bet, I'd say it was a cat.*

This was a different story altogether.

"Should we give it some tuna?" she asked, already digging in her pack. Ram had found a new backpack for her. It said "I'm a Belieber" across the top and had a picture of some boy with tall hair. The whole thing was girly in its way. The coolest part about the pack was that it wasn't just decorative. She carried actual food, and a can opener, and string, and her fancy white dress folded carefully and zipped up tight in a garment bag, and finally an extra shirt. Ram wanted her prepared just in case they got separated.

I don't know if you should hand over tuna just like that. You don't have a lot of food left, Ipes said.

Jillybean looked in her pack: three cans of tuna and one of beans. She didn't like beans much, but figured a cat wouldn't either. "You always find a way to snag up my plans," she groused as if it was the zebra's fault they didn't have much food. "I think we should give it some tuna. Also I think you're jealous that cats are cuter than zebras..."

She stopped and listened. Whatever was on the second floor had crept onto the stairs and was coming in their direction. By the amount of noise it was making it seemed larger than a cat.

Hide! hissed Ipes, all in a panic.

The little girl slunk behind the couch and watched as a shadow emerged from the stairwell—it was bigger than a cat. "What is it?" Ipes whispered. He had his face buried in Jillybean's armpit and wouldn't come out.

"It's a raccoon," she said a moment later, relaxing.

Run! cried Ipes. *They have rabies.*

She didn't run. The raccoon was a pathetic-looking thing, very skinny through the haunches. "Want a cookie?" she asked it. Jillybean had no idea what a raccoon ate, but in her mind she affiliated these sorts of striped and masked creatures with cookies. Ipes watched indignantly as she took a fortune cookie from her coat pocket, stripped it of its clear rapping and tossed it to the rodent.

You know I love cookies, Ipes said, grinding his

[216]

nonexistent teeth.

So did the raccoon. It held the fortune cookie in its little paws and nibbled. It even ate the fortune.

"Oops," Jillybean said as the slip of paper disappeared in the raccoon's mouth. "I forgot about that. I'm sure it'll be ok. It'll be ok, right Ipes?"

I hope he chokes on it, Ipes griped.

She was about to explode in anger at the zebra, but Ram came in then, saving Ipes from a spell in the corner. The raccoon disappeared like smoke.

"There was a raccoon, Mister Ram," she said eagerly. "It ate a fortune cookie and the little piece of paper inside it. It won't choke on it will it?"

After glancing out into the thickening rain, Ram shut the door and then smiled at Jillybean as if just then noticing her. "A raccoon? No, they're like goats; they'll eat anything. Just don't get too close, they carry diseases."

I told you, Ipes whispered.

"This one didn't," Jillybean assured them both. "He was just skinny...hey, what is all that stuff?"

He had come in with a full pack and there was something metal and tubular strapped across the top. It was familiar, however she couldn't place it. "I found us another bike," he said. "It's outside. And this is a pump; and this is a tire patch kit, just in case we have another flat. I don't really want to ride a bike all the way to Atlanta, but it'll do for now."

"And what's that?" she asked with her eyes grown big all of a sudden and her mouth filling with saliva.

"Are you going to pretend you've never seen a Snickers candy bar before?" She shook her head at the question, and she did so with her mouth open, entranced. He went on, "It's about time we ate the beans you've been turning your nose up at. If you eat your entire dinner you can have this."

"Ok!"

True to her word she chowed down her beans faster

than he could believe. The Snickers bar, on the other hand, was nibbled at and enjoyed for half the evening.

The next morning she took her place on the handlebars and allowed Ram to pedal her further south on route 13. After leaving Philadelphia, he had opted to go east around the Baltimore/Washington DC urban area, thinking he would skirt that nightmare by coming down Delaware and crossing the Chesapeake Bay at its narrowest point. This was when he figured it wouldn't be a problem finding a car and a little gas.

It became a problem that they did not overcome. All day he struck out. Every car he passed sat idle, with its gas caps off, exposing its inner workings to the rain.

The houses along the access roads were all open and looted, while most of the businesses were charred remains, as if someone had taken their anger out on them. Eventually Ram got off the main road altogether to give himself a chance at finding something. There was little to find. The further south he went, the less inhabited the peninsula became.

The homes grew larger and were spaced accordingly, meaning he had to go further out of his way to come upon each disappointment. He found odds and ends: a can of soup on the side of the road, a box of candles among someone's Christmas decorations, a decorative African spear with a sharp point that he had to leave behind because he couldn't carry it.

The only good news was that the zombie menace was correspondingly smaller. By now he had an aluminum bat he'd picked up in one house or the other, which he used when he had to.

Eventually they ran out of land altogether. They topped a rise and saw to the west the beginning of the Chesapeake Bay with Virginia a hazy green in the distance. To the east was the Atlantic: a grey table that stretched beyond the curve of the earth.

Jillybean looked out at the spectacular expanse of ocean and said, "My butt hurts."

Her rear had been hurting her for some time, what with the handlebars digging into unmentionable and tender areas whenever they struck a rut or a bump. Yet she had said nothing. After all, Ram had pedaled all day without complaint which she knew must have been taxing. It was only when she noticed he seemed to have a complaint growing behind his eyes that she felt it would be ok to voice one of her own.

Her complaint brought a smile. Tenderly he lifted her off the handlebars and set her on her feet where she immediately, and unselfconsciously, worked the wedgie of her panties out of her crack.

"Are we going by boat now?" she asked, scanning all around. "We're out of road."

"There's a road," Ram said, pulling out a map. He pointed to a thin strip of yellow which went across a bit of blue, joining two areas of green. There was much more to the map: hundreds of little words, numbers, and lines going every which way. However she didn't need to know any of that. The blue was water, the green was land, and the yellow was a road—simple as can be.

Except that it wasn't.

After allowing Jillybean to play at the edge of the rolling surf as a grey rain slashed sideways for a little while to get feeling back into her legs and bottom, he turned them back inland to where route 13 lay waiting. This he took south and when they came to a big green sign dominating the landscape he stopped and stared at it in a troubled manner. Jillybean did the same, trying to reason out the letters.

"What's that say, Mister Ram? I see *bay* and *tunnel*, but what's the rest?"

It says: *Chesapeake Bay Bridge Tunnel*," he said. "The letters were too small on my map. I didn't see the tunnel part. Damn it."

"Is a tunnel a bad thing?" In her mind she pictured the black tunnels beneath Philadelphia; her body shivered. It had been the height of bravery going through them as she did, but it didn't mean she wanted to repeat the experience if she could help it.

"Maybe," Ram allowed. "It there are a lot of stiffs down in them it could be very bad."

This she understood perfectly well. "Can we go around?"

He looked tired all of a sudden. "It's a long way."

She said nothing despite the fear crawling up her insides; it wasn't her place. They went out onto the bridge where the wind ran hard into their faces. Soon Jillybean was curled into a ball gripping the freezing metal handlebars with red hands. After a couple of miles of dodging around cars or monsters, they came to the first of the two tunnels.

One moment they were high up on a bridge suspended over white-capped water and the next moment the road slanted down at the ocean which appeared to have grown a mouth in order to eat them. There was a small, rocky berm of an island around the tunnel, but still Jillybean wondered if the water ever went down into the tunnel during a big storm. She also wondered if the tunnel itself had collapsed at some time during the apocalypse so that they were heading straight into a trap. And, finally, she wondered if the tunnel was on the verge of collapsing even then and that any little thing, such as a small girl screaming, would send it crashing down on top of them.

These thoughts had her shaking. Thankfully Ram stopped the bike just shy of where the road ran down into the opening.

"Looks sturdy enough," he said to reassure her. The tunnel was dead black and there was a half mile of ocean before the road climbed up out of the choppy waters again…if it actually did. Nothing had ever looked less sturdy to her.

Jillybean looked back the way they had come, thinking she would long to run away, instead her blue eyes grew to the size of dinner plates. "Mister Ram, look." Behind them a mob of zombies came crabbing forward through the rain. They had been drawn to the bridge by the movement of the two humans on the bike.

Ram cursed expressively before coaxing the bike down the incline toward where a forever night awaited them. It was such an unnerving sight even that brave man stopped at the edge of the shadow.

"Is that wind?" Jillybean asked. From the tunnel a low howling could be heard. It was like wind on a winter's night. "That's not monsters, is it? They don't make that sound."

"It could be just the tunnel," Ram said. "It could be just the way it sounds."

It could be the echo of a bajillion monsters down there, Ipes warned. *Call to them. If nothing comes out, you'll know it's safe.*

Ram was already starting forward when Jillybean shouted, "Hey you! Monsters, it's me, Jillybean."

Ram rushed back and tried to clamp a hand over her mouth, but she retreated. "If there are monsters in there, they'll come," she said and for some reason she now whispered.

The pair turned to the black and waited. It wasn't long before the howling grew and the first of many zombies came shambling up the incline to feast on the man and the girl. They spun to escape and stopped. In a long line that stretched back to the land, the bridge was filled with the undead.

"We're trapped," Jillybean said in a hollow voice.

Chapter 24

Neil

New Eden, Georgia

"Neil!" Mark cried, sounding more like a ten-year-old who had just had a nightmare than a six-foot tall man armed with a handgun the size and weight of a tool box. "Get down here. They're coming."

Neil hardly needed the warning. From his vantage on the platform high up in the tree he had a perfect view of the land all around, even with only the stars to light the field. There were indeed stiffs flooding in. He had time, not much, but enough to examine the wood planks closer, looking for clues.

There were none. Even with his lighter casting a golden radiance, the pale white boards that formed the platform were clean and fresh, appearing almost if they had been cut and hammered into place recently. There were no blood stains to indicate a struggle. Nor were there scratches suggesting that Sadie had been dragged down against her will.

"Neil, come on, man!" Mark begged.

A glance over his shoulder, told Neil he had run out of time; the zombies had closed rapidly. It was time to go.

He wasn't keen on heights and had it been a normal night, he would have gone down the rough ladder hammered into the tree, clinging to each plank with the herculean strength that only someone nearly paralyzed with fright could manage, however just then his fear wasn't turned inward.

He was afraid for his little girl. She was injured. She was alone. She had disappeared. Neil zipped down the tree like a monkey and climbed into the Rover just inches ahead of the closest zombie. "*Don't* floor it," he ordered Mark, who looked as though he was on the verge of doing just that.

"I want to be able to come back in the light and check for clues…if we don't find her tonight."

His gut told him that they wouldn't.

Her ankle had been so swollen that she couldn't place even the slightest weight on it. That meant she had either been given a ride or she had crawled away—another reason to go slow.

"Back up," Neil told Mark. "Straight back the way we came. She could be out in the field, hiding from the stiffs and the last thing I want to do is run her over."

"Oh, this sucks," Mark whispered as he drove in reverse, plowing over the grey bodies of the undead. "I keep thinking that I'm hitting her."

Neil, who was turned full around in his seat, assured him he wasn't, though he didn't really know. After they retreated to the corn, they stopped and just scanned the field as the zombies came chasing after them.

"She's not one of them," Mark said. He had his high beams pointing full into the face of the horde. There was hope in his voice. Neil didn't feel it.

Of course she wasn't a zombie; she had been safe up in that tree. What could have enticed her to climb down? Someone in need of help? It was true that Sadie was brave to a fault sometimes. Or was it someone looking to help themselves? She had been alone, unarmed, and injured. An easy target.

"Go around the edge of the corn," Neil suggested. "And roll down your window. I want to be able to hear her if she calls out."

The field was a perfect square, measured, very likely, by some long dead Euclidian farmer. Had Neil not been so upset he would have appreciated the perfect rows aligned with the cardinal points of the compass, the symmetry, and the compulsive neatness involved. Now, he barely noticed. His eyes were on the ground just at the limits of the headlights and his ears were dialed in to hear over the moan of the dead and the growl of the Rover's engine.

After a full circuit with nothing to show for their efforts, he directed Mark to drive down both of the two trails that snaked away from the field. The first led through the corn on an easterly course and ended at a lone silo that stood stiff right next to a river bank. It was an eerie and oddly placed sentinel on guard among the trash trees of slash pine and hackberry. Neil yelled for Sadie, somewhat quietly at first, but with growing volume when his initial efforts were in vain. Only zombies answered his call.

The other trail cut northwest, passing by the blackened remains of a farmhouse before debouching onto the highway they had left hours earlier. Neil yelled himself hoarse until even he was sick of hearing the name Sadie.

"She's gone," Mark said. "We should go. We need to hole up for the night. We're just wasting gas out here."

Was this Mark's cowardice talking or was it simple wisdom? After being left to die it was hard to see anything in the man's actions that wasn't related to fear-avoidance.

"We'll look again in the morning," Neil said. "Go back to the last house; the one with the porn and all the beans. She might have tried for that. We'll stay there for the night."

"It was only a cabin," Mark said. "It won't hold up against an attack, and there are literally thousands of stiffs out here."

In Neil's ear the words held all the manliness of a sheep's bleating. He gritted his teeth, saying: "And we've drawn them all away from the cabin. They're roaming the cornfields now and I hope to God Sadie isn't in them trying to hide. You don't have to worry about us, Mark, we'll be safe enough, it's your girlfriend who you should be worrying about."

"I am," he said in a whisper, clearly nervous about how loud Neil was getting. "I'm scared to death for her, but right now I can't do anything to help her and neither can you."

"Yeah," Neil replied. He didn't like being reminded of

his present state of ineffectuality. They drove slowly back to the cabin and, knowing that sleep would be beyond him without a proper inducement, Neil went to the fridge, an old rusting relic from the 50's that was barely four feet tall, and pulled out a warm beer. He then thought better of it and pulled out a six pack, thinking Mark would like one.

Fours beers and two hours later Neil finally slept; his dreams weren't pleasant. They were about being chased by zombies through a black and white world. Upon waking in a sweat, he discovered that his reality wasn't much better. The day was gloomy with clouds, while outside the windows zombies moaned their way down the sunken road in long lines.

"What do we do?" Mark asked in a whisper. "We can't go out there."

"I'm going," Neil said, taking the keys to the Rover from the counter. "And if you don't want me to leave your sorry ass, you'll come with me." It was so strange to him to be the "tough" one in the group, and, oddly, it made him a little cranky. If there was one thing you were supposed to be able to count on with big people, is that they were tough.

"Ok, hold on," Mark said, putting on his jacket and staring out the window. "We just have to wait for a big enough gap."

"We don't have time for a gap," Neil said. "We're going to make one."

Mark looked at him aghast. "What? No way. We can't just run out there…"

Neil did just that. He threw open the door, darted around one surprised zombie, knocked over another who was just turning in his direction, scooted around the Range Rover and jumped in the driver's seat.

Mark hadn't budged.

"Son of a bitch!" Neil seethed. Grey, scabby hands began to bang at the glass. He ignored them. Casually he started the SUV and then tapped lightly on the horn twice as if he was reminding a dawdling wife that they were going to be late for a party. In his mind he began a slow count to ten.

At eight Mark threw open the rear passenger door and dove in, breathing like he had run a race instead of the eleven feet that it really was.

"You're getting better," Neil said. It was in his nature to encourage others, just like it was in his nature to be nice. And truly he hadn't wanted to be alone. Mark might have been an even bigger chicken than Neil, but his bulky presence was somehow reassuring.

They drove back to the solitary tree that stood high in the middle of the turned-up field and, while Mark kept watch, Neil gazed all around the ground. He was no detective but he didn't need to be one: the tracks of another vehicle showed clearly now in the light. It had come up the rows with its tires in the ruts instead of crossing over them as Neil had.

"There was a car of some sort that came through here," Neil said excitedly. "It headed up that way, toward where that burned down house was." A car meant humans and humans meant guns. The two men checked their weapons: A twelve gauge for Neil, while Mark had his hand cannon and an M16.

Slowly, the smaller man drove toward the house, one hand on the shotgun and one hand on the wheel. Across his forehead were beads of sweat, and his ass was puckered tight. Still he looked better than Mark, who seemed ready to bolt in panic.

The trail, a mere pair of grooves worn into the high grass, first went past another silo before ending at the house. There wasn't much left of the farmhouse besides part of a wall and a chimney that was black as soot, inside and out. The remains weren't even warm. While Mark stayed in the Rover, Neil poked around looking for any clues. On the ground there were hundreds of prints, most of which were shoeless and thus probably made by zombies.

Sadie had been wearing black canvas high-tops, size 7. He knew because he had brought them home for her as a gift. None of the tracks looked to have been made by them.

With an over-large shrug, Neil signaled Mark that he hadn't found anything. Meanwhile, Mark was signaling Neil as well. He was frantically pointing behind Neil at a zombie. The creature was a big one, with the emphasis on one. Had there been more Neil might have been worried, but he was no longer afraid of a single zombie, especially when he was hefting a shotgun. Like a veteran, Neil shouldered his piece, thumbed the *safety* to *fire* and took a bead on the fat head of the zombie. It had been eating well and that meant it would make a sizable mess. He wasn't one for messes, even in the backwoods of Georgia.

And the noise might attract more stiffs, Neil thought. The idea made him pause and after a second he lowered his weapon and jogged toward the silo. A split rail fence marked the boundary where the front yard of the burned up farmhouse ended. Remembering to switch his weapon back to safe, Neil climbed over the fence and waved for Mark.

"Come kill this thing," he bawled across the yard. The zombie had reached the fence and in its near brainless state it just ran up on it and was walking in place, stretching out its arms. "You need the practice."

"I've killed plenty of them," Mark replied in indignation. Since it was daylight and there was only a single stiff to deal with, Mark's fears had retreated, while his more annoying personality traits had re-emerged.

Neil glared at him. "First off, shut up. You don't want to get the thing looking your way. And second, you need to practice killing stiffs without a gun. You can use Sadie's *Louisville Slugger*. It's in the back seat."

"But…"

"I said shut up! Being quiet is the first step. Now, this is going to be easy. I'll keep talking and all you have to do is come up from behind and smash in its brain. He's not using it anyway." When he saw Mark reach slowly for the bat, Neil turned to the zombie and said, "Who's not using their rotten brain? You, that's who. There you go, Mark…no. Leave the door open. You don't have to worry that a zombie will just wander in, and it'll be easier to get back to safety…just in case."

The big man walked through the grass, barely breathing, with the bat cocked above his head. He hesitated only feet away.

"Look at me, Zombie!" Neil cried, waving his hands to keep the beast's attention on him. "Now Mark! It'll be easy. Just step up and Bammo! Knock it a good one. Just…whoa…hey…crap!"

Mark had done what Neil had asked. He had put all his strength into the blow and the zombie's head had come apart like a cheap piñata, covering Neil in blood and black brains.

"Shit. Sorry, man," Mark said, before he began smiling. It became a wide grin and he came close to chuckling. "I didn't know it would come apart like that. Did you see it explode? Holy crap."

Don't be mad, Neil said to himself. *He was just doing what you asked.* Aloud, he grumbled, "That was great. Can you get me some water and some paper towels or something?" Afraid to move, Neil stood with his face squinched up until Mark doused him with water and wiped the blood away.

"You did great," Neil said when he felt clean again.

Mark leaned against the grey wood of the split rail fence and sighed up at the clouds above. "I thought I was going fucking wet myself, but, I did it. I really didn't think I would be able to do it, but I did."

Though Mark was smiling over his achievement, Neil was frowning. There was no sign of Sadie. The tire tracks they had been following had joined the trail and the trail had joined the road, which meant she could be a hundred miles away by now, maybe even two hundred.

"You think there's any corn in there?" Mark asked jutting his rugged chin toward the silo. It was the color of iron and had seen some weather, but not as much as Neil would've thought. Everything that was man-made seemed to be aging far quicker than it had in the old days.

"Haven't a clue," Neil admitted. "I'm not even sure what a silo is for. I mean why do you need a three-story high cylinder to hold corn or seeds or whatever in?" He considered, then answered himself: "I suppose it's just the way they do it."

Mark, who was still in a good mood, grinned and said, "Wrong, Mister *City-slicker*. When you store stuff vertically like this, you get the benefit of gravity. The grain gets pressed down by the weight of the grain on top. It allows you to store more in a smaller space."

"That makes sense," Neil said. "Let's see if there's anything in it that might come in handy." The two men went to the silo and found it locked with a deadbolt instead of a padlock which they could've broken off quietly. They went about tapping the outer walls here and there; it sounded hollow.

"Empty," Mark said, craning his head back, glancing up its length. "It looks like they put it in just in time for the apocalypse. A lot of work for nothing."

"And they already had that other one across…wait. Is that normal to have two silos?"

Mark started to shrug as if it wasn't abnormal, but then he stopped. "People have two silos all the time, but they don't generally keep them out it in the middle of nowhere like that other one. It wasn't even on a dirt road."

"Maybe it's nothing," Neil said. "Maybe…the tree! Son of a bitch! The platform on that tree had new boards. I bet you they hadn't seen a single winter. Someone put them up recently, which means someone is living around here, and that someone has Sadie."

"That's a big jump in reasoning, don't you think? It

could've been anyone, maybe it was a complete stranger, who took her or put up that platform."

"No," Neil said as he turned and marched off to the Rover. Over his shoulder he made his points: "That platform on the tree was new. Would a stranger to this area take the time to cut all that wood and lug it up into a tree just for the view?"

"Probably not, but…"

"And wouldn't it be a huge coincidence if a stranger just happened to be close enough last night to come in and snatch Sadie the minute I left?"

The thought seemed to send a shiver down Mark's back. He stopped before opening the passenger door. Lowering his voice, he asked, "If you're right, where are they? The only thing nearby is a burnt down house, a ratty, zombie infested barn, and a couple of silos."

A touch of rain blew across Neil's face as he turned to look up at the silo. It stood as if guarding the trail into the fields. From its top the view must have been all encompassing; it surely stretched to the lonely tree where he had left Sadie to her fate.

Neil climbed into the Rover and pointed it at the heavy door to the silo. "What the fuck do you think you're going to do?" Mark asked.

"Get your gun ready," Neil said. For his part he flicked the shotgun's safety off and laid it across himself: the butt against the console and the barrel out the window. "Here goes!"

Stomping the gas sent dirt and rocks spitting out behind them as he aimed straight on. Mark cursed loudly and stuck out his arms to brace himself. Just before they hit the door, a gunshot ripped the air, and the door to the silo sprang open.

Neil found himself staring down the bores of a half-dozen rifles.

Chapter 25

Sarah

Atlanta, Georgia

Even as she walked out of the main gate of the CDC alone, save for the sleeping baby snuggled in the sling across her breast, Sarah Rivers had to wonder if she was already dying. What horrifying germs had been released? And did the germs travel through the air, or were they coating the ground, or lying invisible on the chain hanging slack from the gate, or were they even then eating into Sarah's exposed skin?

"Just keep walking," she whispered to herself as she made sure for the umpteenth time that every inch of Eve was covered.

The night was spooky as hell even without the thought of germs. In spite of the fact that she had packed in a hurricane of fear, throwing whatever came to mind into the backpacks as fast as she could, she was still the last to leave. There weren't even taillights in view. The very last of these had dwindled to red dots just as she stepped out of the apartment building.

Around her, the city was dark, *black* in fact. That was the category it had been given, meaning there weren't any signs of humanity left. All save the lone woman and the baby, that is. Everything else that moved was a zombie, at least in her eyes, which, due to her fear weren't exactly 20/20. Within minutes of leaving the gate, Sarah almost shot a scraggly myrtle bush with her Beretta—it was right there appearing to jump out at her with its branches looking far too zombie-ish. Then she almost shot her own foot as she was trying to put the gun back into its holster with hands that shook as though she was an old woman suffering from palsy.

"Oh, crap," she whispered, struggling the gun into place

and struggling harder not to cry. It was an urge that gripped her around the face and clutched at her throat. She had never in her life been this utterly alone. Not even at the beginning of the apocalypse. Then, she'd had her parents with her and when they died, she had Neil. He had always been there for her, no matter the danger.

But now there was a whole city of the dead between them. He had left for the suburbs to the south, scrounging. South was the one direction she couldn't go; not without a car. South was where the neighborhoods stacked in on themselves, where the city of Atlanta, once the jewel of Old Dixie, sent skyscrapers reaching high into the heavens, where no live human had set foot in months.

It was rumored to hold upwards of a million zombies within its dark bosom. If she had a car, things would be different. In a car she wouldn't be afraid or, more accurately, not as afraid. In her mind she could picture herself zipping down the center of town and setting out a huge sign along a highway overpass that Neil couldn't miss. It was a silly dream.

She wouldn't be driving anywhere. There wasn't a car for miles that hadn't been checked and then re-checked for gas. Every last one of them was as dry as bleached bone. Most were settling on their haunches as well, their thickening tires leaking air at a rate immeasurable but, nonetheless, relentlessly constant. They were little more than monuments now, gravestones of a failed and dead civilization. Like gravestones they saddened Sarah as she passed them.

How amazingly quick her fate had caught up to her. Only a month before she had stood marveling at the new, expanded wall the governor had erected: twin ten-foot fences in front of a barrier of cars that were stacked just as tall. The wall around the CDC was so well founded that guarding it had become a perfunctory exercise, an excuse for men to sit around and shoot the bull instead of doing chores.

Only at the main gate was there still a real need for men to stand watch.

Now the watchers had all fled and, as Sarah glanced back, she saw the shambling movements of the dead as they moved into their new home. For a moment she felt guilt at not having closed the gate behind her or for not having left a note. In the dark she paused wondering if she should zip back and leave something for Neil. What could it possibly say? *Eve and I have gone and I don't know where we're going. P.S. You could be coated in germs and dying right now, sorry.*

What else could she possibly write that wasn't a lie? She had no idea where to go, or how to get there. She only knew that walking couldn't be the mode of transportation to whatever her destination happened to be; she'd be zombie-chow in no time. In fact, just as she turned from staring uselessly at the gate, a shadow separated itself from the deeper shadow of the building she had stopped in front of. Though the shadow had the vague outline of a human, the fact that it began to moan told her it wasn't one.

Sarah hurried to the far side of a van that sat parked half on the street and half on the sidewalk. It was the kind of van favored by child molesters and FBI agents; it was without windows. This was good in that the zombie couldn't see where she had gone, but was bad in that Sarah could only track the status of the zombie by listening to its persistent moan. As well she could hear it as it dragged something. The zombie made a constant scraping noise as it worked its way around the long end of the van. She hoped it was dragging its own leg along behind, but she couldn't tell by the sound.

She stayed on the opposite side of the van, endeavoring to keep as much of it between them as she could. In this way they went round twice before the zombie stopped and stared down the street back the way she had come.

Attracted by the movement, more of the beasts were heading their way, too many for a van to keep at bay.

Immediately Sarah rushed at a fast walk around the side of the building opposite the van. Burdened as she was, running was out of the question.

"Eh-heh," Eve said with a jutting lip. This was how she was trained to express her displeasure in lieu of crying.

"Not now. Oh, please," gasped Sarah. She stepped off the sidewalk and squatted down against the building in the gloom of some unknown bush. This offered scant camouflage, really none against any zombie heading down the sidewalk. Still, she had no choice, and quickly pulled back the baby blanket that was keeping the damp night off of Eve's face. The problem was obvious. Eve's binky had come dislodged from her mouth and was resting against her round cheek.

"Here ya go, here ya go," Sarah whispered, bouncing the baby as she poked it back between her lips.

Down the sidewalk from her the moaning grew louder.

Sarah looked all around: she was squatting next to an office building, two stories high, with not a single window left undamaged. Across a side street was another set of offices. The sign on the building read: North East Medical Plaza. There was zero chance that it hadn't been looted, however there was a good chance the front doors were unlocked.

A locked door would likely mean death just then.

Up she jumped and, glancing side-to-side, speed-walked across the street to the front door, or what was left of it. It had once been constructed of glass which had since been kicked in.

Behind her the shuffling sounds and the moaning picked up in tempo—there was no need to look back. She knew *what* was coming. She just didn't know *how many*, and had she looked back, she might have given up on the spot and turned the Beretta first on her baby and then on herself.

Instead she headed into the building, feeling the need to cry growing within her.

The shattered glass door she breezed through was nearly as useless for her needs as a locked one. It didn't slow the onrushing zombies for more than a couple seconds, and if the medical plaza had been like so many other buildings a couple of seconds would have been enough. She would have sped through the lobby to the staircase and slammed the door shut on the zombies who were notoriously bad with doors. Instead, the plaza was painfully open and modern: a wide atrium took up the entire middle of the building.

Even the stairs were out where everyone could see; everyone included zombies. Sarah rushed up the stairs with the first zombie breathing down her neck and she actually felt something tug at her backpack, before the beast tripped.

"Too bad for you," she said jauntily, but also with less force than she had anticipated; she was already getting winded. Including the weight of Eve, Sarah was carting nearly fifty pounds around with her. With that in mind she kept anymore comments to herself and concentrated on going up and up. The stairs ran out on the third floor, from which she had a wide open view of the building, and saw that she had effectively trapped herself. The stairs were the only way up or down.

A bench was right there at the top, possibly to cater to out of shape people who dared the stairs. Sarah dropped onto it, silently thanking chubby America. While she got her breath back, she listened to the zombies below trying to navigate the stairs. If she hadn't trapped herself, it might have been a funny situation. The ones further up were constantly falling and bowling over the ones below—it was good old fashioned slap-stick comedy, except the zombies were relentless in their desire to get at her.

On the plus side, they were dumb as bricks. It was Sarah's hope that they would get tired of crawling all over each other and ignore the third floor altogether. For that to happen, she would just have to sit there quietly, and pray.

For some time it looked as though her prayers were

going to be answered. Most of the zombies took to wandering around on the second floor and the few that made the attempt at the next set of stairs seemed to be tackling the challenge for the simple reason that they were in front of them. To the zombies, Sarah had simply ceased to exist in their minds, that is until Eve gave them away.

"Eh-heh," Eve said, sending Sarah's heart into her throat. She dropped to her knees and uncovered her daughter. For a second time Eve had spat out her pacifier.

Sarah once again corked the baby with the little bit of pink slobbery plastic and then leaned over her, whispering sweet, fearful nothings as she listened to the zombies on the stairs begin to make more of an effort to get up.

Still, it didn't sound like many of the beasts had heard the little baby noise and if Eve could stay quiet for a few more minutes, Sarah thought there was a good chance the zombies would fall again and perhaps forget about her. And if that happened...

"Eh-heh, eh-heh," Eve cried, louder now. This was her version of a full on outburst. Something was wrong—she wasn't hungry, Sarah had fed her just before they left. She wasn't cold, either, Sarah was sure she had her bundled properly but, just in case, she drew back the blanket to feel her cheek and that was when the smell blossomed out into the air.

Eve hated to be dirty and as long as she was, she would continue to cry in that soft manner of hers. It may have been quiet compared to other babies, but in that open atrium it was a very obvious human sound and would draw the zombies like flies.

Working quickly with practiced hands, Sarah laid the baby down, popped the binky back in Eve's mouth, swung the heavier pack off of her back, dug through it with one hand while holding the binky in place with the other so Eve wouldn't cry, smiled in a grimacy, semi-reassuring manner, cooed at such a low decibel that a dog ten feet away might not have heard, pulled from the pack first a diaper and then the thin package of baby wipes, snapped it open with just her thumb, peeled back the layers surrounding the baby, handed Eve her own feet to play with, removed the soiled diaper, wiped a pudgy bottom, re-diapered, re-dressed, re-swaddled, and listened as the zombies came ever closer.

A chest-high, partitioning wall separated the stairs from the third level. Sarah was just about to creep away using the wall as cover when her eye fell on the dirty diaper. The mother in her wanted to wrap it up properly, perhaps even double bag it so as not to be in the least offensive and then throw it in the trash. The woman on the edge of death had a better thought.

She took it and threw it, open-faced over the wall so that it landed on the stairs behind the zombies that were clawing their way up. Movement attracted them, but on the other hand smells confused them to no end. The diaper, for instance, stunk of humanity, but where was the human? As one, the zombies on the stairs turned and went for the diaper, while below many others were drawn to the white flash and the odor.

Sarah took what advantage she could. Every door on the third level, but one had been cloven in as though a medieval battering ram had struck them. The one intact door stood out. Even in the dark there was a gleam to its metallic surface that denoted an elevator. Hope surged through Sarah, hope and fear in equal parts.

What if she couldn't get the door open? What if the elevator was there on the third floor? She had envisioned sliding down the cable, but if the elevator was there she'd probably make a lot of noise getting the doors open for nothing. Finally, what if the cable was oily or too far to reach? Could she realistically jump to it with Eve and the backpacks all over her?

All this was counter balanced by the fact that she *knew* she couldn't just find somewhere to hide on the third floor indefinitely. Zombies lingered, sometimes for days on end and Sarah only had so much food and water, and there was the fact that Eve would stir and make more noise eventually.

All this was going round and round in her head as she approached the elevator. Then Eve squirmed in the sling, finding a better position, and Sarah jettisoned her fears. She was out of choices; she only had action left to her.

Step one was to get the doors open. Her first attempt, gripping the seam between the elevator doors with both hands and pulling with all her strength, failed when her right index nail bent back nearly in half. Focused as she was, she didn't even notice. Next she pulled the seven-inch hunting knife from her belt. Everyone carried them, though until this moment hers had been more decorative than useful.

She jabbed the sharp blade deep into the seam and pried the doors as far apart as she could—three inches. It was just enough room for her to get her shoe in and wedged in the gap. Then it was just a matter of hauling on doors that hadn't budged in seven months. She found it impossible to use even a fraction of her strength with Eve across her torso. Still with her foot wedged, Sarah gently laid her down, resting her head on a backpack, hoping the baby was asleep. She wasn't.

Eve stretched in her cocoon and made tiny baby noises. In another time or another place it would have been adorable, now Sarah could only pray that Eve would not start babbling.

"Sshh," she whispered. "Go to sleep."

Eve did not stir again and so Sarah turned back to the elevator doors which were slowly crushing her foot. Bracing herself she heaved, using the muscles of her legs and shoulders. The doors ground back a few inches, the metal squealing as though in pain as it did.

Sarah froze and Eve said, "Ba-da?" into the strained silence that followed.

The silence lasted only another second before the zombies forgot the diaper or whatever they were doing and again made mounting the stairs their main focus. Many had been close to the top to begin with and now Sarah could see the crowns of their heads over the partition.

She bent back to the cold steel of the elevator doors and heaved as hard as she could, causing a torturous scream to erupt from the metal as it slid slowly back. Every zombie in the building was heading up the stairs now.

Finally she had the door fully open and was somewhat gratified to see that the elevator car was not there. It wasn't anywhere as far as she could tell. The shaft was almost physically dark, as though her hand would go through something wet and inky if she were to reach outward only a few inches.

Swallowing her fear, she pawed at the blackness, growing bolder with each swipe and yet not finding a thing. Her mind pictured a cable somewhere just out of reach. She had to cling to the wall and stretch as far as she could before she found it.

How the hell was she going to get a grip on it with it so far away? With the zombies nearly to the top of the stairs, she began a blind sweeping search of the walls of the shaft nearest to her, hoping to find a ladder. There wasn't one; it was bare concrete without a single handhold.

She turned back as the moaning grew louder. A zombie had managed to climb the last of the stairs, while more were only seconds away from the top.

"Crap!" she cursed. Leaving the baby and the packs, Sarah ran at the zombie, pulling her Beretta as she did. With little ammo to spare she hadn't practiced much, thus she closed to within six feet before pulling the trigger. The undead thing lost most of the top of its head with what looked like a black cloud of bees flying up and out.

The zombie toppled and, before it struck the ground with a forgotten thud, she was past it, looking down at the stairs, gripping the partitioning wall as if no other force on earth could hold her upright. The stairs were carpeted in a grey mass of bodies, writhing slowly upwards. There must have been hundreds fighting to get at her.

Panic threatened to erupt within Sarah, however it was then that she heard Eve sniffling in fright. Any other baby would be bawling over the sound of the gun, but not tough, little Eve who was so much like her big sister: brave.

"I can be brave too," Sarah said, trying to pump herself up. She had to be brave because the only way out of her dire situation was a mad leap into the dark elevator shaft. "I can b-be b-brave," she said and this time the fluttering in her chest had worked its way up into her lips. They wouldn't stop jack-hammering up and down. It grew worse when she ran back to the shaft and tossed one of her backpacks down into the void—it seemed to take a crazy long time to land with a soft thud. Sarah turned away.

"There has t-to be a d-different way," she said. There wasn't. Already three zombies had cleared the stairs. They were gaping all about, though not seeing her just yet. She slunk down and looked at her baby.

Her greatest fears kept her from moving: What if I don't catch a hold of the cable? What if I just fall straight down? What will happen to Eve, then?

"She'll die," Sarah said.

From beneath the blanket, Eve turned her head toward the sound of her mother's voice and said, "Ba-da, ma-ma."

Now, although there were eight zombies stumbling about on the third floor, with two heading around the partitioning wall towards her, Sarah found a moment in her panic to smile. "Love you," she whispered and then gently slung Eve onto her back. It wasn't the normal position and Eve immediately began to squirm.

It was a strange feeling as if the baby was trying to get her little arms out to hug her from behind. Sarah reached back, patted the baby's bottom, kicked the second pack down into shaft, and then, without hesitating, she leapt.

It was all faith and literal blind hope.

She aimed for the center of the elevator shaft where something jumped up and smacked her on the side of the face. With flailing hands she grabbed at it in a mad rush as she fell and was able to catch a grip with her left hand. The cable bit into her flesh, searing it like fire, causing her to lose her grip almost instantly, but her legs found the steel and squeezed while, with her left forearm, she crushed the cable to her chest.

Again, the fire was immediate; now it was a line of raging pain up her body. She refused to let go. Instead she gripped tighter and fumbled with her right hand…she missed and there was no time to try again. Instead she hugged the cable with both arms and fairly flew down the line like an out of control fireman; there was a hissing all around her as her clothes added to the friction.

And then with a thud and a sharp pain zinging into her knees she struck the top of the elevator.

"Ow," was all the expression she allowed herself before she crumpled to her knees and attempted to see the pain in her left hand. For all that she could see she may as well have dropped to the center of the earth. Around her was black like she had never experienced.

"Eh-heh," Eve said, in a half-cry of fear.

"We're going to be ok, sweet…" Sarah began to say, but stopped as above her a moan echoed down the shaft.

There was light after all. Thirty feet above her was a grey gloom that pushed feebly at the black. It was just enough illumination for her to see the outline of a zombie. It glanced down once, saw nothing but black and then turned as if to leave, only just then a second zombie appeared. He too made to look into the shaft and in the process knocked the first one in. With a rushing wind it dropped straight at Sarah.

Chapter 26

Neil

New Eden, Georgia

For just the barest fraction of a second Neil considered slamming on the gas instead of the brake. After all he was clearly outgunned by a group of men who had, in all likelihood, kidnapped his daughter.

Then hope sprung up. Maybe they hadn't kidnapped her. Maybe they had rescued her instead. Maybe she was sitting up in the silo with a bag of ice on her ankle and nibbling on hillbilly stew—in the brief instant he had seen the men, he had noted they had a hillbillyish air about them.

Neil hit the brakes, kicking up a cloud of brown dust through which four of the men advanced on them with their guns locked and loaded.

"Didn't know anyone was home," Neil said, getting over his shock quickly. He would describe his fear level as "Mild". In his experience, people threatened with guns but only rarely used them. "We knocked, but I suppose you took us for Jehovah's Witnesses. Ha-ha."

Though the joke fell flat, the men behind the guns lost the dirty edge of their scowls. They still advanced however and not a one relaxed the grips on their weapons in the least. In seconds, Neil and Mark were pulled from the Range Rover, disarmed, and made to kneel in the light rain.

"Whatchu boys want?" one of the men asked Mark in heavily accented Georgia-English. He was a stout man, robust through the waistline, which was something of a rarity these days.

Mark jerked out a feeble shrug, irritating Neil.

"I think you know why we're here," Neil replied for them both. "I'm looking for my daughter. She's about my height with black hair and dark eyes, dresses kind of Goth-like. Have you seen her?" Instead of denying that they had, in any way, the men glanced back and forth at each other—a clear admission of guilt in Neil's eyes. "So you have seen her, he said, trying to appear more nonchalant than he felt.

The bigger man nodded pleasantly. "Oh, yeah and we're very 'cited bout havin' her stay on with us."

The calm way in which he said this sent Neil's fear level close to "Pants Wetting." After swallowing loudly, all nonchalance forgotten, he said in a quavering, indignant voice, "You can't hold her against her will. There may be no real government, but that doesn't mean there aren't any laws. It doesn't mean morals are thrown out the window."

"That's funny," the man drawled. "I'm gittin' a lect-chor on morals from a northern carpetbagger. Seems nuthin' ever changes." He came closer and spat in the dirt not an inch from Neil's hand. Clearly his aim was such he could've spat square in Neil's blue eye if he had a mind to. "Just a bit a warnin' boy, we answer to a higher moral authority than you know, so you may wanna keep your ten-cent bible thumpin' to yourself."

"What authority would allow kidnapping?" Neil demanded.

Just then a man that Neil hadn't noticed emerged from the silo. He was tall and dressed in white linens and wore sandals on his feet. His most striking feature was a beautiful mane of silver hair that came to his shoulders. He stepped around the gathered gun-toters and smiled benignly down so that his blue eyes twinkled.

"God's authority," he informed Neil. "Deuteronomy 24:7 states if someone is caught kidnapping any of his brethren and treating or selling them as a slave, the kidnapper must die." He had an easy southern twang, gentle and rich in tone like a story teller.

Neil looked up at the man, shaking his head. "I don't get it. If that's your law then whoever took Sadie must die. Though, to be honest, I'm not looking for revenge, I just want my daughter back."

"You don't 'get it', because you are ignorant," the man said easily. "That is a natural state that can be remedied. God's laws are beautiful things and not only do they state what they state clearly, they state what they do not state with an equal measure of that same clarity." Again, Neil shook his head and the man squatted down to his level and asked, "Are we brethren? Are we kin?"

"No," Neil replied and then he blinked in realization. "And so you think it would be within God's laws to kidnap me and sell me as a slave?"

"Yes, my son. The law could not be any more clear. However, you have the misfortune to be the odd man out. *He created them male and female*. It is the way to achieve harmony through balance. We do not accept nonbelievers save only in pairs: *They went into the ark to Noah by twos, male and female, as God had commanded*."

"So...I can't come in unless I bring my wife?" Neil asked. "Is that what you're saying? What about Mark, here. He is...um...they are a pair. Sadie and Mark, they're a pair."

"It's an interesting question," the man said, rising easily.

"Dear Abraham, he's an unbeliever," one of the men cried. Neil would've laughed at the man's theatrics if it weren't for all the guns pointed his way.

Abraham put out his hands as though he was about to give a blessing. "Is it your covetous nature or your hypocrisy that wields your tongue, Lenny? I sincerely hope that it is the beam in your eye which is causing you to see things so imprecisely. This gentleman, Mark, is not an unbeliever, yet. For now he is only ignorant. One day, the good Lord willing, he will be a *believer* and then we will welcome him. Give me an *Amen*, Lenny."

Dutifully, and with down-swept eyes, Lenny recited, "Amen."

"About the question of Mark?" Neil prompted

Now Mark came alive. "What about Mark? Don't I get

a say? I don't want to join this bunch of…" He stopped just in time. The eyes of the men around them had gone to squints and Neil's guts began to crawl into his chest.

"I will answer the question of Mark," Abraham said. "Our numbers are even and thus in harmony. Either of you may *join*, as you put it, as long as you come two-by-two. A man and a woman."

"But how do I get my daughter back?" Neil asked.

Abraham looked up to the rain in silence until they were all soaked down to their skin. None dared to speak. Finally he smiled and glanced down at Neil. "You are married? And Sadie is your daughter; that is good."

"We have two daughters," Neil said, hoping to create some sympathy. "The youngest is a baby. She's at home with my wife. We're very close as a family."

"A baby? How fantastic. How old is she?" Abraham asked with genuine interest.

"Eve is about six months. We don't know for certain. Her real mother died shortly after she was born."

For some reason the man found this invigorating. He laughed aloud shaking his head like a dog might shake its body to dry it. Though in this case it only sent his silver hair whipping. "Eve! What a beautiful name. Come, stand up. There you are. What's your name?"

"Neil."

"I know your skepticism, Neil. It's shared by your daughter. I haven't met anyone as headstrong as Sadie! Which is why I fear for her so."

Abraham had been leading Neil into the silo which was surprisingly empty. It held only a ladder that went up to a platform high above their heads. At the word *fear*, Neil pulled back.

"What does she have to fear?" he asked in a manner a pitch away from being surly, which was dangerous around people who were clearly deluded with false religious awe.

The man grew sad and said, "What we all have to fear:

sin. And that which goes with sin, eternal damnation. Let me explain while we walk."

Neil glanced around, wondering where they were going to walk to. They were in a steel structure with but one door and they were currently facing away from it.

Then one of the men bent to the ground and heaved up what Neil had thought was just part of the floor. A wide set of stairs led down into a tunnel—not a tunnel where the ceiling cascaded dirt as it threatened to cave in, nor a tunnel that was roughhewn and black and smelled of human refuse—this tunnel was warm and well-lit by evenly spaced light bulbs. The floor was perfectly poured cement. The air smelled of rain.

"Where are we?" Neil asked. His first thought was that it was some sort of military facility.

"This is my home," Abraham stated, heading down. "It all started ten years ago. The Lord our God came to me in a dream. He spoke like the wind and I was blown this way and that, much like a ship in a tempest, however my ship flew to scrape the heavens. From high up I saw the world beneath me, green and blue as simple as a marble. It was so insignificant that I turned my back on it, but then Our Lord Father showed me the riches that this world possessed: acres of gold, rivers of silver, pearls that fell from the sky in a storm of white snow. Every luxury was to be mine. Every woman, as well."

As Abraham spoke he became animated, his hands describing as much as his words and his face alight from within as if he truly believed everything he was saying. The men around Neil and Mark were equally believing. They stood with their guns and their prisoners forgotten.

The man went on: *Take it all*, the Lord our God said. Though he spoke in the speech of humans, his voice held such power that no ear could withstand it; I was deaf for a month. The next day I awoke stunned so that I lay in my bed for hours as the sun crossed all the way to the west. To me, even at the height of day, the sun was nothing but a dim little disc. For I had seen! Compared to the original light, the sun was nothing more than a candle on a birthday cake. It shed its paltry light as if it were a wicked, greedy little miser."

Here he laughed loudly and clapped Neil on his back. They started walking again down the long tunnel.

"I was happy for the sunset," Abraham continued. "The jealous sun was like a false king. It was all for show and stole the world's attention to itself. When the sun fled the skies, the vast creation—the entire universe of the Lord our God, was displayed to me and revealed just how pathetic we humans truly are.

"Yet, in that entire universe, I had been chosen. Why? For what reason? I was to be given riches. Everything I could possibly want would just be handed to me. As I walked along that night a shred of paper, blown by the wind slapped against my chest and clung there. It was a lottery ticket. I stuck it in my pocket and without once glancing at the numbers I went to collect my winnings the next day: Forty-three thousand dollars.

"Needless to say I was now doubly happy, for here was physical proof that the Lord our God had chosen me. I was to be given everything and it was all true! That night I fell on my knees and thanked him, and then, still on my knees, I slept. Again the Lord our God spoke to me, only now his words weren't an exhilarating wind that lifted me close to the heavens. No! Now his words were a hurricane of fire. It roared over my riches destroying everything: melting my gold so quickly that it boiled away and disappeared into the air, while the river of silver went a dead grey and became a river of death, and the marble of the earth shattered like bitter glass leaving behind green and blue shards."

He smacked his hands together sharply and turned to Neil in a froth. "Do you see what he did?"

Neil glanced back at Mark—the big man looked as though he didn't have a drop of blood in his head. Not only was he white he was sort of tilting as he walked.

"I…I don't," Neil said. So far they had walked over a hundred yards and now they came to an intersection. There had been many just like it, all identical in every way except this one carried with it the smell of cooking food. They turned left and the smell increased causing Neil to salivate.

"Let me tell you," Abraham said. "This wasn't about money. It was about learning a lesson. The Lord our God showed me that a gift, even a gift from God, is wasted if you don't put your faith in that very God. Tell me, how many of us were given the world? How many of us were born here in America, the greatest country on earth; to a stable, affluent, loving family, and how many of us possessed greater than average intelligence, perseverance, and imagination? And how many of us have pissed all that away?"

Neil didn't know what he meant by pissing it away. In his mind, what a person did with their life was their business. If they enjoyed sitting around watching TV all day, then good on them, as long as they didn't simultaneously complain about their life. In retrospect, Neil had to admit there were plenty of people who did just that.

"A lot?" he ventured.

The man smirked. "Try almost all of us." They began passing doors of heavy iron, left and right. Abraham let his long fingers trail across them as he walked. "And we didn't just piss it away, we sinned it away. Sin is what turns the beautiful into the ugly, the pure into the diseased. It was sin that brought us to the point where we are today. The sin of arrogance in the face of a higher power. The sin of gluttony in a world where people starve in the streets. The sin of apathy in the face God's love!"

"But…" Neil said timidly, hoping to steer the conversation without being offensive. "But my daughter. She is none of these things. She's not a glutton, or apathetic. She is very loving to her family, and dotes on her sister."

"Are you saying Sadie is without sin?"

"No, I'm not," Neil said, blanching a bit. Abraham had stopped and put his large hand on Neil's shoulder and squeezed to the point of pain. "But if she has sins they're really minor. Little things, you know?"

The man released Neil and ran a hand through his silver hair as if he was relieved. "Only minor sins, thank the Lord! Tell me, Neil. From your understanding of the bible, how many minor sins equal a major sin?" Neil's mouth came open and hung there to the great humor of Abraham. He barked laughter and commenced to walk again, taking another turn.

"I'll help you on this, Neil. Every sin is an affront to God. Every sin is a slap in his face. Tell me if you were to meet, let's say the Queen of England. Would it be ok if you just gave her a few slaps? A few small ones that barely turned her cheek red? Would it be ok if I slapped you? Not my hardest, just a smart one like this." He lunged at Neil with a raised hand and a sudden rage in his eyes. The smaller man flung up an arm, but the blow did not land. Again, laughter from Abraham, and this time the gun-toting men who had taken them prisoner joined in as if it was the height of humor.

"Do you see? Do you understand? I fear for Sadie because she is a sinner and what's worse, she rejects the Word of God. The punishment for this is death" Without a pause, and in the same tone, he said, "Ah, here we are. I hope you're hungry."

"But…" With Neil's mind spinning over the word death, they came to an open room that didn't seem possible. It could have been a cafeteria in any high-school or large office—bright and clean with windows opening to a view of a pretty green prairie in a long mural. It gave the impression that they were above ground instead of twenty feet below it.

"I believe we have venison sausage and eggs, if you wish," Abraham said, walking in casually and waving to the people. There were maybe two dozen of them sitting at the long tables and the first thing that struck Neil was that not a few of them were leaning toward the chubby side of the scale. More surprising was that they were all clean. Their clothes and their hair and their skin were all scrubbed spotless. Even Sadie was clean. At one of the tables she sat parked in a wheelchair with her foot elevated and wrapped in bandages. The wrappings were crisply white and matched the dress she wore. Except for her eyes, she never looked so pretty than at that moment. Her eyes were guarded and held a warning for Neil.

"I see you're being well taken care of," Neil said with a large fake smile. He came forward and hugged her.

"Careful," she breathed, too low for any but him to hear.

"Of course she's being taken care of," Abraham said jovially. "She will be one of us this afternoon and we take care of our own. There is no hunger in *New Eden*. There's no crime and no poverty, or racism, or any of the nonsense of our old lives. We are born anew! Tell him, Sadie. Tell your father what you've learned."

One thing was certain, she had learned to be afraid and that was something in such a courageous person. She swallowed with a clicking sound. "Well, uh, there are over three-hundred people in new Eden. They have a hospital with, uh, twenty beds. They got two doctors and one is a surgeon. And they have generators and, uh, hot and cold running water. I had a bath last night and one again this morning. That was good."

She faltered and Abraham said, "Tell him about the people."

"Oh. They have, like I said, three-hundred people here and there are nurses and architects and engineers. Things like that."

"What we don't have are any lawyers," the silver-haired man said proudly. "And no politicians and no criminals and no homosexuals and no bankers..." Neil's eyes flicked to

Sadie's before he was even aware of it. Abraham caught the look and asked in a sugary voice. "Are you a banker?"

"I? Me? Uh, no. I was in mergers and acquisitions. We bought and sold companies, depending."

The man nodded as if he knew all this already. "Depending on what? Profits? By the way we don't have profits here either, or losses or overhead, or salaries. We don't deal in money at all. Hard work is a blessing from God, just as is love and family. Money is worthless to us, as are gold and rubies and diamonds. What we find priceless is the knowledge of God's love, and the knowledge that it will never change and never grow less. Not for us. Not as long as we reject everything about our former lives. That's right. We reject everything this country once stood for."

Despite the fire and brimstone manner of the man's words, Neil spoke into the pause, "Everything? Even freedom?"

Here Abraham sneered. "Freedom," he spat out. "It's a lie invented by the Devil. All my life the word freedom was tossed about by every conman ever spawned. In all of history who ever had true freedom? I tell you that it wasn't you, Neil. Nor was it me. From sunup to sundown our lives here in the land of the 'free' were governed by rules and regulations, endless laws, and the threat of the police-state. Where was our freedom? Having the choice between McDonald's and Burger King does not constitute freedom! It was just as well. As man has shown, true freedom and true evil go hand in hand. Look at all the truly free men and you will see the face of evil. Am I right?"

All around Neil the people had sat in rapt silence, now they sent a volley of "Amens" at the man. He nodded before raking his fingers through his hair, displaying a fine sweat at his brow.

He glared down on Neil with wild eyes. "I see your doubt. Think. What is true freedom? The ability to do whatever you want without repercussion, without consequence. Who has that sort of power? Hitler did. And Stalin. And Genghis Khan. Only those with true power can possess true freedom, and look what they did with it! They conquered! They enslaved! They murdered!"

He accentuated each word by smacking one hand into the other and the room was quiet, the people entranced.

"That's why we do not give credence to the false notion of freedom. Rather we adhere to the dictates handed down by Our Lord God through his prophet." He paused, lowering his head so that a silver curtain fell before his face. Still positioned thus he added, "And one of the most important dictates that the Lord our God has shown through me is the Law of the Denier."

The room grew still around them, the air heavy with expectation, but it was not exactly silent. Sadie's breathing was rapid and charged with fear. The man who claimed to be a prophet turned to her. "The law is simple: a denier will be put to death." He made a gesture to Sadie.

"Amen," the people gathered said as one.

"No!" Neil cried in anguish. "I mean, no, she's not a denier. Maybe she's just an Unbeliever. That's what you called Mark and you didn't threaten him."

"Oh, Neil, I see you fear for your daughter. You don't want any pain to come to her, it's understandable. The question is can you understand that I care for her on a greater level than you? I care for her eternal soul."

"But…"

A sharp look silenced Neil. "One does not say *but* to the word of the Lord," the man said. "Right now she is an Unbeliever. At noon she will be baptized into the family of Believers. If she denies her faith, then…" He left off with a sad look and a shrug.

Neil was so anxious that his hands started to flutter. "Won't you give her any time to think things through or even learn what you guys are all about? And what if," he had to pause to collect himself before he asked, "What if she would prefer to come back home to her family?"

Abraham nodded. "We are a just people. All believers go through a period called *The Time of becoming*. It's three months of intensive education, of growing and learning. It's a very exciting time in a person's life. Only after *The Time of becoming* can someone be accused of being a denier. Secondly, Neil, look around you. There is nothing like *New Eden* left on earth! The Lord our God showed me the coming doom of mankind and I gathered my followers. They cast aside their worldly goods and began with me this great endeavor. It's been eight years in the making. Countless hours have been spent excavating, shaping and fortifying every square foot of this valley. We have herds of cattle, and hundreds of goats and sheep. There is nothing that we find wanting."

"Amen," the people called.

The false prophet beamed like a tent-show preacher. "Amen indeed! God is on our side, Neil. America is dead, while we thrive! The world rattles in fear, but we sleep snug and safe! We have light and heat and water! Who wouldn't beg to become a Believer? Neil, I want you and your family to join us. A baby would be such a blessing."

The little crowd had been worked up by the man and now they waited expectantly for Neil's response. "And if I don't want to?" he asked as if only curious, as if there was no way he was serious with such a question.

"Then you go your merry way and we will be all the sadder. We are not savages. We don't conduct orgies or have human sacrifices. Belief is voluntary."

Neil scratched his head. Had he missed something in all this? "What about Sadie? She's not being given a choice."

"God has chosen Sadie," Abraham said in a loud voice. "Lenny's mate was taken by the Devil. He was without a woman and we prayed and lo! Our prayers were answered. Harmony and balance were attained. Sadie is a gift from God as surely as the venison on her plate and she will be baptized at midday."

Behind him Sadie shook her head from side to side along the tiniest arc. Neil caught the movement; it stung his heart. Reaching out a beseeching hand he begged Abraham, "What if I get you another girl? You prayed for 'a girl' but maybe Sadie isn't the one God meant for you. You said she was headstrong, maybe God meant for you to have another."

The crowd began to murmur at the suggestion and the false prophet let them go on for nearly a minute as he considered. Finally he threw back his head, shaking out his long hair; this must have been some sort of cue because the people quieted.

"I have asked for harmony and the gift has been given already," he said, pacing on a short leash; five feet one way and five feet back. "Yet I understand about the love a father has for a daughter. The obvious thing for you to do, Neil would be to bring your family back and join us, so that you could always be together. But…but if you will not, I will allow a substitute, even if it is a baby. Bring us…"

"No," seethed Sadie, interrupting.

Abraham smiled at her though it was with his mouth only. His blue eyes were hard and cold. "Your mind is curdled by unfounded fear, Sadie. A baby would be loved here and protected! She would have a great life compared to how you live. You scrounge around like rats after crumbs. You're dirty and ungrateful and suspicious of kindness. And yet for some reason you look down your nose at how we live? We live as God's children!"

"Amen," the crowd roared.

"Amen, amen," he said, calming slowly. "I did not say it had to be a baby. My only stipulation is that she comes to us voluntarily and since I have a journey to make that cannot be delayed, she must be here by sunrise. Simple right? If you can do this, Sadie will be free to go. If not, she stays, and we can only pray that, for her own sake, she will not deny our teachings."

Chapter 27

Ram

Chesapeake Bay

Jillybean couldn't have been more right. They were trapped like a couple of mice. On one side zombies piled up from the midnight-black tunnel and on the other side they came at a shambling run down from the bridge. On either side of Ram and Jilly the walls were flat panels of cement that were too tall to reach by jumping.

We're going to die here, Ram thought. It had all been for nothing. All his scrabbling and fighting had been wasted. He looked to the little girl at his side, perhaps to apologize for leading them into this trap, but she was staring up at the wall.

"I guess," she said to the zebra she carried under her arm. "But what about Ram?"

"What is it?" he asked with a feeling of sudden hope…as well as a feeling of foolishness. He was relying on a stuffed animal to figure a way out of the trap. "What's he saying?"

"I can escape, but you can't," she said to Ram. Her eyes were huge and wet, and as he watched they pooled. "You have to throw me up there." She pointed at the top of the wall fifteen feet up. A short green fence ran all along the edge except where she had pointed, it seemed to be bent back or broken. "I have to stand straight and stiff in your palm like the acrobats at the circus we saw. You are aposed to throw me, but I don't want you to get eated."

Ram didn't want to get *eated* either, however that wasn't really up to him anymore. But he could save her. With a single glance he saw what the zebra intended. It could work. Standing on tiptoe, with his arm straight up he could reach nearly eight feet, and Jillybean, with her arms stretched could get maybe another five feet. He would only have to toss her three feet to safety.

And then he would get *eated* by a hundred zombies.

"It's a good plan," he said, choking on the words. With no time to waste, he rushed her to the side of the wall, snatched the zebra from her hand and stuffed it in her pack. He then hefted her up to his hip where she began to climb him like a tree until she was on his shoulder. Nervously she stepped onto his palm.

She was quivering like stem in the wind. "Don't be afraid," he said. "I won't let you fall." With his left hand he held her stable.

"I'm not afraid for me," she said, as if it hurt to speak.

"Yeah," he replied softly. The zombies were closing rapidly. Very, very rapidly. "Ready?"

She nodded. He bent at the knees, and then launched her shot-put style straight up. She was so light that she made the top edge of the wall easily. There she immediately began to scramble up and over, disappearing from sight.

Ram would have cheered her except the first of the zombies arrived. The creature wore part of a scraggy white uniform, that of a toll taker. Ram crushed in its head with his bat. A second one grabbed his arm. This had been a woman—it was horribly naked, showing off long, pus-filled lesions which ran up and down its torso. Ram stepped back and whistled the bat at her, Hank Aaron style, nearly taking her head clean off.

He brought down a third with an over-hand chop, and a fourth by hacking like he was trying to fell a tree with an axe. One grabbed his pack and without thinking Ram gave it up, freeing himself to swing harder and faster. Corpses piled at the feet of the walking corpses, stacking higher until Ram grew frantic.

They were all around him with their ragged claws and their biting teeth. A useless panic set in, turning him from a thinking man into a beast, little better than the creatures that swarmed him. In a quarter-second lull in the fighting, he saw a clear area, a circle of cement that was free and open. Pointlessly, he charged through the ring of zombies, desperate to get at it, losing the bat in the process.

When he arrived he found the circle was nothing special or magical and its zombie lined edges closed on him like a vise. He screamed and bashed through the line again, feeling nails rake across his jacket. He didn't care. The virus no longer caused the least fear. They could scratch him all they wanted. It was their gaping, putrid mouths that had his mind spazzing.

Without proper management from his brain, basic survival instincts took over. He ran around, sometimes leaping, sometimes kicking, sometimes screaming uselessly until his voice was hoarse and his throat burned with the ragged breath shooting in and out of him. And then above all the ruckus he heard Jillybean scream.

"Raaaaaam!"

In that instant his panic left him and before the little girl finished drawing out his name in what seemed like an endless piercing tone, he was completely focused on everything around him: he noted that the zombies had filled up both directions of the bridge/tunnel—and the area he had been going crazy in was now so dense with the creatures that it was a wonder he hadn't been pulled down already—and that Jillybean had not been idle on the top of the wall. Somehow she had managed to drag a broken piece of fence to the edge and now it hung out like tartan tongue.

She screamed something, maybe an encouragement to try for the piece of fence, or perhaps a warning that he was within inches of being smothered. He didn't know. His focus, which had been all-encompassing a second before, narrowed to a beam: all he saw was the fence ten-feet off the ground and the ziggy line through the zombies he would have to run to get at it.

In other words: the easy part.

The hard part would come after he leapt up and grabbed

the fence: he would still have to climb up it, while he was horribly exposed, hanging like a worm dangling from a hook, well within reach of the zombies. For how long? Ten, fifteen seconds?

The darkest part of his mind saw clearly what would happen in two scenarios. In the first he would dash forward, only to be met by surging zombies before he could even make the attempt at leaping for the fence, whereupon he would be swarmed and eaten alive.

In the second scenario he would weave through the undead and make a Michael Jordan-esque leap catching hold of the fence and before he could even begin to climb, he'd feel zombie claws gripping his legs and ankles. He'd be pulled down, swarmed and eaten alive.

The choices weren't good, but they were better than just standing there and being swarmed and eaten alive. Without thinking, Ram took off, letting his subconscious dictate his path through the zombies who reached out and tore at his clothes as he passed, slowing his momentum, giving the short sprint a slow-motion nightmare quality. Still, he was young and strong and he made a leap that wasn't in the least graceful but was just powerful enough that his fingers found the lower edge of the fence and hooked on.

Just like in scenario two, he found his legs were immediately attacked.

Unlike in scenario two, Ram went wild, kicking this way and that, feeling facial bones snap and eye sockets cave, but, as he had expected, a particular tough and large zombie caught a hold of his shoe. Ram kicked hard and swung away. As he swung back, he knew he couldn't keep this up. With all his kicking he hadn't progressed an inch up the fence and already the bite of the wire was worrying his fingers loose. If he didn't find some way to relieve the pressure on his hands and get out of reach quick he would be a dead man.

This time, when he swung back toward the big brute, he kicked again but this time the blow struck the thing's chest.

In an instant, an idea shot from his brain to his foot like lightning. He planted that left foot on the zombie's collar bone and then his right went on the crown of its head and in this way he stair-stepped right out of reach.

He was up the remaining part of the fence in a few seconds. Wearing a smile of relief, he was prepared to give Jillybean a huge hug, but she wasn't in sight.

"Jillybean!" he called in desperation.

"Oh, hi," she said from almost at his elbow. She had been bent over in a little crevice among the rocks. Now she struggled up bearing a stone as large as she could carry. "You made it! I'm so happy and Ipes won't believe it. He thought you were a goner. Hold on." The rock was getting heavy so she pitched it over the side where it sounded like it crushed something squishy. "I was going to save you with that rock."

"You saved me with that fence. Was that Ipes' idea? Or yours?"

The zebra was lying on its side in the rocks. Jillybean picked him up. Dusting off his bottom, she said, "The way he talks you would think I don't have *any* ideas. It is a wonder I can tie my shoes without him."

Ram laughed—it was half relief and half because she was so button-cute. She went on talking about the zebra for a few minutes, all nonsense of course, and while she did Ram checked himself for scratches. Thankfully his tough leather jacket had resisted every fingernail.

Euphoria had a good hold of him until he saw a string of zombies picking their way through the rocks toward them. The man-made island consisted only of the bridge/tunnel highway and a rocky hillock. His euphoria dissipated in the chilly rain and Ram sighed looking out at the grey sea.

"It's gonna be cold," he murmured.

Jillybean's lips thinned in anxiety. "Can we maybe go back? You know, sneak along the edge of this island thingy and then make a run for the land."

Even if they could get past the mass of zombies heading their way, it would be a long run, one that he could make if he was alone. There was no way Jillybean could make the run. If she tried she'd die; something he wasn't going to allow to happen. "Naw, it's too far," he said. "We'll swim to the other island, it's only about a half a mile…" Her leg began an anxious, shimmying dance and her lips compressed so much that they practically disappeared. "I'll carry you if you can't swim," he assured her.

"I can swim a little. I had swim lessons at the Holly Pool, by the supermarket. They used to do swim lessons for the *Tadpoles*. That was me, a Tadpole. It was at like early in the morning and it was cold, but that looks really cold and I don't like the waves. I can't swim in waves, I think. Ipes says I can't, neither."

He assured her once more that he would carry her if needed—and it was needed very quickly. Choppy, churning waters, coupled with trying to swim while fully clothed turned out impossible for Jillybean and a torture for Ram, especially when he added the weight of a six-year-old and her sponge-like Zebra.

When she began to sputter after barely twenty-yards, he turned over on his back and pulled her onto his chest. For the next hour he slogged backwards in a one-armed, monotonous, and very slow manner. It would have been quicker to sink to the bottom of the bay and walk through its black mud.

By the time he reached the other island he could barely keep their heads above the water. They both struggled to shore. Ram's muscles quivered with exhaustion, while Jillybean's quivered with early onset hypothermia. She sat on the rocks and hugged herself while Ram went to investigate the highway as it emerged out of the tunnel.

More zombies. They dotted the bridge and, like drunken guards, they went back and forth in erratic lines. The sight of them crushed Ram's spirit. He had spent almost the last of his energy fighting to get to a little rocky island that was, for all intents and purposes, the exact match of the one he had just left.

What was perhaps worse was that in the distance at the edge of his vision he could see another little island where the bridge ended and the highway again slunk down beneath the water.

"Why did they build a bridge like this?" Jillybean asked. He had stared at the impossible route he had chosen for them for so long that she had come wandering up and now she reached out and held his hand. Her fingers were like ice. "It really doesn't make sense and Ipes is too cold to talk or he'd tell me."

"I think it's because we have a navy base near here and they can't get the super big boats under the bridge," Ram explained. "So they built a couple of tunnels and sent them under the water. And now the boats can float on past. It's an engineering marvel, except they didn't engineer it very well with zombies in mind. Look. See all of them out there?"

"Yeah. Ipes is afraid."

"I am too," Ram lied. The truth was that he was too tired to be afraid. "Do you think you might be able to swim some more? I mean without me carrying you?" She shrugged without looking up, meaning she would try but wasn't going to guarantee the results.

"But I'd rather we just take that boat instead," she said, pointing off to the right.

"There's a boat?" Ram demanded. He didn't wait for an answer and took off, hurrying over the thousands of head-sized rocks that made up the little island.

There was indeed a boat: a dinky sailboat of fifteen feet in length that looked part zombie itself. Its hull appeared to have gone over rocks like cheese over a grater, and the sail was in tatters, flapping uselessly in the wind. Even the boom, the pole that jutted out perpendicular to the mast and held the lower part of the sail in place, was bent near in half.

Ram couldn't believe his good luck.

Careful not to accidentally set it free back into the Chesapeake, he climbed onboard and began to inspect his new treasure. There wasn't much to it: in a storage compartment at the back of the boat he discovered two life preservers, an anchor and chain, and fifty-feet of thin cord. In the bow was a crawl space and it too held some items: a heavy fishing pole and tackle box, rags—mostly old t-shirts, a couple of buckets, and a sail repair kit.

"Jillybean, get on in," he said through the driving rain. She was just standing there shivering. "Don't be afraid."

"I'm not afraid, but this doesn't look like it'll go. And look there's water all in the bottom. Won't it sink? Like blub, blub, blub?"

"We'll keep it close to shore at first to see," he said. When he put out his hands to her she allowed herself to be lifted over the side. "We have to get you out of the rain. Get in there." He pointed at the crawl space. "Take off your clothes and bundle up in those shirts."

A minute later she said from in the cubby, "They are kinda stinky. What are you going to use to get dry with, Mister Ram? Ipes says you'll freeze to death if you don't get dry. There's still one t-shirt left."

"Wrap it around your head, Jillybean," Ram ordered. "Don't worry about me." How was he going to get dry? That was a question he would have to worry about later—unfortunately later would equal to one cold, wet night, which in truth was on the verge of becoming the present.

"Hey Jilly, can you hand out that sail kit. It's the big clear bag." She handed it out with a skinny arm that protruded from what looked like a pile of dirty clothes.

"Thanks," he mumbled, trying to see through the plastic for instructions, and not finding any. It wasn't a professional kit. The owner of the boat had collected a mish-mash of items he thought would come in handy, heavy sewing needles, thick, white thread, an awl for puncturing and a square of heavy canvas. At the bottom of the bag he finally found something that gave him hope: a wide roll of *Sail Tape*.

"Hhmm," he said, squinting at the tiny writing on the tape in the fading light. After a minute his shoulders slumped: the sail would have to be dry for the tape to work. He cursed at what he considered a poorly designed product. Seconds later he cursed louder when he pulled back on the sail and saw the extent of the damage. There wasn't enough tape in the whole world to hold together the shreds of white.

"So much for sailing," he said.

"What?" asked Jillybean from in the crawl space.

He squatted in front of the door and looked in; only her eyes were visible. "The sail that's up now is shot. I don't know what to do. We can't really stay here, but we also can't go on."

"You wanna know what Ipes thinks?" she asked, her voice muffled by the t-shirts. Ram had little to lose in hearing advice from a toy, besides the zebra had come up with a few good ideas already. He nodded and Jillybean said, "Ipes says we should sleep here. He says you should push us out a little and drop the weighty thing...the *anchor*! That's it. He says that if we are out a bit the monsters won't be able to get us while we sleep. Is that a good plan, do you think?"

"Are you sure it was Ipes' plan and not yours?" Ram asked.

"Yeah, it was Ipes. He's really smart," Jillybean said. She then giggled and added. "Just ask him, he'll tell you all about it."

"Maybe later," Ram said and then shut the door on the girl.

Moving the boat wasn't a problem. He had gained much of his strength back and the boat fairly shot away from the shore egged on by a stiff southerly wind. Too late he discovered that the anchor chain was a knot of rust, frozen into a ball by oxidizing chemicals. He lost two minutes working it free only to find that the infernal chain wasn't hooked to anything!

The little island seemed small when he glanced up in a panic. How deep was the water, he wondered. It seemed too deep for the length of chain, so he added the fifty-feet of cord to the end, tied it off at the gunwale and chucked the anchor in. Then came another worrisome minute when the anchor didn't catch the bottom as Ram had thought it would.

He figured there'd be a little jolt and they'd be stuck in place. Reality was different. The anchor thumped into the black mud far below and then was dragged along like a reluctant dog on a leash.

Ram could do nothing about it. He sat there in a growing depression, lashed by the cold steel rain and stung by the sharpness of the wind. They would blow out to sea; he was sure of it. They would starve or freeze or the boat would sink under them! Was it his imagination, or was the water in the hull beginning to grow deeper?

After marking the level he stared at the water for long minutes and found that it wasn't getting deeper, or rather it was, but it was from the rain only, which could be bailed overboard. Delighted by this, he looked up to another treat: while he had been busy fretting over the concept of sinking, the anchor had finally snagged on something. They were some two-hundred yards offshore, a little further than he had hoped but on the bright side they were free from the zombie menace.

"Scootch all the way over," he said to Jillybean. The crawl space was the shape of a gently curving triangle with a base of about four feet; there wasn't much room. "Also, can I have one of those T-shirts? Thanks...now turn away. I have to get undressed."

"Are you gonna turn the shirt around and wear it like shorts? Ipes said it was a good idea, but it feels like I'm wearing a diaper."

That was the plan. In a few seconds he discovered that

she was right; it felt very weird. Still, it was better than freezing in his wet clothes—that is, once he got used to dressing after the fashion of an infant.

After he changed, he wrung out their clothes, and squeezed as much water as he could out of Ipes who was a saggy-bottomed little thing. He then brought out the sailcloth from the plastic bag, nervous that it would be little more than a coarse slab of canvas. It turned out, softer and larger than he could have imagined. When stretched out, it was ten-by-ten and big enough to wrap the two shipmates in a warm cocoon.

With the rain pattering, the boat gently rocking, and the little girl snuggled up, snoring lightly, Ram could barely stay awake. He had much to think about and to consider: mainly how they were going to get back to the safety of the CDC. However that question wouldn't stay latched to his thinking. Instead he thought about Jillybean. Her resilience amazed him. She was mostly bone with a thin layer of skin stretched across, yet nothing fazed her for long; she had bounced back from her food poisoning as if it had never happened. The same was true with every fright that came her way.

They made a good team. He supplied the brawn and the experience, while she had an intuition that was decades beyond her maturity level.

"What am I going to do with you?" he asked. Whenever he wondered about this, he pictured Neil and Sarah. They were the logical choice to raise her: they were good parents and the CDC was a safe place, or so he thought.

Once again he'd be "Uncle Ram." He smiled at the thought and as he did his head grew warm and his eyes sleepy.

The night passed without either of them even noticing. One second they closed their eyes and the next a murky light filtered into the crawl space to wake them.

"I don't want to get up," Jillybean said in a whisper when she saw his eyes flutter open. Off the shore as they were there was no need to whisper, but the survival mechanism was clearly ingrained.

Ram grunted, "Yeah, me neither." Getting up would entail another difficult day of survival; of running and hiding, and probably swimming in freezing waters. Staying curled up in the soft material in the semi-dark held a great appeal; it was sort of like playing hooky from school. "But I can't," he moaned. "I got to see if I can get the sail working. Turn away I got to get dressed."

Getting dressed entailed putting back on the damp clothes from the day before—they were absolutely freezing! Jillybean giggled as he fake cursed.

When he was dressed, he crawled out into the morning, stood in six inches of chilly rainwater and cursed for real. The little island was gone. Sometime during the night the knot he had tied to the gunwale had given out and they had floated away, pushed out to sea by the prevailing east wind.

"Where did the land go?" Jillybean asked squinting all around them. His "real" cursing had set off alarms and she had dressed hurriedly.

"I have no idea. That way I think," he said, pointing in the general direction of west. Though the clouds were still heavy and low, the sun's rays filtered through to irritate his eyes when he faced east. "I just don't know how far. It could be really far." He began a quick calculation. "Maybe up to…twenty miles."

This was a lie to keep her from freaking out as much as he was. He judged the wind to be about fifteen miles-per-hour, and they had been in the crawlspace for ten hours. If the knot had let go right away they could conceivably be a hundred-and-fifty miles away from land. Even a middle-case scenario put them at seventy-five miles away.

And Ram did not know how to sail.

He had some vague ideas and figured if the wind turned around he could point them at the wide expanse of the Atlantic seaboard and not fail to hit land. But of tacking, or luffing, or rigging, or even tying knots he was painfully clueless.

Jillybean's lips pursed. This was her *thinking* face and Ram waited patiently for her, or Ipes, to come up with an idea. After a moment she glanced up at the mast, taking its measure.

She then turned away and spoke in a low voice, as though talking to the ocean, "But it's too high. Why can't Ram do it? Oh...I guess." She glanced once more at the mast before addressing Ram. "Ipes says I have to climb up there before we do anything. I have to look around. He says you can't because of your weight. He says you might capsize the boat which means knock it over. But I don't really wanna."

"It'll be ok," Ram told her. "I'll be right here. I'll catch you if you fall."

Nothing other than hearing those words would have got Jillybean up the twenty-two feet of mast. Ram lifted her almost half-way, while the remainder she shimmied, with jutting elbows and frogging knees, until she had the masthead butting into her diaphragm.

Pointing to the south of them, she yelled, high-pitched, "There's a boat."

Ram hopped up on the bow and squinted, but couldn't see a thing beyond rolling grey waves. "Are you sure?"

"It's a boat or a small island. No, wait it's a boat for certain!"

Chapter 28

Sarah

Atlanta, Georgia

The hoist cable saved her. When the zombie pitched forward and fell, its flailing body twanged off the thick wire, sending it thudding down, not inches away from Sarah.

Though they were in a small space, the elevator shaft was so all-encompassing black that she couldn't tell exactly where the zombie was or what it was doing. It was there in the dark, groaning, swimming its feral hands about, trying to feel its way around.

Twice, she felt its claws strike her leg; both times she had to bite the inside of her cheek to stop herself from crying out. For the moment the zombie didn't know it was in a five-by-five concrete square with two humans.

It would know soon enough. Eve wouldn't last. She had begun to squirm. She wasn't used to being carried on Sarah's back, and she didn't like the dark, and she most certainly didn't like the weird action that occurred during and after their fall. She was on the verge of letting out one of her little cries that her parents had worked so hard to teach her in the hope it would keep her safe.

Without something; a low reassuring whisper, a gentle humming, even a caress, she was going to cry and then the zombie would know there was a human nearby.

In the cramped shaft with a deadly creature, this was all the advantage Sarah had. She knew that she had to strike and very quickly. The zombie, on the other hand, was only concerned with getting to its feet. It used the cable to pull itself up. Sarah felt it vibrate and heard it hum.

Then she caught the putrid breath of the creature square in her face. It was standing now, but how close was it? How tall? Where could she strike that would kill it in an instant?

In the black, all she had to work with in order to fix its location was the noise of its moan and the stink of its mouth.

Very slowly Sarah eased her hunting knife from its sheath.

The Beretta was still in its holster, and if she had any chance of getting out of there—not just out of the elevator, but out of the building—it would have to stay in the holster. The third floor was probably packed with zombies by now and a gunshot would have them all running to the shaft. She'd be buried in an avalanche of undead.

It had to be the knife and it had to be quick, only where was she to strike! Anything less than a single accurate, piercing blow to the thing's temple or eye would doom Sarah. It would find her and she didn't like her chances of a brawl in the dark with a baby strapped to her back.

It was this that had her hesitating, even after the zombie found her. A hand brushed against her shoulder. It left for a brief moment and then came back, this time with too much curiosity.

Sarah could not wait any longer. She struck downward in a diagonal and the knife bit into something. There was blood on her hand, while in the dark the zombie moaned louder than she had ever heard one moan before, yet it did not die.

Again the diseased hands reached for her. They clawed at her coat and she took a step away, sweeping the walls with the back of her arm, trying to get her bearings. Just in front of her there was a thrumming from the cable as the zombie struck it. For an instant she had an idea of where the beast was, but then she stepped on one of the backpacks she had tossed down. It was filled with cans that went squirrely beneath her weight and before she knew it, her ankle buckled.

She wasn't hurt, however she was down on one knee with a zombie almost directly on top of her. Its arms were out and searching, and worse, Eve had reached her breaking point.

"Eh-eh, eh-eh," she cried.

The zombie glanced down and Sarah *saw* it!

Tripping on the backpack couldn't have been more fortuitous. From her vantage she could see the zombie's outline against the grey gloom washing down from above.

She could see its hands begin to reach and its mouth open. Acting on instinct she slapped the wall to her left. In an instant the thing turned to the sound and Sarah struck for a second time. Now that she had a fixed target she punched the knife blade to the hilt through the thin bone of its temple. It died instantly, slumping gently to the roof of the elevator with help from Sarah, who guided it down.

Now was not the time to give away her position.

Standing, she pulled her baby around so that Eve was once again properly positioned. "You did great, sweetie."

She soothed Eve until the sound of her sucking on her pacifier came up from beneath the blanket. Only then did Sarah stoop and remove the knife from the zombie's head; as disgusting as it was, there was still a chance she would need it. Next, she found the two packs and set them aside out of the way. She then crouched and ran her hands back and forth on what was the roof of the elevator, searching for the latch to the trapdoor.

After a brief panic she felt under the still-warm body of the zombie and discovered the latch. In a minute she went from the pitch black of the shaft, to a level of dark beyond even that when she dropped carefully into the elevator. Yet she didn't need light to escape. By feel she found the elevator doors and sunk the bloody knife in its seam. With a light grunt she heaved back, stuck her foot in the crack, sheathed her knife, and then put her entire weight into getting the doors open wider.

Her efforts elicited only a single, creaky, metallic shriek, but that just enough to alert the zombies milling about on the floors above and the few still left on the stairs.

They all turned to gaze in her direction, as she sped toward the lobby, but were slower to react than normal. Perhaps they failed to recognize her humanity in the dark, what with the heavy packs slung on her back and the baby hitched in front. Not daring to make eye contact, Sarah walked brusquely past the stairs, looking more like a loaded-down Christmas shopper than a woman fearing for her life.

She barely got past the lower steps before the zombies came alive with louder, excited moans—she'd been spotted! The ones on the stairs, in their haste to feed, came tumbling down and it was Sarah's great wish that they would all break their necks. She didn't stay to discover if this was the result.

Out into the chill night she hurried once again. Dotted here and there along the streets like ill-plotted shrubbery were stragglers, zombies that didn't seem capable of making up their minds which way to go. She avoided these by heading into the maze of neighborhood side streets, where she found herself safe, but lost after only about twenty minutes.

"Am I really lost?" she whispered to her baby, jiggling up and down in the way that comforted Eve. The unfamiliar street signs implied that she was indeed, however the fact that she had no idea where she was going or how to get there, suggested otherwise. Being lost hinted strongly that one either had a destination in mind or some reason to journey. In this case she had neither.

"At a minimum I should know what direction I'm going," she said, looking about. The stars could have told her, only they were hidden by clouds that were clearly in league with the *Fates* who were trying their best to kill her. She thought it best to ignore this negative thought. "Maybe I could orient on…"

She jumped at a very human sound: a slamming car door. Just like that, this simple thump brought out an intense desire for her to run down the street screaming: *Don't leave me!*

[271]

Sarah bit back the urge to cry out, but nothing was going to stop her feet. They took off under her and she was borne along with the great fear that she'd be too late and she would be left behind, again. A minute later, while crossing a wide boulevard she was amazed to discover she knew exactly where she was: the CDC.

Somehow she had managed to come in a big circle. There was the seven-story main lab and the front gates, and right across from it, settled on the median in the middle of the boulevard was a gold Ford F-250. She knew that truck, as well as she knew the big lady who was crouched down inside it.

"Shondra," Sarah said in a barely audible tone as she drew close. Shondra lifted her head just a hair above the level of the door frame; when she saw Sarah her eyes went comically big.

"Sarah! Get in. There are zombies in the CDC. Did you know that?"

Sarah climbed in and as she did she cast a look back. "Yeah, I know and I think some of them saw me."

Ever so slowly, Shondra rose up again to peer over the door frame. "They did! Get down!"

"Get going," Sarah shot back. "Don't just sit there, drive!"

Shondra shook her head. "I can't. I got high-centered trying to turn around. We're stuck." Even as she said this she hit the gas and the back wheels, which were off the ground spun uselessly.

"Then we got to get out of here. We gotta leave the truck," Sarah said, poking her face up to see what their situation was. It wasn't good. The CDC was emptying of the dead and all around the streets were clogged. "Do you have a gun?"

Sarah had her Beretta drawn and held it up. Shondra nodded quickly, her jowls shaking. She took a .38 Police Special from the console and checked the load.

"That's all you got?" Sarah asked in disbelief. A lousy six-shooter wasn't going to cut it.

"I have a shotgun in the back." She jerked her thumb to the open bed of the truck. It wasn't going to do them any good back there.

"Try the truck again!" Sarah cried. Shondra did her best, but the wheels only spun doing nothing but attracting more zombies. While she was at it, Sarah put Eve on the floor at her feet and did her best to cover her up.

"We're going to have to shoot our way out," she told Shondra, who immediately began shaking her head. "Yes. We'll make a gap and try to make it to the..." She had been about to say the lab, but the germs came to mind. "...to the storage facilities on the east side."

"I can't run that far!" Shondra said. She opened her mouth but just then a grey fist struck the window. More would follow, she knew, until the windows were destroyed and then they'd be dragged out. This knowledge had Shondra changing her mind. "Ok...ok, let's do it."

"Please, Lord be with us," Sarah said, thumbing off her safety. She grabbed the handle, kicked open the door and fired off two rounds in quick succession dropping a pair of zombies. At close range she was as deadly as anyone. Five more shots sent the brains of five more zombies ripping into the night yet still the beasts closed in.

"Shondra! Help me," she screamed. The woman hadn't budged from the driver's seat. Under Sarah's withering look, she timidly began to roll down her window. Sarah couldn't spare more than a second to look at the frightened woman, she had to concentrate on the zombies right at her door. With her fear mounting, she counted the spent bullets.

"Eleven, twelve, thirteen..." At fifteen she reached out and slammed the door closed before going through the automatic motions in reloading. Both Ram and Neil had forced her to practice over and over. She could reload blindfolded. Shondra couldn't. Her hands were shaking so badly that she dropped more shells than she managed to put into her pistol.

"You ready to make a dash for it?" Sarah asked.

Shondra shook her head. "It's not going to work. Listen to Eve! She is crying too hard." It was true. With all the shooting, the baby was bawling with the full power of her lungs.

"Then, I'll go alone," Sarah said, blinking to clear the sudden blurring of her eyes. "You stay down and keep her quiet until I draw them off." Shondra didn't argue other than to shake her head in a very weak display of denial.

The zombies were pounding the doors now with dreadful power. It wouldn't be long. Sarah grabbed the door handle, but just then the bigger woman pointed.

"Look!"

A sharp light cut the night. It swept them and then came the roar of an engine. In a second, a motorcycle, not much more than a dirt bike, was in the street thirty feet away, spinning in short arced circles. Immediately the zombies advanced on it, but the man on the bike only spun sharper.

In the dark, his features were loose and hard to define, but Sarah was almost sure she knew the man. "Ram?" she yelled from her cracked window.

"Get down! Get down!" he raged. It was Ram. He was there, unarmed save for a golf club and his motorcycle. When the zombies were within reach, he gunned it forward but only for a few seconds, and then when they closed a second time he spurted on again.

Sarah didn't see after that. She bent to her daughter in the foot well and was soothing her as best as she could when suddenly her door was flung open. She grabbed the gun that she had set aside, but was too slow. A little girl with flyaway brown hair stood there. She too had reached for the gun, but only to keep from being shot. Their hands overlapped on the hot barrel.

"We have to go," Jillybean said.

"Who are…" Sarah began, but Shondra interrupted.

"We can't leave the truck. We'll die out there."

At this the little girl turned sharply and stared into the night, her little muscles bunched, ready to send her flying. After a moment she relaxed. "No, they're all after Mister Ram. It'll be fine."

Just then Ram came flying back on the motorcycle and was surprised to find them all still there. "What's wrong?"

"The truck is high-centered," Shondra said. "We can't leave it. We'll die out there."

Ram spun once looking at the truck, before glancing to the hordes that he had led away. They were heading back and weren't being slow about it. "Can you fix this?" Ram asked the little girl.

She had stepped away from the truck and was now looking at it with her lips tight together; under her arm she carried a stuffed animal. The little girl nodded. "I think so, but we'll need some time."

"I'll give it to you," Ram declared and then spun about again. He headed right for the mob of undead, turning at the last moment to lead them away.

"Have you tried putting it in four-wheel drive?" Jillybean asked. "That's when all the wheels go at once. You see with your truck, it's only the back wheels what are up off the ground."

Shondra looked at her dashboard, searching. "I don't think it has four-wheel drive," she said at last.

Jillybean made a face of disappointment and then unexpectedly said, "It doesn't matter if it's a stupid truck. We still have to get it off of there."

The two adults glanced at each other, before Sarah asked, "How old are you?"

"Six and three-quarters," Jillybean answered by rote. Her mind was clearly focused on something else. She squatted down and looked at the truck's undercarriage, she then climbed up the back to peer into the bed. "We need some help back here," the girl said. "Whichever one of you is stronger."

Sarah was the younger by twenty years. She hopped out of the truck and hurried into the bed where Jillybean stood pointing at the spare tire. "Can you pick that up?"

"I...probably," Sarah said. The tire was much heavier than it looked, and it looked very heavy. First they cleared a path through the chaos in the back of the truck then the two heaved it to a standing position and rolled it off.

"I need you to put this extra tire under one of the tires that's off the ground," Jillybean instructed. Sarah saw what was needed and together they shoved the spare onto the median beneath the jacked up tire but, unfortunately they were inches too short. "The two tires have to be able to touch!" the little girl said emphatically. She was clearly getting nervous at how long the operation was taking. "We need some boards or wood or anything flat."

There was nothing in the bed that would serve. In vain, they pushed aside the heavy fuel cans and the water jugs and the boxes of canned goods that had been haphazardly thrown in the back. Their surroundings weren't any help either.

"What about a shovel?" Jillybean asked suddenly. "Ipes says we can build a quick mound of dirt that could do the trick."

"Ipes?" Sarah asked.

At that moment, Shondra gasped and pointed behind them. Mistaking this for a good thing, Sarah turned, excited, hoping that Ram had returned, instead she was confronted with more zombies heading their way.

"What do we do?" Shondra asked.

It was clear what they had to do. Sarah ran for her gun, pausing only to kiss Eve. When she got back to the end of the truck the little girl was acting strangely.

"Come on, Ipes! Tell me what to do," she demanded. "I told you we don't have anything that'll go under there. What? The gas? It's too big. Oh, I get it...excuse me. Ipes has an idea. If we can't raise the mound we can lower the truck."

"You're going to let the air out of the tires?" Sarah asked. "Will that even work?"

"No," Jillybean said matter-of-factly. "That'll make it worse by increasing the angle. What we need is everything in the back piled as far to the rear as possible. If we're lucky then the truck will tip rearward the few inches we need."

The two women immediately started to climb into the truck forcing Jillybean to remind them of the zombies. Shondra hopped down. The zombies were straggling up and her .38 was good for this sort of work. She began killing them one at a time, while Sarah heaved the gas and the water to the back.

Jillybean watched for a minute, but then she said in a monotone, "Ipes says to put down the tailgate. I think it's that thing." She pointed vaguely at the back of the truck. She then walked away and came back toting Eve in her arms. "Whose baby is this? She was crying."

Sarah almost choked to see this strange girl holding her baby without permission. Eve always seemed like such a tiny thing, but in the little girl's arms she looked to be the size of a sack of potatoes and the girl was holding her like one.

"Oh hey, Honey, don't," Sarah said. "You can't just pick up someone's baby. She was fine."

"She was crying," Jillybean explained. "I forgot to mention, you need to put that stuff on the tailgate." She went to point, but almost dropped the baby. "Oh, sorry. I'm pretty good with babies, normally, you can trust me."

"It's not you," Sarah lied, hopping down and taking back Eve. "She's just safer in the truck. What if a zombie comes up? You see?"

"I have magic marbles," Jillybean said.

It took a moment for the words to sink in, though understanding failed to follow. Sarah asked, "Magic what?

Marbles? Babies can't have marbles. They'll choke on them."

Jillybean sighed. "You don't get it. The marbles are used against the monsters. You see? Not babies. And especially not this baby. She is supposed to be my little sister."

Sister! Who was this kid? None of what the girl was saying made any sense and it caused Sarah to stand there speechless. Eventually, Jillybean sighed again and pointed at the truck. "It's ready. Ipes says to floor it, which means go fast. I'll hold the baby if you want."

"That's ok, but, thank you," Sarah said and put the baby back on the floor, making sure to bundle her tight. She then started the truck and easily drove it off the median. In minutes the back of the truck was righted and a shaking Shondra was in the passenger seat, while a quiet Jillybean sat in the back.

"Are you worried about Ram?" Sarah asked the little girl. "You shouldn't be. He's an extremely capable person. He can take care of himself."

"He can't, not really," Jillybean replied. "He's like everyone else. He can't take care of himself."

Figuring it was best not to get into an argument with her, Sarah only smiled briefly before turning back to the road. They found Ram minutes later. Amazingly, he was leading a black Range Rover that she recognized immediately—it was Mark's SUV!

With a feeling of wild joy, Sarah was out of the truck in a flash and running to see her husband and Sadie…only Sadie wasn't there, and Neil looked like he was about to throw up.

In less than a minute, he explained how Sadie had been kidnapped by a, as he put it, "crazy-assed cult" and was being held against her will. "They'll trade for her though," Neil said as a way of re-assuring Sarah. She had been feeling lighter and lighter in the head with every word her husband uttered.

"But we don't have anything to trade," Sarah cried. How quickly she had gone from joy to crushing despair. She felt like she'd stepped off a cliff.

"No," Neil said, taking her hand. "They don't want stuff. They want…" Just then he noticed Shondra and Jillybean for the first time. He pointed at the two females. "They'll trade for one of them."

Chapter 29

Neil

Atlanta, Georgia

"Hell no!" Shondra exclaimed.

The six of them, Eve was snoring contentedly in the F-250 now that the shooting was over, stood in the middle of an intersection just down the street from the CDC. Shondra still held her .38 Police Special. It had been an afterthought but now she gripped it with two hands, clutched to her bosom.

"You can't make me join into some cult," she insisted.

Neil put out his hands hoping to calm her. It didn't work. His hands shook and his eyes were big circles of crazy. Out of fear for his daughter, he was beyond desperation and into a territory of mental aberration he had never experienced before.

"No, it's not a cult," he pleaded. "I misspoke. They believe in God, sure, but that doesn't make them a cult. It's actually really cool. They have this underground city that is completely safe and the people are happy. And they have food! I didn't mention the food before. They have so much food that some people are getting kind of chubby."

All this spewed out of his mouth in seconds as the sentences accordioned in on themselves, running one over the other.

In the gloom of night, Shondra's normally dark face was impossible to read, but her tone spoke volumes. "I'm sure it's just lollipop heaven," she said, sarcastically. "If it's so great then why doesn't Sadie want to stay?"

"Because," Neil said, his mind floundering. "She is…uh. They want to…uh. I don't know. She wants to be with her family?"

"Find somebody else to trade," Shondra stated flatly.

Just then that somebody else spoke up. "Excuse me,"

Jillybean said, raising her hand as if she were at school. "There are monsters coming from right over there." She indicated an open area; there were indeed a few zombies heading towards them. Everyone followed her pointing finger, but Neil.

He stared at Jillybean in amazement. She was a miracle in his eyes. This was how he was going to get his Sadie back—he just had to play his cards right. With Shondra he had let his emotions, and the crazy sensation that was overwhelming his thinking show on his face. With this girl he would try another track. The little girl wasn't just thin, she looked as if she had just been liberated from a Nazi concentration camp. Her eyes were wide and blue in her thin face, while her cheek bones rose up like little apples. Even the bones and cartilage in her neck stood out in rings beneath her tight skin.

"I wasn't kidding about the food there," he said quietly, wondering if this was how child molesters spoke. "I had the best meal in a year. We had sausage and eggs and toast with jelly. And milk! I bet they had strawberry milk too, but I didn't ask. Do you like strawberry milk, uh…?"

"Jillybean," she said.

Her odd name caused him to pause but only a second. "Do you like strawberry milk, Jillybean?"

Before she could answer, Ram said, "Neil." The one word carried a warning in it. Sarah stepped all over it. She pointed at the zombies and taking Ram's arm she gave him a gentle nudge.

"Can you stop them, please?" she asked. "I've had enough of zombies for one night." She looked it. Neil had never seen her more of a mess. The front of her pink shirt and jeans were covered in tar or oil, and her left hand dripped red blood, while her right was so black with zombie blood it looked as though she had fished about in the guts of one.

Ram glanced at her in surprise and answered. "Sure.

Ok. I'll be right back."

The second he was gone Neil started back in immediately. "They have everything, Jillybean. Like I said they had chicken and hamburgers and milk and bread. Did I mention the bread? It smelled so good you wouldn't believe. You like bread." It was a statement, not a question.

"Yes, I do like bread," Jillybean admitted, guardedly. "But that doesn't mean…"

"And I forgot to mention the animals," Neil said, interrupting. "They have flocks of sheep and cows and goats. Have you ever seen a baby goat? They are darling. I bet they'd let you pet them and feed them. Would you like that?"

She nodded but her face was in pain. "I do, real bad, but Ipes says cults aren't good for me. He says that if the black lady doesn't like them and you don't like them, then I shouldn't like them."

"Ipes?"

Sarah stepped to his side and pointed at the stuffed animal Jillybean carried. "It's the zebra, I think."

"Oh, Ipes said that?" Neil asked. "I bet Ipes didn't know that Christianity was once called a cult too, and now I bet you're a Christian. You celebrate Christmas, right?" When Jillybean nodded, Neil did too. "That makes you a Christian. I'm a Christian also. So you see a cult isn't always bad…"

Shondra made a noise of disgust and said, "I can't believe you're going to try trick a little girl into thinking cults are good things! If it's so good, why don't you want your daughter joining one?"

Neil's eyes flared with heat. "You don't know what you're talking about. Ask Mark. Did anyone look unhappy there, or scared, or abused?"

Mark stood, edged in close, practically touching Neil. "The only person who was scared was Sadie. And it was probably because everything was so new," he said.

"I'm not going to be a part of this bullshit," Shondra seethed. "I'll wait in the truck until you're done brainwashing this poor girl."

For all his life Neil was a *nice guy*. But not then. The life of his daughter hung in the balance and so far he hadn't said anything that wasn't precisely untrue. "Then go," he demanded. "Get the hell out of here, but don't forget the girl. She's your responsibility now, since you care so much."

Shondra hesitated as Neil knew she would. There were no secrets in a community as small as the CDC: Shondra could barely take care of herself. Even owning a cat was beyond her.

Neil sneered and said, "Go on. She's yours. We all know Ram won't keep her. That's not the way he is. And I can't take her; I have my own family to watch over. So it's up to you to feed her and clothe her and protect her from the zombies. Go on, take her." Neil even went so far as to give Jilly a push in Shondra's direction.

The black lady stepped back.

"That's what I'm talking about," Neil said, making his own noise of disgust. He went to one knee and turned Jillybean so he could look her in the face; her skin was now so pale there was a spectral sheen to it. "Here's the truth: I want my daughter back and she wants to come home. Do you understand, Jillybean? About family? Do you understand what a father would do to get his girl back?"

In the second before she could answer Ram arrived in a mood that matched the black blood he was covered in. With one arm he yanked Neil to his feet. "You've got some nerve!" he bellowed so loudly that every zombie within a mile must have heard. Without effort he threw Neil to the ground effortlessly and stood over him with his fists balled.

"He is right, Mister Ram," Jillybean said in a voice that was as quiet as his had been loud. Everyone turned to stare. She stepped back, squeezing the zebra tight to her chest. "My daddy would have done anything to save me."

"That doesn't give Neil the right to act this way," Ram said.

"What way?" Neil demanded. "This is Sadie I'm talking about! Will you cast her away after everything she's done for you? She risked her life for your baby for goodness sakes. Do you remember what you told her?" Ram's anger wilted before their eyes. Neil went on, nodding, knowing that he had won, "You said if there was *anything* you could do to repay her, you would do it. This is something you could do, Ram."

The night was quiet save for the pattering of rain and the distant haunting moans that they had all come to live with.

"That baby is yours?" Jillybean asked Ram, her head wagging in confusion. "I thought she was his and hers."

"It's a long story," Ram told her. "I had a woman and…"

Neil interrupted, "And he gave up his baby when she died. It's not a long story. You told Sadie you could never repay her, but now you can. Ram, please, at least come look at this place before you make a decision."

Sarah touched his arm, adding, "And it's not like the CDC is safe anymore. It's empty. The germs got out and everyone has runaway. We may be too close even now."

"Then why the hell have we been standing here?" Shondra asked, drawing a sleeve to her face.

"Because I need a girl," Neil said. "This place Sadie is at may be a cult, but I don't know if it's a bad one. It's weird. That's the truth. The leader wants balance. He wants there to be a male for every female. It's got something to do with harmony is all I know."

"I'll do it," Jillybean said. Her face was down, her chin resting on her chest. "I thought I was going to live here, with you, Mister Ram, but…but you were going to give me away, weren't you? You said I'd be a big sister. That means you were going to give me to these people."

"I wanted you to have a family," Ram told her. "A real family, with a real mom and dad. Honestly, they aren't normally like this." He scowled at Neil.

She shook her head. "Ipes thinks you're wrong and I do, too. They're always like this, but only for their own babies….not for me. I think I want to go to the cult. It's better than being alone."

"No. I'll take care of you. You won't be alone," Ram said. "Ever. I mean it."

He went to one knee and the little girl crushed into him, but then she drew back, her face wet. "My daddy said that too, and you're like him. You'll end up dying for me and I'll end up alone." She pulled away completely and went to Neil. Without looking beyond the tips of her toes she held up a hand. "You'll take me to that place?"

The hand was so tiny and delicate. Neil was suddenly afraid to take it as if his touch would doom her, as if his skin was poison, as if he was leading her to a sacrificial alter where she would be drained of what little blood her frail body possessed.

She saw the swift doubt and took his hand. "It'll be ok as long as they let me keep Ipes. Do you think they will?"

Neil gave a shrug. "I don't see why not."

"Hold on!" Ram cried. "I haven't okayed this. You just can't take her."

"I don't know if you have any say-so in this matter," Neil shot back, standing as tall as he could, going stiff in the spine. "Ten minutes ago you were going to give her to Sarah and me. Are you now claiming some sort of parental right? We both know that alone you're not really father material." When Ram hesitated, Neil begged, "Come and look at their facilities before you make up your mind, please. That's all I ask."

Ram dropped his head, agreeing without a word.

Chapter 30

Jillybean

New Eden, Georgia

We can escape any time you wish, Ipes said, under his breath so that only Jillybean heard. *Just say the word*.

All during the ride through the zombie-clogged city streets and the hauntingly-empty outer suburbs, the zebra had kept an eye out for a chance to make a break for freedom. He was dead set against the notion of a cult.

It's a doomsday cult, just one with good timing. What would your father think? he asked.

Jillybean refused to answer. Whenever she talked to Ipes, the adults would stop their conversation and glance back with worry in their eyes. They did not understand about Ipes, nor could they hear him.

The adults talked about their days apart. Neil told them about his adventure with the cultist, and Sarah told about being abandoned by an entire fortified base. Shondra spoke about how she had left her CDC apartment to hide some food and had come back to a ghost town.

Ram talked about Jillybean. He talked about how she had saved him time and again—sometimes he went quiet in the middle of a word and it was minutes before he could pick up the story again. He spoke little of his own heroics as if they were nothing.

Eventually, Jillybean fell asleep as Ram was telling how they found the second boat. For her that had been a dull time. It took them an hour to rig the spare sail and then six more frustrating hours were spent trying to eat up the distance between the two boats. They were separated by only a mile, but it took them the rest of the morning, zigzagging across the ocean. Ram wasn't much of a sailor and frequently worked his rudder and boom at cross purposes. He got so cranky that Jillybean thought it prudent not to point this out.

The find, a fully-fueled motorboat, had been worth it. From the moment they boarded it they fairly flew all the way to the CDC; first by the boat and then on the motorcycle. The closer they got the more Jillybean grew excited. Ram had been vague with the details but he held forth the promise of a family and a home.

You'll see, he would say. What he should have said was: *You'll see that I don't really want you*. It was a blow to her heart when she realized the truth.

With the sound of the truck's roar lulling her, she slept for a few hours in a vague, dreamless way until she was woken by Ram. "We're here. It's time to get up."

For a few seconds she had no idea where they were, or what they were doing, or even who the other people were around them, or why she was feeling an elusive sensation of disappointment with Ram. Then the baby gave a little pouty cry and Jillybean's mind kicked back into gear.

She remembered that she was there to be traded: one human for another.

Ram shook her again. "I'm getting up," she said in clipped tones. She kicked off the blanket she had been given and slipped out of the Range Rover into the night…or was it morning? There was an indistinct purple hue to the eastern sky, suggesting the latter.

"Where is this place?" Ram asked, taking a peek at Jillybean before glancing around.

They were out in the country with the only man-made structure anywhere around them being a grain silo. Neil gestured to it. "They're watching right now," he said, waving in a friendly fashion. "Also, they're armed to the teeth so no heroics."

Ram glanced again at Jillybean, but she refused to meet his eye, so he dropped down beside her. "I'm sorry if I misled you about being your father. You saw me on the boat; I have a short fuse. And I don't know anything about raising girls—lipstick and shoes and bras, I'm not good at that sort of thing. But Neil is and Sarah is even better."

"But they're not going to be my parents, are they?" He shook his head at the question. She followed it up with: "Ipes says you sold us a bill of goods!"

"He did, huh?" Ram asked. "Do you even know what that means?"

It means he over-represented the state of things, Ipes told her. When she hesitated, the zebra added, *Or you can just say he lied*.

This she understood. "It means you lied...about the state of things. Now, I'm not even going to be their daughter."

"I haven't agreed to any of this yet," Ram cautioned.

"It doesn't matter what you agreed to," Jillybean said. "I'll never be their daughter. If I don't go through with this and you give me to them, they'll always look at me as the chicken-girl who wouldn't help save their *real* daughter. No thank you."

"You remind me of Sadie," Ram said. "She's very tough and..."

Just then the door to the silo swung open showing five men armed with black weapons. One of them stepped forward and ordered: "Leave y'alls guns in the cars and come forward one at a time. We is gonna frisk y'all."

Run! Ipes cried. *While everyone is turned away! Now's our chance.*

"No," whispered Jillybean. She didn't discount the idea of running, just not yet. First she would check out the cult and if it was too crazy she would pick a good opportunity and run.

Since she wasn't armed and she was mad at Ram and didn't want to be near him just then, Jillybean walked up first. "Do you allow zebras in?"

The leader of the squad was big and quite a bit scarier than she had anticipated. He dropped to a knee and asked,

"Is he carrying a gun?"

"No. Me neither," Jilly replied.

He gave her a speedy pat-down and said, "He can come in if he can pull a plow. Go stand over there."

He pointed next to one of the men and as she went, Ipes begged her to run. *Do I look like a common plough horse? I am a zebra! Zebras don't plough. We're known for our beauty and quick wit. Jilly, you have to get us out of here.*

"Shh," Jillybean hissed.

In short order they were all frisked and headed down into a well-lit tunnel. Ram insisted on walking next to her, but she kept her arms folded around Ipes and tried to pretend Ram wasn't there.

"This isn't bad," he said on more than one occasion. Despite her anger at him, and her anxiety, Jillybean had to agree. Everything was clean, bright and warm—a big change from the last eight months of her life.

Eventually, after a few turns that Ipes committed to her memory, they came to a wide double-door which led into what was undoubtedly a church of some sort. It was a room shaped like an inverted pyramid. Down the many stairs was an altar of white marble and next to it was a pool of water. It was clear and pretty with a shining silver base. It would've been inviting to Jillybean except she had the sinking feeling that they would dunk her in it. She had seen something like that on TV once—it didn't look fun, mainly because everyone went in "backwards" with their noses to the ceiling, something she feared as much as monsters.

Down the rows was a carpeted aisle with a brass banister on one side. Ram let her take the metal in hand as they descended in an uncomfortable silence. Hundreds of people dressed all in white sat looking up at them.

"Come and join the family of Believers." A tall man with gobs of silver hair beckoned from next to the altar.

What a perv, Ipes remarked. *Can you say child-bride?* The sarcasm was lost on Jillybean. The year before, one of her friends, Mary Greenfeld, had been married to a boy name Taylor in a ceremony held under the slide at recess. Though their marriage hadn't lasted a week it had been a fun time.

"What do you think, Jillybean?" Ram asked.

He seemed very, very tall when she looked up at him, like he had stretched somehow. As she stared, she found that her anger left her completely, leaving only a growing fear in its place. She reached out with a shaking hand to grab his steady one and said, "I don't know. Ok, I guess."

"I know what you mean," he whispered. "It looks alright and the people seem ok, but I don't like it." Regardless he began walking down the steps. Behind them the others followed: Neil and Sarah holding Eve, and behind them, Mark and Shondra.

"The Lord welcomes you to his home," the man with the silver hair announced. "Give thanks and praise."

The people in white cried out: "Amen!" as though they had but a single voice like a giant. All the people, save one: a girl with black hair who sat somewhat apart from the rest; she jerked in her seat at the roar of the crowd. She wouldn't take her eyes off Jillybean.

"Are you her?" the girl asked when Jillybean had run out of steps to descend.

"I guess so," Jillybean answered after taking a deep breath. "Is it scary?"

Sadie did an odd thing then: she laughed high and loud even though there were tears in her eyes. "No, it's not scary. At least not for you, cuz you get to go home. I think I'll stay...but thanks for coming. Neil, thanks so much for trying, and Sarah...I love you. Ram, you too. And, can I see the baby one more time?"

This she asked of the man with the silver hair. He nodded easily, not the least unhappy with the choice. Sadie kissed Eve who ogled everything around her with big eyes and tried to grab Sadie's nose with a pudgy fist.

Sarah whispered, "Sadie, no. We have a substitute.

Come home with us."

Sadie hugged her tight and said, "I won't do this to a little girl."

No one knew what to say to this, especially Jillybean. What was happening? Was she going to be able to stay with Ram after all? And did he really want her to? She didn't think so, but at the same time he had such a grip on her hand as if he would never let go.

"I take it, Neil, you won't all be staying and joining the family of believers?" the man with the silver hair asked with disappointment in his voice. Neil shook his head and the man smiled sadly. "*New Eden* is always open to Believers, Neil. This is a safe place for Believers, but only for Believers. Do not return unless you're ready to join, for I now name you Denier."

Neil blanched. "But you said…"

"I said nothing!" the man thundered in a voice that shook the very water in the pool. "I am but a vessel. The Lord our God speaks through me and his word is law. He has twice now shown you his love by allowing you into our midst. You have seen, but you do not embrace his glorious gift! What is that if not denial? The same is true for these with you. Look upon the grace of our Lord and see his bounty, his love, his wisdom. It is through him that we are safe!"

"Amen," the people shouted.

"It is through him that we are fed!"

"Amen," the people shouted.

"It is only through him that we know the beauty of love!"

"Amen," the people shouted.

"Come and join our family," the man commanded with arms raised. "Or forever be hunted as a Denier. And know this, the Lord our God will not be deceived. He is all knowing and all-seeing! You may hide, but according to his desire, you will die at the hands of the blessed. What have you to say?"

Though he addressed all of them, only Ipes answered: *I say you're as nutty as squirrel poo.* Jillybean almost choked. She cowered into Ram's leg and hid herself, just in case "The Lord our God" heard the zebra's blasphemy.

The room was quiet for an agonizing minute, during which the crowd seemed to lean in toward the group. Some even moved into the aisle to block their one line of retreat.

"They have eyes, but they do not see. They have ears, but they do not hear. Nor is there any breath at all in their mouths!" the man intoned, low at first but with growing strength in his voice.

"Amen," the people said—this time without the excited fervor. The word seemed more like a curse.

"Sad," Abraham said. He shook his head to clear the gloom and brought out a fresh smile. Just like that, the mood lifted in the room. "Stand clear of the dead, Sadie, for you are most fortunate. Your friends will die in their allotted time, but you will live forever in the kingdom of God." He came to stand behind her and to Jillybean it looked as though he would pull her throat back and slit it open with a knife. Perhaps it was the low angle that created the illusion because clearly not everyone saw it.

"Wait!" cried Shondra. "I want to take her place." She pushed past Neil and nearly bowled Jillybean over in her haste to get to the altar. "Will you take me instead? Please, I don't want to be hunted. I don't want to go back out there with the zombies. I want to be a Believer."

"That is up to Sadie," the man said. Gone was the thundering voice, now he was pure sugar. "Will you become a Denier and one of the hunted, Sadie? Or will you stay here with your true family?"

Sadie looked about to faint; she swayed like a willow in a stiff breeze. "I…I want to go with them, if that's ok?"

It clearly wasn't. To Jillybean it seemed as though the man with the silver hair was like a toddler fuming into a volcanic tantrum. "Go then. Live your last days as a denier," he said icily. "Today, we will weep for you; tomorrow you will be as the dead."

"Yes, thank you," Neil said lamely. He backed away and shooed the others on. Ram and Mark took positions on either side of Sadie who walked with a limp. They propelled her up the stairs, lagging in the rear, while Sarah led the way at a speed that bordered on a rude dash.

When they reached the top of the stairs, the men who had brought them in did not stop them, nor did they direct them. They only glared. "Thanks, have a good night," Sarah said, wearing a painfully false smile. The glares intensified.

In the corridor they were on their own. "Do they want us to get lost?" Sarah asked.

It was a rhetorical question, however Jillybean didn't understand the concept. She'd been taught that when an adult asked a question you answered, even if the answer was *I don't know*.

"I don't know," she replied, doing her duty. "But you are going the wrong way." Sarah had breezed right past an intersection without slowing. On the way in, they had hung a left here. Jillybean pointed to the right. "We have to go this way."

"No, it's the next intersection," Sarah said. She began to march away and Jillybean reached out and took her hand, pulling her back.

"It's this way, Miss Sarah."

Sarah looked back and forth in confusion for a few seconds before she turned to the slower half of their group. "Sadie, how do we get out of here?"

"I don't know," the teen said through gritted teeth. "This place is a freaking maze and *out* is the one direction I wasn't allowed to go."

Jillybean pulled harder on Sarah's hand. "It's this way," she insisted. "Even Ipes agrees."

What are you talking about? the zebra demanded. *I was*

the one who told you.

"I would listen to her," Ram said.

Ram's influence helped; they went to the right. At the next intersection Sarah wanted to stop again. "I'm completely turned around," she said looking at the four corridors. "They all look the same. I have no idea which way we came in."

Jilly pointed straight forward. "Keep going."

A pained expression swept Sarah's features. "How do you know? If we get lost...and they catch us...I don't want even think about what they'll do. That's why I'm a little nervous about taking directions from a...you know, a kid. Do you have a photographic memory or something?"

"I have a memory of taking pictures," Jillybean said helpfully. "My daddy had a digital camera that he liked very much so. He let me use it all the time; said he liked it because now he could take all the pictures he wanted. I guess before he couldn't. There must have been a law maybe."

Sarah listened to this and then stood blinking for a second before asking, "Which way?"

Jillybean guided them the rest of the way and within ten minutes they were outside and climbing into the vehicles. They took both and not a one of them cared in the least that the truck had been Shondra's. She was a Believer now, and in their minds she was as dead and dangerous as a zombie.

Then they were driving hell-bent for the highway, where they paused to discuss where they should go.

The conversation went like this: "Where should we go?" Ram asked. Each of them shrugged, one after the other, including Jillybean. She didn't know where they should go and frankly didn't care, just as long as Ram went too, and just as long as he continued to hold her hand. He hadn't stopped from the moment they had climbed into the Ford F-250.

Chapter 31

Ram

North Bound

The little group did not flee far in that early morning. Each of them felt complete exhaustion on a physical and emotionally level. With the sun cracking the horizon Neil led them to one of the homes they had explored the day before. It came complete with a pond in the back and its own squad of undead that stood about like sentries in front.

These were killed in a semi-silent mode using bats and golf clubs, and in Neil's case an axe. The sounds of splitting heads, a percussionist's nightmare, left even Ram a little queasy. It was a state he discarded minutes later for a deep sleep.

It was late afternoon before the lightest step woke him. It was Jillybean. Without a single word of discussion she had slept with him, cuddled up for the entire day and now there was a little, warm depression in the blankets and she was creeping away.

He made a noise like a warthog's grunt and she turned.

"Gotta go baffroom," she whispered, swaying a little. He couldn't help but smile at her sleepy state. Her fly-away hair had combined itself with bed-head to leave the impression she had slept in a dryer, while her eyes, one cracked open and the other closed, seemed confused as to whether she was awake or still asleep.

Ram opened his mouth to give directions to the bathroom, but closed it again when he realized he had no idea. They were in a bedroom and they had definitely passed through a front door on the way in, but beyond that he didn't know the first thing about the house.

"We'll find it together," he said, standing and taking her hand. It turned out to be the room next door. That it had been used already was evidenced by the biting odor of urine;

neither Ram nor Jillybean paid the least attention. Instead, as habit, each stood guard as the other went.

"I have a can of tuna left for breakfast," she said. He had lost his backpack on the bridge two days before, but she had clung to her *Belieber* backpack with tenacity. "We can share. I won't eat much."

He knew she wouldn't. "Let's see what Neil has," he suggested. They crept down the stairs, Ram's memory of the place coming awake with each step. They found the kitchen right where he expected and found Neil awake and bustling about—again as expected.

"I'm glad you're awake," he whispered. "The sun's only going to be up for a few more hours and I have a treat planned! After the last few days I think we deserve it. Ram, I need a bunch of firewood cut, but be careful the woods are chock full of stiffs. And you, Jillybean, can you fish?"

Her head went side-to-side but her mouth said, "Yeah. Ipes knows how. But I can learn real fast, too, which is real good because Ipes doesn't like touching bugs or fish, and he doesn't like the water, not really. He says he's more of a *Show-pony*, whatever that means."

Neil chuckled and took the little girl by the shoulder, leading her to the back yard. There he showed her the pole he had already set up and the bucket of dirt and worms he had ready. As Ram watched Neil sat on a log at the water's edge and went over the basics of fishing and what to do when she caught a fish.

Excitedly, she made a few casts with the rod. When she successively sent the bobber further than ten feet, Neil declared her ready for a worm.

Ram watched and the strange feeling of jealousy that would later grow to amaze him was then only a hiccup. He went into the forest, keeping just within the tree-line so he could keep an eye on the girl, though why he felt the need he didn't know. She fished, only partially attuned to the water and the pole, the rest of her keen perception she sent outward. The shadow of a chipmunk couldn't creep past without her knowing.

It wasn't long before she caught her first fish. It was so big that it unbalanced her as she leapt up. She took two wobbly steps into the pond before she yanked back on the pole and began to work the reel.

"I know how to do it," she said. "Jeeze, Ipes. You're not the expert on everything."

Ram smiled and began heading her way to help, however she landed the fish before he had taken a dozen steps. With a great deal of splash and flap, mostly on the part of the fish, Jillybean stuck it, still hooked through the mouth, in a bucket. She took both to Neil.

"What a fish!" he exclaimed. "Who knew a pond that small could hold a whale?"

Jillybean looked closer at the fish and said, "That's not a whale. It doesn't have a hole in the top of its head. The hole is where it shoots water at you."

"Really?" Neil asked as he worked the hook free.

"Yep. This is only a normal fish, though it is pretty. Maybe we should put it back. I don't want to eat a real pretty fish...or we can keep it! We can get an acqairdim...acquararium..."

"Aquarium," Neil prompted.

"An aquarium," she replied, sounding out the word slowly to get it right. "We can get one of them and take him with us."

"Fish don't travel well. They get sick easily," Neil told her. "Here's a deal for you. If you catch five more fish, I'll let you free this one."

Eagerly she nodded. This time, Neil had her bait her own hook so that she would learn. In a minute she was back on her log, peering over her knees with her little feet turned inward so that her toes touched.

Ram went back to cutting wood and as he did he wondered what sort of dad he would make. Besides having been a child himself, he had little experience with children. They were a mystery that he had avoided like the plague. he was sure he had been right to give up Eve. There was no question that he lacked the patience to raise a baby, while the hormone-driven battles that swirled around Sadie convinced him that a teenager would be just as bad.

Frequently he marveled at Neil. Practically overnight, he had gone from confirmed bachelor to husband and father of two. Yet he had not only taken it in stride, he had flourished. It wasn't something Ram felt he could replicate.

Then why was he so drawn to Jillybean? Why did he feel the need to protect her and teach her and love her as a father would? Was it her age? Was she at the "good" age that many people referred to.

She's six? Enjoy it while it lasts because pretty soon she'll be a monster who hates you. How many times had he heard comments just like that?

Was it that Jillybean just happened to be between the "terrible twos" and the "torturous teens" that he found her so charming to be near? If so what would happen in a few years' time? Endless arguments? Fights and then fits of silence followed by her running away or hooking up with some loser that would have Ram mulling over the idea of murder?

"I can't keep her, can I?" he asked himself while watching Jillybean carry on a conversation with her zebra. Clearly its smart-aleck nature had come out because in seconds Ipes was sitting with his nose to the rough bark of a pine tree.

Ram stood there watching the little girl catch fish after fish and all the while his heart was like a great weight. He couldn't ever remember feeling the organ in his chest with such force as when he watched Jillybean. He loved her, pure and simple, but would that make him a good father? He was good at fighting for her and making sure that she was fed and warm, but he wasn't like Neil. He wasn't good at the little things; the day-to-day stuff.

"And besides I have a hero complex," he said, catching sight of a zombie advancing on the little girl. Judging by the fact that she sat frozen in place beside the log, she had seen the zombie even before he had. Her eyes sparked with shrewd intelligence. He could see her calculating the odds of having been seen—about sixty-forty in his mind—and what to do if she had been.

Her coltish legs were coiled beneath her body, ready to spring her in any direction. Whether they would need to spring they didn't find out. Before Ram could take even a step, Neil came flying from the kitchen, brandishing the golf club Ram had picked up outside of Savannah the day before.

"Don't watch," Neil ordered Jillybean. She watched regardless, perhaps fearing Neil's attack with a weapon he wasn't familiar with would fail...which it did.

He struck as fearsome a blow as he could manage, and it was indeed powerful, but misaimed. Instead of striking with the weighty head of the club which was deadly, he hit with the hollow shaft and bent it crooked over the top of the zombie's skull.

What would have given pause to the toughest human barely slowed the zombie.

"Run!" cried Neil, turning to flee. Jillybean didn't budge.

"There's a good rock, Mister Neil." She pointed at a hardy chunk of slate.

Neil ran to it, heaved it out of the ground, and then hucked it at the onrushing zombie with a victorious grunt. The zombie caught it full in the face—a non-fatal blow. It was a stunning shot and both the rock and the zombie rebounded away.

With another grunt, Neil hefted the rock a second time. His follow-up attack was an overhand blow that caved in the top of his enemy's skull. It dropped to its knees and for half a minute it spurted black fluid like an oil well.

"Eew," Jillybean said, making a face.

Neil wore the same face, except his was also tinged with green. "Yeah, eew."

She laughed, thinking he'd been joking, and then as if nothing had happened she went back to fishing and he went back to the kitchen. All the while Ram stood in the forest feeling a little useless and more than a little envious. Quickly he gathered an armload of boughs and went down to the pond.

"That's a lot of fish," he said. It was all he could think to say.

"I gotta get two more in order to free Chedrick. That's the fish all by himself in that bucket."

Ram glanced in at the one. It was a forlorn looking bass, puffing his narrow cheeks in and out. "Chedrick? Is that even a name?"

Jillybean snorted. "That's what Ipes asked and he got in trouble. I think everything should have a name. Mister Neil said I could name a fish anything. He said they don't care what it is as long as they get one because they are only born with numbers. Is that true? Is this like, bass number fifty-six?"

"It's probably true if Neil said it," Ram replied.

"Can I tell you a secret?" she asked. When he shrugged and nodded at once, she let out a long sad sigh and said, "I used to not like fish. No, not at all. It was blechy. I like to catch 'em. That's really fun, but I don't like to eat them. And now Mister Neil is all 'cited about making them for me. I don't want to hurt his feelings."

The aforementioned Neil was suddenly there, bent at the waist so that he was smiling directly in Jillybean's face. "You won't hurt my feelings." He had come creeping up in his bright green Crocs—he claimed they were the most comfortable pair of shoes he had ever owned. They were certainly the silliest he had ever owned, as he would also admit. "I think you will like these fish more than you think.

You like tuna and that's a fish."

"It is?" she asked, skeptically. "It says chicken right on the can."

The two men laughed. "I assure you, it's a fish," Neil said. "They call it *Chicken of the Sea* because tuna is so abundant." When her head tilted quizzically, he added, "That means there are lots and lots of them."

This explanation helped, but what really did the trick was the fish itself: lightly fried and breaded. Jillybean ate an entire fish all by herself. She sat at the table in a perfect state of happiness. Not only was the baby right next to her, but Sadie sat across the table. Jillybean was infatuated by the older girl.

"Did you lose all your clothes?" Jillybean asked, running her eyes all over Sadie's black pants and shirt. "I know where we can get you a new dress." Not only was Jillybean wearing the white dress Ram had found for her, she was also truly clean for the first time in months. Neil had hauled in rain water from a barrel and had heated it with rounded river stones he had set in a pan above the fire. To Jillybean's fear and delight, they hissed like angry snakes as he dipped each into the tub.

After her bath, Sarah had toweled her dry and had weaved an intricate braid through her hair. They had to pull her from the mirror to get her to go down to dinner. Ram had napped during all of this.

"I never wear dresses," Sadie told her, after taking a bite of fish. "But thanks. You look real pretty in yours."

"Ipes says I'm showing off, but he's only jealous. Why don't you wear dresses? That doesn't make sense because you're a girl. I like dresses a lot because my mommy wore dresses and she was real pretty too. Thanks for calling me pretty. Why is your hair like that? All poking up everywhere? Ipes says you look like a Tufted Titmouse. That's a bird, not a mouse at all. It has feathers that make it look like it just got out of bed...that's what Ipes says at least."

"I wear what I wear because that's my style," Sadie explained. "Just like being a princess is your style, and sweater vests are Neil's style and scowling is Ram's style. What's wrong, Ram?"

Ram jumped a little. "What? Was I scowling? I guess I'm just worried a little about the future."

"Yeah, me too," Sarah said. "The CDC is contaminated. We have crazies to the south. To the east is ocean and to the west is a big continent filled with zombies."

"There's Fort Riley," Sadie ventured. "As far as we know it's still around."

"I heard a rumor that it isn't," Mark said. He had only picked at his food and hadn't said much of anything since Sadie had been rescued as far as Ram knew.

"We can't live our lives on rumors," Sadie replied sharply.

"It's just really far," Mark said as way of apology.

Neil cleared his throat before saying, "Distance shouldn't be a factor. Something near can be just as dangerous as something far away. Ok we have one suggestion: Fort Riley, Kansas. Anywhere else? Ram?"

"There's Philadelphia," he answered. "I'm pretty sure the *Whites* would take us in, but with Cassie fueling a race-war I wouldn't suggest it. There's also New York. Supposedly there's a settlement..."

Neil and Sadie looked shocked with the idea that Ram had run across Cassie again. Sarah was shocked for a different reason. "What?" Sarah cried. She had been feeding Eve, now, much to the infant's displeasure she pulled back with a spoonful of peaches only inches away.

"Ay do," Eve said, before propping her mouth open in a little circle. She was ignored by everyone but Jillybean who took over the feeding operations, happily.

"There are people still alive in New York?" Sarah asked. "Why didn't you tell me?"

Ram shrugged. "I heard it from a few people while I was in Philadelphia." He explained about the vaccine and the different ways to get a hold of it.

"A thousand cans of food?" Neil asked, blowing air out of his puffed cheeks. "That's going to be hard."

"Five years of hard labor would be worse," Sadie said. "I'd be old by the time I was done."

"I'm going," Sarah declared. For some reason she touched the wood of the table with the tips of her fingers, tapping lightly as if to reassure herself that it was real. "Yeah, I'm going, and you're going too, Neil. We'll go tomorrow."

"Slow down, Honey," Neil said. "We barely have two hundred cans. I wouldn't want to go with less than three thousand."

Sarah blinked. "Three thousand! Are you kidding me? That'll take months and months. My daughter may still be alive. Brittany was in New York when this all started."

"I know," Neil said. "But we have three girls right here who need the vaccine."

Ram had listened to the conversation unfold around him. Now he laughed. It was barely more than a grunt of self-loathing. He hadn't had a single thought about getting a vaccine for Jillybean. Not one. He was sure he would have eventually, but as always Neil beat him to the punch.

Jillybean raised her hand and said, "Ipes doesn't think the girls should get any shots, especially me and Eve. He thinks it's smarter that the grode-up get the shots because they have to fight the monsters. They could get scratched or bitted...and I don't like shots neither."

Sadie laughed: a gut-busting snorty sound. "You're too precious."

"You're precious too," Jillybean shot right back. After a look from Ipes, who was sitting next to her plate, she added, "I mean thank you. Ipes says I should say thank you."

"I want the girls to get the vaccine," Sarah said. "But I

don't want to wait to go. There's no more danger in going and checking things out first than there is hunting all around Georgia for months before going."

"Then I guess it's settled," Neil said. "We're going to New York."

Mark cleared his throat. "I'm not going. It's too dangerous. And it doesn't make sense. What good would a vaccine have done for you, Sadie, when you were surrounded in that field?"

"It would've done a hell of lot more good than you," Sadie said in a dangerous tone. "Why didn't you come with Neil to save me?"

"I...I...that's not the point. My point is we could get eaten alive just trying to get a vaccine that'll save us from a scratch."

"Then what are you going to do?" Sadie demanded. "You think Fort Riley is too far, Philadelphia is too dangerous, and New York doesn't make sense. So what's your plan?"

Mark took a second to push around the fish bones on his plate before he said, "New Eden." This set the entire table into an uproar, except for Eve and Jillybean who watched with big eyes. "I don't think we gave it much of a chance," Mark explained. "It's safe, you have to give them credit for that. And there's food and light and everything."

"It's safe alright," Ram growled. "Right up until they begin human sacrifices to get it to rain or something."

"Abraham said they wouldn't do that," Mark said, defensively.

"He also said we wouldn't be hunted as Deniers," Neil cried, thumping the table. "Mark, come on! What about the harmony crap they insist on? You'll need a female and no one here is going."

"I know," Mark replied. "I'm sure there are some women who had been at the CDC still nearby."

Sadie shook her head in angry wonder, while Neil

shrugged; his way of giving up. Ram decided he would keep a close eye on Mark until they parted ways. He assumed this would be at first light the following morning since Sarah was so anxious to go. However they were delayed when Neil refused to leave Mark high and dry. Everyone else was happy to take both vehicles, all the food, and all but one of the guns. Especially Sadie, who positively smoldered in anger over the subject of Mark.

At sunrise, Mark and Neil left to find a new vehicle for him. Mark tried to claim that the Range Rover was his, but was ignored. Sadie had given all the argument necessary: "The registration says John Rosen, and that ain't you."

While they were gone, Ram tried to engage Jillybean, however she was too busy playing with Eve, as well as snacking.

"I gotta fill my hump," she explained when Sadie had expressed amazement how much the little girl could put away.

Ram chuckled at this, and he sighed when she kept Eve from crying by blowing in her face, and he straight up laughed when Eve spat her pacifier out onto the floor and Jillybean cleaned it off by sticking it in her own mouth. And he knew it would be time to leave again soon when Neil returned carrying a doll nearly Jillybean's size. It was almost an exact replica of her as well, right down to the peculiar blue of her eyes and her brown, fly-away hair.

"I can't compete," Ram said under his breath. Without even trying, Neil was twice the father Ram would ever be. "I'm just not father material. At best I'm a mediocre uncle, and she deserves so much more than that."

She deserved not only a fantastic dad like Neil, but also a fierce mother like Sarah and a brave big sister like Sadie. Ram also realized that as long as he was around things would be messy.

He packed the truck for one, though no one noticed, as he hid the fact that the Ford's bed was empty by covering it with a blue tarp. The great majority of their worldly possessions was stacked neatly on the luggage rack of the Rover and tied down tight.

At about ten, they left Mark standing in the doorway to the little house. The man whined incessantly about how little they were leaving him to get by on. Sadie pointed out that they were leaving him with an entire pond full of fresh fish and all the zombie meat he could stomach. When Neil commented on the harshness of her statement, Sadie rounded on him quickly.

"He left me to die," she said. "One day he's telling me he loves me and the next he abandons me. And he did the same thing to you, Neil. He let you run out into that field all alone. And now he's abandoning all of us! He's lucky we even let him keep a gun."

"We don't know his heart and we don't know what he's been through," Neil said. "I won't judge him."

"Besides, his leaving may help you guys," Ram said. "It's one less person bidding up the price of the vaccines."

No one caught the fact that he hadn't said *us*.

All that day they wound through the maze of roads heading north through Georgia, the eastern shank of Tennessee and up into Kentucky. Ram drove the truck with only Sadie as a companion. Jillybean rode in the cargo area of the Rover, which Neil had turned into a combination crib/playpen. She, Ipes, and Eve spent the day playing, or napping, or just staring out the window.

That night they made camp east of Lexington in what Ram felt was an appropriate and nostalgic local: a big red barn. It was safe and warm and for Ram, sad. It would be the last night Jillybean ever slept curled up to him.

At first light they took to the fog-bound mountain roads of the Appalachians. Though there were a number of places where the roads were partially blocked with cars or fallen trees, they made better than average time since they weren't stopping every ten minutes to hunt for gas or food. They had plenty to get them to New York...or Philadelphia. Ram decided that he would have to begin his hunt for Cassie once more. She had to die and not just to satisfy vengeance, but also to save lives. Without her hate fueling the race war it would likely die out.

In Harrisburg, Pennsylvania Ram flashed his lights and pulled in behind the Range Rover.

"Was I speeding, Officer?" Neil joked as any real dad would.

Ram could barely muster even a polite smile, his insides were too torn up. "I just wanted to say good-bye."

Chapter 32

Neil

New York City

"You ok, Jillybean?" Neil asked in a gentle voice. There was a pause before Sadie glanced back to the cargo area at the mass of soft blankets and children's toys.

"She's 'sleeping', the poor thing," Sadie said, using air quotes.

"Damn it, Ram," Neil swore in an undertone. Sarah reached out and squeezed his hand, reassuring her husband. He could barely muster a curl to his lips as way of a smiling back.

Losing Mark had been more of a blessing than anything else. Despite all of Neil's propping, he was always going to be a chicken-shit.

Slowing the Rover to slalom around a jack-knifed semi-truck, Neil let out a snort of derisive laughter. Who would have ever thought that he, Neil Martin, the world's biggest wimp, would ever be in a position to call another man chicken?

It was good riddance as far as Mark was concerned, but Ram's departure was another story altogether. His leaving to hunt down Cassie was bravery to the point of foolishness. It was terrible timing as well, especially as Neil figured he would need a good dose of foolish bravery on his side when they got to New York.

New York scared him. Before the apocalypse, it had been the most densely populated city in America, a fact that would suggest that now it would hold the greatest number of zombies.

Cassie's not worth it, Neil had rationalized.
Let sleeping dogs lie, Sarah had suggested.
Kill the bitch, Sadie had said through gritted teeth.
Neil had pleaded with Ram, but his words were

meaningless compared to what was left unspoken.
Jillybean's wet, blue eyes had begged: *Don't leave me!*

"You know there's a bad person in Philadelphia I've got to deal with," Ram had told her, getting down to one knee to look her in the face. "If she's not stopped, more people will die. I can't let that happen, just like I can't leave you all alone. You'll have Mister Neil and Miss Sarah. They're the best parents in the whole world. And you'll have Sadie. You can trust her with your life."

"You need me," Jillybean stated baldly.

"I need you to be safe and cared for," Ram told her. "When I'm done with Cassie, I'll be back." At this, the little girl had fled to hide in the back of the Rover, where she refused to speak or even peek out of thr blanket fort she had made there.

When Ram had finished kissing Sarah and Sadie goodbye, Neil pulled him aside. "What's going on for real?"

"Cassie is a danger...but it's also Jillybean," Ram admitted. "I'm not father material, remember?"

"I was wrong," Neil said. "I was going out of my head out of fear for Sadie when I said that."

Ram had blown out like a bull. "You weren't wrong. I'm not father material, but you are, Neil. Jillybean needs that. The problem is, she's too attached to me. I figure a clean break would help; just for a week or two. I'll take care of business and come back. By then you'll have stol...you'll have worked your magic, I mean. And there won't be an issue."

He had ended the conversation with an awkward hug for each of them. The only one going without was Jillybean. She had burrowed into the blankets so deeply that only some of her wispy hair showed.

Since then she hadn't budged and Neil got the feeling she had slipped from fake sleep into actual sleep. They all drowsed as the sun dipped ever lower in the west.

It had been Neil's plan to drive for two hours before

looking for a place to hole up for the night. The state of the roads changed the plan. With every mile closer to New York the obstructions became fewer. When his two hours had expired he was just west of Manhattan seeing the old familiar view of the city skyline. Had this been a family vacation in the year 2012, he would have woken Jillybean to let her see. Instead he let her sleep. The city looked dead and depressing, like an immense graveyard. It gave him a shiver.

They drove without interruption all the way to the George Washington Bridge and here Neil fully expected to find the way blocked. Instead the cars had been pushed aside forming a single traffic lane that fed them directly into the city.

"Does anyone else feel like we're heading into a trap?" Sadie asked.

"A little," Neil said. "Though from a business point standpoint it makes sense. You want customers to be able to come right to your door."

The lane did just that, though it wasn't exactly inviting.

New York was no longer a city of lights and garish neon, or of hustle and bustle. It was grey. The entire city from the buildings, to the streets, to the zombies was lifeless and grey. Everything but the deep shadows that pooled at the base of the buildings. These were black and cold. They stirred as though alive with the movement of the undead.

As Neil feared, there were plenty of zombies. They were like grey waves that washed around buildings and stalled-out cars. They swept up to the fencing that penned off the lane and bowed it in. Where it looked like the fence wouldn't stand the onslaught of the undead, Neil stomped the gas, leaving them to struggle to catch up.

Sometimes the odd one would squeak under the fence by accident. If they got in Neil's way he would grind them under the wheels of the Rover; if not they went ignored.

With their speed they crossed to east side of the island very quickly, finding themselves at a stretch of concrete.

"The FDR," Neil said, fondly. "I was in a taxicab that was car-jacked on the FDR six years ago. Yeah, this guy just came up with a gun and kicked out the driver, but for some reason he wouldn't let me out. He drove me all the way to the Bronx. The messed up thing was that the cab company made me pay the entire fare, even the part up to the Bronx! Isn't that funny?"

"Yeah, that's funny," Sarah said. She wasn't smiling however, instead she chewed at the inside of her lip. "Neil...where's Long Island?"

He pointed straight ahead. "All of that's Long Island. It goes for like fifty miles. Maybe more. If your daughter's not at wherever this lane leads to, we'll need an address if we're going to have any hope of finding her. Not to mention a way to get across the East River."

Just at the moment they had only one option when it came to driving: a hard turn south on the FDR. The highway hugged the East River, hanging over it for a spell; they followed it for only a mile before they came to a massive set of iron gates that stretched across the lane.

"That's new," Neil said, unnecessarily. The gate opened as the Rover approached and closed again the second they had cleared the track.

On this side of the gate the debris on the highway had been pushed back forming what appeared to be a large square parking lot. From a squat shack of new concrete blocks at the back of the lot, a man in a black uniform emerged. In one hand he carried a clipboard, while the other rested on a gun at his hip.

"Is this where we get vaccines?" Neil asked, with a polite smile.

"Do I look like a fucking nurse?" the man replied. Before Neil could do more than splutter, the man shoved the clipboard at him. "Fill it out completely."

"Wait," Neil said in a rush. He jumped out of the Rover and hurried after the man who was already halfway back to the little building. "Wait, I don't know if we want to go in just yet."

"Well, you can't stay here," the man replied. He pointed ahead to where there were two more of the huge gates. "You got two choices: that way sends you back out into the world and the other one sends you onto receiving where your items are inventoried for trade."

"Can't I leave the car here for a bit?" Neil asked. "You see, we don't know if we want to go in or not. I'd like to check it out."

The man gave Neil a long look, before glancing back at the shack. Making sure they wouldn't be overheard, he said in a whisper, "Maybe we could cut a deal. Ten bullets buys you an hour of free parking. You still got to obey the rules though, no weapons inside."

Was that a good price? Neil wondered. Ten bullets seemed like a lot to leave his car sitting in an empty lot. "Six bullets," he countered. "Or I come back in the morning and take my chances with the next shift."

"Fine, I'll take six, but one hour only. After that, I'll have you towed."

"Good, good," Neil said, eager to please. From his spare clip, he thumbed out the brass and dropped them into the man's hand. He then went back to the Rover and put his gun on the driver's seat. "He's giving me an hour to check this out, he said to Sarah and Sadie.

"Do you want me to come with?" Sadie asked. "Someone should watch your back."

Neil shook his head. "Better you stay and keep Sarah company. I don't want her out all here by herself. Besides, I think everything will be cool. They're traders, right? Not mercenaries." Under his breath he added: *"I hope."*

The man in the black uniform frisked Neil and then pointed him along a walkway that extended straight down to the river and to what looked like a cruise ship. It wasn't one of the mega-ships; still he found himself, minutes later, high over the water on a gangplank that swayed under him as he walked. It shimmied as well, as though it were held together with string.

Neil's hands gripped the rope runners on either side of the footpath and an actual sigh of relief escaped him when he made it to the ship.

It was a close vessel with not a lot of room to spare and what room Neil could see was taken up by people. People of every sort leaned against the white hull, or stretched out on the decks, or squatted in passageways that were so narrow Neil had to turn sideways to get by. There were so many people that the boat stank of them.

Along with the stink, what stood out the most was the proliferations of signs. The majority were unofficial, asking if anyone had seen this or that person—usually offering a reward for verifiable information. These notes were of every color, shape, and size and were hung on every available surface, giving the cruise ship a Gypsy air.

More formal signs sent him to a converted casino, and though they were official looking--uniform in size and color, the signs didn't make much sense:

Receiving: Less Than Minimum
Receiving: 1-3 K
Receiving: Over 3 K
Receiving: Manservant Category A
Receiving: Manservant Category B
Receiving: Manservant Category C

Neil wandered around the casino in a daze, oblivious to the sudden stir he caused about him. When his confusion meter went into the red, he found another man in a black uniform.

"Can you help me? I'm looking to ask..."

The man cut him off, "Where is yellow form?"

"My form?" Neil asked. The man had a thick Russian accent that turned *form* into something that sounded like *foam*. "Did you say form? It's, uh, my wife has it back at the uh, where you do the uh..." Neil pointed back the way he came.

"You can't get far without form," the man said. "Though at time like this you won't get far at all."

"A time like what?"

"Huh? You cannot read?" The man gestured with a wave of his arm toward all the signs. Neil made to complain but then saw that the man had finished his gesture by pointing at the smallest of the signs: *Receiving Hours 9-6*.

"What about to..."

"No exceptions to rule." Abruptly he left.

Neil turned to watch him go and came face to...chest with a very tall black man. The smaller man turned his pallid brow up and gaped.

The stranger stared back angrily. "Neil Martin?" he asked as if it was an accusation.

"Yes, that's me," Neil said. The thought of lying didn't enter his head even for a second.

"Follow me."

Through the thicket of humanity the man marched off with strides so long that Neil had to jog every fifth step in order to keep up. "Where are we going?" he asked, puffing with the urgency of their speed. "And how do you know me? Excuse me? Sir? Can you slow down?"

The man ignored him and went on with his particular pace until Neil was red in the face, as well as completely baffled as to where they were or really, where they had been. Finally Neil lost his patience. "Look! Mister, I'm not going any further until you tell me what's..."

Before Neil could utter the last word, the man had spun and seized Neil by the collar of his coat. "Listen up, you little shit. You're coming with me and that's that, and if I get any more of your lip you'll be sorry."

Neil wasn't the coward he had been in the old days. In the last eight months he had found a modicum of courage within his heart, and now, with so many people staring at the sudden entertainment, he didn't feel as though he should back down so easily. After all there were more of the black-garbed men in attendance. They had to represent some sort of authority.

"I don't think what you say is altogether true," Neil said, doing his best not to stutter with his fear. "I will decide where I go and when."

Though a ghost of a smile played on the man's lips, his eyes were hard, as was his voice: "The only choice you have is if you come along with your teeth still in your mouth or not."

"In my mouth, I think," Neil said, having reached the limits of his courage.

Before the black man could resume his march, he was accosted by two more men. They swaggered up, clearly military men by their garb and their bearing. Neil was astonished to recognize one of them: Colonel Williams—the same man who had stolen everything Neil had possessed and set him loose in a zombie-infested forest without a weapon. The same man who had tried to turn Sarah into a whore by holding the safety of her parents against her.

He was probably the last person Neil wanted to see just then. Hoping not to be recognized, Neil dropped his chin and edged closer to his kidnapper.

"Everything ok here?" the colonel asked. The man with him was a burly sort. He rolled his head on his thick shoulders and made a display of rubbing the scarred knuckles of both his heavy hands.

"We're great," the black man replied in a snarl.

"Is that so?" Williams asked. "It sure looked like there was some sort of issue here." He turned his gaze on Neil and the smaller man had to suppress the urge to shudder.

Neil shook his head. "No, just a misunderstanding. We're good, but thanks."

This was a surprising answer to the black man. He coughed a little and then made a show of wrapping his arm around Neil's shoulders. "You see? Just a misunderstanding. So, if you don't mind."

He began to push past the colonel, when Williams stopped Neil. "I know you from somewhere. We've met before, right?"

Neil attempted an innocent shrug, considered answering in a thick Jersey accent, discarded the idea, and then shrugged a second time without really answering the question.

"He doesn't know you," Neil's kidnapper replied, before trying again to shepherd Neil away.

Williams stopped them a second time. He took hold of Neil's coat and dragged him around so that they were face-to-face. "But he does. I know you, but from where? It must have been…" Williams blinked as recognition flooded his face. "You're the corporate guy from Jersey! The Wall Street pirate."

"That's me," Neil replied in a squeaky voice.

"So you lived," Williams said, looking impressed. "Good for you, and what about that little fireball you had with you? The punk zombie hunter?"

"She's alright, I guess."

"That's just great," the colonel said with fake enthusiasm. Though he smiled, he had the cold, calculating eyes of a snake. "We should get a drink and talk about old times."

The black man grabbed Neil's arm and said, "He's already going to have a drink, with me."

"But we're old friends," Williams replied. He flicked his eyes to the black man and then back to Neil—a clear warning to Neil that he was in danger.

"I—I guess we could have a drink, Colonel," Neil replied in confusion. "But only one. I'm, uh, double parked outside."

"Excellent!" the colonel cried, slapping Neil on the back with enough force to knock the wind out of him. "I hope you like *Coors*. It's piss, but it's cold piss."

The black man watched in anger as his victim was directed out of his grip and up a set of stairs. When they reached the first landing Williams slammed Neil up against the wall. "What the hell is going on?" the colonel demanded. "What did that man want?"

"I—I really don't know," Neil said. "I just got here when he accosted me."

"They must want something," the colonel replied. "They'll get it, too, unless you align yourself properly."

"They?" Neil asked in confusion.

"That was one of the *Blacks* from Philadelphia. You ever been there?" The colonel watched Neil close.

"No. Never. Not even in the old days. I always thought…" Neil's words came to a dribbling halt. Up to this point he had been sure there was some sort of mistake being made and that when everyone realized he was just Neil Martin, they would leave him alone. However now he knew better.

He had never been to Philadelphia, but Ram had. He was after Cassie, the Queen Bee of the *Blacks*—a woman who hated Neil with a passion. That was the connection.

Williams couldn't help but notice the pause. "What is it?" he demanded.

"Maybe we should take that beer somewhere private," Neil suggested.

"In here," the colonel said after a quick glance around. "You'll be safe, but only as long as you play square with me."

They ducked through a door—the only one Neil had seen so far that was guarded. Bracketing the door were two black-uniformed men; both were armed with machine guns. They weren't the colonel's men. Williams gave them a nod but it wasn't with his normal easy, familiar manner.

The door led to a plush suite of executive rooms. These were markedly different from the sweat smelling gypsy world of the main part of the boat. Everything here was dark mahogany, shining brass, and thick carpeting.

There were a number of people seated around a long table. They had been staring at each other in an uncomfortable silence, but now they turned their silent faces toward the colonel. A man at the head of the table swiveled toward them and smiled.

"Punctual as always, Colonel." The man was blonde and pale in all respects save about his eyes which were swarthy and hooded. He had a pronounced Russian accent so that there was a lag after everything he said as the people around him tried to make sense of his garbled words. "We are missing a few of guests, so please, if you could make yourself comfortable. Oh, and do leave servants outside."

"Actually, I need just a moment to discuss things with my associate," the colonel said. "Can I use…"

"You are one who call meeting and now you wish its delay?"

"It'll just be a minute or two, Yuri," Williams assured.

"A few of minutes?" Yuri shrugged and turned to the group of men seated at the table. "What of you? Do any begrudge a few of minutes?"

Not many looked happy at the delay, but none raised a fuss, though one had a simple request.

"When you are done with him, Colonel, I'd like a word as well."

Neil blanched at the sight of the speaker: white linen robes garbed his tall frame, while upon his head was layered hair that resembled silver waves. It was the false prophet of New Eden.

"You…" With his surprise and fear mounting, Neil could barely speak. "H-how did you get here?"

"The truth is I am here by the will of our Lord God. Though, as a *Denier*, I'm sure you are probably seeking more of a mundane answer: I arrived by car. We had a talk with your friend Mark yesterday morning, not long after you left him to die. How strange that our destinies and our destinations are so entwined."

The colonel put his arm out to Neil and gently thrust him back, saying, "They aren't entwined yet, *Jesus Christ Super-star*. Right now he's mine."

"No! Hold on," Neil cried, trying, and failing, to disentangle himself from the colonel. "Don't I get say-so in all of this? I am my own man!"

Even as the words left his mouth, a newcomer entered the room, and where a second before Neil was trying to get away from the colonel, now he nudged in close.

It was Cassie, but not the Cassie that Neil remembered. In the half-year since he had last seen her she had matured: she stood tall and straight, and across her muscular shoulders she wore a leopard print shawl. Her rich dark skin was bejeweled with diamonds and on her arms were bands of gold. When her eyes flashed it was with the power and surety of a modern day Nefertiti.

"That's where you're wrong, Neil," she said. "You was never a man, and now you is even less of one. Yuri, I wanna purchase him."

The world began to spin in Neil's eyes. "You can't do that," he said breathlessly.

"I can!" Cassie declared. "You ain't aligned with any faction. Three barrels of fuel-oil should do it."

"Unless there is a counter-bid," Yuri said, looking to the colonel and Abraham.

"One second," Williams said, pulling Neil as far to the back of the room as they could go. "Come clean with me, Neil," the colonel whispered. "If you give me the truth, I'll let you keep half of what you have. You may not think that's a great deal, but it's better than losing it all to her. The rumors out of Philadelphia are horrible. I heard she'll chop your balls of and choke you to death with them."

"My b-balls?"

"That's what I've heard. So what do you have that they

want? Fuel? Ammo?"

The colonel had grown loud in his excitement and was overheard. Cassie snorted: "It ain't what he gots, it's who he is."

A man at the table with a grey-streaked beard looked disgusted as he asked, "Are we trafficking in human beings now?"

"For the right price, *da*," Yuri said. He then called to one of his guards, speaking in Russian. The guard left at a run.

Abraham watched him go and then said, "I care nothing for the Denier; his fate is just. I shall put my bid in for the infant who's been traveling with him. Sixteen-hundred cans of food."

"I'm not selling her at any price," Neil growled as rage flared within him, pushing back against the fear and the helplessness he'd been feeling.

"I was not offering it to you," Abraham scoffed. "But to our host." He inclined his head to Yuri. "We are, for the moment, within his domain and our lives are in his hands to dispose as he wishes."

"Can you help me?" Neil whispered to Colonel Williams.

"Perhaps. Tell me you have more than just a baby."

"I do," Neil told him. "I have about sixty gallons of fuel and two hundred cans of food. It's not much, but you can have it all if you help me."

The colonel rolled his eyes. "Two hundred cans? Is that a joke? You aren't worth one can." Williams shook off Neil's pleading hands and went to his seat at the table.

Only one person said anything in Neil's defense: the man with grey in his beard. "Are we really going to let this *pretend Jesus* buy a baby? And this bitch buy a man? Do any of you even care what's going to happen to them?"

"Listen to me, *Denier*," Abraham said. "Eve is a gift from our Lord God. She will sit at my right hand. She shall be revered among my people. She shall be queen!"

Cassie laughed at this. "You mean you is gonna pedophile her as soon as she can walk? You is one sick white boy."

Glowering in rage, Abraham asked, "What about you? Tell us what you plan do with this man."

"Prolly carve the white off him. That or burn it off. Whatever I do to him he'll deserve it.

Neil swooned and clutched the wall just as his family came in.

"My Eve!" Abraham exclaimed, rushing forward.

Sadie was perplexed about what was happening, nonetheless she saw danger approaching and before anyone else could react she stepped in front of Sarah, who held the baby clutched to her bosom.

"What do you want?" Sadie demanded aggressively through clenched teeth. Abraham might have been a false prophet, but Sadie was a real hell-cat and her claws were out. Prudently, the man stopped just out of reach. He was pushed aside by Cassie who looked Sadie up and down in astonishment.

"Surprised I'm still alive?" Sadie asked. "Thought you had killed me? Wrong, bitch."

Cassie's face went fiery with anger, but then she smiled in an evil manner. "Yuri, three barrels for her, too. And where is Ram? I'll give three barrels for him as well. Keith, was there anyone with them?"

Neil's family had been escorted in by one of Yuri's men and followed by one of Cassie's as well. "This is it," Keith said. "I saw them arrive. One man, two females and a baby. Sorry."

"It's alright," Cassie said. "He'll show soon enough. So, Yuri, do we gots a deal? Three barrels each for these two?"

"What's happening?" Sarah asked in astonishment. "Are you being sold?"

Neil dropped his chin to his chest so his nod was a bare

movement. "Yeah. We all are. Everyone but you."

"No…not Eve…not Sadie," Sarah said breathlessly. "Not you."

Now the bearded man rose and pounded the table. "This is preposterous! We came here for a vaccine to help our communities and now we're buying and selling people like slaves?"

"Sit down, John," another man said. "If you're against slavery, don't own one."

"But she's just going to kill them!" John shouted.

"It does seem a waste," another agreed.

Cassie sneered at them. "For a thousand years you treat my people like monkeys and sell us like cattle and now when we finally have power you're gonna pretend you gots morals? What a fuckin' joke. I gots me oil, White-boy. I gots me a whole fuckin' train full and what I do with my property is my business. If I wanna buy this mother-fucker who's gonna tell me I can't? What law? There ain't no law but power. But, shit, you don't have to watch what I'm gonna do with 'em if that's what you're worried about."

"Maybe we should watch," Colonel Williams said as he got to his feet. "The reason we came to this meeting is that we needed some proof that the vaccine actually works."

Yuri threw his hands up and cried, "You each had a demonstration!"

"Only on rats," Williams countered. "What I suggest is that we get a zombie from off the street and have him bite each of these two." Here he gestured to Neil and Sadie. "One will be vaccinated and the other will be our control subject. If only the vaccinated one lives, then we know for sure that your vaccine works."

"Will I get to keep the one that lives?" Cassie asked, warming to the idea.

"And I get the baby?" Abraham asked. "She won't be harmed, you have my promise."

Yuri nodded and said, "Da, we can do this. It is settled.

Tonight, we vaccinate one of these two in full view of everyone and tomorrow we let them each get bit. The only question is which will get vaccine?"

"I will," Neil said, before Sadie could even open her mouth.

"What a chicken-shit," Cassie sneered.

"Yeah, that's me," Neil replied, dropping his gaze; hoping that Cassie hadn't seen the fire of determination there. He was sure that Sadie's death from the fever would be a hundred times easier than his own.

Chapter 33

Ram

Philadelphia, Pennsylvania

At the moment Eve was being torn from Sarah's grasp, and Sadie was throwing around haymakers in vain, Ram was just finishing applying his make-up. He checked himself in the rearview mirror and grunted.

On the way into the city he had stopped at a garishly decorated store: *Party Palace*. Anything of real use had already been looted, but there were still Halloween costumes by the hundreds—including a fine assortment of zombie costumes. Compared to the real thing they were a bit of a joke, however with a little bit of makeup and some fake blood he would pass inspection, he hoped. "Here goes nothing," he whispered.

Ram slipped out of the truck and with a last look around began to stumble along as any zombie would. Everything he knew about zombies suggested that the thinking part of their brain was destroyed. This meant that they had to identify humans based on an unchangeable paradigm imprinted into the dregs of their memory. To zombies all humans walked a certain way, they held themselves erect, their heads swiveled quickly and they generally carried things. Even if their hair wasn't combed, their skin was generally clean of blood and filth, and their clothes were almost always intact.

In order to go, unmolested, on foot in a city the size of Philadelphia, Ram had to change all of the human things about himself. Thus the make-up and the limp and the ragged clothes, and of course the hidden gun. It had to be good, because not only did he have to fool the zombies, he had to fool the humans as well. He had found out the hard way that Cassie kept her petty kingdom well guarded. They would be watching every avenue into the city, however they wouldn't be watching for zombies. That was like keeping an eye out for flies at a picnic.

"My first test," he mumbled after a minute. A zombie had angled slightly toward him, perhaps alerted by something Ram wasn't doing correct.

"Uuhhhh," the zombie moaned, as it closed the distance.

There it was. Ram was being too quiet. "Uuhhhh," Ram said. He made sure to watch the zombie from eyes that were half-cracked. It paused as it got closer and then after a moment of deliberation turned aside. Ram kept going, aiming for the school where Trey and Jermy had trussed him up.

There had been a guard station near there somewhere. They had undoubtedly watched Ram come tooling right up like a fool. He was a fool no longer. With his training, he picked out the perfect vantage point where a car could be seen coming from half-a-mile away. With it as a beacon, he moaned and schlepped his way slowly along, sometimes coming within feet of real zombies. Their proximity gave him the shivers on a subconscious level. Outwardly he went on without the least flinch.

Then he was at the base of the building; it was three over from the school and close enough for Trey and his crew to have zipped down and sprung their trap.

Here's where things get messy, Ram thought. Blood and tears would be spilt. It wasn't going to be pretty.

He abandoned his zombie gait, opting instead to move with all the stealth of a panther under the moonlight. In his right hand he carried a three-pound hand sledge, which was basically nothing more than a heavy-headed hammer. It would do for both human and zombie opponents. In his left hand he gripped a Beretta that Neil had given over without the least qualm.

It was growing dark as evening turned to night, but the staircase was like midnight in a cave. By feel alone he worked his way up, finding something strange just after the second level. After a minute he risked giving away his position by flicking open his *Zippo*. What he found was nothing more than a desk shoved sideways onto the stairs. Though a zombie would never be able to get past it, Ram scrambled over it easily.

The desk meant he was on the right track and not two minutes later he heard the first of the voices. There were two: a man and a woman. They were on the seventh floor, in an apartment that faced east. Ram oriented on their voices, and crept to the edge of the room.

Other than to hit hard and fast, he didn't have a plan. Without the smallest battle cry he rushed into the room. The man was bigger, stronger, and faster than the woman, however Ram picked him out for his first assault simply because he was closer.

Down swept the hammer in a deadly arc. Its speed was such that it would crush bone and go straight into the skull— Ram turned the head and pulled the stroke at the last second. He couldn't kill a stranger in cold blood if he had a choice.

There was a crunch and the man went down without a sound. The speed and unnerving silence of the attack caught the woman so completely by surprise that she did nothing but watch as Ram turned on her next.

"No," she squeaked. Ram stayed his hand and her head began to wag from side-to-side in confusion. "You're not a zombie?"

"No. Turn around. Hands behind your back."

"Ok…ok. I didn't do anything, Mister. I just keep watch is all. They make me, really. I used to like your kind back in the day. You gotta believe me."

"Shut up," Ram said softly. He bound her hands with a coat-hanger, twisting it slowly down to the point she cried out; he did the same for her feet. Then he bound the unconscious man as well, before dragging him into another room. There he splashed water on him until he revived and looked at Ram blearily.

"What da fuck?" he asked.

Using his knife, Ram cut away a couple of swaths of the man's shirt to make a crude gag. "Open up," he ordered. When the man hesitated Ram held the knife to his cheek. "I can pry your teeth open if you wish." The man clearly did not wish this and reluctantly accepted the gag. "Here's what's going to happen," Ram said in a low voice. "I'm going to ask you some questions and I'll ask the same questions of your friend in the other room. If your answers don't match, I'm going to crush your toes with this."

He held up the heavy hammer.

"Do you want to go first?" Ram asked, pulling out the gag.

"Whatever, you fuckin' Spic."

"I'll take that as a yes. We'll start easy. Where's the building that you *Blacks* have fortified?" Ram could see the lie forming in the man's eyes. "Remember it's not just your toes that'll get crushed. It's the woman's as well. Also, please keep in mind that I have a lot of questions. That's a lot of toes. You don't want to go around being a cripple in this day and age."

"Look man, please don't do this…"

Ram punched him in the face and then said, "I don't want to have to do any of this. Tell me where the building is."

"On Stanford Avenue. It's about eight blocks from here. Go west four blocks and then south eight."

"Good," Ram said. "Let's hope your friend gives me the same answer."

After re-gagging him Ram went to the woman. She was such a pitiful sight that he had to keep from looking at her as he explained the "rules" of her interrogation. "Just give me the same answer as him and you'll be alright."

Her face glistened with tears and fear-sweat. When he took off the gag she began to plead. Ram could not bring himself to hit her. He settled for shaking her very hard and screaming the question in her face.

"What if he lied?" she asked. "He prolly lied and you're gonna bus-up my toes. Please don't take it out on me."

"How about this: You tell me the truth and I'll go back to him with one more chance."

"Stanford Avenue," she hissed. "That's the truth! If he lied then…"

"It's what he told me as well. It seems he doesn't want you hurt. That's nice, right?"

"Yeah. That's nice," she said in a shaky, relief-filled voice.

Ram then asked how to get there and she repeated exactly what the other man had said. "You're doing great. Now comes the hard part." She braced herself for something serious, but he only asked where she lived in the building. "I'm trying to get a feel for the layout. If you want you can tell me where your friend lives instead."

This she did readily enough, and she didn't stop there. With simple prodding she explained the entire floor plan of the building; exactly what he needed.

He thanked her and went to her companion. "Did she go on and on, or what?" Ram asked trying to show what a genial person he could be in spite of the circumstances. "Now it's your turn and here's the bad part, if you try to mix up truth with lies, you both are going to be in big trouble."

Just like his counterpart, the man described the layout of the building in minute detail. If their stories ever varied Ram would ask him if he wanted to "re-think" his answer. He did every time. "One last question and we'll be done," Ram said. "Where in all of this does Cassie sleep? Where are her quarters? She's the only one I'm really after."

There was a hesitation that perked Ram up. "Top floor. Take a left outside the elevator doors. It's at the end of the hall."

"And are there any guards?"

"Just one."

The man had lied somewhere in his answer. "Anything you want to change?" Ram asked almost sadly. The man claimed he was telling the truth, and the woman gave essentially the same answer and she too had left something out.

"That's not what he said. I'm sorry." Ram went to reach for the hammer.

"She's not there," the woman said in a rush. "Is that what he told you? I'm so sorry, but you asked me where her room was and I answered that truthful. But you didn't ask me where Cassie was so I just didn't answer that because it wasn't really part of the question. Please don't hurt me."

Her honesty was now evident, which was a relief to Ram. Hitting her with the hammer was the last thing he wanted to do. "Where is she?"

The woman didn't hesitate: "New York."

The two words bored a hole in his belly where it felt like his stomach and then his heart fell through. His family was in New York—Neil and Sarah and Sadie and Eve…and, "Jillybean," he whispered.

"Huh?" the woman asked.

"Nothing. You did well. So well that I don't think anyone's going to get hurt. Not today." Ram stood and glanced around at the room they had set for keeping watch. There was a food and some water; he ate and drank, and thought about what he had to do. It wasn't hard. He had to get to New York before anything terrible happened.

"I have to go," he told the woman, standing and stretching.

"You're going to leave us here? All tied up? You can't do that! Mister, come on, we answered everything you asked."

"You'll be fine," Ram said, looking out into the early night. It was freshly dark, seeming blacker than a normal night. "I'm sure your replacement will be here soon enough."

"Not till morning and by then my hands will rot off. Please, Mister. I can't feel my hands or my feet. You'll be clean away by the time I have any circulation. Please don't leave…"

Ram wanted to go, but he gave in. "Fine," he said and began to undo her hands. "I'm taking the guns. They'll be downstairs, but I have to warn you I will shoot to kill if you try to follow me." Not trusting her sob story completely he cinched down the wire on her ankles, knowing that it would take her five minutes to undo it and another five minutes to free her friend. By that time he'd been in his truck and heading northeast to New York.

"Were you really going to bash my toes in?" the woman asked as she massages her hands.

"At first," Ram told her. "I think so. I was pretty pumped up but after a few minutes I didn't think I could."

She grunted an understanding. "Cassie says that the other races are weak and we are weak when we associate with them. She says they undermine us by using compassion and that we would have been stronger if we had never accepted the first promise of forty acres and a mule."

"Probably," Ram said with a final grunt. When he looked up from her bound feet he found himself staring down the dark bore of a short-barreled pistol, the make of which he didn't recognize. "You know Cassie is crazy," he said.

"She's not. Undo the wire right now. And know this: I'll splatter your brains at the first twitch." Ram saw that she wasn't joking; the trigger was already halfway back and he could hear the sound of the spring tightening up.

Even working slowly the wire was off her before he could think of a single plan to escape. She then disarmed him completely and had him free her friend. At no time did she give Ram the slightest opening to snatch her weapon.

When the man was free he punched Ram in the face and then worked him over with his fists—it wasn't unexpected.

Perhaps because the man had been brained by a hammer not long before, the beating wasn't prosecuted with much enthusiasm.

"What are we going to do with him?" the man asked. He rubbed his head seeming more in pain than Ram was.

"I ain't taking him back with us," the woman said. "We'll be fucked if it gets out that we spilled all that we did. Cassie won't care if we were tortured or not."

"So turn him into grey-meat?" the man suggested. She agreed as if there wasn't any other choice. He went to the window and whistled. "There's a fuck-load of them down there tonight. Looks like you're in luck, asshole. They'll be like piranhas; you'll be dead in no time. Five minutes tops."

Ram had his hands bound behind his back with the same wire he had used on them, and because of this he was escorted down the stairs. The man carried a flashlight in one hand and had Ram by the collar in the other, while the woman led the way. She had traded out her pistol for a shotgun—a more certain weapon against zombies.

Below the third level Ram was basically heaved over the desk where he knocked the side of his head enough to make him dizzy. He moaned in pain.

"Stop your fucking faking," the man said and began pushing him on. "Or I'll give you…"

Just then a horribly familiar sound came to them from somewhere on the second level. It was the sound of a marble bouncing. Goose bumps flashed across Ram's skin. They weren't of excitement; they were of dread. There was only one reason for a marble to be bouncing just then…but that reason couldn't be possible.

Yet in his heart he knew that it was possible.

"Jilly! Don't do this," he cried at the top of his lungs. In the silence that followed, the bouncing marble kept going, clacking about merrily. "Run away! Get out of here."

There was no sound but the marble and the wailing of the undead outside.

Chapter 34

Jillybean

Philadelphia, Pennsylvania

"He will die without me, Ipes," Jillybean had said earlier that afternoon.

The stuffed animal shrugged. *I like Mister Neil better. I know he tried to give you to the cult, but he's actually very nice aside from that. And, he's very complimentary to zebras, which is a mark of an advanced and fully mature mind.*

"If you like Mister Neil so much maybe you should stay here," Jillybean countered.

Ipes waived his stubby arms. *But they will give me to Eve, and she slobbers*, Ipes groaned. *I swear she must have Basset Hound somewhere in her ancestry.*

"Then I guess you're coming with me," Jillybean said. She watched as Neil pulled Ram aside to chat. "Now's our chance." Sarah was busy changing Eve and Sadie was watching the two men and had her back to Jillybean.

With deft movements, the little girl buried her new doll in the blankets, leaving only her hair showing. She then grabbed her backpack and hurried to Ram's truck. There was no use being coy about what came next—she would either be caught or not. In a quick move she climbed up the side of the truck and slithered beneath the blue tarp.

Now what? Ipes asked.

"We wait."

Ipes tapped his toe or rather he tapped the part of him that represented a hoof, either way it was a silent tap and one that was all for show. *Do you think he's in need of saving yet?* Ipes wondered aloud. Jillybean blew out in a huff. Ipes went on, *Why don't you admit what this really is?*

"What this is," Jillybean said with her eyes blazing, "is a zebra on the verge of getting a spanking if he doesn't stop being a pain!"

Nope. This is you trying to force yourself on a grown man. You can't adopt an adult just because he reminds you of your father.

Jillybean did not like the way the conversation was going, however she was in a mood about being abandoned by Ram again, and said, "Why not? Why is it only the adults who get to go about adopting people? If he was a kid, people would be like: oh, he's all alone, we should adopt him. But since he's a grode-up we just have to let him be all alone? That doesn't make…"

Just then she heard Ram walking back to his truck; he sighed continually. Then they were off and despite the tarp flapping above her, Jillybean was very soon cold enough to take out her fancy dress and throw it on over her jeans and ugly *Eagles* sweatshirt.

They stopped after an hour or so and Jillybean peeked out to see where they were. "*Party Palace!*" she exclaimed. "I've been here before."

Don't you mean we've been here before? Ipes reminded her. *I was there as well.*

She ignored him. Her mind was far away remembering the fairy costume she had worn a year and a half before on Halloween. It had been pink and silver with gold trim on the fairy wings. Her mom had taken five thousand pictures and had made Jillybean walk back and forth shaking her wings.

What's he got there? Ipes asked a few minutes later. He had his long nose sticking out of the tarp. *Ha! He's got a monster costume. What's he going to do with one of them?*

Jillybean felt a silly disappointment. Deep in her heart she had hoped that Ram had stopped in at the store to get her something. He watched him try on his costume and later after they had made it into the city she saw him put on makeup.

This is called betting on the wrong horse, Ipes said. *Ram's gone crazy. Neil isn't crazy, you know. Neil isn't going to a costume party at night in the middle of a zombie infested...*

"Shhh," she hissed. Ram had finished his makeup and was right next to the bed of the truck. He took a couple of deep breaths and then began to act like a monster as he walked away.

Maybe I was a bit premature in my diagnosis of his mental facilities, Ipes allowed as he saw what Ram had done.

"Come on." Jillybean crawled out of the truck and went to the cab which Ram had left wide open. After taking off the dress and folding it neatly, she slapped on makeup, making herself look like a sad little monster. Next she happily shredded up her *Eagles* sweatshirt so that it hung off her in tatters. Her hair was already going in every direction and so there was nothing left but to tuck Ipes into the pocket of her backpack and go lurching out into the night.

The hard part was catching up to Ram when she had to go at a monster's pace. When they weren't after prey, they moved with all the speed of a vacationing sloth.

She would've gone at the dangerous pace of a slow walk if it hadn't been for Ipes. The zebra kept her focused. *Slower! Swing one arm. You look too much like a girl; are you trying to get us killed?*

After an agonizing time they passed right by the building Ram was in and kept going, unaware. She was halfway down the block when a cry of someone in pain stopped her in her tracks. It had come from behind her. Jillybean wasn't the only one attracted by the sound. The shadows all around came alive with monsters.

Slower! Ipes cried. She had begun to go faster than was prudent. However she couldn't go slower. The cry had come from Ram's lips. He was in trouble just as she knew he would be.

"Sorry, Ipes," she said as she pulled a magic marble from her pocket, kissed it, and chucked it across the street.

Every monster head turned at the sound of the bouncing glass ball. Jillybean took off at a sprint back the way she had come. In her wake the monsters weren't fooled for more than two seconds, but it was enough.

Jillybean pelted up to the building, turned the corner and immediately went back to monster-mode: moaning and shambling her way to the front and into the lobby. Behind her monsters came and began milling around, searching the corners or behind the stray cars or just staring blankly.

You've trapped us, Ipes accused. *What are we going to do when we want to come back out?*

"We'll see," Jillybean replied. She didn't have the luxury to dwell on what might happen in five minutes when there was so much danger immediately ahead in the next two. Like a shot she sped up the stairs. Her legs were too short to go two at a time so instead she pumped them furiously and arrived in time to hear two people, a man and a woman discussing Ram's fate.

"What are they going to do to him, Ipes?" she asked. "What do they mean by grey meat? Are they going to turn him into a monster?"

Yes, I think so. But we...they're coming! Back down stairs, he hissed. The pair rushed back the way they came. *Stop*, Ipes ordered just after they slid over the top of the desk. He studied it for five agonizing seconds—its height, its width, the edging scarred with age and abuse.

"What is it?" Jillybean asked.

The zebra hushed her for being too loud and yet not a second later he practically screamed: *This won't work at all!*

"Work for what?"

My plan.

"What's your plan?"

Ipes grabbed his spiky Mohawk of a mane with both hooves and cried, *I don't know! We have to separate Mister Ram from his attackers. If he goes outside with them, he'll die for sure.*

"What?" Jillybean asked, confused. "If he goes out all alone, he'll die too."

Don't be silly, Ipes said. *He dressed like a monster, remember? Just like you. So what we need is to get them to let Ram go out alone.*

"They won't do it," Jillybean replied. "They'll want to watch him die. They'll..." Five floors above them they heard Ram and his captors on the stairs.

We have two minutes, Ipes hissed. *Think of something!*

"Me?" Jillybean cried. "You're the one who always comes up with the plans."

I'm all out of ideas, Ipes said in a little voice. *Sorry.*

"There has to be something," Jillybean said. "We'll try in here."

The door to the second floor hall had been yanked back and lay cockeyed, half off its hinges. The little girl went through it and found herself in a typical hall of a high-rise apartment building—other than doors and ratty carpeting it was empty. She rushed to the first door on the right, which also sat open.

Her eyes ran over the debris of someone's life. The place had been ransacked for food or weapons, however beneath the chaos was a normal apartment: In the main room a TV on a stand was the dominant feature, all the furniture pointed its way. In the dining room was an old table sitting on older tile. In the kitchen there was a spray of spilt salt on the counter beneath cabinets with their doors hanging open like so many gaping mouths. On the walls were pictures and a calendar and knick-knacks and dust.

There's nothing here we can use, said Ipes gloomily. *Too bad. We can hide here at least. Maybe gather up those clothes and bury ourselves until...Jillybean? Hello?*

The girl was standing still, a magic marble held very tight in her clenched fist, while her mind worked with the exactness of a Swiss watch; each piece of her shaky plan coming to her, unfolding one after another, fitting together seamlessly.

First the table. It had to be cleared and one corner of it raised. A book was too much, but the blade of a butter knife too little. With a grunt she turned the knife around and set the table leg on it. She tested the marble; it rolled too quickly.

Ipes saw where this was going. *The salt in the kitchen!*

Jillybean rushed to the other room and scraped up all the salt she could. It was barely a teaspoonful. It wouldn't slow the marble down enough unless...

You build a track, Ipes said finishing her thought. *But you better hurry.*

She couldn't spare even a second to say: No Duh!

Breathless, she ran to the table and spread the salt down it in a long thin line—it was very sparse, which meant she would be cutting things close. Next, she grabbed up a pair of pants from the floor and a sock and two shirts. These she stretched out right next to the line of salt, leaving barely an inch gap.

Lastly she went to the high end of the table and stood poised with the magic marble ready to roll.

Do it! Ipes screamed in her mind.

"Ssh," Jillybean said. "I'm trying to listen." The three people on the stairs came closer and closer, and all the while Ipes was going crazy.

Now! Roll the marble, please, before it's too late.

With her stomach knotted, Jillybean counted to five and then let the marble go. It bumped over the salt, shuddering with each grain and picking up speed with agonizing slowness.

Jillybean couldn't afford to watch its progress. Stooping to snatch up a black sweater she sped for the stairs, arriving while the three were only a flight above her head. Without checking her momentum she ran upwards.

Wrong way, Jilly! Ipes wailed.

Five steps along she found the desk wedged sideways, it

was little more than a solid shadow in the dark. By feel only she clambered around it and curled herself in the space where a chair would normally go and then the adults were right there.

A grunt sounded in the dark, which was followed by the soft sound of someone light sliding across the top of the wood a bare two inches over Jillybean's head. A light flashed; the beam making crazy angled shadows in the cubby. Then there was a louder thud on the desk, causing her to jump in fright.

They had thrown Ram over the desk. He began to groan.

"Stop your fuckin' faking," the man who had taken him prisoner said after he slid over as well. "Or I'll give you…"

Finally the marble had made its way to the edge of the table and now threw itself onto the old tile. It was a loud sound in the still night, but not as loud as Ram, who began yelling for Jillybean to run. In the commotion she peeked out from her hiding place and saw the two people with Ram: a man and a woman, both of whom were black. The man had a scoped deer rifle across his back, which he promptly yanked free and pointed outward. The woman had a shotgun that was so large it looked like a bazooka to Jillybean.

"Shut the fuck up," the man said as he bashed Ram in the stomach with the butt of his gun. Ram dropped to his knees on the landing and started to make a noise as though he couldn't decide whether he wanted to throw up or choke.

"He brought someone with him," the woman said, keeping her voice low.

"No shit," the man replied. "With a name like Jilly, it's probably a girlfriend. Watch him. Bash him in the face if he says anything."

The man turned off the flashlight and before Jillybean could get her night-eyes back he had disappeared down the hall, moving with such soft steps that the sharpest ears could not pick out his tread. Whether it was the loss of the man's presence, which was significant, or the loss of the light, which was greater still, the woman quickly grew afraid. She swung her head from Ram on the edge of the landing, to the man creeping down the hall.

Jillybean began to squeeze from her hiding spot—*Wait. Not yet*, Ipes warned. *Count to twenty. Let the man get further away.*

Waiting would have been nice and it would have been safe, but only for her. She knew with a certainty that when Ram caught his breath he would yell out to warn her. When that happened he'd be hit on the head with a weighted hunk of steel and wood by a woman whose blood was primed with adrenaline. At the least, Ram would be concussed and would have trouble walking or even talking. At the most he would be knocked out. Being knocked out equaled death since Jillybean wouldn't be able to move him in time to keep him from being pitched out into the street with the monsters.

With all the natural skill in her lithe body, Jillybean stole out from her hiding place just as Ram began to get his wind back.

"Jillybean…"

"Shut it or so help me I'll bash your head in," the woman said with the shotgun raised to strike.

With the sound covering her movement, Jillybean stepped away from the desk and rushed full on the woman with the only weapon she possessed: the black sweater she had grabbed from the apartment.

The charging shadow, which seemed far larger than it really was, caught the woman's attention. She yelped and, with her heart hammering, she moved with the speed of panic, stepping back and swinging the gun around to shoot. Both actions contained all the commonsense common to panic. There was no room left on the landing to step back and within a second Jillybean was too close to shoot with a shotgun.

This didn't stop the woman from trying both.

Her right foot came down on air just as she pulled the trigger. The shock of the gun blast helped to propel her tumbling backwards down the stairs in a jumble of cries and grunts and sickening thuds, while above Jilly's head the air fizzed with the passage of the shotgun's pellets.

Before the woman came to a bone-breaking crash at the bottom of the stairs, Jillybean was urging Ram to get up. "Hurry, Ram. I've got you," the little girl cried, straining with all her might to help him to a standing position. In seconds they were hurtling down the stairs in the dark while above, the man with the rifle came rushing like a hurricane wind.

"Reba," he bellowed.

Reba was on the landing below, moaning like one of the undead. Both Jillybean and Ram tripped on her sprawled form, but neither fell completely. They had one set of steps to go before light flicked down.

"Reba, shit!" the man cried. With his flashlight and his unbound hands, the man was faster. They could hear his feet skipping down the stairs coming two, three at a time. It would be seconds only before they were within range of his gun.

"Jilly, shoot him!" Ram yelled, unexpectedly.

"But I don't have a..." Jillybean started to explain that she wasn't armed when the man above them shot his gun blindly. It sounded like a stick of dynamite exploding. Defensively, he shot again, more or less at nothing but the dark. The bullet whined nowhere near Ram and Jillybean.

"Come on," Ram said under the noise.

At the bottom of the stairs they burst through the door leading to the lobby. This space wasn't much more than an open area with two banks of elevators and the door to the stairs. Ram paused to get his bearings and to think of a plan. There wasn't time.

"Out here, Mister Ram," Jillybean said pulling him toward the front door.

"But the zombies," he said.

In the dark he missed her shredded clothes and the make-up on her face. "I'm like you," she said moving up close. "I'm a zombie, see? And I can act like a zombie, too."

He gazed down on her fondly. "Zombies don't smile, Sweetheart. Now, we better hurry."

Just as their enemy came tentatively into the lobby, they stepped out into the night. In a second, zombies came at the pair. Ram took the lead, lurching awkwardly and moaning loud and pointedly to make sure Jillybean understood to follow suit. She did, though making sure not to get as carried away as she thought he was.

Their disguises worked. In seconds they were part of the crowd that gimped about in front of the building and when the man with the rifle stuck his head out they acted just like the rest and moved toward him until he retreated back inside.

Only then did the pair act their way back toward Ram's truck.

"You're crazy," Ram said as Jillybean struggled with the wire. His bindings were far too tight for her soft fingers and her skinny, malnourished muscles, but they weren't strong enough for her mind. Using a flashlight to illuminate the wire, she studied it before pulling out the can opener from her back pack. Using its tiny teeth she was able to grip the wire and use the strength in her entire upper body to loosen them.

"There, you're free," she said, rubbing her fingers where the metal had bit. "But I don't think I'm crazy. That's what means insane, right? Cuckoo for cocoa-puffs? That's not me."

"Then you're the bravest girl ever," Ram said. He too sat rubbing his hands where the wire had dug cruel and deep.

"I don't think that either. I was really ascared the whole time, especially when that guy shot his gun. My ears still hurt."

Ram groaned at how she kept refusing his compliment, though he smiled as he did—he couldn't seem to help smiling at her. "Well you are very brave to me," Ram told her.

"Ok. You're brave to me too, except Ipes thinks you're not very smart coming here all alone like that. You need me, Mister Ram. So don't try to leave me anymore. Ok? And why do you keep smiling?"

"Because I..." Ram stopped in midsentence and his face fell in sadness. "Because I think you're a very special girl."

He was going to say something else, thought Jillybean.

Whatever it was Ram kept to himself. He grew from sad to grim as they sat there. "Are you thinking about leaving me again?" Jillybean asked, misreading the look.

"No. I'm just not done saving people. We're going to New York."

Chapter 35

Ram

New York City

Driving on dark streets populated with dead humans and dead cars, led to a premonition of coming death for Ram. He had, for too long, tight-roped across the knife's edge; his luck would not last forever. Nor would Jillybean's.

She lay at peace as the tires thumped and the engine churned out its white noise. When the trip northeast had first begun she had chirped nonstop like a tireless bird, but then the stress of the evening had caught up with her. Down dropped her lids to cover over her blue orbs and then, gradually, her breath stopped forming words and lightly whistled on the outflow instead.

She was beautiful. Even covered in zombie makeup she stirred Ram's heart with her button nose, soft cheeks, and pointy little chin. He wanted to kiss each of her features as if she was his own daughter.

With difficulty he refrained.

"Not yet," he said glancing away from her long enough to correct his course. "Maybe if I live through the night, I'll tell you that I love you, little Jillybean."

But not before. There was just too much of a chance that he wouldn't make it and she was already far too attached. What would it do to her to hear *I love you* from him right before he died? Would she blame herself? Would she push away Neil, or any other father figure? What if it just plain messed her up for life? After all, everyone who had ever told her they loved her was very likely dead.

He wasn't going to take the chance of giving her a complex just so he could die without feeling all alone.

Was that what his feelings for her were all about? Was she just a cure for his loneliness?

Ram couldn't get a handle on his feelings and while he

wrestled with them the city came into sight far to the east. At night there wasn't much he could see of it. It was simply a horizon of angular shadows against a starry background. As he drew closer, the empty buildings and the sorrowful wail of the zombies added to the aura of death that he felt surrounding him. It seemed very close now, like an invisible glow coming from his exposed skin and hovering about like a shroud.

The single lane between the endless shambling mounds of grey flesh didn't help the feeling either. It was as if he was being herded to his doom and so, very uncharacteristically, he followed the lane without once considering deviating from it. If he did, where would he go? New York was huge and he had no idea where Neil and Sarah, or even Cassie, were.

It was true he could get out and walk the streets as a zombie, but for how long? In Philadelphia he had walked a half-mile and passed two hundred zombies, which had felt like a lot. Now he knew that it was nothing.

In New York City the numbers of undead were astronomical. Their smell was like an invisible fog that coated everything, including the inside of his mouth. It made him want to gag.

Why would any human stay here? Ram wondered. If there was an answer it lay ahead…and not much further ahead. There in his lights were heavy iron gates that undoubtedly led to his destination. Further on he could see a brilliantly lit ship sitting next to a pier. Across from it, tied to the dock, in tandem, were two Staten Island ferry boats that crawled with live people.

This was it.

Ram brought his Ford to a stop right before the gates which did not retract as they had for Neil earlier. When he saw the guardhouse flicker with shadows he tapped lightly on his horn. The sound stirred up the zombies nearby. *En masse*, they pushed forward, and so great were their numbers that the metal poles leaned and the fencing bowed dangerously.

"Read the fucking sign, asshole!" someone called out above the moans.

Now Ram saw the sign:

Gates will not open after sunset. No exceptions!

"Son of a bitch," he swore under his breath. He felt the pressing need to get his fate over with one way or the other and the idea of a delay only added to his anxiety.

Sitting there, with his intuition trending darkly, he forced himself to relax and decided to use the time to come up with a better plan. His only plan at the moment was to go in friendly, smile pretty, and then blast Cassie the moment he saw her, and let the chips fall where they may. It wasn't a good plan, but having been born with an action oriented personality, Ram had never been much for plans.

After a few seconds of gazing down at the brilliantly lit cruise boat, he came up with a new plan. He'd sneak aboard, find Cassie, blow her to hell, and let the chips fall where they would.

"Good enough," he said as he turned the truck around.

"What are you doing, Mister Ram?" Jillybean asked. She rubbed her eyes and then yawned in imitation of a tiny grizzly.

"I think I found where Neil and Sarah are. Back there at those boats that are all lit up."

She squinted at the retreating lights. "Then why are we going this way?"

"They won't let us in until morning," Ram told her. "I have a bad feeling that Neil is in trouble, sooo…" He paused after drawing out the syllable and gave her a guilty smile. "So I'm going to find a different way onto the boat while you stand guard with the truck."

"You mean you don't want me to come with you," Jillybean said with her chin sunk to her chest.

"It's not because I'm mad at you or anything," Ram

said quickly. "It's just you're so small and this is really dangerous. I don't want you to get hurt."

"But everything is dangerous now," Jillybean said. "And I'm always going to be smaller than you, and I don't want to get hurt either. But I also don't want you to get hurt, and neither does Ipes though he doesn't say it."

"This is extra dangerous," Ram tried to explain. "It's the kind of dangerous that I may not be able to come back from. Do you understand?"

"You mean you might die," Jillybean said, her face starting to twist beneath the make-up. "Then don't do it! Stay here with me."

"What about Eve? And Sadie and Miss Sarah and Mister Neil? They could be in trouble right now. And, even if they're not, somebody has to stop Cassie." Somebody has to be *good*. That was the real reason behind his foolish heroics. Ever since the apocalypse, the concepts of *good* and *honor* and *duty* seemed to have been thrown out the window.

"But what do I do if you die?" Jillybean asked. Her lower lip stuck out and quivered while her eyes grew bigger and wetter with every passing second.

"Come here," Ram said, gathering her into his arms. "Don't worry about that. You are such a smart and brave little girl that I think you'll be fine. Just make sure you keep Ipes near. I can tell that he helps you be smart. And he's a good friend, right?"

"Yes, b-but he's not the same as having you," she said with her thin chest beginning to hitch. "I'll b-be all alone again."

"Yeah," Ram breathed. He had no idea what to do. On one hand, it would be insane to take a six-year-old with him into what could be a gun-battle. On the other hand to leave her all alone in a city plagued with so many zombies was horrible and cruel.

There was only one person he could turn to for advice. "What does Ipes say you should do?"

Ipes always had an opinion. Jillybean paused, as if actually listening, sniveling up buggers and wiping at her tears uselessly, since more followed in a steady trickle. When the zebra was done she cried even harder.

"He thinks you should stay in the truck, doesn't he?" Ram asked, holding her.

She nodded without looking up. "He says people are mean, while zombies are just monsters. He says I should take my chances with the monsters. They're easier to understand and easier to handle."

"Ok," Ram whispered and patted her leg, glad that he had been let off the hook. It was a decision that he couldn't have made on his own. "Ipes is very smart and I know he makes you very smart too. We should listen to him." His use of the word "we" had him thinking a ridiculous thought. "What does Ipes think I should do?" Ram asked. He even glanced down at the stuffed animal as if expecting the zebra to speak.

Jillybean nodded gently, her face growing resigned. "He says if you don't go to help Neil, no one will. And he says I shouldn't try to stop you. He says I have to let you go and hope that you make it back."

Ram marveled at the answer. What part of Jillybean's six-year-old brain was mature enough to formulate such a response? Was she channeling her father through her subconscious? Was she naturally precocious? Or had her intelligence blossomed due to the extreme conditions she found herself living in?

The answers didn't matter. He hugged her fiercely for a moment and then pulled back to look at her. Despite that her eyes still dripped tears, she smiled bravely and he hugged her a second time so that she wouldn't see that his own eyes had grown misty.

He cleared his throat and said, "Ok," before setting his face forward and putting the truck in motion once again. They back-tracked, looking for a stretch of fencing on the east side of the lane that looked weak enough that he could bash it down with the truck. Since all the fences were reinforced with stalled-out cars, Ram had to drive further than a mile to find a spot.

"Buckle up, Sweetheart," he warned Jillybean when he reached a space that looked promising. He then floored the truck and sent it spearing through the fence in a great crash and shriek of metal-on-metal. The fence wasn't his only obstacle. The Ford jounced over the undead like a tractor carving up a New England field.

Eventually he came to a place near the river where the dead were fewer in numbers. Ram stopped the truck and the two of them hid under a sleeping bag as the zombies came up to inspect the vehicle. When they didn't see humans they moved on.

"It's time," Ram said, after peeking above the edge of the door to make sure the coast was clear. "I should get going. Now remember, if I don't make it back...listen to Ipes. He'll know what to do."

Jillybean agreed she would. "Are you ascared?" Jillybean asked. She clearly was scared for Ram.

Ram had to smile at the realization. "You're scared for me, but I'm sacred for you. We're funny aren't we?"

She smiled sadly. "Butterfly-kiss for luck," she said, and came right up to his face so he could feel the subtle wind of her breath. A second later her giant lashes whisked up and down on his cheek. It was the greatest thing he had ever felt in his life.

"Your turn," she said, pulling back and then presenting her cheek to him.

He had never done this before, though he guessed he did it right when she began to giggle.

"Ok, time to go," he said again. He didn't want to go. He wanted to tell Jillybean that he loved her and that he would take care of her and that they could go away and be a family. He would be the dad and she would be his little girl.

Instead he squeezed her hand and said, "Bye."

"Bye," she said right back in a little voice.

He left then, and after looking back once and seeing her tiny upturned face staring out the truck's window he couldn't force himself to look back a second time. Whatever noble reason he had for leaving couldn't compare to the idea that he was abandoning a little girl on a dark night in a city of the undead.

Chapter 36

Neil

New York City

What started out as a simple affair—a demonstration of the viability of a vaccine—became a scene straight out of Mad Max.

Since no one trusted anyone else, every faction kept an observer near the two prisoners which made for a cramped and uncomfortable setting. Arguments were nonstop and fights frequent. Because of the friction Neil and Sadie were brought to one of the Staten Island ferry boats that were moored across the pier from the cruise ship.

In the center of it, where cars were normally parked, was a cavernous open space, lit only by a few low-watt bulbs high-up on the ceiling. There the two prisoners were chained by the neck to the floor just out of reach of each other. They had only enough links in their chains to stand and even then the metal bit into their skin.

To make the proceedings seem more official and less like a circus, Yuri had them inspected by a physician. Their scratches and scrapes were documented, their temperatures were taken, and blood was drawn, but for what test it was never revealed.

Sadie seethed in her chains at her coming death. At first she was like a wild animal, but Neil advised her to save her strength just in case there was an opening to escape. Escape was a pipe dream. It would be impossible. There were eleven separate factions from all over the country and each was willing to pony up a wealth of goods for a vaccine, but only for a vaccine that worked. With a real demonstration as the only true test they would do their best to thwart any escape.

Within an hour, news of the demonstration had circulated around the boat twice and such was the curiosity that a separate viewing area had to be created to keep people back. It was low-rent fancy. Tattered, red, crushed velvet ropes were appropriated from a nearby theater and strung down the length of the boat, allowing people to walk by and stare at the two prisoners. Most just looked while others heckled:

"Let's see your face!"

"What did you two do? Kill someone?"

"Is it true you guys are father and daughter?"

"I heard he's going to let her die."

"I heard he was nothing but a coward."

"Don't listen to them, Neil," Sadie said, coming to his defense as always. "I know how brave you are."

He laughed softly. "If I'm so brave then why do I feel like I'm about to piss myself?"

"Because that's who you are," she replied. "You're the most frightened person I know, but there isn't a fear you haven't overcome. I know you'll be tough for this, too."

"Probably not," he said. "I won't have anything to be tough for." Conspicuously absent from the crowd were Sarah and Eve, and of course, Jillybean whose disappearance was a mystery to them all. He had failed as a father and a husband. This certain knowledge made it hard to look anywhere near Sadie. Her death would be on his shoulders.

Sadie dropped her head. "It's going to be ok. I hope. I love you, Neil."

"Love you too."

The spectators razzed them for this display and there were more taunts and insults. For some reason people thought it was proper to spit at the pair. The guards did nothing until someone threw a battery at Neil. The man received only a warning.

At just after ten, when the moon hung, quartered, in the sky, Yuri and the faction leaders, along with as many people as possible, crammed onto the ferry boat. There seemed to be thousands of them. They whispered like snakes and pointed and joked and laughed like hyenas.

Yuri did not make a speech. He raised his hand and in it was a syringe. "The vaccine!" he shouted. The people cheered. The Russian advanced on Neil, who sat waiting docilely. Sadie couldn't stop herself. She raged against the chain sending out flailing kicks and when that proved fruitless she spat at Yuri and cursed him for a coward.

The crowd roared its approval and began to chant for her to get the vaccine in Neil's stead. Unable to shout above the noise Yuri shook his head and then pointed at Neil.

"Boo!"

"Give it to the girl!"

Yuri did not. Her death had already been bought and paid for. He held up his long pointer finger and wagged it at the crowd as if they were naughty children for even suggesting such a thing. He then went to Neil and the crowd was so loud that not even the closest to them heard Yuri say: "Good luck."

When the shot was given the crowd quieted and watched Neil, looking for signs of his immunity. Eventually some began to depart, but, like an Emcee under the big top, Yuri cried out: "Now for the monster!"

The crowd buzzed with excitement and then a woman shrieked and people pointed.

A zombie, wrapped in chains, was brought down the center of the boat, causing people to crush in on themselves to keep away. There was little danger. Though it was a large and healthy male, and although it moaned and snarled and gnashed its grey teeth theatrically, it had four handlers who kept it in check.

It was chained just across from Neil and Sadie so that the three of them formed a triangle. Slowly, link by link the zombie was given room to move. It leaned towards the pair going back and forth, testing the chains.

This entertained the crowd for a few minutes; they cheered and jeered, but just when they began to grow quiet again with the show seemingly over, Yuri clapped loudly twice. It was a signal, clearly, and the crowd began to look back and forth expectantly.

It was not long before a second zombie was brought forth. This one was more subdued.

"What's it for?"

"Why are there two?"

"One for each of them?"

Sadie glared at Yuri for his sick ways and tried her best to inch closer so that she could give him a swift kick in the balls if the opportunity presented. It did not.

The zombie was brought forward and, unlike the first who was wrapped across the torso, this one only had a chain around its neck, while its hands were cuffed behind its back. And, again, unlike the first, this one was soaking wet: it dripped water and red blood onto the steel of the deck.

"That's a man!" someone shouted.

It was a man. Neil felt his legs go wobbly when he recognized Victor Ramirez beneath the grey makeup and new wounds. He was shackled by the neck to the deck and his cuffs were removed.

Yuri held up his hands for silence. "We have uninvited guest," he said in his accented English. "Is there a faction who will claim him or perhaps I let him go?" Neil saw the Russian's eyes flick to Cassie who stood with the *Blacks*. The question had been for her sake—Ram wasn't going to be let go, not when Yuri could make money off the deal.

When Cassie saw who the bedraggled person was her eyes flew open. "I'll give you three barrels of fuel-oil for him."

John, the leader of the *Whites* raised his hand. "I'll give you four!"

Almost as one, the crowd blinked. They had never seen a person auctioned off like this—no American had in almost a hundred and fifty years.

The crowd grew so quiet that Cassie didn't need to raise her voice to say: "Five."

"Six," John shot back.

"He don't have no six barrels," Cassie screamed, in fury. "Yuri, he's lying. He don't have no six barrels of fuel-oil. I don't think he gots any."

Yuri shrugged. "He would not lie to me. He needs my vaccine too much to even think about lying to me. So, do I hear seven barrels?"

John raised his hand again, but not for a bid. "Listen, Cassie, I'm willing to go to nine barrels, but I'll retract my bids if you give me the girl. Really, do you hate them both so badly that you are ready to pay out this much?"

Cassie looked torn between her different hatreds. "If I do, how much will I owe?"

"That'll be between you and Yuri," John said, scratching his head beneath his *Phillies* cap. "This wasn't a formal auction. He's just playing us to get the most out of the situation."

"Cut her loose," Cassie ordered, snapping her fingers. "I'll give you four for this man and not a drop more."

At first Yuri's face went hard at losing his chance at a bidding war, however he waved a hand as if to say it was nothing. "Four it is, but that's on top of the three you promised to pay for this small man and of course three for girl from before." When she nodded he grinned at the haul he had bargained for. "You are generous to your enemy. A fine display for a leader."

"Yeah, I can be generous," Cassie agreed. "But he will be worth it. Having him as my slave will be well worth it."

Colonel Williams, who had been standing alongside the other leaders, smirked at this. "Wrong. He won't be your slave. If he's taking the girl's place, he'll be dead of the fever by this time tomorrow."

"No, I want them switched," Cassie demanded.

"But we already inoculated this little man here," Yuri said. "By sunrise he will be immune. And girl is no longer yours. We cannot let her be victim unless you buy her back.

No, we will have this other man die of fever. It will be good, he is big."

Cassie's large doe-eyes went to slits as she realized she wasn't going to get everything she wanted. "You white boys trying to play me?"

John laughed nastily. "Hardly. What's happening is that your hatred is getting in the way of your common sense. You're more interested in death than in life. We should be protecting women and children. We should be freeing these people not..."

The colonel interrupted, "Slow down, cowboy. Unless you're going to volunteer we're going to need someone to step up and test the vaccine. Are you going to do it?"

"No," John said. "But I still want the girl. She was part of the deal."

Deal or no deal, John didn't get her just then. Everyone rightly assumed that a free Sadie was a dangerous Sadie. She stayed the night chained just out of reach of two men she loved and a zombie that tore open the skin at its neck trying to get at them. Their only consolation was that after many hours it crushed its own larynx with the chain and could no longer moan.

The crowds slowly died away and the three of them, and the zombie, were left with an oversized guard of fifteen men. Three were Yuri's men, armed with M4s. The others were basically paranoid babysitters who watched each other more than they watched the prisoners.

"Alright, Ram. Tell me this part of some master plan to escape?" Neil joked. His joke was flat, but he still barked out a high laugh that betrayed how nervous he really was. Though it wasn't exactly a secret; his face was as pasty white as it could get and his insides were all a jitter.

Ram dropped his chin to his chest. "I wish. They have every way onto this boat watched. They were on me before I could even stand up. Philly was a little better, except I almost got killed there. If it wasn't for Jillybean I would have been..." He stopped at the shock on their faces. "I'm sorry. I forgot to mention she stowed away with me. I bet you were worried."

"Is she...?" Neil couldn't bring himself to finish the sentence.

"No, she's alive," Ram said after a quick look over at the watchers. "North of here by the river, in my truck," he said in such a low whisper that it was easier to read his lips than it was to hear his words. "She should be ok for a little while. But what about Sarah and the baby? Please tell me they got away."

Neil swallowed and opened his mouth but when that was all he could manage, Sadie intervened, "That evil fake Jesus has Eve. He bought her as if she was a freaking goat. And Sarah...I don't know. They took us away and I haven't seen her since. But if I had my guess, I would bet the colonel has her. That rat-bastard was eyeing her real hard."

They lapsed into a long silence that was broken only by Sadie fingering the length of her shackles in a constant rattle. It was a simple length of chain hooked to itself twice with padlocks, once in a loop around her neck and again after passing through a ring set into the floor.

"If we had a screwdriver we could escape," Sadie said. She had given up on the chain and was inspecting the ring bolt attached to the deck. "Anyone got a screwdriver?"

"We'd also have to get past them," Ram said, lifting his chin at the watchers.

Neil cleared his throat. "I think we have to admit to ourselves that we're not going to be rescued. We've been in our fair share of scrapes, and one of us always came through. But I don't think it's going to happen this time. Sarah's our only chance and she's not a fighter. She can't take on this many guys, and I wouldn't want her to try. Maybe...maybe we should pray."

"Yeah," Ram said in a choked voice.

The two men went quiet for a long time. Sadie clicked

her chain until she couldn't take it anymore. "I don't know what I should be praying for," she burst out in a rush. "I want God to kill them all. I want him to sink this boat, and I know that's not right, but it's all I can think about right now! It's not fair that you two...that you two..." She broke down sobbing and Neil cried with her.

His coming torture formed a black mist on his mind making it impossible for him to think beyond it. He cried quietly, ashamed of his tears and thankful that the dark hid them. He cried deep into the night until the stars had crossed the sky.

By first light, as individuals began to claim their spots for the coming event, Neil was all cried out. He was still afraid, but now his fear was mingled with disgust. Like spectators at a football game, people had brought blankets to spread on the cold steel decking, and one couple had brought a pair of folding chairs. Most brought food and all chatted happily. The zombie finally turned away from salivating over the three prisoners and swung about to take in the larger mass of humanity. It stretched out on its chain and began snapping its teeth like a guard dog. Neil had to wonder if he did have a screwdriver just then, would he free himself or would he free the zombie and let it go hog-wild on the people?

Time went slowly by and each minute was an agony of waiting. Every ten seconds or so Neil scanned the crowd anxiously. He didn't know whether or not he wanted Sarah there. Part of him desperately needed the moral support, while the other part couldn't bear to see the pain in her eyes he knew he would see.

Ram passed the time meditating, breathing deeply and focusing on floor just in front of his knees. Even when the faction leaders came in he didn't stir. It was only when Yuri declared: "Now for the test!" that Ram glanced up.

"Do you want to go first?" he asked Neil. The three humans had moved as far from the zombie as their chains would allow. The beast, on the other hand, was having its chain lengthened.

Neil shook his head while simultaneously nodding. He then swept the crowd for the hundredth time, looking past each of the leering faces, searching for someone who wasn't there. He knew on a certain level that they weren't going to be rescued and yet there was still that part of him that held out hope. That part of him demanded to know, where were the explosions? Where was the gun fire? Where were the commandos rappelling down from silent helicopters at the last minute to save the day? He even looked for little Jillybean.

"No one's coming, Neil," Ram said, seeing the look on his face. "Like you said, it's just us this time."

The zombie was pushed toward Neil; he flinched back so that its teeth snapped just inches away and its vile breath coated him in a horrid mist. They were so close to each other that Neil could see right down its black throat.

"Step right up!" Yuri cried with flair. "Come! Let it have a taste or we let out its chain even more." The crowd called for more chain to be released regardless. They wanted blood and lots of it.

"Do it, Neil. Right now. Get it over with." Ram ordered like a drill-sergeant. "Do it! Don't let them see you're afraid."

It was easy for Ram to say. He never seemed to be afraid of anything. Neil was the opposite. Everything scared him and this, being eaten by a zombie, scared him the most. He looked down at his hands—they were curled in toward his chest.

"Just do it," he whispered to himself. This was going to be nothing compared to what Cassie was going to do to him. This was only a bite...a horrible, diseased-filled, deadly bite, but still just a bite.

Grimacing in fear he stuck out his left forearm. The zombie did not hesitate. It retracted its black lips and launched itself on the flesh, sinking its teeth deep and shaking its head side to side like a rabid pit-bull. The pain was immediate and intense. It overrode Neil's ability to think straight. A high scream, one that would embarrass him later, ripped from his throat, causing the crowd to roar with laughter. He barely heard. His mind was on the pain. Instinctively, he began to beat the zombie on the face with his right fist—and all the while the crowd laughed and pointed.

Though it seemed like ages to him, the zombie tore out a hunk of Neil's flesh in seconds only. It then chewed loudly inches from Neil's tear-stained face while he held his arm gingerly. He could almost feel the disease running up his veins. When the zombie finally swallowed it was prodded back by guards holding long poles and then sent toward Ram. He didn't flinch as Neil had. Instead he stepped forward and where the zombie was bound, he had his hands and arms free. With a quick move he grabbed the monster's head in both hands and spun it around to face the crowd. The move so surprised them that those in the front row gasped and flinched back.

"This is what you created," Ram said in a voice that carried over the crowd's babble. "Look at it. This could've been your father or your brother. It could've been your best friend. It could've been anyone, but now it is the face of hate and greed! And let's not forget fear. You're all so afraid that it's turning you into the monsters. This is what I see when I look at all of you."

The crowd heard and began to glance at each other—some skeptically, some with strained smiles, some with a tinge of fear, some with wisdom in their eyes. These last were few in numbers and they alone nodded at the truth.

Yuri was quick to intervene before Ram undermined him any further. "He is wrong! People, you must not listen to him. He says the opposite of truth. He says lie. We are here to save you from becoming like this thing." Yuri pointed toward Ram and the zombie, but which he meant wasn't clear. "But if you do not want vaccine, then you are free to leave."

No one left, though many shuffled their feet and refused to meet Ram's gaze.

Shaking his head in disgust, Ram allowed the zombie to bite him. Just like Neil he gave up his left arm, though he did not flinch or cry out. When his blood ran and colored the floor he tore his arm away.

Sadie watched this with hatred in her eyes. Without thinking she strained against her chain. Ram shook his head at her. "It's done," he said.

This simple statement ended the spectacle. The zombie was killed with a blow from a bat and disposed of; callously it was flung over the side of the ferry. Then it became a matter of waiting and few hung around for very long. Neil pleaded for Yuri to release Sadie, but in a fit of depression she refused. "Where would I go? My place is here, at least for now."

What should have been a long miserable day of waiting turned out to be only miserable. Just when they wanted time to stand still, the hours flew by. At one in the afternoon Ram was unchanged. The same was true at three. He told them the story of how he'd been scratched in Philadelphia and how he had lived. There was hope and determination in his brown eyes as he recounted that day.

The people who came to stare, now did so with an air of disappointment. Sadie usually lashed them with her tongue:

"Keep walking, ghoul!"

"You sorry he's going to live?"

By six even Yuri was getting nervous. He had Ram's temperature taken and then retaken. "Doesn't look good for sales, does it?" Sadie asked, not bothering to hide her malice from any. "Who's going to need your fancy vaccine when both of them live?"

By seven Ram's eyes were fever bright.

Chapter 37

Sadie

New York City

"Come on, Ram, fight it," Sadie whispered. She was like the cut-man in a boxer's corner. "It's nothing but a few germs. You are tough. The toughest man I know."

The encouragement was useless. Within the hour the delirium had him raving. "Don't look at me, Trey," he screamed at Neil. "Stop it! Stop looking with your bug eyes full of bugs. Full of bugs."

Neil turned away to look at the wall with gritted teeth and wet cheeks. He stared uselessly at a seam in the old boat. It was a natural seam created by time and weather which, extending from the top of a girder, made its way down its length, gaining in width as it did so. "This world is falling apart," Neil murmured.

"Full of bugs," Ram whispered. "The world is full of bugs like fishing bugs and zebras and monsters. Trey knew it. Trey, that stupid fuck!"

"It's going to be ok, Ram," Sadie soothed. She didn't know the name, Trey, however she did understand about zebras and fishing bugs and monsters, all of these alluded to Jillybean. It was a subject that she felt had to remain secret. "Trey's not here. Do you know where he is, Ram?" she asked to change the subject.

He nodded, his face coated in a sweaty luster. "He's gone fishing. He's drown face down in the brown. I killed him. He drown in the brown. In the brown! There was water and I said it would be ok and he said we would drown. Like a clown, in a gown and a frown and hound and a mound..." His words tapered off.

Ram was quiet for a minute until one of the ghoulish spectators threw a pencil at him. "Come on! Let's hear more about the hound and the mound." The people with him laughed, until Sadie, quick as lightning, zinged the pencil back at them full force. One of them gave a shout of pain, much to her dark joy.

"Hound, mound, found, round," Ram said. His eyes swam in his gently rocking head; he turned them to Sadie. "I'm sorry, Julia. I love you and I could love you more, but my head hurts...it hurts so bad. Do you believe me?"

"Yes," Sadie whispered. Her throat was dangerously near to closing all the way. She could feel the emotions gripping her right where she breathed.

"I'm sorry," Ram said.

"You have nothing to be sorry about," Sadie replied. She prayed then. As a sign of her lack of faith, she prayed that Ram would die quickly because in her mind he was so far gone that not even God could save him. "Why don't you lie down and sleep," she suggested.

His fevered mind found the suggestion agreeable and he slumped over with his face on the steel decking. More people came to gawk and though quite a few made snide or evil remarks, Sadie refused to respond, fearing to wake the man.

At half-past eight Ram began to make guttural noises from deep in his throat and a little while later he awoke. He turned his cadaverous eyes on Sadie and then launched himself bodily at her. Only the chain kept him from rending her to shreds.

Sadie went to her knees and cried, with the zombie that had once been her friend stretching out his fingers only inches away. "I'm done!" she screeched to the guards. "I can't do this anymore. Let me out! Let me out!"

Neil tried to yell with her, but his voice locked and cracked; he could only pound on the deck until Yuri showed up.

"Finally," the Russian said as he saw what had become of Ram.

"Please kill him," Sadie begged.

The idea seemed to insult Yuri. "What? How you say this? I can not kill my exhibit. He and this little man are now exhibit. They show my vaccine is good. Da. They stay put until black woman go away tomorrow morning, and then I don't know what. Not good for little man, I suspect. Big man? He is already dead so nobody cares."

"Then release her," Neil said, indicating Sadie. "She's not yours and she's done nothing wrong."

Yuri considered: "This, I could do, buuuut..."

"There is no but," Neil said cutting in on the Russian's drawn out word. "The *Whites* bought her. She should be free to go to them."

Yuri nodded in a tepid manner. "Yes, is true, but the *White*s they are not so strong. I think your little girlfriend is better here. She keep you company. Is nice, da? Is safe."

"Safe?" Neil asked. "Is she in danger? I thought no weapons are allowed on board. Not even knives."

"What is it that I can say?" Yuri asked with an over-done shrug. "The *Blacks* have much oil. It gives them much power. Things happen. Now there are more and more bodies in river every day. I do what I can, but this girl is special. The queen black, she hates this girl. Is only safe right here."

"Maybe he's right..." Neil began.

Sadie cut right across him, "No. I can't stay here, not with Ram like this. I can't, it hurts too much. And besides I don't want to stay on this boat." For a brief second she held her hand at waist height. Neil nodded his understanding.

"Let her go," he said to the Russian.

When Yuri left to get the keys to her shackles, Sadie moved as close to Neil as she could. The crowds were beginning to trickle back to see the final outcome. In a whisper she asked, "What do I do?"

Neil's face was puffy and red and in the dim light he barely seemed himself. He tried to smile and it was achingly sad for Sadie. "Run," he said. "God gave you beautiful, fast legs. Use them! Find Jillybean and make a run for it."

"What about Sarah and Eve?" she asked. Her voice then dropped an octave, "What about you?"

"I think it's best if you forget about me," he said. "And Sarah, if she's with the colonel. And forget about Eve, too."

Sadie couldn't believe this. "You want me to just give up. Look what they did to Ram for Christ's sake!"

Neil didn't look at the beast that was swinging its strong arms just inches away. "What do you think I'm trying to keep from happening to you? I don't want you to end up like him, and I definitely don't want you to end up like me. You heard what Cassie has in mind for me. She's going to skin me alive and probably hang me out..."

"Stop!" Sadie whispered harshly. Her face felt hot except where newly formed tears ran streaks down her cheeks. "Don't say that, please."

"Then listen to me," Neil pleaded. "You don't have a chance to save Sarah or Eve, or anyone. From what I've overheard, the colonel brought at least thirty men with him, and his is not even the strongest faction. Cassie probably has more, while Abraham is the leader of a whole bunch of religious fanatics. They think he comes from God! They may be the most dangerous of all. And what do you have? The *Whites*? All they have to defend you is moral outrage. The truth is you're all alone. Yes, you're smart and brave and fast as the wind, but it's just you against a whole boatload of people. Take Jillybean and run."

Before she could say anything, the Russian returned, waving to the eager crowd who cheered him. "Here is proof that my vaccine will save you! Look at little man. Him, healthy. Vaccine save him. But not big man. Now we begin. Tonight! First come for vaccine, first serve. We will open the docks for unloading in five minutes."

Many in the crowd rushed away; Sadie guessed they were people who didn't belong to any of the factions. The Russian dropped his cheerful demeanor and, walking in a wide circle around Ram, said, "I have keys, but I think it is waste. Are you sure you want to be free?"

"Yeah," Sadie replied. The second she was released she ran to Neil and hugged him fiercely and didn't want to let go, ever.

After a few seconds, Neil took a deep breath and pushed her away. "You have to be quick, now. If Yuri is correct..."

"I am," the Russian said.

"Then it won't be long before someone is after you."

"Your warning comes too late," Yuri said. He pointed to where his guards and the faction guards were standing. There had been two members of the *Blacks* off to themselves. Now there was only one.

Neil's eyes bugged. He shoved her. "Go. If Sarah is with the *Whites*, then take her and make a run for it. If not..."

Sadie understood. Despite a growing alarm that had her stomach churning she hugged Neil one last time and then turned to the crowd. They ranged before her, filling her vision from left to right, a dense thicket of humanity unbroken by the slimmest path between.

They watched her with curious eyes and with hating eyes and with greedy eyes, and a few with sad eyes. All these eyes beguiled her and she lost her wits, forgetting how close real danger actually lurked.

Ram grabbed her.

By accident she had taken one step too close and now his hand was like a vice on her wrist. Even in death he was exceedingly strong. Slowly he dragged her closer to his gaping mouth.

"Nyet!" Yuri cried. "Nyet. Stop!" Bravely he waved his hand in front of Ram's face. Mindless now, Ram turned to attack the closer flesh and let go of Sadie, who, shaking all up and down her body, took only a single step back.

"Get out of here!" Neil cried, also trying to distract Ram.

Sadie turned to go. People blocked her way. Some

stepped back remembering old manners, while others tried to edge closer, almost eagerly. These she ran from, pushing roughly through the crowd. Saying over and over, "Excuse me, excuse me."

Someone called her name, but in the crush she couldn't tell who it was. Everyone seemed a villain. She was jostled and knocked; a hand grabbed hold of her coat from behind. It was a black man—one of Cassie's men—he was recognizable by his yellowed, jaundiced eyes and his particular anger which he wore as a mask over his handsome features.

He had Sadie's coat in one hand and in the other was a jagged flash of bright silver. The one hand on her coat pulled her close, attempting to impale her on the barely hidden knife.

With a shrug, Sadie let her coat slide from her shoulders and the man was left holding nothing but cloth as she sprinted away. Using every bit of her speed she ducked and dodged through the crowd. When she had almost made it to the end of the boat, and perhaps to safety, another man grabbed her hand.

He was a white man and, for a brief second, Sadie mistook his skin color to represent some sort of haven or safety. But his grip was crushing and his lip curled.

"What are you doing?" she asked in confusion as he began to pull her back toward the man with the knife, who was even then fighting through the crowd to get at her.

"Sorry," he said, clearly not meaning it. "But money is money, even if it is oil."

Desperately, she yanked back, her arm extended. There were cries and yells all around, but no one helped. They only retreated so as not to get caught up in someone else's business. One woman was too slow; she flinched and made a face, but otherwise stood her ground. Sadie reversed her pull and went straight at her. With her arm and the arm of her attacker stretched, they struck the woman across the midsection—the woman went berserk in fear. Like a feral cat she scratched and bit to break the connected hands.

In seconds Sadie was free once again and running. She made it to the front of the boat which she found packed with people. Some were hurrying away to have their goods registered, others were coming to see the freshly made zombie. Others were coming to collect a bounty.

"She's right there," a woman screeched, pointing.

Instinctively Sadie dodged to the right, away from the woman, and up a flight of stairs toward the passenger deck of the boat. Halfway up a blur of silver caught the moonlight as it passed within inches. It clanged against the railing to drop on the stair in front of her. Without losing a step, Sadie scooped it up—it was a hunk of scrap metal that had been honed to razor sharpness.

It was not balanced for throwing, which was likely why it missed her, yet she didn't hesitate to throw it herself. The black man with the yellow eyes was on the stairs behind her. One-on-one she knew she would lose against him, which meant she had to keep her distance, she had to evade. At the top of the stairs she turned and very deliberately hurled the knife end over end at the charging man.

Even in the dark he saw it coming straight at his face. He threw himself to the side and the knife whizzed harmlessly past. When he looked up again, Sadie was out of sight.

She was small and she was speedy. Running, crouched over, she slipped through the upper deck crowd, most of whom could not possibly know she had been freed. Most...

As she slipped by the door to the pilot house it swung open and before she could leap away a man with hard, brown eyes and deep brown skin slapped a hand across her mouth from behind and brought one of the steel shanks up to her eye. In a single fluid move he slipped her into a darkened room and shut the door behind her.

Chapter 38

Sadie

New York City

Sadie fought the innate desire swelling in her to fight the man who had her from behind. She could've bitten his hand, or stomped his foot, or perhaps reached back to try to crush his testicles. However the knife point was so close to her eye that *any* movement beyond the simple act of breathing would send it slicing into her.

"I take it you are Sadie?" the man asked in a whisper.

"Dat is a dumb question," another voice said. It originated from a female and was thick in its accent. "Dere can be no utter dat looks like she."

The knife withdrew, but the hand stayed for a moment longer. "We're friends of Ram's," the man said in a low voice. "Or we were. It's terrible about what happened."

Now Sadie was released and she slowly turned to look at the people standing in the little stairwell that led to the pilot house. There were three of them and all were very much black. She couldn't help remarking on that fact.

"But you're black."

"And proud of it. But don't worry, we're not associated with those idiots in Philadelphia. They're a damned embarrassment to black people everywhere." He blew out in a sigh and then rubbed his beard. "My name is Steve; this is Donna and our quiet friend is Ray."

Before Sadie could say *Hello* or *Thank you*, Donna nudged Steve to the side and asked. "Oh Cherie, what of the lil' chi-al?"

Sadie blinked at the question. "Chi-al? Do you mean child?" When Donna nodded emphatically, Sadie answered, "Are you talking about Jillybean? Ram's says she's north of here, somewhere near the river. I have to get to her, only everyone on this boat seems out for my blood."

"There's a bounty on your head," Steve told her. "Enough to pay for half a vaccine shot. It's turning people into killers."

"I think they already were killers," Sadie said, darkly. "Or worse. They were all savages, every one of them, regardless of color. Did you see what happened to poor Ram? It was like something out of Roman times."

"We saw, Cherie," Donna said, reaching out and touching Sadie's cheek. "It twas a sad ting."

Strangely, grief was not Sadie's most immediate emotion and neither was hatred, though it was a close second. It was fear, fear for Sarah, Jillybean, and Eve took up most of her heart. "Tell me, have you heard anything about our friend Sarah or her baby? They were taken yesterday."

Donna's face clouded over and she dropped her head. Steve answered, "There are all sorts of rumors running about. People buying people. Families being torn apart, that sort of thing. Everyone has heard about the baby, she's with the people from New Eden, but I don't know anyone named Sarah."

"She's older than me. About my height," Sadie said, holding her hand up at head height. "Blonde, blue eyes, very pretty. Does that ring a bell?"

Just then the door started to open. Quickly Steve pushed Sadie behind him, smushing her into the wall where she was pinned. He asked the new comer, "You need something?"

A man's deep voice, asked, "Anyone come through here? A white girl? All got up in black clothes?"

"No, we just checked up here," Steve said. Next to him Donna kept slipping fearful peeks at Sadie, who pressed herself to the wall, trying her best to remain still and unobtrusive. She even went so far as to hold her breath.

"Shit!" the man cursed and then left in a huff.

When the door clicked shut, Steve sent the dead bolt home and then leaned against the frame. "Jeeze. They aren't going to rest until you're dead."

"I know," Sadie replied. She was unconcerned with herself however. "What about the blonde? Do you know if there's a woman with the *Whites* or with that Colonel from the *Island*?"

"No," Steve answered. "At least I know there's no girl with the *Whites*. They're all on the main boat in the lower deck. I went through there a few hours ago to see if they needed any help, but they couldn't see past my skin color, not that I blame them. The *Blacks* are shanking them left and right every time they step out of their little corner."

"So what are we to do wit dis girl?" Donna asked. "She can't stay wit us, and she can't stay here. Not for long, no how."

"Hiding won't help me," Sadie said. "I have to get to Jillybean, which means I need to get off the boat."

"How?" Steve asked. "By now they'll have both exits covered. There's only two ways off, you know, unless you want to jump over the side."

"Then I go over the side."

Shocked faces greeted this. "Are you that good of a swimmer?" Steve asked. "Nighttime in a river is no joke."

Though she loved the water, in truth she was not a good swimmer in the technical sense. A weak version of the breaststroke and the sidestroke were the only two styles she had mastered and she was not particularly fast in either of them. Where she excelled was swimming underwater.

"I just need a clean shot to the side of the boat," Sadie said, trying not to think about how she wasn't the biggest fan of heights. She'd just jump and know that it was better than getting shanked in the dark.

Steve rubbed his beard, thinking. After a few seconds he began a slow nod. "You know we can't be seen with you, but, I think we can help a little. Me and Ray can run some interference. From here it's probably only fifty feet to the side of the boat. Just take off for it...and don't look down.

It's probably only a twenty-five-foot drop but it may look like more."

"An' I can keep watch," Donna said. "I'll jes tap on de door when de time is ripe. Good luck, Cherie."

"Thanks," Sadie said.

The three Good Samaritans left her in the dark, where her imagination quickly exaggerated the height of the ferry boat to ridiculous proportions. "Just jump. Don't look. Just..." A tapping on the door told her it was time.

With a huge breath, Sadie slammed open the door and sped to the right. Between her and the side of the boat, there were many people and they were all blurs of different flesh colors, each representing the cruelty of her fellow man. None was special. None was inherently good.

Like a kaleidoscope, the colors oriented on a single point—Sadie. From the second she opened the door, every face turned in her direction, sparking a cry that reached into the ears of her enemies, and, as though she were a magnet, there was a general surge of humanity toward her. They were all too slow.

She was a blur, herself. In seconds she was at the rail and, finding it higher than she expected, vaulted over it. There was no time for her to fear falling. There was only a moment where she gasped and held her body rigid before the icy water ran up her body to cover over her.

Two strong kicks propelled her to the surface and then she was swimming at her fastest rate straight away from the side of the boat and into the dark. At first, Sadie feared being shot at more than anything, but then she heard the sound of a heavy splash behind her. She looked back to see someone churning the water with arms that pin wheeled with such precision that he seemed more like a machine than a man.

With her limited skills she saw was not going to be able to out swim such a person, nor, judging by his size, was she going to have much chance at outfighting him either, especially if she remained in his element. After a huge breath, she turned neatly in the one direction that would give her the slimmest advantage: down.

The water was cold and black as she dove deep. She turned with the current hoping to put as much distance as she could between them, but above, her enemy guessed her intention and turned as well. It was a smart move on his part. With his superior speed it behooved him to keep her upstream of him where he could relentlessly hound her until she was too tired to go on...and then what? Would he drown her? Or would he drag her back to the boat and let Cassie skin her alive? All these thoughts went through her mind in a blink and the sum of them boiled down to the very frightful reality that she was going to die, if she didn't do something completely unexpected.

From beneath, Sadie could see her pursuer as a lighter shadow against a deep background. His long body cut the water elegantly like a power boat. She was more like a torpedo rising up unseen and unheard; she went right for his midsection. He was completely surprised and, with his perfectly mechanical motion, which included properly timed breaths, completely unprepared as Sadie came up, grabbed his jeans at the waistline and pulled him down.

In the span of one second he went from elegant to epileptic. Fear of drowning was so ingrained instinctually that his precise technique failed him; he flailed and kicked.

For as long as she could, probably no more than twenty seconds, Sadie held on, sticking to his underside, barnacle-like, until she too felt the urgent need for air. Releasing him she came up to the surface, took two large breaths, and then, ducking back under the water, chased him back toward the boat. In the brief attack he had breathed in water and now wanted nothing more to do with her.

She didn't pursue more than a few strokes, before turning north; her business wasn't one of revenge, but of rescue.

Slogging against the current, she slowly put enough

distance between her and the boats to chance going to shore. There she staggered on, holding her dripping body in a vain attempt at retaining heat and at the same time keeping an ear out for zombies.

There were many of them; so many that she couldn't muster up enough energy to fear them unless they actively turned and rushed at her. When that happened, and it did with an exhausting frequency, she would dash into the water where the zombies displayed all the swimming skills of drowning kittens.

Because of these interruptions, it took her an hour to find Ram's truck. With the world of humanity eroding like a snowman under a fine drizzle, the Ford stood out like a sentry on a little bluff over the river.

"Finally," she whispered, careful to keep her voice barely above the sound of her own ragged breathing. Very near at hand was a pipe, which Sadie figured was part of the sewage system. She gave it a wide berth, because coming from its hollow throat were the moans of many zombies. She tried to slip past, using a crumbling concrete barrier as cover, but they saw, sending up a dreadful echoing howl.

"Shit," she cursed. Now she had a quick decision to make: did she run back into the water for the twentieth time, or did she try for the truck just up the hill? The water was just too cold and the truck too alluring. "Hey, Jillybean!" she called as she huffed up the hill with the zombies scrambling behind—there was no need to be quiet now. "Open the truck, Jillybean. Quick, it's me Sadie."

The truck flashed its blinkers and the girl breathed a sigh of relief. She had been deathly afraid that after all her troubles in getting here, she would find the Ford abandoned—which, within three seconds was exactly what she found.

Sadie hauled back the heavy door and, with the first smile she had worn in ages, said, "Thank God, you're still..." She choked on her words. The truck was clearly empty.

Somebody had beaten her there and had taken everything, including a six-year-old girl. It was a kick in the stomach.

Feeling her body and mind go numb, Sadie climbed into the cab and shut the door behind, locking it just in case a zombie got lucky with its fumbling hands. She had only just begun to hide herself in the foot-well when she remembered that the truck had flashed its blinkers. That hadn't happened on its own. Someone had the keys and had used the remote car door opener purposely, clearly trying to draw her in and trap her there. Even as the thought struck her, the locks shot up on their own, just as the first of the zombies began climbing up the side of the truck.

Chapter 39

Jillybean

New York City

"Hey," Jillybean said, as she opened the truck's door.

Sadie went crazy, kicking with her feet while simultaneously trying to claw herself out of the truck.

"What are you doing?" Jillybean asked, giving her monstrous face a scratch. For the most part the make-up went unnoticed, however if she moved her face too much or sweated, as she had huffing up the hill, it started to itch like mad.

You scared her, duh, Ipes said. *Sure is funny looking, though*.

"I guess I did. Hey, Sadie it's just me, Jillybean. I'm not a real zombie if that's what's got you all ascared about. It's just Halloween make-up, see?" The little girl pulled back on the shredded up *Eagles* shirt to show her normal pale skin beneath.

"What?" Sadie asked, bewildered. "But, how?" She peered over the top of the dash back the way they had come. "Where are all the rest of them? Weren't there lots of zombies in that pipe?"

"Oh, them," Jillybean said with disgust. "They're all stuck behind this grate a few feet back. They were good for camel-flog, but..."

Camouflage, Ipes corrected.

"Right, camouflage," Jillybean said. "But they sure were annoying. So did Mister Ram rescue you? He was gonna get you and Mister Neil and Miss Sarah and the baby. Do you think he'll be back soon? Some people came and robbed us. That's why I had to hide in that pipe and it's been real, real boring. Hey, what's wrong with your eyes? Huh, Sadie? Why are you crying?"

"Ram is dead," Sadie said, running tears and mascara

down her already wet face. "They made him into a zom...zombie."

Jillybean sat back stunned for a moment, but then she burst out in peals of laughter. "No, they didn't. He was just wearing a costume like from Halloween. See? Look at mine. It fools the monsters. Once for Halloween I was a fairy. The dress was pink and silver, but the wings were..."

Unexpectedly, and with the speed of a striking snake, Sadie grabbed Jillybean and crushed her in a hug. Sadie dribbled tears and rocked back and forth in misery.

Confused, Jillybean went on, "...The wings had gold on them all along the edge. And you know what? The costume came with a wand! My daddy said the Chinese didn't know the difference between a fairy and a fairy godmother. Which is real funny. Is that a real thing? A fairy godmother? Ipes says it is, but I think he's trying to be a jokester."

Sadie went on crying, with a slight hitch in her chest.

Eventually Ipes rolled his eyes and said, *There are godmothers, but no fairy godmothers.* He then followed up his argument, asking, *Does she smell weird to you? She smells like the river. I don't think that's the cleanest water. Remind me not to go swimming in there.*

"Stop being bad," Jillybean scolded the zebra, despite secretly agreeing with him. As a consequence of possessing an ill-mannered tongue, Ipes was set on the far end of the truck's dashboard.

"Look Jillybean," Sadie said in a husky voice. "Ram is really dead. I watched him get bit by a zombie, and...and...and I saw him t-turn into one."

"For reals?" Jillybean asked. She felt strange all of a sudden—her body went completely numb all except her ears which tingled and rushed with the sound of TV static.

Sadie nodded with blank eyes. They were dark and black, save where points of light, like sharp needles seemed to shoot out. "For reals. And yes, there are godmothers. They raise a baby just in case something happens to a parent. I can be your godmother if you want me to."

The static grew, making Jillybean's head feel filled with it, like a scarecrow with its hay. "But what about Mister Neil and Miss..."

Jillybean watched as Sadie suddenly burst out in fresh tears. Her head rocked back and then out of the blue she slapped herself, leaving a four-fingered mark on her cheek.

"You ok?" Jillybean asked.

"They're gone too!" Sadie shrieked. "Damn it! Damn it! Fuck!" As soon as she cursed, Sadie's black eyes flew open and she stared at Jillybean, realizing it was a mistake.

"Those are bad words," Jillybean said, blinking. Her monster makeup was streaked with tears that she didn't feel. Just at that moment she couldn't understand what Sadie meant by *gone* or really what she meant by Ram being *dead*. These were abstract words to Jillybean. Their meaning kept changing in her mind as *what ifs* sprang up: what if she was wrong? What if she didn't see it correctly? What if Ram was faking? What if Ram could get better?

These answers fell into the category of what she didn't know. What she did know as fact was what her father taught her. She knew *rules*. Rules were black and white, and concrete in their meaning. And one of the rules was that people weren't supposed to say bad words!

"You're right," Sadie said, making a sound that was a combination of a cry and a laugh. "Neil would say the same thing."

"Cept he's a monster, right?" Jillybean asked trying to grasp more concrete ideas. "And monsters can't talk."

Sadie blew out a long breath through puffed cheeks and then told Jillybean everything that had happened, which only led to more uncertainty.

"You're too ascared to go save Mister Neil?" Jillybean asked.

There were parts of Sadie's story that were very heartbreakingly sad and others that made her little teeth clench together as though they had been welded shut, and others that were confusing, especially this one point. If Neil was alive, but chained to the open deck of a boat and a simple tool would free him, why didn't she want to go?

"Do you think it's too dangerous? I told Mister Ram that everything is too dangerous now, even just living, and he believed me."

The older girl wiped her eyes, saying, "And look what happened to him. What good did it do?"

"He saved you. That was good," Jillybean said. "I think so, and so does Ipes, though he thinks you smell too much like that green river."

"It doesn't matter anyway. We can't save him because we'd never get on the boat," Sadie said after making a noise like she was flicking dirt from the tip of her tongue. "Ram couldn't. They're watching every way of getting on board."

Jillybean's lips pursed as she recalled the short pier and the boats tied alongside of it—she saw all of it in her mind as though she was there looking down on the scene. On the right side of the pier was a white boat. It was brightly lit; tall and long. On the other side were two orange boats—*ferries* the word popped into her mind—tied side by side. The two ferries had platforms running from the dock to the lower decks allowing people and vehicles to get on board. She also saw the highway and the fences and the zombies and the little guard house and the men on guard. And she saw a way past all that.

Stop, Ipes ordered. *We aren't going to try to save Mister Neil. Not after what happened to Ram. It's too dangerous. He...*

Like shutting a door, the little girl closed her mind to the zebra. One second he was there, pointing out how dangerous going on to the boats would be, and using Ram's death as an example, and the next second he was simply a toy sitting on the dash. She decided she wouldn't think about danger. Danger was what happened to other people. And she wouldn't think about Ram either. Thinking about Ram hurt far too much--it was like a knife in her heart, a fist in her gut, a hand crushing her throat. It was like all the pain in the world being crammed into her soul...

She would think about something else.

"They're not watching every way," Jillybean said. No, they weren't, and why would they? Ram was dead. Neil and Sarah were captured and Sadie had been forced to flee. Why would they keep too tight a lookout? "We can get on the boats, but first we need to change your look. You'll need to do something with your hair if you're going to pass. And, of course, you'll need a dress, maybe a pink one."

No, not a dress, Ipes said, suddenly there again in her mind, cutting in on Jillybean's vision of Sadie in her full potential. *If we're going to do this we're going to do this right. No one wears dresses anymore, not even Miss Sarah. Besides we have to deal with getting her passed the monsters first. Her hair is perfect for pretending to be a monster already so at least you don't have to change that.*

"Ipes, hush!" Jillybean gave Sadie an embarrassed smile. "He has some silly ideas. Now let's get you costumed to look like a proper monster."

"Are we really doing this?" Sadie asked. When Jillybean nodded the older girl added, "Neil is going to be pissed."

Giving Sadie the look of a monster took almost no time. Jillybean shredded her clothes with her little pocket knife and applied the makeup as though she was wielding a trowel. It took minutes only. Teaching her how to act like a monster was another matter. For so long, Sadie had used a hyper-aware state to stay alive: she had the quick, nervous eyes of a mongoose on the hunt, while at the same time her head swung about as though on a swivel.

"Try half-closing your eyes," Jillybean suggested. "And maybe stare at the ground for the most part. Watch me do it." Jillybean did her best monster impression.

"But how do you see them coming?" Sadie asked. "With your hair all down like that you won't see them coming."

"It doesn't matter if you see them coming. You're not aposed to. You just go along and pretend you're a monster. Come on, I'll show you with real monsters."

Jillybean took Sadie's reluctant hand and began to walk back to the FDR highway, looking for zombies, but strangely, in a city full of them, there weren't any around. They crossed the highway, simply stepping over the fencing that Ram had destroyed the day before, and on the other side slipped through a gap where a zip-tie had let go.

They proceeded south on a course parallel to the FDR, heading toward the pier and the colony of boats. They didn't need signs or directions; sound drew them on. The roar of heavy machinery carried in the still night air and, like an infernal summons, it attracted every zombie within blocks. Finally they saw some late-comers staggering on.

"I'll go first," Jillybean said. They were ducked down behind a car, watching the stragglers slowly moving south. "Just do what I do." She took a second to adjust her pack beneath the flayed sweatshirt and muss her hair even more before stepping out in a slow, gimping manner. To show Sadie that there wasn't anything to worry about, Jillybean went straight for a lone zombie and passed within inches of it before heading back to the car.

"That's so crazy," Sadie said, somewhat in awe. "It didn't even give you a second look."

"Yeah, just be one of them and you'll be fine. Now it's your turn."

Sadie did her best. When it wasn't good enough and a zombie would come close, drawn by some peculiarity, Jillybean would let out a human word, or throw a magic marble, or otherwise draw attention away from the older girl.

As they drew closer to the pier, Sadie's acting became more stiff and human-like, however the zombies were very much focused on what was happening in the lot that had been erected near the pier and didn't notice. A pair of forklifts, piled high with crates that were filled with guns, ammo, fuel, and food, buzzed back and forth among hundreds of trucks and SUVs parked in the receiving area.

There were people there as well; men in black uniforms were sifting through the goods that people were putting up in exchange for the vaccine.

"How are we going to get in there?" Sadie asked in a breathy whisper. "And how on earth do you think we'll get by all those people?"

Jillybean went stiff that Sadie would dare to break character, surrounded as they were. "Shhhuuuushh," she moaned loudly. She then grabbed Sadie's hand and pushed through the crowd of undead. The closeness of the creatures, the touch of their slimy skin, the fetid and dank odor drifting out of their open mouths was mind-numbing in its horror, yet Jillybean persevered with a not-altogether single minded determination. Ipes was there in her mind as well, urging her on in a voice that reminded her of Ram's:

Hurry Jillybean. Cassie will be at the front of the line to get her vaccines. Time is short if we have any chance of saving Neil.

In truth she didn't need to be reminded. Inside her heart was a fear countdown that was rushing towards a conclusion. It forced her on faster than she thought prudent. Still she arrived unmolested at her destination: a corner of the fence where vehicles were lined up close, conveniently blocking them from view of the workers.

"How..." Sadie began, again in a whisper.

Jillybean waved her arm in the older girl's face to shut her up and Sadie responded by gesturing at the barbed wire that ran along the top of the fence. Her question was obvious: how do we get past the fence?

"Fooolloooow meeee," Jillybean intoned and then she actually squirmed between the dead where they bowed out the fence. Suddenly she dropped to her knees, crawled forward at a fast clip until she was at the very edge of the fence, and then rolled under it. When the press of zombies bowed it out, they created a slim gap at the bottom.

Sadie followed right behind and came up smiling. "That was cool," she said in her normal voice. There was no need to be quiet now, when the zombies were making a hell of a racket. "So what's next?"

"We change back into people," Jillybean replied, scanning the vehicles. "There it is, Mister Neil's rover-thingy." Keeping low, they scampered to the Rover and found it had been pawed through and that everything of any real value had been taken already. Still there were baby-wipes left to clean the makeup off their faces, and brushes to run through their hair, and clothes of Sarah's for Sadie to change into so that she looked very pretty in Jillybean's eyes.

Jillybean didn't have extra clothes to change into except her white dress. Against Ipes strong opposition she happily put it on.

"You're not going to stand out at all," Sadie said sarcastically.

"No one is looking for me," Jillybean replied. Ipes was quick to point out that Abraham of the doomsday cult would probably snatch her up if he got the chance. She chose to ignore the zebra just then, rationalizing: "Besides I don't have anything else to wear."

"I guess not," Sadie said as she watched the people work. They were very methodical, sorting, cataloging, and storing what goods they wanted from each vehicle. They buzzed quickly through each in a matter of minutes. They were far out-pacing the forklifts which had a line of thirty crates waiting to be picked up and moved.

The six-year-old watched as well. "Are you thinking what I'm thinking?" she asked.

"Probably not," Sadie said with a laugh. "What I'm

thinking is that we're going to get caught right off the bat if we try to get down that ramp. I guess we could say we left something in our truck?"

"What?" Jillybean asked incredulously. "No, that won't work. Even in Miss Sarah's clothes you still look like you, which means we can't have anyone see you up close. I say we use those wood boxes. We can climb in and get a ride onto the ferry. Should be no problem at all."

Sadie looked unconvinced. "What happens if they pop open the crate the second we get on the boat?"

"We say we were playing a game," Jillybean suggested. "You know, like hide-and-go-seek. They might yell at us but that's about it."

"Seems like a plan," Sadie said with her half-shrug. "Let's do it."

Gaining access to the crates was a simple task as it was only a matter of timing. They waited for the forklifts to bear away their burdens and then they just climbed into the next crate in line. The crate smelled of fuel and oiled metal which made sense since they were sitting next to a little gas-powered generator, while all around their feet were bullets of all calibers crammed into ammo-crates, as well there was a wicker bushel basket filled with roundish objects that caught Sadie's attention.

"Put these in your backpack," she said dropping three of the items in among Jillybean's candles, and string and other oddities.

"What are they?"

"Hand grenades. They're like little bombs, so don't even think about using them," Sadie said with a stern, motherly glare. She hooked two of them to her jeans under her white, buttoned up shirt.

Jillybean wouldn't dare use them. She was afraid to even move with them in her pack and when the crate was lifted and jostled by the forklift she had to hold her hand over her mouth to keep from crying out.

After a short ride, the crate was set down in a dark, noisy area. Sadie peeked out and then swore under her breath.

"We're on the wrong boat," she said, opening the top of the crate and lifting Jillybean out. "We wanted the one on the other side. That's where Neil is."

Their crate, along with dozens and dozens more, was in an open area of the lower deck. Men and women worked there: some hefting supplies to other parts of the boat, some directing the forklifts, and others installing a string of light bulbs to illuminate the dim proceedings. For now, the dark hid the two girls, but, as an extra precaution, they snuck around to the back of the crates and crouched.

Sadie poked her head up again to find a way out. "I think we can make a run for it after the next forklift comes in."

With her pack filled with bombs, Jillybean didn't want to run anywhere. "How about instead we try to see where those stairs lead," she said, pointing at a set of stairs that sat in the middle of the vehicle deck. It brought them dangerously close to where the men were working on the lights, however their focus was on the ceiling.

The older girl nodded, took Jillybean's little hand in her soft, cool one and led her to the stairs making sure to keep low and quiet. Sadie started up, but Jillybean didn't follow. She was looking down.

"Those won't go anywhere," Sadie said in a hoarse whisper. "That's the engine room, I bet. We don't want that…Jillybean? Hey, we can't just stand here, they're gonna see us."

Jillybean wasn't just standing there. She was thinking.

On the next ship, where Neil was, there were guards—according to Sadie probably three or four, too many for Sadie to fight, which meant that in order to free Neil they would need a distraction. A big one.

A fire is big, Ipes suggested.

In her mind's eye she pictured where the stairs down would lead: a room, long and low, but very well lit. Machinery with pipes and knobs and blinking consoles would run from one wall to the other. These were the engines. Engines ran on fuel, and fuel burned.

"And you want to start a fire?" She could envision the boat engulfed in flames with people running and screaming. People were going to get hurt.

Ipes was unfazed. *Ram got killed and they did nothing. They aren't nice people and besides it'll be a slow fire with lots of smoke. At least it will start that way. We just need a couple of those gas cans to get it going.*

Sadie was tugging on her shirt and saying something, but Jillybean ignored her, turning to see a line of jerry cans just feet away on one of the crates.

"We need two of those," she said to Sadie.

The older girl's eyes bugged. "For what?"

When Jillybean explained, Sadie's eyes went even wider, but she didn't argue. Instead she crept back to the crate and after a look around, grabbed the heavy cans one at a time. Grunting, she heaved them to the stairs and then lugged them down into the engine room where Jillybean was already standing, staring all around with her blue eyes at squints.

"You ok?"

This time Jillybean snapped right out of it. "Yeah, I was just looking for where the gas comes in for these engine things. Ipes says it's right over there." She led the way to the fuel import lines.

"What happens if this stuff explodes?" Sadie asked with a crooked little smile and a little laugh as she began dumping the fuel all over the import lines and the machinery.

"I don't know," Jilly said with a shrug. "Ipes says we should get another one of them cans and make a trail out of here and then light it from a distance or we won't be able to get away in time."

"This is crazy," Sadie replied before running up the stairs. When she returned, Jillybean directed her to pour a line of gas in a great loop around the machinery.

"Just like the movies," the little girl said, holding up a lighter. However, before she let Sadie grab it, she pulled her hand back as Ipes had another idea, one that made her stomach go queasy. "Really? That's what you want to do?" she asked. From her pack she pulled one of the hand grenades and rolled it at the gas cans.

"Jeeze," Sadie said.

"Ipes says it'll cook off like a bullet. Whatever that means. He says it'll give the workers something to think about if they decide to get too heroic." Jillybean calmly bent down and lit the line of gas herself, though it took both of her small hands to do so. "We better go."

Chapter 40

Neil

New York City

After so many hours chained to the steel deck, Neil discovered that he had long ago run out of any position that he could describe as comfortable. His arm ached where the zombie had bitten him and the bones of his ass were two raw points—he turned on his side and tried to fall asleep to the constant growls and moans coming from what was left of Ram. It was not exactly soothing and yet Neil had been without proper sleep for so long that he was actually lulling off to it when a sharp *Bang* vibrated up from the deck.

Everyone perked up at the noise, even the zombie, which had been slowly tiring at the end of its leash.

"What the fuck?" one of the guards asked. He wasn't the only one voicing the rhetorical curse. The question was a common one before the cries of "Fire" began to drift down. Neil stood and looked about, however his vantage on the lower deck was extremely limited. The same was true of the three guards.

"One of you should check it out," the sole armed guard said in a Russian accent. He was one of Yuri's men and it would take a lot more than a few cries to get him to budge from his post.

"We're not going any…" one of the men began to say.

Bwammm!

The first noise could've been anything: a dropped pallet, or a forklift crashing into something, but the second could only have been an explosion. Neil could feel it through the soles of his shoes. The men only stood and looked at one another. "Someone should do something," Neil said as the cries of "fire" turned to screams of panic. He was convinced that if a fire broke out he would be left to burn up along with what he now chose to call "the zombie".

"I'll go," one the *Blacks* said. He wasn't gone long. "That whole mother-fuckin boat right next to us is covered in smoke!"

"You have to release me," Neil cried immediately. Already the smell of burning diesel could be detected despite the fact that the wind was running down the length of the boat instead of cross beam.

Neil was ignored, though it was done studiously. It was as though everyone knew he was right, that he should be released, and yet no one had the courage to do it. So they just pretended he wasn't there.

"We should get out of here before the fire spreads," the one man who had seen the smoke said—there was a twitchiness to his voice that hinted at panic just beneath the surface.

His fellow *Black* shook his head. "You need to chill, Ron. This is a steel boat; it's not going to burn." As emphasis he banged on the hull with a dull thump. "I was in the Navy and I saw a ship like this burn for three days. It never did sink. So chill, we're going to be just fine. Trust me on this; it'll be worse if we leave our post."

No one felt fine and for sure no one chilled. Minutes passed and the smell of smoke only grew and the cries became more insistent.

"What happens if the ship blows up?" Neil asked. All eyes went to the ex-navy man for answers.

He was reluctant to answer, perhaps because it was Neil who had asked the question. His friend Ron had to goad him before he would answer, "Diesel doesn't explode. It burns like a mother, but it doesn't explode."

This seemed to calm everyone but Neil, of course he was the only one chained to the boat. "I've heard different," he said in something approaching a babble. "Like in World War two, boats blew up all the time...I mean after they were on fire. That was a thing, I swear it."

"It's true," Ron said, licking his lip. "I heard the same

thing. Why the hell are we staying here, Jimmy? We should be getting the hell off this goddamned boat."

"Chill out, mother-fucker," Jimmy said. He wasn't as chill as he wanted to appear. Even in the midnight dark, there was enough light from the dim bulbs overhead to catch the sweat glistening on his forehead. "Those mother-fuckin' boats blew up because they had mother-fuckin' munitions on board. That's why."

The Russian guard opened his mouth as if a thought had struck that made him want to puke. "Munitions is what they have been loading for the past three hours on that boat."

They all looked west and each was silent as though trying to hear the sound of munitions about to explode. Instead they heard the beginning of a gun battle. Everyone literally hit the deck.

"What the fuck?" Ron cried as bullets sprayed everywhere clanging off every metal surface. "What the fuck is going on?"

"It's the ammo cooking off," Jimmy said. His words were garbled because his face was pressed flat against the deck as though he was being stepped on. "We got to…"

A new explosion, and one with far greater force, shook the boat. This was followed by a series of eruptions like giant hammers. They rang out into the night so that even Ram stopped his moaning and stood as if paralyzed by the sound.

The second there was a break in the explosions, both Jimmy and the Russian dashed for the railing and jumped out into the water. Ron ran to the rail and looked out but could not bring himself to jump.

He turned to Neil and cried, "I can't swim."

With the bullets continuing to pop off and muffled explosions shaking the six-thousand-ton boat, Ron was practically blind in his panic; right next to him was a life preserver.

Neil pointed at it. "It'll float. Just hold onto it,

and...wait! Don't leave me!" In the instant Ron had seen the preserver, he had grabbed it and started to climb over the rail. "Please, don't leave me!" Neil screamed. Ron wasn't the only one panicked. The very air was beginning to shimmer with the heat of the fire in the next boat.

"I don't have the keys to the lock," Ron said. "I'd let you out but I don't have them." Once over the railing, the man clung to the side of the boat long enough to say: "Sorry."

Then Neil was alone...for all of ten seconds. In the time before Sadie and Jillybean arrived out of breath and worried, he gave up. He sat on the thrumming deck and looked at Ram. "I'm sorry, too," he said. "You were the best friend I ever had."

"Neil!" Sadie said, rushing up. Despite the mayhem she was grinning and crying. She flung herself into his arms and he squeezed her for the span of time it took to take one huge breath as if he could breathe in her living soul.

"You did all this?" he asked as he pulled back.

She shook her head. "No, Jillybean did." Sadie pointed at the girl who had been running along looking like an angel—a ray of innocence in a night of terror. Now she was standing just a few feet away and only inches from Ram's hooked fingers. Her face was frozen in a mask of misery as if she were experiencing a thousand deaths in that one second.

Sadie went to her and held her, gently turning her head until it rested on her breast. "Don't look at him. It's not Ram anymore. Ram is in heaven. Do you hear me? Ram is in heaven. That's only a monster." Jillybean nodded her head as a fat tear streaked out of one blue eye. "Good girl," Sadie said and then turned her around and began to dig through her pack.

"Here we go," Sadie said, holding up a heavy Phillips head screwdriver. She turned, took one step toward Neil and then was lifted off the deck of the boat as the biggest explosion yet erupted. Everyone and everything was thrown to the side—and that included the boat itself. Neil sat up and found the deck leaning slightly toward the water.

"What the hell was that?" Sadie cried.

Neil shook his head to clear it before saying, "There was talk about a missile launcher. Someone had one, maybe that was it."

"Are we going to sink?" Jillybean asked. "Ipes says that a missile can sink a boat."

"Let me have that screwdriver," Neil demanded. The ring on which his chain was looped was attached to the deck by four screws. If he could loosen them, he'd be free.

Sadie watched him grunt at the resisting screws for only a few seconds before she said, "I'm going to go get Sarah or Eve, or both if I can. Meet me north of here at Ram's truck. Jillybean knows where it is."

"Shouldn't you take her with you?" Neil asked. He gave a little sideways smile and added, "We might just sink."

"She'll be safer here. There are life preservers against the rail and Neil...you'll be fine. Remember you're a hero. Get yourself free and get north." Taking only a moment to kiss them both, Sadie then ran off and Neil watched her go, noticing the deck was tilting even more as she fled.

"I better hurry," he mumbled. With gritted teeth, he went to work on the first of the screws, fighting with all of his strength against the rusted metal.

"Try hitting them with the butt of the screwdriver," Jillybean said in the voice of an army sergeant. "It might loosen them."

Neil banged on each with a growing anxiety in his gut. What if they didn't come loose? What if the ferry sank with him still attached? The thought lent him strength. With both hands on the tool he twisted with his full power not realizing that the screws hadn't been loosened in twenty years and were so rusted in place that for all intents and purposes they were welded to the deck. He twisted until the skin of his palms tore and still, nothing happened.

For a moment he sat panting. An old soda can rolled past him and he watched with a sudden feeling of dread, as it gained speed until it hit the metal wall. Only then did he notice that the ship's list was at thirty degrees. It was beginning to get so steep that Neil had to plant his palms on the deck to keep from sliding down.

The metal was hot under his hands. There was a fire in the deck below his!

"You have to go, Jillybean," he said. "Leave me here. Go get a life preserver and…" Even as he pointed toward the water he saw a blue-green sheen floating on its surface. A second later, flame spread from around the side of the boat to light up the night like a giant's torch. Jillybean's one escape route had been cut off.

"The fuel tanks must be ruptured," Jillybean said in a ghostly voice. It was like she was empty and the air just whistled out of her in the form of words.

"Son of a bitch!" Neil screamed in anger.

Jillybean shook her head at this as she leaned further back to compensate for the growing list of the boat. "That's a bad word." Her voice had transformed into such softness that it was a wonder Neil could hear it. Butterfly wings made more noise and yet the sound, in all its oddness came to him, drawing his eyes from the growing fire to her tiny form. She was utterly still and staring down at Ram, and yet Neil was certain that she wasn't seeing him.

"We're going to die," she said in the soft lilting manner of a child in a dream.

"No, we're not," she answered herself in a deeper voice. Neil's skin flashed with goose bumps at the voice that was coming from her full lips. It was Ram speaking. "There's a way to get out of this. Find it, but you have to hurry, Jillybean. Look around at what you have to work with and find a way out."

She stared around at the tilting boat for three seconds,

her blue eyes huge and unblinking. She then pulled off her "*I'm a Belieber*" backpack and searched through it. Of all the things that she could have pulled from it he was surprised to see she had a pair of scissors in one hand and in the other was a green item that had Neil blinking in wonderment.

"Is that a hand grenade?" he asked.

"I need your shoelaces, Neil," she said in her Ram voice. "And hold this for me." Jillybean slid the clip of the hand grenade onto Neil's belt and then before he could splutter nonsense about having a bomb sitting on his hip, she left.

The tilt was bad now and getting worse. The entire boat, groaning as if in mortal agony, was slowly tuning on its side, forcing the little girl to walk with her left hand running on the deck. She went across what had once been car lanes searching back and forth with scanning eyes.

"What are you doing, Neil?" he asked himself. Was he really going to let a six year old girl rescue him, employing a hand grenade of all things? "You're a smart man. You went to Columbia for goodness sakes, surely you can figure a way out of this."

He looked around to see what he had to work with: a sinking boat surrounded by fire. And his shoelaces. And a hand grenade. And…and he had no clue how to make an escape or what on earth Jillybean was doing. Yes, a hand grenade could blow off the chain, however he was attached to it; barely four feet away.

"Just don't think about it," Neil said to himself, going to work on undoing his laces. He decided that if Ram had trusted her he would as well. From a certain point of view, it was an easy decision since he had no other choice. As he got the first lace undone Jillybean knelt and began working at something with her scissors.

By the time he got the next lace off she was hurrying back with a circle of metal, the rust of which was marring her dress. Only he seemed to notice or care. She handed him the disc.

"There's no time for this," she said, fearfully, in her own little girl's voice.

"No time for what?" Neil asked.

Jillybean ignored him completely. "Why can't I just…" she started to say, but then she cocked her head to listen.

Neil realized she was taking orders from either her zebra or Ram, on some ghostly level. He had to resist the foolish temptation to ask her what he was saying.

She began to nod. "I suppose I understand…"

Just then she almost pitched forward down into the water as the boat heaved again. Neil snatched her, almost dropping the metal disc in the process. With his hands occupied he slid to the end of his chain.

"Uaghh!" The noise ripped from his throat as the metal dug into the soft flesh of his neck. Jillybean regained her footing and shoved him up with all her strength, while he kicked with his feet.

"I'm g-good," he said a second later when he could breathe. "Go do what you need to do."

What she needed to do was to get a shirt, a roll of tape, and a candle from her backpack. Neil could only sit and wonder at how that was going to help in anyway. She went right to work, showing him. Since the boat was now at a sixty-five-degree angle, Ram had fallen to the end of his chain as Neil had and was now almost choking. What prevented the zombie from strangling to death was that he had his hands up under the chain.

Jillybean simply slid down on her bottom so that her feet landed on Ram's broad shoulders. She was practically sitting on his head. He turned to look up and, in mid-growl, she shoved a thick candle in his mouth. A second later she threw the shirt over his head, and then in three quick passes wrapped it there with the tape.

"Oh," said Neil, comprehending. She then slid down Ram's body until she was at the rail where the fire was licking up. Moving as fast she could she ran for the next life preserver on the short wall. For a single dreadful moment, Neil was sure that she was going to leave him and he felt a monstrous panic explode in his chest, but then she turned daintily and made her way back.

With one hand holding the preserver, she used Ram as a pseudo-ladder. He sort of kicked a bit, but with his head and hands bound he couldn't hurt her as she climbed up him.

"Lift your foots, please," she said to Neil a second later.

"What?" Neil asked. She had the life preserver at his feet and wanted to run it up around his body. His mind was a whirl of thoughts and still he was clueless. Did she think he couldn't swim? It was his neck that was the problem, not his hands.

"Lift them, please," she demanded. "Hurry or the boat will fall over on us." He did his best to lift his legs, then his butt, and then his torso as she worked the heavy foam circle up his body before running it along the chain all the way to where it attached to the ring. With the last of the tape she secured it there above his head.

"Shoelaces," she said, holding out her hand. He lifted them to her and, along with the tape, she made a little basket out of the life preserver. Now the boat was practically at eighty degrees. It rocked from unseen explosions, making Neil slip to the end of his chain where he began to choke. The sound of his gagging went unheard by Jillybean. Around them, the boat was buckling with metallic screams.

By sheer luck Neil found a seam in the decking that hadn't been there moments before. He was able to stand on the tiny ledge and gasp.

Jillybean didn't have time to pity him. "Give me the round metal thing!" she cried. Somehow he had kept a hold of it.

She was like a monkey. With one hand holding onto the chain she reached down effortlessly and accepted the plate. This she set in the basket she had created from the life preserver, and finally Neil saw what she was doing. The thick life preserver and the metal plate would absorb the blast of the grenade...hopefully.

"Do you want the hand grenade?" He was already pulling it from his belt.

Jillybean took a tired breath and said, "Not yet." She then began to climb up the deck of the ship using the new seams as hand holds until she reached, what at one time had been the divider between the car lanes, but was now basically their roof. A fire extinguisher sat on the wall.

Once it was in hand she leaned back and slid down the boat to Neil. "I need you to pull the pins on both the extinguisher and the grenade. I'd do it, but Ipes says they're really hard to do." He went to pull the pin from the grenade, but she stopped him. "The fire extinguisher first! I don't want to accidentally blow us up."

"You just want to do it on purpose," Neil said, trying to make a joke to show he wasn't scared. He was petrified. If the grenade didn't kill him, he was going to slide down into a river of fire...which brought to mind a question. "Why don't you go use the extinguisher on the fire now and I'll toss the grenade in the basket you made."

She climbed up the chain, saying, "Because you can't *toss* the grenade. If you miss, the chain may not break and if it bounces out it'll roll right down to where I'll be." She was on his shoulders now. "Hand me the fire extinguisher, please."

"Don't you think you should spray the fire first and then..."

"Please, Mister Neil!" she begged. "We don't have time."

Her fear was obvious, but so was his. He was the one who was going to slide into an inferno seconds after a hand grenade went off just a few feet from his head.

"Trust me," she said.

He handed up the fire extinguisher, and then, when she

murmured, "Hand grenade," he pulled the pin and, still holding down the spring, gave it to her. As if time was a fiend, the next few seconds dragged out in a slow-motion, fear-filled misery. With his heart ramping up in speed, he heard the spoon safety lever of the grenade bounce away; he saw Jillybean zip by as she slid down on her *I'm a Belieber* backpack; he cringed down at the end of his steel tether letting it choke him all it wanted because he was afraid his eardrums would burst from the blast. Both hands were on his ears, crushing inward while he crimped his eyes to distorted slits.

The seconds drifted by like clouds on a hot summer day, taking their time as if all the world was theirs to meander their way across the...

The sound of the hand grenade, detonating so close to him, was something indescribable. The noise was so sharp and so all-encompassingly loud that his brain basically shut off. Down the side of the boat he tumbled rather than slid and into the foamy water he plunged. Somehow he had lived through the explosion—the pain in his head told him that he was indeed alive, but now he was in the fire. The water was scalding, but the flames...were not there. He found himself in a semi-circle of white foam, as Jillybean raked back the flames with the extinguisher.

Neil, blinking like an owl, tried to flounder a bit. With his brain all ascatter he would have drowned two feet from the edge of the boat, but Jillybean handed him half a life preserver that was black in parts and riddled with holes.

"Now what?" he asked, not realizing he was shouting. "We're still surrounded by flames and the boat..." he paused to look back to see if the boat was still there or if it had disintegrated in the blast. It was still there and barely scorched where the grenade had gone off. "And the boat is going to sink on us."

"Ipes is right, you are silly," Jillybean said, smiling now that the hard part was done. "We still have this to get us through the fire." She held up the fire extinguisher. "I barely used any, and the fire only goes about fifteen feet."

She was standing on part of the railing, a beautiful little angel against a background of hell—an enormous column of billowing black, backlit by a golden glow rose for miles into the air while closer the boat loomed as if at any moment it would simply fall over onto them.

Jillybean looked back at the body of Ram, her chin dropped and she drew in a big breath. It looked like she wanted to say something to him, but instead she turned away and toed the water. "That's not so bad," she said. "It's like a nice hot bath, with bubbles."

Chapter 41

Sadie

New York City

Other than the man chained to its deck and the little girl scampering around trying to save him, Sadie was the last to leave the outer ferryboat. Despite the smoke and the searing heat that caused everything to shimmer, it was an easy thing to do. The two ferries were crushed into each other. She simply leapt across into an inferno of hell.

The heat of the deck turned the soles of her Converse sneakers soft and the raging fire made opening her eyes nearly impossible. The best she could do was cringe behind her hands and make her way to the far end of the boat.

Even the dock was on fire. Midway between her and the safety of land the entire wooden structure was going up in flames. Almost too late the *Nordic Star* was trying to pull away. Its engines churned the green water to white foam, however in their haste to get away, and perhaps inexperience in emergencies, many things were going awry.

The gangway hadn't been unchained and now hung down the side of the boat, trailing the first few of its steps in the river. Much worse than that, especially with a tremendous fire raging not thirty feet away, was that not all of the mooring lines had been detached. Both the forward and aft spring hawsers, great, arm-thick ropes, were still tight around their cleats on the pier.

Because it was attached in one quarter, the *Nordic Star* was now pointing to a bend in the shore. In spite of this, the 5000 horsepower engines could be heard revving powerfully even over the fire. The strength of the engines, coupled with fire had the dock swaying on its pilings.

Sadie realized that one way or the other she was going into the water.

Holding the two grenades hooked to the waist of her

jeans to keep from losing them, Sadie leapt out into the river and immediately began swimming for the cruise ship. With everything going on: the water heaving, the engine revving, the fire, and the explosions, it was unnerving for the girl to approach such a creature of metal as the *Nordic Star* was.

It seemed alive and, like a skittish horse, it felt to shy away from her as she reached out for the swaying gangway. The waves made it doubly dangerous. With what felt like evil intent they picked her up and slammed her against the side of the boat and before she could barely recover from the shock they smashed her against the metal gangway.

Thankfully, the white blouse she wore got hooked on a shard of twisted metal and she was able to hang on. Seconds later, winded and battered, she was on deck with one of the Russian guards staring at her. From her vantage he seemed tall as a building. He had opened his mouth to say something, however he was now in a state of mental pause. He stood there with his mouth open, staring at the sheerness of her wet shirt.

"Um," he said, pointing in the general direction of her breasts, while trying to keep his blue eyes on her dark brown ones. "Your, um…"

"Thanks," Sadie said, wrapping her arms around herself. "Where's the Colonel? You know, the army guy from *The Island*. I need to know where he is."

"The Colonel is on Promenade deck, one floor up, in starboard cabins," the guard answered. Sadie gave him a quick: *Thanks* and made to leave, but the man grabbed her. "You should not go there. You are prisoner girl, da?"

"Yeah."

"Is no safe for you. Come, we must hide you." He dragged her to the stairs. "Bottom floor is med deck. Tell them Nico say is ok. I am Nico." He added this last with a smile, patting his own chest just in case his English had failed him.

"Thanks, Nico, but I don't have time for safe," Sadie

said. Gently, she pulled back and he let her go. With a last smile she turned and ran for the stairs leading to the Promenade deck. As she ran she pulled one of the grenades from her jeans.

There were many people on the deck watching the boat struggle against the pier or gazing in awe at the fire. Sadie gave the inferno a glance, which turned into seconds of gasping fright. The nearer boat was now sinking in an odd manner. It seemed to be falling beneath the second ferry, causing that boat to lean far over on its side. Higher and higher the near edge went and she was sure that it would topple over at any time.

She tried to calculate how long it had been since she left Neil—two minutes, maybe three. Had he gotten free?

"He got free. He had to have," she whispered. "They were just screws."

Her words were unconvincing, even to her. She was just wondering if she should go back to help him, when a man in an Army uniform walked right by. In that second, she decided that Neil and Jillybean would have to make it on their own.

A few steps behind, she followed the soldier to a plush set of rooms right where Nico had directed her. She was so close to the soldier that she entered the suite right after he did, causing him to jump slightly in surprise. When he turned she presented him with an even greater surprise: the image of her holding a grenade in one hand while the other had a very firm grip on the safety pin.

The soldier's eyes bugged. "What the…?"

"I want to see the colonel," Sadie explained through gritted teeth. "Where is he? You're going to tell me right now or so help me God, I'll blow you the fuck up."

Inadvertently the man's eyes flicked to his right. "I…I don't know. Just don't pull that pin. There's no coming back if you do. You understand?"

"I'm going to count to three," Sadie said as way of

reply. "One…"

"Colonel!" the soldier yelled. "There's someone here to see you."

A door that led to another part of the luxury suite opened and Colonel Williams stepped into the room. His uniform was starched stiff, but his smile was easy.

"Well, the zombie hunter is back," he said coming closer and giving her a scrutinizing eye, barely glancing at the grenade. "Maybe I was wrong about not taking you on. You got balls…for a girl that is."

"Where is Sarah? Tell me or else."

The colonel waved his hand as if he didn't think there was any chance of that happening. "You won't pull the pin so don't think you're scaring anyone."

In answer, Sadie pulled the pin. Suddenly the hand grenade seemed to gain in weight, and perhaps in heat. Her hand certainly began to sweat more, making it slippery, which in turn added to her mounting state of anxiety, because what if the damned grenade just slipped out of her grip like a bar of soap?

"Where is she?" Sadie demanded, brandishing the green bomb.

"Still not scaring me," Williams said. "You won't throw it, because you know you'll die as well."

"Did you happen to see that boat on fire out there?" she asked. "I did that. Now tell me again how afraid I am."

Williams laughed. "I definitely screwed up not getting you while I could. You want Sarah? Fine, she's all yours. I'm done with her anyway." The colonel nodded to the soldier Sadie had followed in. The man left quickly, leaving the colonel and the Goth girl alone to stare at each other.

"What did you do to her?" Sadie asked. She was afraid of the answer, or more accurately she was afraid what she would do when she heard the answer.

"Stuff," he said with a shrug. "No one else wanted her so I took her in, and as you probably know, there's a price for my protection."

Sadie's dark eyes went black with hate. "You son of a…"

"Uh-uh," he said, wagging his finger. "Don't be like that. You're getting her back, more or less in one piece. If I hadn't taken her in, out of the goodness of my heart, I can guarantee she would've been killed by that damned Cassie. She's the one you should have a beef with."

"The goodness of your heart?" Sadie raged. "Let me tell you about *my* heart, I have enough room to hate both you and Cassie. Don't you…"

Sadie caught her tongue as Sarah came in.

"See?" the colonel said, wearing an evil smile. "Good as new."

Sarah walked slowly, hesitantly, as if either she was unsure of herself or that every step was a painful experience. Or both. In wonder, she looked at Sadie with swollen and blackened eyes. "I thought you were dead," she said in a blurry whisper through swollen lips. "Where's Neil?"

Who knew the answer to that question? The sight of the ferry practically on its side, so soon after she had left him and Jillybean did not bode well. But she wasn't going to add to Sarah's pain, not then.

"Let's get out of here. I'll tell you later," Sadie said, coming forward and offering her left arm, making sure to keep her right—her hand grenade throwing arm—free.

"We have to get Eve," Sarah declared. "She's with Abraham."

Sadie did her best to keep her face neutral. She was pushing her luck to the edge just trying to free Sarah who seemed exceptionally frail and in no condition to take on a doomsday cult.

"Oh yes," Colonel Williams said. "Go get that fruitcake and all his fruitcake followers. I'll even help. He's got the suite just above us. Stairs are right around the corner. Good luck."

"Fuck you, Williams," Sarah said, turning to glare. "There'll come a time when I take my revenge and…"

Just then the boat lurched forward. Sarah went to her knees with a cry of pain while Sadie barely kept her feet.

"Maybe you should put the pin back in that grenade before you blow yourself up," Williams suggested. "I mean you don't want to do that until you find Abraham, right?"

Sadie hadn't known that re-pinning a grenade was even possible. She pushed the little pin back in its hole, watching the colonel as she did. By his reaction it was clear the bomb wouldn't blow up now.

"There's a good girl," he said.

A hundred angry retorts sprung to mind, but she didn't have time for a single one, not if she was going to rescue Eve. Gently she helped Sarah to her feet and then backed out of the room into a bewildering night of people screaming, and yelling, and running.

In confusion, Sarah's eyes went round and round at the smoke-filled sky and the raging fire. Sadie's confusion was even greater. Sometime in the last two minutes the *Nordic Star* had turned and was now pointing directly at the river bank not a hundred feet away. They were drifting sideways to it and it took the girl a few seconds to realize that the engines weren't throttled up anymore.

"What's going on?" Sadie asked the first person who would glance her way. It was a shirtless man who was just coming back from leaning out over the stern railings.

"Those fools cut the mooring lines in the wrong order and now they're tangled in the propellers." He seemed to want to say more, but after a look at Sarah's face he just gave them a quick nod as way of a goodbye and left.

"Did we get attacked by the Navy or something?" Sarah asked. "All I could hear was all these explosions and machine guns firing nonstop."

"No. That was Jillybean's idea of a distraction. But we can't worry about that now." Sadie pushed against the stream of people. The boat was normally crowded, but with the terrific events occurring, the decks teemed with crowds. She yanked Sarah along by the hand, slipping past people until she came to the stairs and then she stopped dead in her tracks.

Lounging on the stairs, insolent and radiating a revulsion for the mostly white passengers were the *Blacks* of Philadelphia, Cassie among them. Not a second passed before Sadie and Cassie locked eyes and stared at each other in mutual hate.

The connection lasted until a tall man shoved past Sadie and started up the stairs. Just like that the two young women sprang into motion.

Cassie stood and screamed, "The girl in the white shirt! Get her!"

Sadie spun, thrust Sarah back against the wall, and pushed the grenade into her startled hands. "Hide!" Sadie hissed. She then took off running, using her speed and nimble feet to outdistance her opponents who relied on brute force, which in a ship as crowded at the *Nordic Star* was not a good strategy.

Still there were many of them and the ship wasn't of great size. Gradually, Cassie got her men in order. Over all the commotion, Sadie could hear her bawling out commands. A man was stationed at each stairway and on every level. The rest of them she formed into a squad that searched as a coordinated unit.

Ever lower into the bowels of the ship where few people trod the corridors, Sadie was herded. She felt like a fox being hounded to her death and she ran in a growing fear until she found herself in a corridor at the bottom of the boat. It was then that she remembered the Russian guard, Nico. She was supposed to drop his name, however there was no around.

She banged on the first door she came to. "Anyone in there?" she called. When no one responded, she tried the knob, found it locked, and moved to the next door, repeating the process until one opened. It was one she had already passed and it was a black man who answered.

At first her heart caught in her throat, but then she saw it was Steve, the man who had helped her the day before.

"You?" he asked in surprise. "What are you doing back on…"

An explosion somewhere above them stopped his words. It was distant and muffled, but no less frightening.

"Sarah," Sadie whispered, feeling dread bloom in her stomach like a poison that leeched out into her limbs, weakening them. She staggered and caught the door frame.

Steve did not notice. His eyes were to the low ceiling. "That sounded like it was on this boat! Are we on fire too?"

"No, it was…it was nothing. Can you hide me? Cassie is after me."

Steve looked pained, but took her in nonetheless. The room was tiny, no bigger than a walk in closet, and yet it held a single bed on one side of a two foot walkway and a bunk bed on the other. Donna, looking afraid with the covers up to her chin, sat on the single.

"I'm sorry about this," Sadie said. "I was trying to save my…my mother. Sarah's my mother." The words felt strange, but right.

"You can only stay for a little bit," Steve said, listening to the door. "They know I helped you before, or at least they have guessed that I did."

"Can you give me a half hour to…"

Just then the sound of voices slipped through the cracks of the door. They could hear sporadic knocking and then Steve's door was thumped upon.

"Under the bed," Steve hissed to Donna. He then pointed Sadie to the closet. It was nothing more than a broom closet.

"Yes," Steve said, louder. "One second. I'll be right there." His voice was high and it shook with nervousness.

From the closet, Sadie heard the door open.

"Where is she?" a gruff voice demanded.

"You mean Donna? She's out. What with all the commotion…"

"Cut the shit. I'm talking about the white girl."

"Just search the place," Cassie said.

Sadie, realizing that she was caught, opened the closet door. She had meant to brandish the hand grenade, but she was caught up in a dress of Donna's and was slow to step out. There was no question she was seen, however. Cassie looked her dead in the eye and said, "Kill the race traitor."

There was a man in the room with them. He was very large and strong, with shoulders that were wider than the door itself. Before anyone could voice the slightest peep of protest and before anyone even noticed the grenade in Sadie's hand, the man stabbed Steve in the chest with a makeshift knife. He acted so fast that all Sadie saw was a flash of dull metal as the blade went deep into Steve's flesh.

Steve keeled right over.

At Sadie's horrified look, Cassie smiled a wicked smile. "Don't worry. I won't kill you so fast. You'll wish…" Now Cassie saw the grenade.

For the second time, Sadie pulled the pin. This time the bomb did not cause the slightest unease in the Goth girl. She dropped the pin on the carpet where it bounced once and then gleamed up at them. It was trod upon as Sadie stepped forward.

"Is that real," Cassie asked, slowly backing into the hall. As answer, Sadie opened her hand, letting the spoon spring back.

"Shit!" the large man cried. He turned to flee, and Sadie, with a feeling of utter calm, tossed the bomb over his shoulder and into the hall.

There came a pause in which Sadie slammed the door shut and threw herself onto the bed and covered her ears, thinking, as she did, that she hoped that Sarah had felt this very same tranquility when she had detonated her grenade.

A second later, the bomb discharged, torturing the very air with its violence. Even in the next room Sadie felt a moment of disorientation, however she knew she didn't have more than a moment. She jumped up and rushed to the door. There she was forced to step over bloody bodies to get by. Unbelievably the most horrid one began to move. It was the man who had killed Steve.

With an odd, womanly grunt he moved to the side, but then Sadie saw that it was Cassie who was moving the body. She had used the man to shield herself.

"I'm gonna kill you, bitch," Cassie growled in a voice that wasn't human. Her face was bloody and wild and so thoroughly filled with evil that Sadie fled instead of attacking her when Cassie was probably at her weakest.

It was a fatal mistake, one that she would come to regret

In a full out sprint Sadie booked down the hall and right past one of the guards that Cassie had set in place. The man gave chase, but Sadie had the fear of the devil in her and she raced away from him as if he were standing still. She went up three flights of stairs and as surely as she had been energized a minute before she now hit the limit of her endurance…just as she ran into another of the Cassie's guards.

There was no doubt he recognized her. It was one of the same men who had kept guard over her, Neil, and Ram all the night before. He looked her up and down, then, unbelievably, he turned his head to the side and began to pick at the wall.

"You better get off the ship and fast," he whispered as she edged by.

She had no idea what to say to that, so she didn't say anything. Instead she staggered on, heading further up the stairs, going slower and slower with the weight of her exhaustion. She had only one goal in mind: find Sarah and, hopefully, Eve.

She did not find them. Instead she found Cassie. "You is so stupid," the black girl said.

Sadie could only muster the breath to ask, "How?"

"How did I get here so fast?" Cassie asked. "The elevators work just fine, dumbass." With that, Cassie launched herself at Sadie and began to pummel her with punches that came thudding home.

Sadie had never been much of a fighter, while Cassie had been raised on the streets where violence was a way of life. The black girl was not only a very good fighter, she was also stronger and fresher. She hit Sadie three times before the Goth girl even knew what was happening. After that Sadie could only try not to get hit square while hoping that someone would come to her rescue.

No one did. A hundred people on the deck watch Sadie bleed and not one lifted a finger. They either didn't care or they were too afraid of Cassie. Sadie didn't blame them. Cassie was crazy and rabidly dangerous.

Now that Ram was dead, the only person she knew who would stand up for her was Neil. And he did not come riding in to save her on a white horse. Neither did odd little Jillybean, or Sarah.

Sadie was on her own with just her wits to save her. They weren't enough either. Out of desperation, she took a punch to the temple just to get close, in order to grapple Cassie. Sadie held on tight, intertwining her fingers in the black girl's hair. Only when she was sure Cassie wasn't getting away did she launch herself off the boat.

The two of them fell over the railing with a splash, and both came up spluttering: Sadie, because her limbs were like lead weights; Cassie because of the surprise move. She wasn't surprised for long.

"You think this will help you?" Cassie asked as she swam at Sadie. "You think cuz I'm black I can't swim?"

Sadie felt a foolish moment of guilt because the thought had crossed her mind. She had hoped to prevail in the water, however Cassie turned out to be the better swimmer. In desperation Sadie tried the trick she had used earlier: attacking from below.

Cassie met her under the water and the tables were turned. The stronger girl held Sadie below the surface until the need for air was too much. Sadie bucked and twisted and squirmed and in the end her need to breathe overcame her rational mind—she sucked in the green river water, and when that didn't satisfy she sucked in more and more until the water before her eyes went from green to black, and her body went completely still, inside and out.

Chapter 42

Sarah

New York City

The grenade was thrust in her hands so suddenly and so unexpectedly that Sarah immediately dropped it on the deck with a heavy clunk. It was a strain to bend down to get it. The black eyes she sported for all to see looked bad, however they didn't give her anywhere near the pain that seared her insides where the colonel had rutted with a vengeance.

It hadn't been sex for him. He had aimed to hurt her and he had succeeded, repeatedly.

As Sarah crouched with the hand grenade partially hidden in her hands, Cassie came by, glanced down at her battered face and moved on without recognizing her one time companion.

"I must look like shit," Sarah said in a whisper. A woman next to her agreed, though she was pleasant enough to help her up. "Thanks." Sarah's voice was guttural and there were purple marks on her neck where the colonel had gripped her until she thought she would pass out or die.

"You're welcome," the woman answered. "Looks like you're having some man trouble. That's a damn shame, but what can you do? Things are different now...and...and is that a hand grenade?" When Sarah nodded the woman gave her a shrug and added, "I guess you got it covered."

As the night had been exciting enough for her, the woman took her leave. Sarah hid the bomb beneath her shirt much the way Sadie had, and then slowly, painfully, walked up the stairs to the next level. She was basically devoid of fear at this point. In her mind Sadie was too quick to be caught, so she didn't waste any time worrying on her account. Neil and Jillybean had each other. And Sarah had her bomb. She touched it gently, almost as though she were caressing a tiny baby beneath her shirt.

Still gimping, Sarah went to the doomsday cult suites. They weren't hard to find: A robed man stood out front.

"I'd like to see Abraham."

Again, she went unrecognized. "A new convert? Abraham will be so pleased." She was led into his presence. As always he was robed in white and his hair was so perfect that Sarah wondered if it was in fact a wig he wore. The fake messiah raised his hands in a welcoming manner until, that is, he discerned who it was under the bruises.

"I see you are living the fate of a Denier," he said as if her appearance saddened him.

"I'm here for my baby," Sarah announced. She produced the grenade, holding it in two hands. Immediately Abraham's followers leapt in front of him, protectively.

Abraham shook his head so that his mane flowed easily. "I would sooner hand Eve to the devil himself. Why should I make deals with one of his handmaidens?"

"You don't understand," Sarah said, pulling the pin on the grenade. "I'm taking my baby or I'm taking your life."

Abraham stepped forward with his hands raised to the ceiling. "It is you who does not understand. You cannot hurt me." He glanced to one of his followers and then touched him on the shoulder. "Timothy. Show the Lord our God your full devotion."

Timothy was a portly man with thin hair that hung like a greased curtain from his head. He was extremely unattractive, the kind of man who, in the old days, would have been more likely to worship a beauty such as Sarah than any dusty preacher. Now was a different time.

He came up to Sarah, nodding gently, with his hands out for the grenade.

"I'll blow us up, I swear!" she cried, backing to the corner of the room. Unbelievably, Timothy kept coming and she saw that she would be forced to either give up the grenade or use it. She wasn't going to give it up. Sarah tried to heave the heavy bomb but Timothy was quick enough to grab her wrist as it went back.

Now she couldn't throw it. The best she could do was to drop it behind her and hope that some of the metal pieces would hole Abraham through the heart. She let the grenade go and then tried to run to the other side of the room.

Timothy showed his devotion like a true believer. He dropped on the grenade and cuddled it to his body. When it exploded, the force of the blast straightened him out, and, of course, killed him immediately. Sarah was thrown to the floor but Abraham was untouched.

In fact, Abraham was all smiles. "What a beautiful soul our dear friend Timothy possesses! Lord, we thank you for the blessing of Timothy."

"You're messed in the head," Sarah said. Just then it was she who felt messed in the head. The colonel's fists had given her a number of concussions and now the hand grenade's explosion had only added to the addling of her mind.

Abraham looked down on her with sorrow. "You were a good mother. Eve is perfect. For that I will not have you killed by fire as all witches should be. Instead we will let your soul be cleansed in the purifying water that the Lord our God has given us."

"Huh?" she asked.

"Tie her hand and foot and throw her overboard," he said to one of his minions. He then breezed out of the room leaving Sarah speechless. In moments, the curtains of the suite were shorn of their ties which went around her wrists and ankles. She was then hefted to the window and dumped out like a bag of trash. Fortunately for Sarah, it was a straight shot to the water below, unfortunately, her foot hit the side of the boat on the way down adding a ninety degree rotation to her fall. She struck the water flat on her back with, what was in her mind, a thunderous slap.

She was so stunned that she could only lay there,

floating, as the water infiltrated her clothes and shoes. Slowly, she settled deeper into the river until eventually its green water slipped into her mouth. She could barely muster up the energy to care.

Suddenly there was another explosion from inside the ship. Due to the nature of sound through different mediums, the explosion was far more urgent for her out in the water than if she had been in the boat.

"Sadie," she whispered. Sarah had been so focused on Eve that she had barely given thought to the other girl she claimed as a daughter. With a groan she rolled in the water and began a style of swimming that resembled the crawl of an inch worm. Her destination: a strange run of metal that hung from the side of the *Nordic Star*. As she got closer she was surprised to see it was the stairs of the gangway.

They were nothing short of a miracle.

With her hands tied behind her back she could barely float, but the stairs not only afforded her a platform to rest on, it also sprung dangerously jagged slivers of metal in all directions from the rough treatment it had received.

With a will, Sarah went to work on the cloth binding her hands; they ripped relatively easily. In a minute she had freed herself completely, and, wasting no time, she began to climb the ladder. Halfway up, she heard a scream and a splash. At the other end of the boat Sadie and Cassie were in the water, battling for their lives. In seconds it was clear that Cassie was the better swimmer and the better fighter and as Sarah watched, her daughter was thrust under the water and held there…and held there…and held there, until bubbles gushed to the surface.

Ignoring the pain in her body, Sarah dove into the water. She may have been average with guns and dreadful at street fighting, but Sarah Rivers was a shark in the water. For three years she had captained the Danville High swim team and for seven years she'd been the ultimate blonde lifeguard, turning heads and saving lives.

Sarah knifed through the water and almost took Cassie unawares. The leader of the *Blacks* was so busy holding Sadie's limp body beneath the river that she barely turned in time to confront this new menace. Having not seen Sarah's power-boat-like stroke, Cassie turned confidently and foolishly. She reached out to deal with the blonde with her strong right arm, thinking she would drag this woman under the water as she had Sadie.

However, being attacked in the water was nothing new to Sarah; life guards are frequently attacked by panicked swimmers and they are trained to expect it.

Sarah took Cassie's arm at the wrist and forced it across the front of her body, turning Cassie almost ninety degrees as she did so. This was standard for saving lives and had this been a rescue instead of a killing, Sarah would have turned the girl all the way around and settled her onto her firm bosom where Cassie would have calmed rapidly.

Instead she turned the black girl with one hand, scissor kicked upwards with her legs so that she rose up out of the water practically to her navel, and then plunged Cassie beneath the surface of the water with her right hand, using all the strength in her shoulder and back. Cassie was strong as a lioness and fought like one, however her strength was more than balanced by Sarah's position on top of her.

As Sarah held the struggling woman under the water, she had a second to weigh her options, to weigh life versus death. Her daughter was face down in the water not seven feet away. By Sarah's estimation the girl had not taken a breath in a full minute and Sarah knew that every second she waited to attempt to revive her would make the job that much more difficult.

But saving Sadie meant allowing Cassie to live, and who knew how many more lives that would cost in the long run?

The decision had to be made in the next few seconds, but Sarah didn't know which way to turn. She knew what

Ram would say if he were still alive: he would vote to kill Cassie. His motivation would be revenge. Neil would go the opposite direction: he would vote to save Sadie, but only out of selfish love. But what would Sarah Rivers do?

The old Sarah Rivers had been a foolish optimist and would try to do both…and so would this new one.

Killing would have to come first and if the reviving had any chance, the killing would have to happen sooner rather than later. To facilitate it meant taking chances. Sarah took a huge breath and reached down into the water with her right hand searching for Cassie's throat. The black girl immediately attacked the arm, grabbing it and using it to pull herself up. Sarah allowed the move, knowing that if she got to the throat and squeezed, Cassie would find it impossible to hold her breath.

In seconds their positions were almost reversed, however Sarah used her legs in the opposite manner than Cassie had. The black girl had been trying to force her way up, but Sarah kicked down, deeper into the murky water. It was unexpected and frightening, and since Cassie hadn't had a good breath in twenty seconds she tried to break away. In order to do so she had to push off of Sarah, which was exactly what the older woman had hoped Cassie would do.

Cassie's hand reached out to push and Sarah grabbed it and swung it neatly aside, much as she had done when they were on the surface. Now, instead of trying to hold her under, Sarah sent her fingers clawing for the larynx, digging at Cassie's throat with desperate strength. One vicious squeeze was all it took.

A gush of bubbles shot upwards. Now, getting frantic for air herself, Sarah broke away, angling for Sadie's limp body and hoping that Cassie wouldn't be able to recover from sucking in a lung full of water, eight feet below the surface of a river.

A glance back told her that the girl wouldn't. Cassie was just a dim shape bucking beneath the water. Sarah turned to her next job. She broke into the air right next to Sadie and immediately turned her over, going into CPR mode: tilt the head, pinch the nose, fully seal the pale blue lips with her own and breathe, and repeat, and repeat, all the while kicking like mad with her legs toward the shore.

Once her feet hit the rocky bottom things went much faster. "Sadie! I'm right here. You're going to be fine," Sarah cried out. But she wouldn't be fine. A very large part of Sarah knew her daughter had never stood much of a chance. Seven years of lifeguarding through high school and college had taught her the harsh lesson that very, very few people were saved when they had been submerged that long.

Sarah had personally brought back six people from the brink—five of whom had been submerged for less than thirty seconds. Of those who had been under longer than thirty seconds she had saved only one in her eight attempts.

She had no choice but to try. Roughly, Sarah turned the girl over and watched the water drain from her lungs. She then lowered her back down, gave two breaths and began CPR again. Like a robot she went at it: thirty chest compressions followed by two breaths. She did this four times and after each sequence her hope faded a little more.

She was in the middle of the fifth when a man came wading up, carting an orange bag high on his shoulder. "You must is step back, now," he said in the thick Russian accent common to most of Yuri's guards.

He unzipped the bag and pulled out an AED, which Sarah knew was basically a portable defibrillator. With practiced hands he attached the leads to Sadie's body and started the machine.

There was a pause as it charged and Sarah asked: "What is this? I mean why?"

"You make Yuri much money. Sit back and do not touch girl." The man pressed a red button and Sadie jerked.

Anxiously, Sarah and the guard looked at the readout that monitored her heart: it blipped once and then went flat.

Automatically Sarah breathed for the girl and began more compressions as the machine charged again.

"This girl lose money," the guard said. "Yuri bet American Colonel three hundred gallon of fuel she win fight with black queen. Sit back." He pressed the button again and Sadie jerked just as before, but now her heart began to sputter on the read out. "Damn! One more do trick...I hope. Breathe for her."

Sarah did and the guard went on, "Yuri lose and is very mad. He is sore loser and so he bet double or nothing on you. You win and he is much happy. I ask to help you with girl; he say yes."

"What made you want to help her?" Sarah asked, suspiciously. Too many people were working too many angles as far as she was concerned.

The guard was a handsome young man with nice eyes. They crinkled when he smiled. "She is very pretty. Maybe we go on date. Ok, let's hope this work."

The machine sent its charge into the girl, resetting the rhythm of her heart, which began a peppy beat. In seconds Sadie blinked and didn't even seem to see Sarah.

"Hey Nico," Sadie said in a whisper. "What are you doing in my bedroom?"

Epilogue

Sarah

Philadelphia, Pennsylvania

The many bruises that decorated Sarah's body were all fading to green and yellow. On the outside she thought she was hideous. On the inside she feared she was rotting or had been corrupted. Every day she cleaned herself thoroughly...perhaps more than thoroughly, perhaps she did so manically; it had become a compulsion for her. In the week and a half since her rape at the hands of Colonel Williams she had douched three times a day and had kissed Neil a total of four times. A part of her was afraid he would know what had happened simply by touching her. She didn't like to look in the mirror.

She was not the only one bruised and battered. Sadie was confined to bed with broken ribs, a fractured orbital bone, and persistent double pneumonia. Neil had run a low-grade fever from the moment he crawled out of the East River. His arm where he had been bitten, was infected and slow to heal. But their wounds were "natural" as Sarah saw it. Theirs would go away in time while she would be forever stained.

Only Jillybean had come through virtually unscathed. Sarah thought her an odd girl and had yet to bond with her. She was afraid to get too attached. Being a mother hadn't been anything like it was supposed to be for Sarah Rivers: one daughter probably dead, another practically dead, and a third abducted by a cult of fanatics.

Sarah was simply a horrible mother, and for Jillybean's sake, she had made every excuse in the world not to be alone with her, but now she was stuck. It was May first and the little girl had declared it to be her birthday.

They were living in Philadelphia, though not in the

compound of the *Whites*. Sarah's group of misfits was a political hot potato. Yuri had been pleased about winning his spur of the moment wager, however when he heard a rumor that Sadie had caused the fire that had destroyed so much of his livelihood he had instantly put a bounty on her head.

Understandably, the *Blacks* were not well disposed to the group either. In order to recoup some of his losses, Yuri had declared them equally responsible for the fire and had seized their goods. With the loss of their leader and six of their best men, the *Blacks* had asked for a ceasefire and the *Whites* were not going to jeopardize the opportunity for a permanent peace. They did what they could for Sarah's family, but they did so on the sly.

This was why they were hiding out in Jillybean's house of all places. It was not a particularly safe structure. The house relied more on high bushes to keep their movements unseen rather than on sturdy doors to protect them. Yet they had no better option.

Nico did his best; installing deadbolts on the doors and shutters on the windows when the zombie numbers were at their lowest in the bright afternoons. In Sarah's mind he was the only good thing that had come from the fiasco in New York. In the strange way of this new undead world he had fallen straight away in love with Sadie.

That love had saved their lives. Weak, injured, hunted, and possessing nothing but the clothes on their backs the group surely would have perished in New York, however Nico had come through for them, stealing a Dodge Ram with an extended bed filled with goods from his former boss.

Now the pair of love birds had matching bounties on their heads and were nearly inseparable. Except, that is, for that morning.

Jillybean, using all the manners and sweetness she could marshal, had asked for a special birthday favor—of Neil, not of Sarah. Neil was a soft touch as everyone knew.

This was the reason Sarah and Jillybean were sneaking

up a creaking staircase in some unknown Philadelphia suburban house, while Nico was out front guarding and smoking stale cigarettes. The house was altogether unremarkable which had Sarah wondering why on earth they had wasted the gas to come out to it.

"Was this a relative's house?" Sarah asked. "Your grandmother's place? Or was it…" The engine of her mouth came to a halt as they entered a girl's bedroom and she saw what it was that Jillybean wanted. "Wow."

It was a dollhouse of huge proportions. Jillybean had to go up on tiptoes and still she couldn't peer down into the chimney. Not only was it impressively large, it was beautifully decorated, hand painted and furnished like a French palace.

"Can I keep it?" Jillybean begged clasping her hands and intertwining her fingers. "I know it looks real big, but Ipes says all we need to get it out of here is a hexagonal driver."

"A what?"

Jillybean dug in her *Belieber* backpack and pulled out something that resembled a screw driver but with an odd tip. "This. It's a hexagonal driver. It unscrews those things there on the hinges. Ipes found it for me. He wanted me to tell you that on account of you being so pretty. I think he likes you."

Sarah touched her own face. She couldn't feel the bruises but she knew they were there. Just like the stain was on her insides. "Well, tell Ipes that…" Sarah had to stop herself from carrying on a conversation with a zebra. "You know Ipes isn't real, right?"

"Yes he is. This is him right here." Jillybean held the zebra up as proof. Sarah looked at the ceiling as she tried to find the right words to explain herself, but Jillybean didn't need the help. "Ipes says that he's the outward expression of my subconscious mind, which I think is a funny thing for him to say, because he's actually a zebra, though only a toy one."

"Yeah, that's what I meant," Sarah said. She realized that she had been about to disabuse a sweet child of an innocent game. "He sure is smart for a toy zebra."

"That's what he says," Jillybean replied as she went around to the back of the dollhouse. "He'll talk your ear off about the inherent wisdom of zebras. Do you know he thinks that the instinct of animals is the highest form of reasoning? He says instead of wasting time on conjecturing and figuring and stuff like that an animal automatically knows what to do in any situation. He says they bypass reason and get right to what's important. I think he means that animals are smarter than people, but I don't know about that."

"He sure is smart," Sarah said again. "In fact Ipes seems smarter than Neil and that's saying something."

Sarah sat down on the floor next to the front of the dollhouse, and ran her fingers lightly over its features: the shutters beside the windows, the shrubs in the garden, the mailbox, whose door would come open like a mouth. She was fingering a tiny potted plant the size of a pencil eraser when, for some reason, a great feeling of melancholy swept her.

"Is there any way I can talk to Ipes alone?" Sarah asked, suddenly. "I mean without you hearing?" Neil had told her about his rescue from the burning ship, about how the little girl seemed almost possessed by Ram. Just then Sarah needed and missed Ram badly.

Jillybean was quiet for a spell and then said, "Yeah, maybe. Is something wrong? Did I do something wrong?"

"No sweetie, no," Sarah said. "I just need to talk to someone about private stuff and I don't have anyone. No one who will understand."

"Ipes will do it, but he says that grode-ups are weird."

"Yeah, that we are." When Jillybean didn't respond and there was a long pause Sarah asked, "Ipes?"

"Yes?"

The voice wasn't Ram's as Neil had described. Instead

it was Jillybean's but flatter, less childlike. Sarah took a deep breath before asking, "Can she hear you?"

"Our conversation will be stored in her long term memory, but will be irretrievable unless she needs it. For instance, if you were to tell me you were going to kill her I would alert her as soon as possible. However if you want to talk about your rape then, no it will be as if she had never heard it. So, in essence the answer is both yes and no."

"How did you know about the rape?" Sarah was stunned by the words coming from the girl's mouth. As far as she knew, only Sadie knew and it wasn't something she would blab to a six-year-old about.

"Jill is very observant. She saw the bruising and how you've been behaving. She knows something is wrong, but it is only on a subconscious level that what occurred is understood. Before you ask, *how* or *why* I will answer. I protect her innocence as well as her life. I suspect the same is true with the subconscious of most people, but I can't be sure."

Sarah couldn't resist a sudden desire that had welled up in her: she had to see Jillybean. She had to see if the little girl had changed in the last minute. She had to see if there was a grown up version of Jillybean sitting on the other side of the dollhouse? Rising off the floor she craned her neck over the roof and there saw a little girl with fly away brown hair staring unblinking at the dollhouse.

Sarah sat back down. "I don't want to talk about the rape. What good would it do? What I need is advice," she said in a whisper, feeling like a catholic in a confessional.

"About your plan to leave?"

Air caught in Sarah's throat. "Yes."

"And you want to know which of your babies you should go after first? Brit or Eve. Have you considered Jill? She needs a proper mother and father."

"She's not my baby," Sarah insisted. "I don't love her."

"I think you mean you refuse to love her." Sarah

shrugged at this and the zebra somehow knew. "My advice is don't go after either. Look at what happened to Ram when he went off on his own. He wound up dead and you will as well. However, since I know you are set on this, I will tell you that Eve is clearly the better choice and for two reasons: you know for a fact she's still alive, and you know exactly where she is."

Just like the colonel and his men, Abraham and his band of whackos had been free to leave after receiving their vaccines.

"Eve it is. Thanks," Sarah said, nodding now, feeling right inside for the first time in a week. "Do you promise not to tell Jillybean about this?"

"I told you that my job is to protect her. If she knew where you were going, she would follow you and attempt a rescue. She's wonderful like that. It's too bad you can't see it."

"I see it," Sarah said. "But I can't feel it. I'm broken now. That's another reason why I have to go."

"Good bye Sarah," Ipes said. "Don't ask for me anymore."

"I won't."

"You won't what?" Jillybean asked. She came around the dollhouse and stood next to Sarah and, in the manner of small children who weren't learned in the lesson of boundaries, she leaned against Sarah and took her hand, tracing the lines on her palm.

"I won't go back home without this dollhouse. That's what."

"Really?" the little girl asked, jumping up and down. She paused with her head cocked as a puzzled expression swept her pert features. "That's silly! Ipes says that maybe I shouldn't hug you, but you look like you need a hug."

Jillybean hugged Sarah and though she sensed the contact and the squeeze and the warmth on a certain level, it didn't penetrate past the first layer of her mottled skin. Sarah didn't feel anything. It was almost as though she were dead inside. Whenever that dreadful numb sensation struck her, and it did any number of times a day, Sarah would put her hand to her hip to feel the one thing that mattered to her anymore: her Beretta 9mm.

If she couldn't feel the warmth of life, she could sure as hell feel the cold of death.

The End

*

Author's note:

The story continues with The Apocalypse Outcasts, but before you run off to the bookstore to snatch up your copy could I ask a favor? The review is the most practical and inexpensive form of advertisement an independent author has available in order to get his work known. If you could put a kind review on Amazon and your Facebook page, I would greatly appreciate it.

Peter Meredith

The story continues in The Apocalypse Outcasts:

There are no Happily-ever-afters in the new Undead World. There are no vacations or time-outs or do-overs. There is only the endless daily grind of living or the shockingly horrific fact of death that hangs over every living creature left on the face of the earth. For some that death lies in a single mistake or a moment of bad luck, or simply in fate.

For others that hard death hounds them day and night, relentlessly.

Peter Meredith

When a huge bounty is placed on their heads, Neil Martin's misfit family is set upon by ruthless bounty hunters. They are pursued by sociopaths, sadistic ex-soldiers and of course the warped Believers of New Eden. There is no refuge, no place of safety, no shining city on a hill that will take them in. They are outcasts and doomed to flee from their enemies until they're forced to make one great stand.

Fictional works by Peter Meredith:

A Perfect America

The Sacrificial Daughter

The Horror of the Shade Trilogy of the Void 1

An Illusion of Hell Trilogy of the Void 2

Hell Blade Trilogy of the Void 3

The Punished

Sprite

The Feylands: A Hidden Lands Novel

The Sun King: A Hidden Lands Novel

The Sun Queen: A Hidden Lands Novel

The Apocalypse: The Undead World Novel 1

The Apocalypse Survivors: The Undead World Novel 2

The Apocalypse Outcasts: The Undead World Novel 3

The Apocalypse Fugitives: The Undead World Novel 4

Pen(Novella)

A Sliver of Perfection (Novella)

The Haunting At Red Feathers(Short Story)

The Haunting On Colonel's Row(Short Story)

The Drawer(Short Story)

The Eyes in the Storm(Short Story)

25098956R00239

Made in the USA
Middletown, DE
17 October 2015